DARK ROADS

Also by Chevy Stevens

Never Let You Go
Those Girls
That Night
Always Watching
Never Knowing
Still Missing

DARK ROADS

CHEVY STEVENS

ST. MARTIN'S PRESS
NEW YORK

First published in the United States by St. Martin's Press,
an imprint of St. Martin's Publishing Group

DARK ROADS. Copyright © 2021 by Chevy Stevens. All rights reserved.
Printed in the United States of America. For information, address
St. Martin's Publishing Group, 120 Broadway, New York, NY 10271.

www.stmartins.com

The Library of Congress Cataloging-in-Publication Data is available
upon request.

ISBN 978-1-250-13357-1 (hardcover)
ISBN 978-1-250-27787-9 (Canadian)
ISBN 978-1-250-13358-8 (ebook)

Our books may be purchased in bulk for promotional, educational,
or business use. Please contact your local bookseller or the Macmillan
Corporate and Premium Sales Department at 1-800-221-7945, extension 5442,
or by email at MacmillanSpecialMarkets@macmillan.com.

First Edition: 2021

10 9 8 7 6 5 4 3 2 1

For Jennifer Enderlin and Mel Berger

PROLOGUE

No one ever wakes up thinking, I'm going to die on a dark road tonight, *but that's the point, isn't it? You're young and free, with your entire life ahead of you. You're busy falling in love, arguing over stupid things with your family, thinking of the perfect witty comment for Instagram. You take chances. You drive too fast and drink too much. Time unwinds in front of you like a luxurious, brightly colored ball of yarn. You think you have years to get it right. Then, all of a sudden, you meet the wrong person, and it's over.*

Death didn't come for me with a beautiful burst of light or angels singing, or anything, really. It was sharp, piercing pain, his eyes staring into mine as he choked me, and surprise. Even as my throat collapsed and blood vessels broke in my eyes, I thought someone was going to drive down the highway. Someone was going to see. There would be headlights and screaming.

Well, there was screaming. Until, like I said, he choked it all out of me.

I'm not the only one here. Many of us are still waiting, lingering in the air like whispers. We don't talk about our deaths, or how we each made our fatal mistake, but I imagine we all knew about the Cold Creek Highway long before our bodies were dumped in a ditch or buried in the woods under a blanket of damp moss. You couldn't grow up in the North without your parents warning you, or the clerk at the gas station telling you to watch out, or walking past posters of the victims with their sweet, hopeful smiles. All those grainy photos lined up in rows like they were in some sort of tragic yearbook. Graduating to nowhere.

How many victims are there? The newspapers will tell you that twenty cases have been connected to the highway, more than half were First Nations, all of them young. Truth is no one knows for sure. Their bones are scattered, their names a brief note in a missing persons file.

You're wondering how someone could get away with all these killings unnoticed. It's a fair question—if you've never driven the nearly five-hundred-mile highway that stretches west through the mountains to the coast in a long, undulating swath of gray. The towns and First Nations communities are small and far apart, with no buses or other sources of public transportation.

The forest is a wall of thick impenetrable trees and dense underbrush that scratches at skin already welted from blackflies and mosquitoes. The mountains are sheer, the ravines deep and lined with jagged rocks or loose gravel that can slide a body all the way down and never return it. The rivers swell with rain and swallow anything in their path. Bears, cougars, and wolves carry off bones. Shrubs and ferns grow over the rest. The land is made for hiding.

There are only a few police stations, some with a handful of officers. It wasn't like it is now, with computers and databanks. There was no communication, no obvious pattern to the murders. Or maybe it was just blatant racism that had the police overlooking the problem. What was one more missing First Nations girl to them? Thousands were already missing or murdered across the country. White victims were given more attention, more press.

By the time the RCMP realized that someone was hunting more than deer in the North and formed a task force, the cases went back decades. Witnesses forgot crucial details. Evidence was lost or destroyed. DNA had been recovered, but there were multiple samples that never matched to anyone. The original suspect was thought to be a trucker or a logger, someone transient. They speculated that he'd died and one, or more, had taken his place.

The town erected a billboard warning women not to hitchhike. As if that would stop a girl hell-bent on running away or looking for a good time. *The police promised to step up their patrols, while vigilantes with shotguns took nightly drives and swore that they'd put an end to it. But women still went missing. Sometimes from the highway, other times from nearby communities. They were seen at a party or walking home, then never again.*

Northerners said that there was something evil in those mountains. The highway was haunted, and so was the town of Cold Creek—the last real stop for gas and provisions before taking your chances on the dark road ahead. It was also the last place several women had been seen.

Others said danger was just part of living in that rugged and remote terrain. Death of some type was always certain. Bored kids would get into trouble. Poverty led to violence.

Tourists spoke about blinding headlights in their rearview mirrors that disappeared just as quickly. Teens told stories around fires and scared each other on shadowed trails, then giggled in relief when their friends leapt out. The highway was a favorite topic for sleepovers and Ouija boards. Every year someone dressed as a killer truck driver on Halloween.

Maybe you're thinking, Why would anyone ever visit such a terrible place, let alone live there? *Well, the North taketh away, but the North also giveth. The valley between the mountains is rich with soil, and crops flourish. There is hunting, fishing, and cheap land, unencumbered by pesky neighbors and city rules. Most of the townspeople are third- or fourth-generation, but others come searching for work in logging and mining and never leave.*

I imagine it was easy for them to tell themselves that it was only unwary women and girls who fell victim to the highway. They had been too trusting. Too reckless. People were wiser now.

And they were right, for a while.

Several years passed without any girls having the bad luck to get murdered. The town relaxed, which was its first mistake. The heat rose that summer, broke records, and teenagers flooded out to the lake for the weekends. Girls walked to the bathrooms alone, skinny-dipped in the moonlight, and flashed truckers, until another body was found in the long, yellowed grass by the side of the road. An unfortunate motorist had stopped to pick wildflowers and got more than he bargained for. The dead woman was suspected to be a drug-addicted prostitute.

There was a public vigil and there were community safety meetings, but in private most people thought that it was the woman's lifestyle that led to her death. Who was to say it wasn't her pimp or her drug dealer? But then, not two years later, a high school girl disappeared from a party in a cattle field bordering the highway. No evidence, no arrests. Days later, the farmer's dog uncovered her decomposing body in a culvert. Her photo was added to the posters.

Amateur sleuths hit the internet, opening Facebook groups and Reddit threads, tracing license plates and old prison records. Journalists wrote in-depth articles and scored book deals, hoping they'd succeed where the police had failed. But they haven't. No one has.

Our families and friends keep our roadside crosses painted and bring fresh flowers, teddy bears, and LED candles. The candles flicker for weeks until their batteries run out. People say silent prayers as they drive past. We hear them, and then we watch you leave us behind.

You want to know which one I am, where I fit into the timeline of broken lives. Does it matter? We all share the same story, even if our killers are different, and we want to tell you our secrets. But that's the thing with whispers. You have to listen closely to hear us.

PART ONE

PART ONE

CHAPTER 1

Hailey
JUNE 2018

The door creaked open behind me. Footsteps shuffled across the floor to where I lay on my side, facing the wall and scrolling through photos on my phone, videos. He stopped inches from the bed. He thought he was being sneaky, but the mattress dipped as he leaned over, breathing across the back of my neck, stirring the hairs there. Little puffs of bubble-gum-toothpaste-scented air.

"Hailey? You awake?"

I rolled over, met my little cousin face-to-face. His brown eyes were delighted, his dark hair damp and spiking out in all different directions like he'd rubbed a towel over it. He climbed up beside me, sprawled on his back, his head on my other pillow, and kicked one of his legs in the air. He was wearing shorts and his knees were scratched. He smelled of suntan lotion.

"Are you still sad?"

I blinked hard. "Yes."

He flipped onto his side, squirmed closer, and ran his toy car up my shoulder to my neck with a *vroom, vroom* sound. "Mommy said I'm not supposed to bother you."

"So why are you in here?" I narrowed my eyes, but he just giggled and bumped his head under my chin, his fine hair tickling my nose.

"Can I come with you if you go to the doctor?"

"What are you talking about?"

"Vaughn said if you didn't get better soon, they would take you to see the doctor. They have toys in the waiting room." He looked at me hopefully.

"I'm not sick."

Lana's voice called out from the kitchen. "Cash? Where are you?"

His eyes widened. "Here, you can sleep with Billy. He's my favorite." He shoved a red truck into my hand and scurried out of the room, socks sliding as he rounded the corner.

I put the truck on my night table. My water glass was empty, and I needed to go to the bathroom. I sat up and hung my head, tried to run my hands through my hair, but it was all in knots. My phone buzzed on the bed. I swiped my thumb across the screen. Jonny.

Come to the lake tonight.

I texted back. *Not in the mood, loser-face.*

It might help, lame-ass.

I pushed the truck back and forth with one finger, its wheels squeaking on the wood surface. The lake. I hadn't been there for weeks. The water would be getting warmer. I listened to the noises out in the kitchen. Lana banging dishes, Cash pleading for more cookies. They smelled good. Maybe I'd feel like eating today. I took a shaky breath and messaged Jonny back.

I'll think about it. Text you later.

The hallway was lined with photos of Cash as a baby, then as a toddler, the most recent one with his baseball bat over his shoulder. Photos of Vaughn and Lana on their wedding day. Cash standing between them, holding their hands and smiling proudly in his suit. A painting of an RCMP officer on the back of his horse, next to an official certificate. I peered closer.

Erick Vaughn. I'd forgotten his first name was Erick. Even Lana didn't call him that.

I walked into their country-cute kitchen with the scrubbed-clean butcher-block counters, the cheerful yellow bowl of red apples.

My aunt Lana was standing at the counter, blending something. The ice made loud crunching sounds as it broke up. She spotted me out of the corner of her eye and shut off the machine.

"Hailey!" She gestured to the green slush. "Want to share a smoothie?"

"I could use some coffee."

"Sit, sit. I'll get you a cup."

"Thanks."

She set down the coffee, then flitted about the kitchen, cutting fruit and arranging pieces on a plate with cookies. She carried it over and placed it in front of me. She'd peeled an apple and orange, slicing them into careful sections as though I were six like Cash.

She sat across from me. Her hair was as black as my mom's had been, but Lana's was cut in a sleek bob that skimmed her toned shoulders. She did yoga and Pilates, got up early and made Vaughn breakfast. Ironed his uniforms, always greeted him at the door. I wondered if it was hard being the sergeant's wife. If she worried that he might not make it home one night. I used to worry about Dad when he drove up the mountain alone. Turned out I was right to be scared.

Cash looked at me from where he was building something with Legos in front of the TV. I stuck my tongue out. He grinned, all gap-toothed, then he saw my cookies and frowned at his mom.

"No fair!"

"When you clean your room, you can have more too." Cash groaned, and she turned back to me. "Remember, before you shower, that you need to leave the window wide open. We haven't gotten the fan fixed yet. If you need more shampoo and conditioner, soap, let me know."

"I can buy my personal stuff. I was hoping to get a job at the diner."

"Oh, if you want, but there will be a little money after the estate settles, and Vaughn was planning on investing some for your college fund. Maybe get you a car."

"There might not be much."

She set down her fork. "We should start sorting through your dad's belongings."

"Can't it wait?"

"Well . . ." She looked so uncomfortable that somehow it made it all seem worse. More final, if that was even possible. "Vaughn thinks we should list the house soon, so it can sell this summer for a good price. He knows someone who wants to buy your dad's tools and—"

"No." When I saw her startled look, I added, "They're mine."

"What are you going to do with tools?"

"Store them at Jonny's."

Lana wrinkled her forehead at the tone of my voice. "I'm sure Vaughn wouldn't mind if you wanted to put them in our garage."

"I don't know . . ." I mumbled. "He keeps it so clean."

She searched my face. "He makes you nervous."

He made everyone nervous. I shook my head, but I couldn't meet her eyes, and she sighed.

"I know you kids call him the Iceman, but he's not always like that. You see how he is with Cash. He's only tough because he cares about this town."

Yeah, Vaughn seemed okay with Cash, considering he wasn't his father, and didn't complain about the toys left lying everywhere or having to watch the same Disney movies on repeat, but when Vaughn was in uniform, he'd ticket someone for doing a few kilometers over the limit, then get them for having a burnt-out license plate light. He had tossed people in jail overnight just for *arguing* with him. I'd never met Lana's first husband, some photographer in Seattle who left her broke. He didn't visit Cash. When she moved back a couple of years ago, she met Vaughn at a memorial for the highway victims. Now she only had to work part-time at the florist's, drove a shiny Acura with leather seats, and lived in a four-bedroom house. It was like there were two Vaughns. I didn't want to be around either of them.

"Everything's just so different."

Lana reached over and held my hand. "I know, give it some time. We don't have to clear out the house right away. It's so beautiful. It will sell fast."

I shaped my lips into a polite smile. "Thanks." I pulled my hand away slowly, hoping she wouldn't notice anything was wrong, but she was still giving me that concerned look.

"Vaughn has a Moose Lodge meeting tonight. How about we make popcorn and watch a movie? Or we could just talk?"

"Some of my friends are going to see the new *Avengers* at the theater and I thought I might meet up with them. I'll take my bike, so you don't have to drive me." I didn't want to lie, but I had to get out of here for a few hours. Jonny was right. I needed the lake. The woods.

"Okay. Well, don't stay out too late." She searched her mind like she was trying to think of an appropriate curfew for a seventeen-year-old. "Maybe eleven?"

"It's a long movie and we might get some food after."

She looked at me, hesitating, and I realized she wasn't sure if she should be firmer. It was just as weird for her as it was for me. This new relationship.

"I'll text you."

"That would be great." Her face relaxed. I got up and took my dishes to the sink, put them away, and slipped a couple of cookies under my sleeve.

"I'm going to have a shower." Before I left the living room, I crouched beside Cash, dropped the cookies into his hand, and whispered into his ear, "Thanks for the truck."

Four texts—one asking if I'd gotten to the movie theater okay, another asking me to text her when the movie was over, then two more when she thought I was at Dairy Queen. *Hope you're having fun!* Moments later: *Let me know when you're on your way home.* Except that their house wasn't my home. I texted that my battery was dying. I'd try to be back by eleven.

I shoved my phone into my bag, wrapped my arms around my knees, and pressed my face against my cold skin. Was this what it was like to have a mom? Would my mom have texted all the time? I didn't remember much about her, little things like her reading me stories and doing cute voices, the smell of her oil paints. Dad said she was easygoing and fun, but she died when I was five. Maybe she would have changed. Maybe we would have argued.

Dad would say I should give Lana a chance. It wasn't her fault she wasn't around for most of my life. When Mom got sick, Lana had called every day, sent flowers, and she visited at the end, when Mom was dying, and stayed for the funeral. She tried to keep in touch, but Dad and I were happy doing our own thing, and by the time she did move back, we were strangers.

My thoughts were broken by a scream as one of the girls

leapt off the dock into the lake—a black abyss at this time of night. People stood around with flashlights and lanterns. More splashes, then laughing. Music pulsed across the water—southern rap with a lot of bass. I squeezed my eyes shut, focused on the heat coming off the bonfire, the flickering orange light. My shirt was almost dry, the bikini top string tangled in my hair, but my bottoms were still damp under my cutoffs.

Someone sat beside me, bumped my shoulder. I opened one eye—then both when I realized it was Jonny. His chest was bare, tanned flesh in goose bumps, and his board shorts dripped onto the sand. He stared into the fire with his arms resting loosely on his bent knees. I dragged my fingers through the fine grains, swirled them into a motocross track.

"You need to improve your speed on the corners." I pushed a finger hard into a groove. "I went over the video from your last race. You kept your foot on the rear brake too long."

Jonny glanced down and grinned, his white teeth flashing. "Thanks, Coach." He wore his dollar-store Ray-Bans on top of his wet hair, deepened from its usual soft brown to chocolate. He was letting it grow out in tousled waves, like a surfer, his sideburns blending into the shadow along his jaw. His shape felt bigger next to me. I didn't know if it was because he was putting on more muscle from working longer hours on the farm, or because I felt so small lately.

He met my eyes. "You okay?"

"Yeah."

We watched the dock for a few moments. He tapped out a cigarette from a pack, squeezed it between his lips as he searched his pockets for a lighter. I frowned.

He shrugged. "It's my last pack."

I looked hard at the side of his face. He sighed, plucked the cigarette from his mouth, and jammed it into the sand. I took the pack from him, poured the rest of my beer over it.

"Jesus, Hailey. I just bought those."

"Dumbass."

"That's my middle name." He spread his arms wide until I forced a smile. If I didn't react, he'd keep putting himself down. I hated that as much as he hated when I was sad.

"I have to get back before Vaughn comes home."

"I still can't believe you live with the Iceman."

"Tell me about it." My knees wobbled when I stood and swung my bag over my shoulder. Two beers. Enough to give me a buzz, but not so much that Lana might notice.

"You taking the logging road? No moon tonight."

"I have my flashlight."

Jonny squinted at me. "Maybe you should get a ride with someone." I glanced at where they were putting tents up, rolling out sleeping bags. Most of them planned to spend the night, and there wasn't anyone I wanted to be stuck with all the way back into town.

"I'll be fine."

"Okay, text later." He thumped my calf muscle with a soft fist.

My mountain bike tires were quiet on the dirt road as I passed groups of campers sitting by their fires and propane lanterns, playing cards at a picnic table. No one noticed me. The road was pitch-black as it led out of the campground, the music fading. I leaned forward and flicked on my flashlight strapped to the handlebars. When I reached the highway, I stopped and looked both ways. No headlights. I shifted my backpack straps higher on my shoulder. I had to bike a few miles to the old logging road on the other side—a shortcut back to town. It would still take thirty minutes.

My pace was easy for the first mile, but when I reached the

yellow billboard, I stood up and pumped harder, my breath coming out in huffs. I didn't like riding by the sign during the day, and it was even creepier at night, the way the women's faces and names shimmered, the words glowing white. WOMEN— DON'T HITCHHIKE. DANGEROUS HIGHWAY! "Missing" posters for some of the women were still attached to stakes around the billboard like gravestones. Even the air seemed colder out here and chilled me to the bone underneath my hoodie.

When the sign was behind me, I slowed my pedaling and coasted for a bit. With one hand, I grabbed my cell out of my front pocket and checked the battery. Five percent. I turned it off to save the last bit of juice. A car came over the crest, but I saw it in time, its headlights lighting up the sky. I dropped the bike in the ditch, tires still spinning, and hid behind a bush.

The car passed. I got back on my bike. The highway began to slope up, a gradual hill, then it flattened out to a long bridge, with cement barriers on each side to stop vehicles from rolling into the ravine and the creek below. I was traveling faster now, wheels humming, backpack bouncing against my shoulders. It felt better to be in my body instead of my head, the exertion familiar—breathe deeply, flex my leg muscles, work against the pain. Then, halfway up the hill, a new noise. The rumble of a large vehicle. Coming fast. Headlights flooded the road in front of me. Damn—no way I could get out of sight.

The pitch of the engine changed. It was slowing.

Someone who knew me? One of the guys from the camp-ground? Probably on a beer run. I glanced over my shoulder. The headlights were high and blinding. Definitely a truck, but I didn't recognize the grille, and I couldn't make out the driver.

I turned around and kept pedaling. The truck was almost at a crawl. If it was one of the guys, they would have stuck their head out the window and said something. Unless they were trying to freak me out—in which case I was going to kick their ass. I pressed down hard with my legs and kept my gaze focused where the cement barrier ended a few yards ahead.

Tires close beside me. The heat of the rubber. The scrape of the window being rolled down.

I dared a glance, nearly losing control as my front tire hit a pothole. A white Chevy truck. Stripes of blue, yellow, and red down the side. Light bar on the roof. Not a creep. Just a cop patrolling the highway. My relief ended as soon as I heard the voice.

"Hailey? What the hell?"

I let the bike slow to a stop and looked through the open window. Vaughn's face was barely lit from the dash, but I recognized the blond hair cut so short you could see his scalp, the pale blue hooded eyes, and the frown that made my stomach tighten.

"Were you at the lake?"

What was the point in answering? He already knew. There was no other reason to be out here, and the ends of my hair were damp. We locked eyes. Vaughn's frown deepened.

"Put your bike in the back."

I dropped the tailgate and lifted my bike into the box. He'd switched on his hazards, the red light pulsing across the road, flashing onto my arms and face. He didn't get out to help, which was a good thing. I needed time to think how I was going to explain this. I opened the door and climbed in. He watched as I pulled on my seat belt, then blasted the heat, adjusting the vents in my direction. He put the truck in gear and pulled back onto the highway.

He glanced over. "Lana said you were going to a movie."

"We came out to the lake after."

"Did you tell her that?"

"My phone died." I rubbed at my cold legs, fiddled with my necklace, carved pieces of elk bone on a leather string. Dad had given it to me. The last time I'd ridden in Vaughn's truck was when he'd come to the house to tell me about the accident. He'd pulled in so quietly I hadn't heard the car engine, just the knock on the door. Then his words like static on a radio.

Went over the bank. Driving too fast. Died on impact.

I took a few breaths, blinked away the hazy dots, and shuffled my feet. They bumped into something. A black tote bag on the floorboards. I moved it to the side.

"Careful. That's camera equipment." He looked at me again. I wished he'd pay attention to the road. Every time his eyes met mine, I felt a clutch of uneasiness. "Why were you alone?"

"Everyone's staying at the campground." I kept my gaze focused on the white line. "I thought you had a meeting at the lodge."

"I left early. Got a domestic call."

"Oh." I chewed my lip, wondering if I knew the people involved. There were only summer cabins and a few farms past the lake. It was odd that Vaughn hadn't sent another officer out on the call, considering he wasn't even in uniform, and I was surprised he hadn't stopped at the campsite. The Iceman loved busting kids for anything—he didn't need an excuse to hassle us.

He gave me a hard look. "You been drinking?"

"I'm underage." I dropped my head against the seat and closed my eyes partway. The seat fabric smelled like oranges, something citrus, but with an earthy undertone. A woman's perfume? It didn't smell like Lana. Maybe he'd cleaned recently. The dash and door were shiny. I glanced at him from the side. His square jaw jutting out, that long stare down his nose, his large hands flexing on the wheel. Jonny said Vaughn liked to make people feel powerless, and it worked. Ever since I'd moved into his house, I felt like I had to get everything approved by him.

"Don't bullshit me. I can smell the beer."

"Dad wouldn't care."

"For God's sake, Hailey. You know how many girls ruin their lives when they hit your age? They hang out with the wrong guys, drink, do drugs."

"Not me."

"Sure." He laughed. "And Jonny Miller's a saint. Been a few thefts lately. If we raided his dad's farm right now, bet you we'd find all kinds of stolen dirt bike parts."

My stomach did a hard flip. The truck felt hot. Vaughn's cologne mixed sickeningly with that fruity perfume smell.

He paused, let out a frustrated sigh. "Listen, you think you're all grown up, but Cold Creek is rough. I've seen a lot of bad things, okay? It's easy to get into trouble around here. Someone like you, a pretty girl without a dad, you have to be even more careful."

I stared out the window. Dad used to call me pretty, but he didn't sound like that when he said it. Like it was a bad thing.

"How you look, what you wear, it attracts attention." Vaughn shifted in his seat. I glanced over. He was looking down at my cutoffs. "People get the wrong idea."

Heat climbed my throat, my face. Why was he saying these things? My shorts weren't tight or cut too high. Half the girls in town wore them so the front pockets showed.

"I was only on the highway for a few minutes. I was going to take the logging road."

"You think someone can't kill you in a few minutes?"

"Nobody's going to kill me." I tried not to roll my eyes, but he must have heard the sneer in my voice, because his head snapped around.

"You think this is funny? Lana's friend was murdered on this highway, remember? She was just having fun at the lake too, and look what happened to her."

"She was hitchhiking," I mumbled. "It was a long time ago."

"Yeah, and more girls have been killed since, so while you're living with us, there will be no more parties, and no more lake."

"Like *ever*?"

"Not without me or Lana."

"That's crazy. Why can't—"

"That's the rule. If you break it, I'll lock up your bike, understand?"

I clenched my jaw so tight I could feel my teeth grinding together. He'd been wanting me out of my room, so I finally go out for a couple of hours, and this is what I get? Served me right for thinking anything could be the same again. I should have stayed in bed.

We drove in silence until we were off the highway and through the quiet neighborhood where they lived. He pulled to a stop at the end of their street by the mailboxes. I could just see the white trim of their house in the distance. I looked over, confused.

It was dark in the truck with the dashboard lights off. His body close. He was big, his shoulders bunched. He had turned the radio down. I didn't remember him doing that.

"I'm going to the station to fill out a report." He stretched his arm across the back of the seat and twisted toward me. "I'll keep tonight's adventure between us."

"You're not going to tell Lana?" What was going on? He'd just handed down his stupid rule, and now he was giving me a pass?

"Your aunt doesn't need more problems. She has enough to deal with, don't you think?"

Right. Another mouth to feed. A headache. A kid neither of them wanted.

I nodded.

"Good girl." He patted my leg, then reached across me. I flinched, pressed back against the seat. The door swung open. "Go on. I'll wait until you get into the house."

I slipped out of the truck, closing the door softly so that I didn't wake Lana in case she was sleeping, and got my bike. It wasn't until I reached the front steps that I heard the truck drive off. When I glanced over my shoulder, I caught a flash of red taillights through the trees.

Lana was curled up in a chair in the living room, book in hand, her face lit with a soft glow from the lamp. "Hi, sweetie." She gave me a warm smile. "You have a good time?"

I hovered in the doorway. I wanted to get to the bedroom and put this entire night behind me. "Yeah. Sorry I'm late. Battery died."

"You must have thought I was a lunatic with all my texts." She laughed. "Guess I have to get used to it. I thought it would be a few more years before I had a teenager in the house." She looked at her watch and yawned. "I should get to bed. Vaughn's meeting is running late too."

I forced myself to smile and say good night. While I brushed my teeth, I thought about what she had said. Vaughn must have told her he was going to be late *before* he picked me up because I never saw him using his phone. So why didn't he want Lana to know he was out on a call tonight? What was the big deal? He went on calls all the time. Unless that was a lie too and he was really somewhere else. Then I remembered that faint perfume scent on his seats. I stopped brushing my teeth and stared at myself in the mirror, my eyes wide as it sank in.

He wasn't covering for *me*. I was covering for him.

CHAPTER 2

The vinyl seat on my bike was burning hot as I slid a leg over. I squinted against the bright sun and coasted around the building, my chocolate-banana milkshake balanced on the handlebars. The parking lot bordered a small rest area with picnic tables and totem poles. The tallest one had an eagle on top, wide wings outstretched, the carvings painted in red, black, and white.

Mason's Diner and Dairy Queen were the only places most of us hung out because we could afford the food. Jonny was sitting on the open tailgate of his truck, with Andy and a couple of other guys standing around. I'd gone to a movie with Andy once, mostly because he kept asking. A failed experiment.

Two girls walked over, staring at their phones, thumbs flicking. Motocross bunnies. The only time they talked to me was if they thought I could hook them up with Jonny. Everything about school had been a waste of time, and it was going to suck even more without Jonny next year. At least he wasn't going away to college.

I stopped in the shade behind the building, tugged my cell free from my pocket, and found my last conversation with Jonny. We'd texted after he got home from the lake, but I was waiting to tell him about my ride with Vaughn. I could barely look at Lana this morning. I'd stayed in the bedroom for hours, then told her that I was handing out résumés around town.

My finger tapped across the keyboard, adding to our long thread. *Hey, loser-face. Can't get through your fan club. Meet you at the workshop.*

Jonny looked down at his cell, laughed, then glanced around the parking lot until he spotted me. He gave a thumbs-up. Over his shoulder I noticed a flash of white coming down the street. Vaughn's truck? I wasn't waiting to find out. I spun around so fast I hit a girl in the legs with my wheel. She lost her balance on the edge of the sidewalk and nearly dropped her burger. Simone, I realized when I saw her inky black hair and hipster glasses. Andy's sister.

"Hey! Watch it."

"Sorry." I wheeled away, darted between the buildings until I was out front by the picnic tables. Kids were laughing, pushing and shoving each other as they waited for their food. I used them to block any view of me, glanced over my shoulder to make sure the coast was clear, then cut across the baseball field and disappeared into the woods. I'd take the trail, then stay on the side roads. Jonny and I had a few secret routes. We used to race our bikes home before he got a truck.

Cold Creek was small, even smaller if you knew how to get around on a bike. The downtown was really only a few streets, with a truck stop, the diner, a motel. The rest of the area was rural, with large farms and people who didn't much like other people. Those houses usually had a few pickup trucks in the yard, collapsing fences, tarps on the roof, loose chickens, and a dog or two. I didn't cut across those properties or I'd end up with shotgun pellets in my back.

Ten minutes later I was zipping around the corner near my neighbor's house, my brakes clenching so hard they squealed. I coasted up their driveway, shushing their dog when he barked, and crossed through the trees to my house. At the edge of our property, I stopped to look around. No white truck. My heart slowed, my skin cooled, breath returned to normal. Stupid. Of course Vaughn wasn't following me. I leaned my bike against the railing and climbed the steps.

Lana was right—my house was beautiful. Dad had converted an old orchard barn, built a rock fireplace by hand, and refinished all the wood floors. They still smelled faintly of apple. It was impossible to think of someone else living here. What would they change? Would they paint the walls? Rip out the sky-blue cupboards and the nook Dad had made from the barn doors?

I'd come over a few times since the funeral, once with Lana for more clothes, a couple of times with Jonny. We sat in silence, played video games, *Fortnite, Call of Duty*. When I couldn't see the screen because I was crying too hard, he pulled my head down onto his shoulder.

Dad's red plaid coat was on the hook by the door. The one he wore when he was burning brush or splitting cedar. I slid my arms through the sleeves, breathed in the smoky smell, his Old Spice cologne. His coffee mug was on the sink. I wrapped my hand around the mug, placing my fingers exactly where his would have rested, and carried it with me as I walked around the house.

My favorite photo of me and Dad was still on his dresser. The two of us standing on a pebbled shore, our canoe behind us, bright red against the blue-green northern lake. Our old hunting dog, Boomer, spent most of the time snoozing while we reeled in fish. We were unstoppable that day. Dad said it was almost unfair to everyone else, we were such a good team. He let me hold the biggest of our catch, a rainbow trout, and leaned down with his arm slung over my shoulder, our heads pressed together. Same strawberry blond hair, same green eyes, same freckles. He liked to say we had the same heart too, but his had stopped beating, and now mine ached all the time.

Beside the photo of me and Dad, there was one of my parents on their wedding day, the silver frame engraved with their names and the date. *Finn & Rachel McBride. Two Become One.*

Dad looked young in his suit, only twenty-three, his usually wild hair neatly trimmed and slicked back, my mom smiling up at him, all raven tresses and white skin, her dress with belled sleeves. An ethereal fairy creature who had somehow fallen in love with an awkward Irish lumberjack.

I glanced at my mom's paintings displayed around the room, pretty landscapes, all local scenery. When I was ready, I'd ask Lana if we could put my mom's artwork and some of the household stuff in storage. It was hard to think of a day when I'd have my own place. What would it be like with no parents? My future was a long bridge hanging over a dark hole.

I sat cross-legged on the floor in front of the fireplace, where I used to sprawl with my iPad or watch TV while I waited for Dad to come home, listening for the crunch of his tires on the gravel, the slam of his truck door. I closed my eyes, imagined him walking in, excited to tell me about something he'd seen in the woods, a black bear, a new trail, a good fishing spot.

Why were you driving so fast on the logging road, Dad? You knew it was dangerous. We had plans. You and me against the world. That's what you said. Losing Mom to cancer was supposed to be the worst thing I ever had to go through, but now you're gone too, and I don't know how I am going to make it. Why didn't you get the will changed? How could you leave me with him?

I waited. Maybe there'd be a knock, a mysterious cold breeze. People talked about that. How they got messages from family or friends after they died. But the house stayed silent.

The shop was behind the house, in what used to be a storage building for the orchard. Dad had put windows in and insulated it, added a workbench. He'd said that every man needed a wolf den. His throwing knives, four of them, were still stuck in the target. I tugged them out and got into position. I was wearing a tank top, so my biceps were able to flex smoothly. I held my breath, then released the knife. My goal was to cut a piece of twine. I'd nicked a corner. Not good enough. Back in position, I raised my arm, but a knock on the side window startled me and the throw went wild. The knife hit the wall. Jonny made a face at me through the glass.

I opened the door. "Took you long enough."

"Had to make a stop." He pulled up a stool beside the workbench and reached down for the glasses and the whiskey we'd hidden behind the old paint cans. He poured us each a splash and we clinked our glasses. Dad's last bottle.

I leaned against the bench and studied the target, the frayed piece of twine.

Jonny followed my gaze. "Your ninja moves need some work."

"You're just jealous because your aim is shit." I swished some of the whiskey through my teeth like I'd seen Dad do sometimes. I felt him even more in the shop. His tools were still on the bench, his crossbow and fishing rods hanging over the gun safe, his hip waders and outdoor coats on their hooks by the door. His quad was still caked with mud from his last ride.

"Did you sign up for the race?"

"Yeah."

"That track has a lot of sand on it, so keep your weight back." Jonny was fast and daring—the bike floated when he came off a jump, his legs in the air behind him, one hand gripping his seat. He just needed to win a few more events, get a sponsor, and he could turn pro.

He nodded. "Let's go to the pit next weekend."

"Okay." I looked at my dirt bike leaning on its kickstand. "I want to ride up to the silver mine one day too, but I can't go anywhere until we fix my bike." Dad knew everything about the mountains around there, but he never showed anyone except me how to find the old miner's cabin. So deep in the forest, so hushed and quiet, it was like being in another world.

"Your wish is my command." Jonny pulled a newspaper-wrapped bundle from his backpack, lifted it into the air like a trophy.

"You got the carburetor! Was anyone at the farm?"

"Just the dogs. I almost got bit!" He laughed.

"I told you to use smoked salmon. Did you see the puppies?" I took the carburetor from him, checked it over. For months I'd been slipping into Cooper's barn at night, visiting with the dogs and playing with the mom, a pretty border collie. She was due a couple of weeks ago. I'd wanted to buy one of the puppies for Dad's birthday, but Cooper kept raising the price.

"They're cute. You want to sneak over and look?"

I shook my head. "We need to lie low. Vaughn busted me last night. He pulled right up beside me and just about gave me a heart attack."

"Holy shit." His eyes widened, pools of blue in his tanned face.

"Yeah, and he knows about the thefts. He was talking about you."

We hadn't meant to become thieves, but bikes were expensive. It took me two summers working with Dad to pay for half of my Honda CRF 150, and Jonny fixed everyone's bikes and lawn mowers to get his 250. We were always needing parts and gas. We hit the rich people, the people we didn't like. We weren't short of targets. There were a lot of jerks in Cold Creek.

"The Iceman." Jonny drew the words out long and slow. He was thinking about last fall, when Vaughn caught him riding his dirt bike on the paved roads. He was only crossing a short section, but Vaughn still impounded his bike, and made him walk home carrying all his gear.

"If you have anything on the property, get rid of it."

"Yeah, okay." He frowned. "What else did he say?"

"He was lecturing me about how I dressed, and he was staring at my shorts. Right *here*." I spread my hand across my thigh.

"You think he was creeping on you?"

I pulled the knife out of the wall, remembering how Vaughn had looked at my legs. "More like he was warning me. But now I can't go to the lake without him or Lana."

"That is so messed up. What was he even doing out there?"

"That's the strange part. He said he got a call about a domestic. Then he told me that we could keep it between ourselves, but I think he didn't want Lana to know he wasn't at the Moose Lodge meeting. Swear to God I could smell perfume in his truck."

"He's cheating on her."

"Maybe." I spun the knife, like how Dad taught me, the silver flashing. The knife soared end over end, stabbed in dead center. I walked over and tugged the knife free from the target.

"Are you going to tell her?"

"I don't have any proof." I shrugged, thinking of Vaughn's other warning. "I don't want to cause problems. I'm going to keep my mouth shut."

Jonny looked thoughtful. "You could try to catch him."

"Hell, no. I'm staying out of this—and you are too." I pointed the knife at him. "You going to help me fix this dirt bike or what?"

I grabbed Dad's toolbox without waiting for Jonny to reply, slid to my knees in front of my bike, and began unbolting the old carburetor. A moment later I felt Jonny beside me.

The first time we'd worked on a dirt bike together, I was eight years old and our dads were talking in our driveway—Jonny and his dad had come to get deer sausages. Jonny was a shy, skinny kid, wearing hand-me-downs from his brothers.

Nothing ever fit right. He was a grade ahead of me, but I knew who he was, saw him sitting by himself at recess or following his brothers around. I'd been trying to tighten the chain on my dirt bike and sensed he was watching me. After a few minutes of his feet scuffing the gravel as he slowly moved closer, he'd crouched near my tire.

"What are you doing?"

"Don't you know anything about bikes?"

He'd shrugged. "I know about tractors."

"Grab a wrench."

He'd glanced at his dad, and in a low voice said, "You got snacks?" So I'd raided our fridge, then showed him how to change the spark plugs, clean the chain and the air filter. He started coming over after school, on weekends, and I taught him to ride. Soon he was better than me.

Junior high, he got taller, stronger, and gained a reputation for kicking anyone's butt if they teased me. Girls decided they liked his blue eyes and dark eyelashes, his tanned skin, and his cheeky sense of humor. Everyone admired him for his daring on the racetrack. He had lots of friends, but I still kept to myself. We spent all our weekends together. It was like at school he felt he had to be cool Jonny, but with me he could talk about how his brothers were giving him a hard time, or how his family was having money problems. We shared our dreams. I was going to have a log cabin on a lake, my own dog. Jonny was going to race all over the world. No one would stop us.

I wanted it to still be true.

CHAPTER 3

Mason's Diner smelled like burgers and homemade bread, bacon frying in a skillet. It was perfect, and painful. Dad and I went for lunch at the diner at least once a week. Sometimes he'd pull me out of school for the rest of the afternoon so we could take the canoe and catch the evening bite. *Come on, you need a break. Let's go get some fresh air in our lungs.* There wasn't much of anything that Dad didn't think could be fixed by spending time in the woods.

I thought the diner would be slow on a Wednesday, but most of the tables and booths were filled with loggers, road crews, construction workers. Then there were the truckers, their caps and shirts emblazoned with company names. Johnson Hauling, A&D Transport, Northern Freight. One of the stools at the counter was free.

I slid into the open spot between a couple of old guys. Amber noticed me right away and paused beside my shoulder, menus under her arm.

"Hey! You staying for lunch?"

"Maybe." I hadn't planned on it until I saw her. Usually she worked the night shift. Her white peasant blouse gaped to show smooth, tanned skin, layers of dangling necklaces. She smelled like coconut lotion and looked like a folk singer with her long, cherry-colored hair, a nose ring, no makeup around her bright blue eyes. Beaded earrings. She'd been at the diner for a couple of months, but I didn't know her whole story—she wasn't from around here.

"Is Mason working?"

"Of course. That man doesn't miss a day." She rolled her eyes. "He's in the stockroom, but he'll be out in a minute. I better go help this table." I watched from the side as she walked away, her faded jeans loose and sitting low on her hips.

Mason came out wiping his hands on a towel. "Haywire, nice to see you."

"You too." I relaxed a little. He'd used my nickname, the one he'd given me after watching me ride my dirt bike at the track. Mason might be a retired logger and rumored to have been in a biker gang at one time—he rode a sweet Harley—but he was more like my favorite uncle. Salt-and-pepper hair, a beard streaked gray, and serious brown eyes that made me feel like he was really listening when I talked. When he bought the diner a couple of years ago, he asked Dad to tell him the history of each black-and-white photo on the walls. There was even a shot of the miner's cabin. I thought it was cool that Mason didn't rip out all the old décor.

"What's this?" Mason pointed at the envelope I'd set on the counter.

"My résumé. I don't have much experience, but I'm a quick learner."

"I could use a hard worker for the summer." He picked up the envelope and slid my résumé out. I was about to tell him that I was willing to take any position—dishwasher, cook, waitress—but he'd turned toward the door, his shoulders stiff, the friendly smile gone.

"Afternoon, Officers."

I snapped my head around. Vaughn had walked in with another cop. Constable Thompson. Younger than Vaughn. Maybe thirty? Tall, with tidy dark hair, clean-shaven, and the only First Nations cop in town. He'd arrived at the beginning of last summer and a lot of people thought it was to ease tension because of the highway, but it just got worse after the last victim was discovered. Her mom was First Nations, their family well known and liked. Thompson seemed okay. He'd shown up at a few parties, even the racetrack once or twice, but he didn't hassle anyone.

I got to my feet. Too late. Vaughn was already coming over while Thompson found a table. Vaughn glanced at the résumé in Mason's hand.

"Looking for a job?"

"Yeah, but I should get going. Lana needs help." I grabbed up my wallet, turned to Mason with a polite smile. "My cell number is on my résumé. I can start anytime."

"Okay, kid. I'll be in touch."

"Awesome." I began to move away, when Vaughn's hand clamped down on my shoulder.

"It's a hot day. I'll give you a lift."

"I've got my bike and—"

"We'll put it in the back." He turned to the other cop. "Coffee another time, Thompson?"

"No problem." The cop gave me a polite smile. Amber was at his table, leaning against the side of the booth, her head dipping toward him as he asked about something on the menu. Mason had moved to the cash register. No one noticed that Vaughn's hand was still on my shoulder, his thumb pressing against my neck as he guided me toward the front door.

Then I saw her—a girl from my school. Our eyes met. Her name slipped through. Emily. Black hair, pixie cut, lots of dark makeup, a ring in her lip. She'd left school early, something about drug dealing. Her gaze lifted from me to Vaughn, settled on his hand on my neck. Her eyes went blank and her mouth flattened like ice spreading across a lake.

She shifted toward the old couple at her table, hiding her face. I didn't get a chance to see if Vaughn had noticed; we were already at the door, and he was pushing me through.

Now we were at the truck. He nodded at the passenger door, unlocking it with a remote key. I climbed in and sat stiff in the front seat while he threw my bike into the back.

The girl watched out the window as Vaughn drove away with me.

He hummed along with the radio, his hand loose on the wheel, sunglasses covering his eyes as he guided the truck through town. He was *acting* calm, but the air in the cab felt thick, even with the air-conditioning going full blast. Was he still pissed about picking me up Saturday night? He'd been working the last few days, so I only had to see him at dinner, when Lana was home.

I sat pressed against the door, waiting for another lecture and wondering if this was going to be my whole summer, riding around with Vaughn in his truck. As the minutes passed, I started to relax. Then he switched off the radio.

Vaughn glanced at his phone on the mount, tapped out something with one finger. "We have to make a run out to the lake. Possible squatter near the cabins."

The lake was twenty minutes out of town. I'd be stuck with him for nearly an *hour* before we got back. "I was going to help Lana with chores."

"You want to be an outdoor guide, right? Like your dad?"

I frowned. It wasn't a secret—everyone knew I helped Dad—but I didn't understand why Vaughn was bringing it up, and I didn't like that hollow dizzy feeling I got when I remembered me and Dad talking about the future, designing our logo, imagining a website.

"You ever consider becoming a conservation officer? Better money. You'll go on calls like this, catching poachers, off-season hunters. This will be good experience for you."

"Lana is expecting me, and—"

"Text her." He turned his head toward me, dark sunglasses covering his eyes. "Never mind, I'll do it." He lifted his phone, pressed the keypad with one hand. I wanted to call him out for breaking the distracted-driving laws, but the less we interacted, the better. The message whooshed. He was driving so fast we were already at the outskirts of town.

"Listen, Hailey. You can't work at the diner."

"Why not?"

"Too many lowlifes hang around there. Tell you what, how about you help us out with Cash? We'll add the money to your college fund, give you a bit for an allowance."

He wanted me to babysit. My mind blurred, a rush of confusion. I'd be stuck at their house all the time—and what did he mean by *allowance*? Like I couldn't spend my own money?

"But at the diner I'll make tips."

"Yeah, and you'll have men harassing you constantly." He looked at me. "Then what? You're going to ride your bike home at night? In the morning when the roads are empty?"

This couldn't be real. He couldn't be this paranoid.

"I've done it for years."

"You want to end up like her?" He pointed through the windshield. I knew who he was talking about without seeing the guardrails ahead, the silver culvert. Shannon Emerson. We'd gone to school together. She was cute, with big brown eyes and brown hair. Eighteen. Only a year older than me. I would have been at the party too—the cattle-field campout was an annual event—but Dad and I had gone on a fishing trip. Now the farmer didn't let anyone into his fields.

The cross on the shoulder was still fresh white, her name, birth date, and the date she died written in black. Her photo was anchored to the bottom in a gold frame. There were other crosses along the miles of highway. Whenever Dad and I had to travel to Forgotten, the next town to the north, I would sneak glances at them, not wanting to see them but feeling like I had to. They were so eerie and lost-looking. The rotting wood covered in moss, names worn away, flowers dried out. Mildewed teddy bears falling over.

Someone had left Shannon fresh flowers, a bundle of pink and white carnations. Her parents had left town, but they came back for the memorial walk last month. All the victims' faces were familiar to me, their names. I'd been a little kid, or not even born, when most of them died, but I'd grown up with their photos and stories. Dad and I attended the memorial together.

"It's coming up on a year," Vaughn said, "and this anniversary is going to trigger a lot of people. The smell of summer, a bonfire, a hay field. It will bring that night back. Maybe they'll remember seeing headlights. A truck that was in the wrong place. Maybe they overheard an argument that they didn't pay attention to at the time. Something made Shannon take off."

I didn't want to talk about Shannon, or anyone, with Vaughn, but something struck me strange about what he was saying. "You think it was someone at the party?"

He shrugged. "Don't know, but it's never sat right with me. I'm going through all the statements again, having another talk with some of the kids who were there."

I stared at the side of his face. "Everyone says it was the highway killer."

"There's never been *one* killer on that highway. There were at least two, maybe even three over the years, but this is someone new. I got to her body first, and there wasn't much left of her, but that image is still burned into my brain. You ever hear the term *overkill*? Coroner said he beat her so hard he broke bones, then he strangled her. Whoever this guy is, he liked hurting her, and he's not going to stop now." Vaughn was taking the corners fast, tires squealing, my body forced against the door. "My bet is that he's already looking for his next victim."

I felt sick, acid burning in my empty stomach, lurching into my throat. I gripped the door handle as he took another bend. "Why are you telling me this?"

"You think you're safe as long as you don't hitchhike, but I'm telling you, this killer is different." He jerked a thumb over his shoulder to my bike rattling in the back. "You know how easy it would be for a guy to knock you off that? He just has to tap it with his bumper and you're on the ground."

"You're trying to freak me out."

"I'm trying to keep you alive." He gave me another look through his sunglasses, turned back to the windshield. "You don't like me much, do you?"

I blinked, held my breath for a minute. Did he actually want me to say something? There was no way I could answer that without lying.

"Hey, I get it. Cops are the enemy, right? We bust up your parties and ruin your fun. But you and me, we have more in common than you think. My dad took off when I was a kid, and my mom had problems. She dated a lot of men, okay?" He slid his sunglasses up onto his head and gave me a quick, hard stare. "I tried to look out for her, but she still got hurt. It's why I became a cop. I take care of my people. This *town* is my people. When I married your aunt, you became my people." I shifted my gaze to stare at my feet. He was wrong—we didn't have anything in common. My dad and mom loved each other, and Dad didn't *take off*.

"My ex-wife and I broke up because she didn't want kids, and you know what? I still go by her house and make sure everything is okay. I still check up on the guys she brings home. I watch out for my *people*." He punctuated each word with a slap of his hand on the steering wheel and met my eyes, unblinking. "You understand what I'm saying, Hailey?"

Yeah. I understood that he had a hero complex and he was expecting me to be grateful that he'd chosen me as a project. "You want to keep me safe."

He slapped the steering wheel again. "Now she's getting it." The truck slowed. We were at the entrance to the campsite. I looked at him, confused.

"I'm going to take a run through here first." Vaughn pulled in slowly, cruising down the center road, his eyes darting from side to side. Checking out tents and campers.

He stared at a group of girls. A little older than me, in booty shorts and crop tops, sipping from their red party cups, probably full of cider or hard iced tea.

"See them? They're going to get drunk, wander off into the bushes alone or down to the lake for a last swim, then they'll pass out cold in their tents for anyone to mess around with." A shake of his head. "They're asking for trouble."

"They're having fun. It's not their fault if guys are assholes."

"If a mouse is dumb enough to walk in front of a cat, it's going to get eaten."

I wasn't going to keep arguing with him. I just wanted to get this over with. Frowning, I stared out the side window. We'd circled the campsite and now we were heading to the lake.

We drove down the highway, bumped onto the gravel road that ran behind the lake. Trees blocked out the sun and cast long shadows. I chewed the inside of my cheek.

We passed cabin after cabin. He stopped at a couple of them, looked down their driveways, and told me what he was checking for—broken windows, vandalism, garbage.

"Renters are always leaving stuff behind. Makes a mess and

brings bears. Most of the owners are decent. They call me to check on things. You get to know them over the years."

At every stop, I stared out the window and ignored his voice. I couldn't stand listening to any more of his theories, but we were almost around the lake. He turned down a narrow, overgrown lane. I had to grab on to the dash to keep my balance. He stopped in a clearing.

The truck was facing the lake, the shore blocked by bulrushes, shrubs, and ferns. At the back of the lot, near the tree line, a run-down shack slanted forward. Someone had spray-painted their initials on the side. Half-burnt logs sat in a fire ring, and a truck bench seat was on one side.

"Sometimes people camp here." He shut off the truck. I knew there were parties on this side of the lake, but it was where the headbangers and druggies hung out. We stayed away from that crowd.

"It's private land," Vaughn said as he got out. "Doesn't seem to stop them, though. I come out almost every day in the warm months. Last thing we need is a forest fire." He gestured to me. "Come on. The view is pretty from here." The door slammed, making the truck rock.

I hesitated, my hand on the door. I didn't want him to think we were going to be friends, but it was hot as hell in the cab without air-conditioning. Better to play along, I guess.

When I climbed out, he was looking out over the lake. "Lots of birds out here. Eagles, herons. I've got some good shots." He glanced back at me. "You like photography?"

"Not really."

I moved to the front of the truck, a few paces away. We were across from the beach on the other side. Had he been here the night of the party? I couldn't see much from that distance, but he would have been able to see the bonfire. He hadn't ordered us to put it out.

At the moment, he was walking around the lot, staring down at the dirt, moving things around with his boots. What was he looking for? Cigarette butts? Needles? He picked up a beer can and tossed it into the firepit, then shone a flashlight through the broken door of the cabin.

"Can we go back now?"

"In a rush?"

"I'm hungry."

He walked toward me, and I thought that meant this strange trip was finally over, but then he stopped and leaned against the hood of his truck. The sun beat down overhead, making his blond eyebrows almost invisible, his pale eyes opaque.

"Your dad and me, we had some talks. He left you on your own too much."

"Dad knew he didn't have to worry about me."

"Yeah?"

"Yeah." I bit out the word. "I know how to shoot a gun."

"Guns are no good if a man gets you on the ground."

"He won't have a chance."

"You think you can take on a man double your size, hopped up on adrenaline and God knows what else? The moment he gets you down, you have to react. Don't stay quiet thinking that he'll let you go after he's done. Go for his eyes, nostrils, testicles. Use your teeth and nails."

"I *just said* I can protect myself. I don't need the lessons." He was trying to make me feel helpless, trying to creep me out. He'd been testing me the entire drive and I was sick of it.

He gave me a measured look, then stepped toward me. In one smooth motion he gripped my shoulder, swung behind my body, and pressed me back against his chest, with his arm across my throat. I struggled to twist away. He breathed in my ear. "Try and get out of it. Go on, try."

I scrabbled at his arm, flailed my legs.

He grunted. "Raise your shoulders, tuck your chin. Reach up and get your thumb in my eye, hook my nostril. Give it a try."

"No! Let me go!"

"Come on." His voice growled into my ear, my skin prickling, his gun belt hard against my back. Panic made me lunge forward. His arm tightened, forcing my chin higher. I kicked back—hoping to get him in the groin—but he hooked his leg around mine. I thudded onto the dry ground. My breath whooshed out and my spine was jarred so hard my teeth clicked together.

He flipped me over and straddled my hips, lifted my arms on either side of my head. My shoulder sockets made a popping sound as the tendons slid over bone, stretched tight.

His face, right over mine. His eyes, icy blue. He looked triumphant—and terrifying. "See how easy that was? He's going to want to get you down fast. Most women buck up, but you have to roll to the side, into their elbows." I tried to squirm free, but his legs were steel, his face so close I could smell his aftershave and see the beads of sweat on his face.

"That the best you can do? Try harder."

"No." I turned to the side, refusing to look him in the eye.

He let go of my wrists and got to his feet. With the sun behind his head, his face was all in black. I lay sprawled in the dirt, trying to catch my breath, and rubbed at my shoulders.

"If this was a real situation, you'd be dead by now." He stepped over my body and headed to the truck.

He sped down the highway, braking hard on the curves, tires squealing. His mouth was a thin line, his sunglasses covering his eyes, but I couldn't get a handle on his mood. He never spoke to me once and finally screeched to a halt at the end of his driveway. I scrabbled at the door. He reached across and gripped my knee, holding me in place.

"Someone stole a carburetor from Cooper's farm. You know anything about that?"

I shook my head and tried to keep my expression flat.

"What was Jonny doing Sunday night?"

"Don't know."

"Jonny isn't a minor anymore."

"So?"

"So he could be pulled over at any time, his truck searched. He could end up in jail."

"Why are you telling me this?"

"I don't want you with him anymore."

"You don't get to just—"

"I can do whatever I want." He spoke with no anger. No force behind his words. He didn't need to prove himself. He looked at me as though I were *nothing*. A breeze in a tornado.

He held my eyes for a few more beats. "Got it?" He waited until I nodded, then unlocked the door. I yanked on the handle, almost falling out, and climbed into the back to get my bike—tossing it to the ground. He didn't leave until I was inside the house.

My phone vibrated in my pocket.

Lock the door behind you.

CHAPTER 4

Lana and Cash were asleep. Vaughn was due home soon. I rolled off my bed in the dark, tiptoed to my closet, and opened the door slowly. Clothes brushed the top of my head as I huddled on the floor and pushed aside shoes to make room. My phone lit up the small area as I called Jonny.

"What's going on?" Jonny's voice was hushed on the other end. I imagined him in his room, his parents sleeping upstairs, his two brothers down the hall.

"Vaughn says we can't hang out—he took me to the lake, like patrolling or whatever, and drove through the campsite, talking about the murders." The words fell out in a rush, anger twisting my tongue. "He was showing me one of the cabins and acting like he was trying to give me self-defense moves but he dropped me on the ground—*hard*—and pinned me."

"Are you kidding?" He wasn't whispering anymore. I imagined him sitting up in bed, flipping on the light. "I'm going to kill him."

"Shut up. You're not doing anything." It made me feel better. The offer. Dad would have gone over with a shotgun. But if Dad were alive, Vaughn would never have dared touch me. "He knows about the carburetor—he was asking questions. You have to get rid of it."

"Why is he screwing with you like this?"

"Because he's on a power trip? I don't know, but he's legit serious. He could put something in your truck."

"Don't worry about me. I can handle him."

"Cops plant stuff all the time. Drugs, stolen goods. It would mess up your chances of getting sponsors." He was quiet this time. He knew I was right. "Delete all our texts. We can communicate through Facebook Messenger. I'll make sure I'm always signed out of everything."

I didn't think Vaughn would take my phone—he needed to check on me when I was babysitting.

"I don't want you getting in trouble over me," Jonny said.

"I won't. I just have to figure out if he's cheating on Lana. Then I can get some sort of proof, and he'll have to leave me alone or I'll tell her." The homes past the lake were mostly farms, run by married couples, or a few men from town, like Mason, who had a big property. It had to be someone who was staying in one of the cabins. The perfect cover.

"You're going to blackmail him?"

"That's the plan."

He blew the air through his teeth in a long whistle. "I'll ask my dad about the Moose Lodge. He knows a couple of guys who belong. Maybe Vaughn has missed other meetings."

"That would be good. Like if there is a pattern or whatever."

"If he's doing *anything* shady, we'll find out," Jonny promised.

"It might be hard. He's probably careful."

"Guys like him never think they're going to get caught."

"I don't want *you* to get caught. When can you get the carburetor off my bike?"

"I have to work tomorrow. I'll go over as soon as I can."

Sunlight streamed through the sheer curtains and made a checkered design on the far wall. The clock above the bed said it was nine. I kicked off the blanket, rolled over, and stared at the door, listening to Lana and Cash moving around, talking. They had an appointment at the salon to get Cash's hair trimmed. Lana asked last night if I wanted to come along, but I'd passed.

I didn't know when Vaughn had gotten home, but I'd heard him walking around an hour ago, dragging the recycling and garbage to the end of the driveway. He'd come back inside to say goodbye to Lana. *Have a good day, honey. Need me to pick up anything on the way home?*

Now the sound of the garage door sliding up as Lana left, her car engine fading away. I got up quickly and checked the garage and the driveway to make sure they were gone, then snuck into Lana's room. I sniffed every bottle of perfume, lotion, and body spray. None of them had that musky orange scent. In the master closet, I went through the pockets of Vaughn's coats, examined his lapels for strands of hair, rummaged through his drawers. Nothing.

I poured a cup of lukewarm coffee, ate some organic cereal that looked and tasted like chunks of cardboard—Lana shopped online from a health food store. I saw the receipt once and couldn't believe how much everything cost. The more I thought about it, the more I wondered how Vaughn had so much money. Their TV was top-of-the-line, they each had iPads, including Cash, and the latest iPhones. Everything in the house was new—appliances, furniture. They bought it all right after they got married. I understood wanting a fresh start, but it was like they won the lottery and went on a shopping binge. Last year they'd gone to Cancún. Lana said their hotel was amazing, and Cash had a blast in the kid's club. She'd touched Vaughn's arm when she was telling me this, gave it a squeeze like she was thanking him. He'd patted her hand.

Lana probably didn't earn a lot at the florist shop. How much could Vaughn make as a sergeant? I wanted to see one of his pay stubs, but I couldn't find any paperwork in the house. Not even one utility bill. They must do everything online. Frustrated, I took a break for a shower.

When I stepped out fifteen minutes later, the bathroom was full of steam and beads of water dripped down the walls. I hadn't opened the window. I'd wipe the marks off and hope no one noticed. I was pretty much the only one who used the main hall bathroom. Cash had his own off his room, and the master bedroom had a suite with a double shower *and* a huge soaker tub.

I wrapped a towel around my body and slid the window up. The long rectangle gave me a clear view of Gray Shawl Mountain—so called because of the way the clouds settled around the peaks. Today it was hazy in the sun. I clenched my hands into fists. I should be up there. Nothing smelled like the woods in the summer, warm earth and pine needles. I should be riding my bike with Dad and Jonny, then coming home to grill fresh-caught salmon with them.

I thought about all the times we'd driven out to the West Coast and brought back huge chum salmon, which we'd smoke in the fifty-five-gallon drum barrel that Dad made, or the traditional First Nations way—over an open fire. We'd butterfly the fish, marinate it in salt brine, and rub it down with brown sugar or maple syrup. Sometimes we used berries and herbs, wild garlic. When it was ready, we'd weave cedar skewers through the meat, and slowly cook it over alderwood. My favorite was candied salmon, long sticky strips of it.

Vaughn bought salmon at the grocery store, threw it on the grill like it was a special treat. I stared out at the garden shed that he used for his office, tucked into the far corner of the yard. It was pretty, with blue siding and white trim around the windows, two hanging flower baskets. The house behind it was blocked by a few trees and a fence. I imagined the shed was a quiet place to work. Lana said Vaughn kept it locked.

Sometimes he has to bring home sensitive material about cases, and he doesn't want Cash to see anything.

Like what, autopsy reports? Evidence bags with bloody clothing? Wouldn't that be kept at the station? It didn't make sense. It wasn't like Cash was going to read his files. Even if there were photos, all Vaughn had to do was put them in a cabinet or a drawer.

Vaughn usually went outside as soon as he got home, and then again after dinner. If he was having an affair, he had to be communicating with her somehow. I'd seen him come home with a laptop case, but he never left it around in the house. It had to be in the shed. At the very least he might have a filing cabinet and credit card bills that I could look over.

I tugged on a pair of shorts, a T-shirt, and, with my hair still wet, hustled out to the backyard. When I got closer to the shed, I realized that there was a dark film on the inside of the windows. Was the tinting to block out the heat? Or for privacy? It seemed kind of extreme. I pressed my face up against the glass and shaded my eyes. Everything inside was murky.

I gave the door handle a try. Definitely locked. I searched above the wood frame, the top of the windows, inside the hanging baskets, under a few rocks nearby. It was possible the key was inside the house somewhere, but I doubted it. My bet was that Vaughn kept it with him.

I stepped back with my hands on my hips, looking up at the roof. There didn't seem to be a skylight or any vents, and it was unlikely to have an attic. Only way in was through the front.

A noise behind me—the back door opening.

Just as I spun around, Lana stepped outside with a bag in her hand. I hadn't heard the garage, or the car. I should have been paying better attention.

"There you are." Her voice was cheerful as it carried across the lawn and she smiled, but her gaze flicked from me to the shed door.

"A wasp flew into the rafters." I pointed to the shed roof. "I was checking for a nest."

"Wasp!" Cash ducked under her arm and sprinted to my side, peering up at the roof.

"Yeah, but I don't think there are more."

"Can you push me on the swing?"

"Sure." I ruffled his hair, which had been trimmed and styled neatly, making him look like a little accountant. He sprinted to his playground and I glanced back at Lana.

She raised the bag. "I picked you up a few products. They'll bring out your gorgeous copper highlights."

"You didn't have to do that." My face was already hot, but now it was fully lit. She was always so generous and kind, and here I was, thinking of ways to blackmail her husband.

"It's nice having a girl to spoil." She gave a little shrug. "I'll put them in your bathroom."

"Thanks."

"Did you want something to eat?"

"I'm okay. I was going to ride into town later and drop off some résumés."

Her eyes widened. "Oh, I thought you were going to nanny . . ." She glanced at Cash.

"I was thinking maybe I could do both. You know, a few shifts at the diner would help me with tips and it gets me out of the house. Might be good for me."

She quirked her lips into a smile, but it looked strained and didn't meet her eyes. I wondered what Vaughn had told her. "Sure. We just want you to be happy."

Another tense smile, then she spun around and disappeared into the house.

I pushed Cash on his swing. He flew up in the air, screaming, *Faster!* at the top of his lungs. I glanced back at the house and caught a movement, through the bathroom window I'd forgotten to close, a swish of color. Lana, her cell phone to her ear. She was talking as she placed two plastic bottles on the counter, then she walked out of the room still talking into the cell.

Vaughn. She could tell him whatever she wanted. There was nothing wrong with working at the diner, and it wasn't like he could force me to babysit.

Meanwhile, I'd come up with a plan to break into that shed.

The diner's parking lot was nearly empty. A slow time, between lunch and dinner. Vaughn's truck was nowhere in sight, but just in case, I parked my bike in the alley beside the dumpster.

When I pushed open the door, a few people turned to look at me. Some with curious expressions, others sympathetic. One man gave me a chin nod and touched the brim of his cap. I knew it was out of respect for Dad. He'd grown up in Cold Creek and was a wilderness guide for years, legendary for his skills. He'd outsmarted cougars, bull moose, and grizzlies, and once nearly froze to death in a snowstorm, but survived it all, only to die on a hairpin curve.

I ran my hands over my hair, wiping a few tendrils off my face, and hoped I wasn't too flushed and sweaty from riding my bike in the sun. Most days I lived in T-shirts and jeans, but I'd made some effort and was wearing clean white shorts, a teal-blue shirt, my hair pulled back into a high ponytail. I'd even put on some lip gloss and mascara.

Just as I sat at the counter, Amber came out of the kitchen with two plates and smiled when she saw me. I reflexively smiled back and was surprised at the flutter in my stomach.

"Hi! I'll come talk to you when I drop these plates off, okay?"

"Okay." She was talking like we were friends or like she'd

been waiting for me. I watched after her. Mason came out from the kitchen.

"Haywire. It's nice to see you."

"I was hoping we could talk about that job."

He winced, the corners of his brown eyes squinting in a pained expression. "Sorry, kid. I can't hire you. Vaughn doesn't think it's a good idea and I don't need the hassle." I could tell by the way he was looking at me that he was sorry for a lot more than a missed job, but it didn't matter. Vaughn had won again. "Get you something to eat?"

I shook my head. I didn't want to burst into tears in the diner, but my throat was so thick I thought I might choke. Amber came up beside me, looked into my face, and casually leaned her hip against me as though holding me up. The warmth felt good, the solidness of her body. The ache in my throat eased enough that I could get a breath. I blinked hard at the tears.

"Mind if I take a break?" Amber said to Mason.

"Yeah, sure. It's slow."

She smiled at me. "Want to get some fresh air?" When I nodded, she said, "Meet me in the alley. I have to get something."

Outside, I waited against the warm bricks, studying the rusted green dumpster in front of me, flies buzzing around. Amber pushed the side door open and leaned on the wall beside me.

"Do you need a smoke?" She held out a rolled joint.

"No, thanks. Makes me cough."

"God, some days it's the only thing that gets me through." She brushed her bangs off her forehead. "I keep a baggie in the ceiling of the storage room. One of the panels slides off." She grinned. "I climbed up there one day and blew my smoke out the roof vent." She laughed.

"Seriously?"

"I told Mason I had girl things to take care of." She laughed again, and I liked that she was normal around me. I tried to laugh too, but it sounded strained, like something I had forgotten how to do. She reached out and let her hand drift down my arm. It made me shiver.

"It must be hard living with Vaughn," she said, and now I felt cold all over.

"Yeah. I want to get my own place."

"That's cool. Maybe we could be roommates." She gave me a cheeky smile, a quirk of her lips. Flirty. I imagined being around her all the time. It was a stupid idea, impossible.

"I should get back to work." She paused. "Why don't you hang out? I'm almost done with my shift. We can go to the lake."

Lana was expecting me home. Vaughn might look for me. It was risky.

"Yeah. Okay."

After we went inside, Amber cleared a booth in the corner, and brought me a cup of coffee and a slice of lemon meringue pie. "On the house." I texted Lana that I'd met with some friends. Did she mind if I went shopping? She texted back, *OK!* And I sent her a smiley face.

I scrolled through Craigslist on my phone. There weren't many rooms for rent, and some sounded like they might be a closet with a hot plate. I'd still take that over living with Vaughn. Most of the jobs were in town or on the farms. Either way, I'd be biking a lot. I bookmarked anything that sounded promising. I'd send them my résumé, then figure out how to get there.

Amber and I sat on top of a picnic table at the end of the campground where the sand formed a narrow beach, out of sight from the dock. I could hear laughing, splashing as people jumped into the water, and I remembered the last time I was here with Jonny. The night Vaughn picked me up.

"You okay?" Amber's voice pulled me back. I turned to

answer but was struck silent by the way the breeze whispered her hair across her cheeks, nose, and lips. We were wet from the lake, towels wrapped around our lower bodies, bikini tops showing. She'd lent me one in a flowery blue paisley pattern, strings on either side of the hip and around the neck. Hers was black with a bandeau top. I tried not to stare at the goose bumps scattered across her breasts.

"Yeah."

She laughed. "You don't say much, do you?"

My skin turned warm. I studied the pink flowers at the edge of the lake. "I like listening."

"Those are wild roses," she said, pointing to the bushes. I looked at her, and she smiled. "Guess you know that. You probably know every plant and tree."

"Probably not." I got off the picnic table and plucked a few of the rose heads, their petals silky. I offered them to her, and she smiled wide, showing her crooked incisor, and pulled one flower free, then tucked it behind my ear. The touch of her finger across my cheek made me shiver, and this time it was she who glanced at my chest, then away, her cheeks flushed. I sat beside her.

She buried her nose in her bouquet and lifted an eyebrow at me. I felt another tug in my belly. Was this how it was supposed to feel? Exciting and scary all at the same time? I wanted to be around her for hours. She made me dizzy. Her smell, the way she laughed, her confidence.

"Let's take a selfie." She wiggled closer so that our thighs touched and held up her phone. I liked seeing our faces together, hair blending, eyes lit with sun. She took a few photos. We made funny faces. "I'll text you copies," she said, and I gave her my number. The photos whisked through and hit my phone with a ping. I smiled at them, scrolled through.

"Most of my selfies are with Jonny. You're a lot prettier."

She laughed, but her voice was serious when she said, "Did you and Jonny ever date?"

I shook my head. "It's not like that with us. I've dated guys, but I don't know. I never connected with any of them. Guess I've been waiting for someone special." Our eyes met. "What about you?"

"I've liked boys and girls." She shrugged. "I just feel things and I go for it." This time it was a warning tug in my stomach. Maybe she could feel something for someone else tomorrow, or another day. Maybe this moment at the lake didn't mean all that much to her.

"That's cool."

She held my hand. "I feel something *good* when I'm with you." She rubbed a circle on my palm with her thumb. "It's like, I'm sad for you because of your dad . . ." My hand stiffened. She smoothed the tight muscles and met my eyes. "But I'm happy, because I'm with you."

I curled my fingers and touched the delicate gold bracelet on her wrist, felt the soft flutter of her pulse. She only had a single charm on the link. A small green turtle. "It's pretty."

"It's from Hawaii. I went there with my family."

"Where are they?"

"Vancouver. I only talk to my sister." She was still holding my hand, but I could tell by the tone in her voice, something fragile and achy, that it hurt her to say it out loud. "I ran away."

"Serious?"

"Sort of. They know I'm here, but they're angry that I dropped out of school, and for partying, dating girls." She met my eyes. "They found Jesus when I was a kid, started going to church twice a week, prayer group. I got so sick of it—the lying, how fake everyone was. I was going to the Yukon to meet friends and stopped here for gas. Mason had a sign in the window. . . ." She shrugged.

"How old are you?"

"Eighteen last month. Anyway, let's not talk about serious stuff, okay?"

I scuffed my sandal against the picnic table. Why did I have to go and wreck the mood? I could feel her body cooling beside me, the light in her eyes dimming. "Sorry."

She hooked her finger under my chin and drew my face toward her. "I just want to think about you." Her finger was warm, her voice husky. She leaned forward, and I realized she was going to kiss me. There were voices in the campground. People could see us, but she didn't care, and then I didn't care—because this beautiful girl wanted me.

Her lips were soft and tasted faintly of peach from the cider we'd shared. I lost myself in the velvet of her mouth. I felt a little high, a little drunk, a little bit of all the good things in life.

Vibration, against my hip. My phone on the table. I ignored it. Tried to lose myself again. The phone kept going. She paused and pulled back. "Do you need to get that?"

"No." I shook my head, and the vibrating stopped. My phone chirped with a text message. Jonny was probably at the racetrack. What if he'd gotten hurt?

"Just a second." I picked up my phone, swiped my finger across the screen.

We need you to come home and watch Cash. I stared at the sentence. Vaughn. I didn't want to leave Amber. I set the phone back down, but it chirped again.

Amber was watching my face. She frowned. "What's going on?"

"It's Vaughn. They want me to babysit."

"I guess you have to go." She didn't say it like a question. She must know what Vaughn was like, and for a moment I was tempted to tell her everything. Maybe she would understand.

But then it might change how she acted around him at the diner. He would get suspicious.

"Yeah, I should."

She slid off the table, brushed pine needles from the back of her towel. We'd left our shorts on the hood of her car to warm in the sun. "Okay."

We drove back in silence. Her car was a silver Mazda with a sun-faded dashboard and ripped seats, but it was tidy and smelled like her coconut suntan lotion. A small stuffed unicorn hung from the rearview mirror, white with a silver horn. I made it twirl with my finger. I wanted to tell Amber that she made me feel like magic, floating and spinning, but I kept quiet.

When we passed the billboard, she made the sign of the cross. "I think about her," she said. "That Shannon girl. I hope she didn't suffer."

"Me too," I mumbled, but after what Vaughn said, I knew Shannon had probably died in a lot of pain. She must have been so scared. That was the part that upset me the most. Wondering what she thought about in those last moments. Did she give up? Did she fight all the way to the end? I glanced over at Amber. "Don't travel this road alone, okay? And don't stop for anyone."

She gave me a nervous look. "You're freaking me out."

I didn't like that I'd said almost the same thing to Vaughn, but this was different.

"It's important. Promise me."

"Okay." Her voice was soft, her eyes wide. "I promise."

We were at the road near my aunt's house. "Can you let me out here? Vaughn . . ."

"Sure, totally." She pulled over, put the car in park. "Text you later?"

"Yeah." I hoped she might kiss me again, but then another text message chirped. I pulled my phone out of my side pocket and turned it off.

"Are you going to be in trouble if you don't answer?"

"No, he's just telling me to get home." I shrugged and gathered my backpack, acting like it happened all the time. "Talk to you later."

I walked around the corner and the house came into view. The driveway was empty. If neither of them was home, why had he texted? I looked back over my shoulder. Amber was already gone. Gravel crunched under my feet as I walked toward the house. Crickets chirped in the grass. Cash loved to catch them. I'd help him for hours, just to avoid being inside.

I used my key and let myself into the house, hung my backpack by the door. When I turned my cell back on, there were no new messages. I plugged my phone into the charger. Maybe Lana had parked in the garage. I called out, but she didn't answer. The house was empty.

There were a few plates and glasses on the counter, so I slid them into the dishwasher, popped in a detergent tablet, and turned it on. Even though Lana said I was family, it still felt like I needed to earn my keep. I hadn't forgotten how Vaughn had called me a problem.

I found a bag of chips in the pantry and was walking out of the kitchen when the front door opened, then closed with a slam. Vaughn, wearing jeans and a black windbreaker. I stopped abruptly. I hadn't heard his truck over the sound of the dishwasher.

He set his camera bag onto the table, his gaze going to my wet hair, then down my body. I was in Amber's bathing suit, my T-shirt overtop, everything damp. I crossed my arms over my chest, the chips hanging loose from my hand.

"You said you needed me to babysit."

"We're going out."

"Lana's not here."

"You didn't ask if you could go to the lake." He grabbed a beer out of the fridge, pulling the tab and taking a swallow. I stood near the counter.

"It was a last-minute thing."

"The way you were kissing Amber it looked like you've spent a lot of time together." He took another swallow of his beer. "Stopped to take some photos and saw it all."

My cheeks flamed. The best thing in my life, the truest thing, and he'd been watching. I couldn't talk. I couldn't say a word. I looked at his camera case.

My cell chirped on the counter. A text. I spun around, but not fast enough. He grabbed my phone. The screen was bright. It hadn't locked yet.

"That's mine!" I tried to snatch it from his hand, but he stepped back.

He was swiping his finger up my screen. Reading my text messages, and all I could do was watch and seethe. Thank God I'd erased my conversations with Jonny. Vaughn tapped at the screen, swiped some more, tapped again. My photos? Facebook? What was he looking at?

After a moment he lifted his head, his ghost eyes narrowed. "I thought you were a smart girl, Hailey. You can't rent a place without money, and I know every business owner in this town. You think they want to hire a messed-up kid? I'll make sure they don't."

"People *know* me. I've lived here my entire life."

"That doesn't mean anything. Children's Aid won't put you in a foster home either. Not when you're already in a stable home." He dropped my cell onto the counter, spun it with his hand, and watched as it slid toward the edge. "Should've cleared your search history."

I was breathing hard. Like he could do this, shrink my life down to nothing? I lunged toward my phone, but before I could take two steps, he was there, grabbing the front of my shirt in a handful, wrenching me toward him, almost lifting me off the floor.

"You've just lost your bike privileges, and you aren't going anywhere until you prove I can trust you. Not alone, or with any of your trashy friends."

He let go, and I stumbled back. "My friends aren't *trashy*." My phone was on the counter, finally within reach. I grabbed it and clutched it to my chest. "You can't lock me up."

"You sure about that? Maybe I should go by your dad's shop and have a look at your dirt bike. If I find Cooper's missing carburetor, that would be a big problem."

"You're *threatening* me?"

"It's called leverage. Stay out of trouble and you have nothing to worry about."

My chest was so choked up with rage I could barely get a breath out. I scrambled for a response. "You wouldn't do that. You don't want to upset Lana."

We held gazes for a few tense moments. I'd pushed him too far. Called his bluff. I waited for him to lose it, but his face stayed smooth and cool.

"I don't know what you think you're doing, but you don't want to play this game with me. You'll never win." He took his beer and walked down the hall. I thought he was going to the master bedroom for a shower, but a moment later I heard the back door shut.

From my window I watched as he disappeared into his office outside.

CHAPTER 5

Cash skipped around the playground and climbed the slide, then headed over to the monkey bars. He grinned at me, his eyes bright and sparkling. He hadn't stopped moving since we'd arrived. Occasionally he'd come over for noisy slurps from his water bottle, then he'd sprint off. I wondered what would happen to him with Vaughn for a stepfather. Would he grow up mean? Would he become a cop too? His real father was out of his life, so it wasn't like he had any other role models. He'd already started collecting toy cop cars and staged high-speed chases, begged Vaughn to turn on the siren in his truck. I hated the idea of sweet Cash thinking that Vaughn was his hero.

For the last few days, I'd been staying out of the house with Cash, walking to the water park or the playground. I'd taken a screenshot of Vaughn's shift schedule, but he could stop by anytime to check on me. I'd find signs that he'd come home for lunch. Bread crumbs, a pot in the sink, dirty Tupperware containers. Lana knew Vaughn had locked up my bike because I'd gone to the lake—and lied to her. I apologized the next morning. "I'm sorry. We were *going* to go shopping, but it was so hot, and I didn't think it would be such a big deal if we went to the lake."

"Two girls, alone at the lake? It's not safe." Her eyes shifted away, like she couldn't meet my gaze. I wondered what else they'd talked about. Had he told her about the kiss?

"I *need* my bike."

She shook her head, her lips a tense line. "I know this is a difficult time, but that's no excuse for lying. Cash is at an impressionable age. He looks up to you." She stood, began to tidy the kitchen, and didn't offer me breakfast. The real punishment was clear. She'd offered mothering, and now she was taking it away. Fine by me. It would make the next part easier.

Meeting Jonny at the park like this was a risk. My body was so tense it felt like I'd been riding for hours on a mountain trail, my stomach muscles washboard-tight. I had no doubt that Vaughn would make good on his threats if he caught me. I only phoned Jonny from the closet late at night, and I deleted my call history. We didn't text—we sent messages through Facebook, but I deleted those too, and made sure to sign out. Thankfully he'd gotten the carburetor off my bike.

So far Cash hadn't noticed Jonny standing on the other side of the tree with a baseball cap pulled low, but I kept close watch of him while Jonny and I talked.

"Vaughn's skipped a few lodge meetings, or he arrives late," Jonny said. "It's been going on for a while. No one complains because it's Vaughn."

"God, he's such a dick. He *has* to be cheating on her. I'm going to break into his office and find proof." Leverage. That's what he called it. I swished the word around in my mouth.

"How the hell are you going to do that?"

"I still have my dad's lock-pick set." Dad was always losing his keys. I'd taught myself to use the picks too. "I'll do it today. Vaughn's at a safety presentation."

"You *sure* he doesn't have an alarm?"

"I didn't see any wiring." There were no motion cameras on the corner of the shed or the house. The house didn't even have an alarm. Vaughn didn't think anyone would mess with him, and he definitely didn't have to worry about Lana disobeying his orders. He was her sun, moon, every damn thing. I swear she would stop breathing if he told her to. She was always dressing up for him and getting her hair done—spritzing perfume on before he got home. When she served him dinner, she barely touched hers until he took a bite first. The only time she seemed relaxed was when he made her his "special" martinis on certain nights, acting like it was romantic when he was really just getting her sloshed so she'd go to bed early. Then he'd go out to his office.

One night I walked into the living room, looking for my iPad, and he was standing there, scrolling through it. He handed it to me without saying anything, but I knew he'd read the messages between me and Amber. We'd been texting every night, and we added each other as Facebook friends. Amber Chevalier. Even her name was beautiful. I looked through all her photos, found some of her sister, Beth, who was pretty too, but in a more serious way. Blond hair, usually in a high ponytail, wisps around her face, light makeup, a thoughtful expression. Only a few photos with her smiling. She had a crooked incisor like Amber. Beth wanted to be a lawyer, and Amber said she was super-smart. Maybe I would meet her one day. The three of us would go for lunch at the diner, laughing, happy. Amber would hold my hand at the table.

She asked if we could hang out again, and I told her that Vaughn had grounded me—I'd felt stupid admitting that. Dad *never* grounded me. I told her I'd come up with a plan. I was too scared to sneak around. My only chance was if I could beat Vaughn at his own game.

"He'll notice anything out of place," Jonny said.

"I'm not planning on screwing up. I'll phone you later."

After he was gone, I called Cash back to me and stopped to pick up a tub of ice cream on the way home, cherry vanilla to hide the taste of Benadryl.

Once Cash had finished a full bowl and was asleep on the floor in front of the TV, I sneaked out to the backyard. It took me a couple of minutes to pick the lock, forcing my hands to be steady and listening hard, before the shed lock released. With a quick glance over my shoulder to confirm that Cash wasn't coming, I opened the door and stepped into the office.

It was small, with a portable air conditioner humming in the corner, and laminate floors. Shelves lined both walls and a reading chair was tucked into a corner with a lamp. I'd never seen Vaughn pick up a book in the house. Nothing personal on his desk. No photos of him and Lana or Cash. No papers or notepads. Two file cabinets were on one side, but they had combination locks. If I tried to mess with those, I might scratch the metal.

I sat in his chair and flipped open his laptop, rubbed my sweaty palms on my legs. The Mac screen appeared, desert dunes, and a white rectangle. Password-protected. Of course.

Lana's name didn't work. Neither did their phone number. I didn't know their anniversary or birth dates. I stared at the white space, then closed the laptop. Before I left, I put the chair back the same way and checked that none of my hair had fallen onto the desk. Last thing I needed was bright copper strands advertising, *Hailey was here!*

When I sneaked back into the house, Cash was still asleep in the living room. Lana would be home soon, but I had a little time. Jonny picked up on the first ring.

"His laptop is password-protected," I hissed into the phone as I loitered in the hallway, close enough to see Cash but hopefully not wake him. "I can't get into his file cabinets either."

"Shit." Jonny was quiet, thinking it through. "Okay, you have to shoulder-surf. Like how people steal passwords at gas stations or bank machines, you know?"

"Dude. I can't spy through his window—it's tinted."

"Set up a motion-sensor camera and aim it at his desk. Watch him type in his passwords."

"Where can I get a camera? How much will it cost?" Vaughn

banked all the babysitting money I earned, and Lana only gave me twenty-five dollars a week for anything personal.

"I'll get it. Hang on for a couple of days."

"Okay." I erased my call history and tucked my phone into my pocket.

Vaughn missed dinner. I could tell Lana was scared, though she didn't say anything. She paced, nudged the silverware she'd set out for him, glanced out the window. Finally, she picked up his plate and covered it with foil, placed it on the counter. I was on the couch, scrolling through my phone, and pretended not to notice. But when our eyes met, she gave me a half-hearted smile.

We both heard the crunch of his tires outside at the same time. She flew to the front door, and I bolted down the hall. I hadn't made it into my bedroom when I heard the door open.

"Vaughn, I was getting worried!"

"Sorry, babe. Long call. Meant to text you, but . . ."

"It's okay. Hungry? I made pork chops."

"Sounds great. Let me grab a quick shower first."

"I've left it on the counter. I have to run to the store for milk."

"Cash asleep?"

"Yeah. Hailey must have gone to bed too. She was here a minute ago."

"Drive carefully. Lots of deer on the road." A long pause during which I guessed they were embracing. I slipped into my room and quietly closed the door behind me.

The garage door opened, and her car drove off. The TV went on in the living room. Sounded like sports. Maybe hockey. Something with loud cheering. I stared at my doorknob.

Footsteps came down the hall. I tensed, but they didn't slow. The back door creaked. I went to the window, lifted the edge of the curtain, and peeked out. Vaughn was unlocking the shed door. A light flicked on in the shed, a soft glow, probably the desk lamp. I watched until the light went off a few minutes later, then I dropped the curtain, hurried over to the bed, and listened as the back door opened. Footsteps going to the master bedroom, water running. Finally.

I leaned back against my pillow with the iPad balanced on my rib cage. Good. He had no idea I had been inside his office. I sent a message to Jonny through Facebook, then tapped the albums. I'd saved some photos of Amber there—in case Vaughn ever took away my devices.

Wait. Footsteps. Coming closer. I sat up. A sharp knock on my door, and then it opened. Vaughn stood there. I pulled my legs against my chest, turned the iPad screen away. His face was a blank mask as he leaned against the doorframe, thumb loosely hooked in his pocket.

"How about you come out and watch a movie with me and Lana?"

"Um, no, thanks . . . I'm watching videos."

"Everything okay?"

"Yeah. I'm just tired."

He came into the room, glancing around in a way that made my stomach clench. He sat on the bed by my feet, the mattress sagging under his weight. "You sure? Anything you want to get off your mind?" He was holding my gaze. I couldn't tell if he was serious or if it was his creepy way of telling me that he knew I'd been in his office.

"I'm fine." I shrugged. "Still dealing with everything, I guess."

"Well, if you want to go fishing one day, I can take some time off."

"No, thanks. It wouldn't be the same without my dad. He

was the best." It was a blow, but Vaughn didn't take the bait, and only narrowed his eyes slightly.

"We appreciate everything you've been doing with Cash. He says you've been taking him to the water park every day. I'm sure it's boring for you."

Was he getting suspicious? He was being so nice all of a sudden. It felt like he was leading up to something, but I didn't know what.

"I like watching him having fun."

He noticed me fiddling with my iPad. "What have you got there?"

"I was going through some photos."

"Yeah?" He grabbed it out of my hands before I could stop him and began scrolling through my Facebook album. "You have a good eye."

"Give it back."

He just held it high, out of my reach. My cheeks burned. Amber had sent me selfies—in bed, her hair draped over a pillow, eyes sleepy. I'd sent one back, standing in the bathroom mirror, bikini, dim lighting, my back arched. She'd replied with a row of hearts and flames.

He shook me free of his arm. "This is dangerous, you know. Someone could hack in, next thing you know your photos are all over the internet. Doesn't matter if you take them down. There'll be a thousand screenshots."

"I'm careful."

He held the iPad up, showed me the selfie of Amber and me at the lake. "This one is nice." How could he make something sound so terrifying without showing anything on his face? Amber had posted that photo on her Facebook page, with the caption "My Lady of the Lake." I'd been nervous but excited too. She'd made us public. She wasn't ashamed like Vaughn was making me feel. I scrambled forward, yanking at his arm again, and stretching toward the iPad.

The sound of tires on the gravel driveway, the garage door scraping up. Lana was home.

Vaughn gave me back my iPad and stood up. "Make sure you keep that in a safe place. If I've learned one thing, it's that you can't let down your guard. Even with your closest friends. You never know what they're really up to." He smiled. "Have a good night."

CHAPTER 6

Vaughn was on shift; Lana had taken Cash to his swimming lesson. The second her car disappeared around the corner, I went outside to pick the lock on the office shed. It had taken three days for Jonny to find a small enough security camera, then we practiced at the park—taking videos of each other, his truck—until we knew the best distance for a clear shot.

I used Vaughn's chair as a stool, balancing carefully, while I placed the camera on the shelf beside his desk. I tucked it into a dark corner, perched on top of a book. Using the app on my iPhone, I tested the camera and made sure the lens was pointed at his keyboard from the side.

If all went according to plan, the camera would be triggered by Vaughn walking into the office, and I'd be able to watch over his shoulder. Then I'd have his laptop password.

After dinner, I complained about stomach cramps. Lana brought me Advil and a cup of tea, offered me a hot water bottle for my stomach, which I accepted with a fake-tired voice.

"It's probably just stress," I told her when she felt my forehead with a worried expression. It wasn't a complete lie. I'd barely been able to eat any of the pot roast she'd made. Vaughn, though, had had seconds, praising Lana for the tenderness of the meat. *Don't even need a knife to cut through this, babe*, and she glowed with happiness.

I lay in the dark and waited until everyone went to sleep. I'd almost given up, my eyes drifting closed. Vaughn wasn't going out to the shed tonight.

Then I heard it—or felt it. The sense that someone was moving in the house. Was that a door clicking open? I frowned, trying to figure out if it was a bathroom or the back door. When I didn't hear anything else, I crawled to my window.

I stared into the dark, waiting, and was rewarded when a soft light flicked on in his office. He might be calling the other woman or emailing her. Something I could get in a screenshot. I couldn't wait to get inside his laptop. Ten minutes later the office went dark. I hurried into my bed.

The back door opened, and his footsteps went down the hall to the bedroom he shared with Lana. I stared up at the ceiling. Tomorrow I'd find out what he'd been doing in his office.

My phone vibrated under my hand, waking me. Facebook Messenger. Amber. I blinked in the dim light and glanced at the clock. Six. She'd be going to the diner soon. I rolled onto my side, head on the pillow, and opened her message. *Good morning, beautiful. How's prison life?*

Oh, you know. Bars on the window, stale bread under the door.

Don't eat gluten. Can you FaceTime?

Vaughn hasn't left yet.

Mason asked about you. I told him that you can't go anywhere.

What did he say?

He just shook his head, but swear to God, I think he burnt Vaughn's burger on purpose. I better get ready for work. FaceTime later?

OK. Later! XO

The water was running in the master bathroom. Vaughn showering. Lana was in the kitchen, opening and closing the fridge. Making coffee. Her slippers whispered down the hall. She was bringing him a cup. Like she did every single morning. Then she'd pour one into a stainless-steel thermos for him to take in his truck. The shower turned off. The murmur of voices.

Vaughn's deep timber, hers light, laughing about something. The closet sliding. The jingle of a belt. Normal daily sounds. Nothing that would hint at his secret nighttime activities.

When they went silent for a moment and Lana softly giggled, I realized they were kissing and pressed the pillow over my head.

They passed my room. Vaughn's aftershave drifted under the door. Cash chatted with him in the kitchen, spoons clattering. Vaughn promised they would play video games later. When he finally left, I used the bathroom, then headed straight for the coffee.

Lana turned from the sink where she was washing dishes. She was humming a cheerful tune. "You're up! Here, I made muffins." She set one on a plate and slid it in front of me.

So much for escaping back to my room. I slumped into a chair. "Thanks."

Lana sat across from me and launched into questions about my house. Like did I want any dishes, my mom's paintings, and she told me that she'd gone over with boxes and began to sort through Dad's personal belongings. I gritted my teeth at that. We had agreed to wait.

"Vaughn thinks we should put your dad's outdoor equipment on Craigslist, but we need to do it soon. He said the house is a target with no one living there now."

"I just woke up. Can we talk about this later?" This was the second breakfast in which Lana had tried to use her baking to soften a hard conversation. It didn't work. The idea of Vaughn going through my dad's things, deciding on prices, talking to people, all smooth and polite as he made them a deal, gave me a gnawing, desperate feeling. He didn't have the *right*.

"Of course. Sorry."

I got up quickly, my knees hitting the table and the chair sliding out loudly behind me. Lana winced, probably thinking about her wood floors. I washed my plate, refilled my coffee. I glanced over my shoulder. Lana was watching me with a concerned expression. My tone had been too abrupt. She might tell Vaughn I was rude. He might find some new way to punish me.

"Do you need any help with chores?"

Her face brightened. "That would be wonderful."

We did laundry, changed all the bedding. She vacuumed while I dusted. We even washed the windows, which she was thrilled about. "Vaughn loves coming home to a clean house." It already seemed clean to me, but I smiled and kept scrubbing. Lunch passed, and I ate a sandwich while I hung sheets up outside in the sun. I kept looking at the shed. I wanted back inside.

I was wiping the shelves in the fridge when I bumped into the new jug of milk and it fell out onto the tiled floor. It flowed everywhere in a white tidal wave.

I dropped to my knees with a cloth. "I'm so sorry, Lana."

"It's okay." She crouched beside me and wiped at the cabinets. Cash had run over when he heard the noise and looked at me accusingly.

"You spilled my milk!"

"We'll go to the store," Lana said. "I need a few things for dinner anyway."

Perfect. She'd be gone for at least an hour. I kept my expression flat and worked on soaking up the puddle of milk.

Cash wandered back out of the kitchen, flopped onto the couch. "I want to stay here. I'm watching my show."

Lana got to her feet. "Do you mind? It would give me a chance to run a few errands, and I'd love to stop by the salon and get a manicure."

Shit. Of course she'd want time alone. Going anywhere for a couple of hours without a kid was probably a luxury vacation for her. I tried to think of an excuse, but I had no good reason for not being willing to hang out with Cash for a while. No school. No other job.

"No problem."

I made Cash popcorn, poured some juice, and checked how far he was into his movie. I'd watched *Cars* so many times with him I almost had it memorized. There was an action scene coming up. If I moved fast, I should be able to get back inside before he needed anything.

"Hey, Cash. I'm going out to weed the garden for a bit, okay?"

"Okay." He dipped his hand into the popcorn bowl and didn't look up. Good. I grabbed some gloves, Lana's bag of garden tools, and dropped them in the flower bed.

A glance over my shoulder, a minute to pick the lock, and I was inside. The camera was still in the same spot. I pulled it down and played the video. Vaughn sitting at his desk. His shoulders were hunched, and he was wearing a ball cap. He moved in quick motions, flipping his laptop open and typing in his password with one hand. I paused the video and typed the series of numbers and letters into notes on my phone. They didn't form a word or code that I recognized.

Something filled his screen, a website or photos, dark colors. He took his camera out of the case, which was sitting on the desk, and plugged in a cord. He was transferring photos.

I tried to make out the images, but all I could see were the thumbnails, and they were too small. He plugged something else into the computer. Maybe a portable hard drive.

After a few minutes, he removed it and closed the laptop. He never checked emails or made a phone call. Never opened a file cabinet. All he did was transfer those photos. His large shape moved toward the door. He paused and looked back, and for a terrifying moment I forgot he couldn't see me. This was recorded video, not live. The screen went black. He'd turned off the light.

I sat in his chair and typed the code into his laptop. His desktop screen came into view. It worked! Now, which folder to try first? I clicked on a few. Taxes, banking info. One of the files was labeled "birds." I opened it and found a series of other folders. Numbered—no names. My heart had begun to beat fast, my mouth dry. What if it was dead bodies?

My hand hovered over the tracking pad, then I clicked. Thumbnails. I opened one and a hazy black-and-white image filled the screen. Like from a video still. I wasn't sure what I was looking at, then I realized it was a bathroom—and the photo was aimed between a woman's legs.

On autopilot, I clicked through more photos. Women's legs, underwear pulled down, a flash of a tattoo on someone's lower stomach, bright colors, the hollow of a belly button. No faces were ever shown. I click opened another folder labeled with numbers. New images appeared. A girl sleeping in a bed, the shots grainy and blue. Then I recognized the bedding.

My heart stilled, no longer able to keep up its frantic beat, exhausted from shock. I clicked through the photos. My face was never visible, like he hadn't wanted to see *me*, just my body. My white tank top, nipples showing under the thin material, my bare legs kicking out. My underwear, the shadow between my thighs. The shots were taken from above, at an angle. I couldn't see the window or the dresser or the closet. The camera was only aimed at the bed.

There were shots of me riding my bike, close-ups of my butt on the seat, my bare legs, the back of my thighs. And in the bathroom. I'm undressing, pulling off my T-shirt, stepping out of my underwear. Drying off after my shower, the towel draped loosely around my chest, my wet hair on my shoulders.

Others showed me in the distance. Sitting on the shore in

a bikini, looking down, my face in shadow. The lake in the evening light. I peered closer. Jonny stood on the wharf with some of the guys. Was he wearing those shorts the night of the bonfire, when Vaughn picked me up?

I opened the next folder. Amber and me on the picnic table—not our faces—just our mouths pressed together, hands in each other's hair, towels around our waists, breasts touching.

A loud slam echoed across the yard—the back door. I jerked to my feet.

"Hailey! Where are you?" Cash.

I signed out, slapping at the keys, closed the laptop, and shoved the security camera into my pocket. When I stepped out of the office, Cash was marching across the lawn, his gaze fixed on the flower bed on the other side of the yard, searching for me.

"What's going on, buddy? Movie over already?"

He stopped, hands on hips, his bony kid's chest bare, camouflaged shorts oversized and showing the band of his dinosaur underwear. "Why are you in Vaughn's office?"

"I'm not. I was checking some plants behind it."

"What plants?" He was walking toward me now, curious. I forgot you can't lie to kids, not easily anyway. They wanted proof of anything different.

"Itchy ones. They sting."

He stopped abruptly with his eyes wide. "Sting?"

"Yup. Stinging nettles." I headed toward him, reached down for his hand, and swung it lightly. "Let's see if there's any ice cream left."

He peered up at me, his face scrunched. "Your hand is shaking."

"I'm excited for ice cream. Come on, race me to the house."

CHAPTER 7

I stared blankly at the TV. Cash leaned against me, laughing at the movie as if he'd never seen it before. Then he climbed down to play with his toy cars on his racetrack and asked if I could put him to bed tonight because he liked it when I read his favorite truck book. "You make the best engine noises!" But his voice seemed to be coming from far away, and I wasn't sure if I answered.

He was still hungry, even after the ice cream, so I got him a bag of chips, and changed the channel to *Spy Kids*. "Back in a minute, buddy." I went into my bedroom and acted as if I were casually gathering a few things—phone charger, lip balm, a pair of socks—all the while hunting for Vaughn's camera. It had to be near my bed. The dresser, window, and closet weren't in any photos. Then I noticed the wall clock, lined up with my mattress. Of course. The asshole.

I made myself walk back out to the living room. How could I ever shower again in this house, lie down in that bed? I thought back to the times I'd spoken on the phone and FaceTimed with Amber. Did the videos have audio too? I was glad that I had hidden in the closet when I called Jonny. I wanted to talk to him *now*. I had to tell him. My uncle had naked *photos* of me. What had he been doing with them? I thought about him touching himself while looking at me, and my body recoiled into the corner of the couch as Cash ran his toy trucks over the cushions.

Vaughn must have been transferring the photos the night I spied on him. Creepy guys had online forums. The dark web.

My photos could be on porn sites. Men all over the world might be looking at me. Fantasizing. Masturbating. And who were all those other women?

He hadn't taken photos—that I knew of—from the living room, but I still felt like I was being watched and kept my legs crossed and my arms over my breasts. From my spot on the couch, I glanced around. What would the camera look like? It could be hidden in anything. I was scared that somehow, just by how I walked or acted, he would realize I knew his secret. Should I take a chance, get the laptop and take it to the police?

I didn't have a car. Cash would follow me outside.

Vaughn would kill me.

When Lana came home, I thought I could escape for a while, but where could I go? She was in a rush as she dumped her purse onto the counter and said, "Can you help with dinner?" She opened the fridge and passed me vegetables.

I chopped. I ripped lettuce. Behind me, my aunt moved around the kitchen. How could she not know that Vaughn was a creep? Wasn't she suspicious of him at *all*? She'd even reminded me to keep the bathroom window open. I felt sick with hurt. Like she had betrayed me.

The salad was finished. Lana glanced at it with a smile. "You're an angel." She asked me to strain the noodles, and explained how she made the sauce, pointed out the spices. I frowned at the bubbling liquid and fought back tears when I realized she was being motherly and passing on her recipe. Lana scooped spaghetti sauce onto a bowl of steaming pasta and passed it to me.

"Ta-da!"

I held the bowl, staring down at the food. My throat was so tight I couldn't imagine trying to swallow a single mouthful. "I'm not really all that hungry."

She gave me a look. "What have you eaten today?"

My thoughts fumbled. *Had* I eaten? The morning felt like years ago. The day was a void. Cash yelled, "She didn't eat anything! Not even ice cream!"

I smiled weakly and set the bowl on the table, moved back to the kitchen to help Lana serve the rest. I might be able to get through it. I'd watch TV later and pretend to fall asleep on the couch. I'd send Jonny a message and meet him somewhere tomorrow. Vaughn was supposed to be working late, but then I heard the truck and turned to look out the front window.

"Can you give this to Cash?" Lana was holding out another bowl.

"Vaughn's home." I almost choked on the words. Did he know I'd found the photos? What was he going to do?

"Oh, good! He must have finished early." She made a small motion with the bowl to get my attention. I took it and set it hard onto the wood table in front of Cash, who was playing a video game on his tablet. He looked up, startled, but I was already turning away. I'd go to the bathroom, say that my stomach cramps were back.

Too late. Vaughn was coming through the door, his dark shape looming in the hallway, boots heavy on the hardwood. I was caught between the dining table and the kitchen.

He was holding a bouquet of roses, his other hand around the neck of what looked like a wine bottle in a paper bag. His eyes skimmed over me, then lit up when he saw Lana.

"There she is!"

She spun around, laughing. He handed her the roses, pulled her in for a hug, and danced her a couple of steps around the kitchen floor. Cash giggled. I couldn't make a sound, couldn't move. I was paralyzed again. How could he seem so *normal*? It was awful watching Lana with him. She had to be oblivious, to let him touch her like that.

When Vaughn finally released Lana, she turned to me with

a smile. "Can you put these in a vase while I finish dishing out everyone's food?" She passed me the roses in their plastic wrapping.

Vaughn leaned against the kitchen counter, stealing bits of garlic bread while Lana admonished him. Their voices were low, intimate. I snipped the bottom of the roses. Thorns stabbed into my thumb. I gripped until blood swelled, then dropped the flowers with a cry.

"I need a Band-Aid." I rushed to the bathroom—the suite off Cash's room—where I sucked at the air in heaving gasps, splashed cold water on my face.

I pressed my palms hard against my face, squeezed my cheekbones, and stared at the side of the tub until my vision came back into focus. One of Cash's toy trucks sat on the edge. He'd asked me to read to him later. I picked up the truck, spun the wheels, and formed a plan.

When I felt calmer, I made my way back to the kitchen, slid into the seat beside Cash, who said sweetly, "You okay, Hailey?"

"You bet." I kissed his cheek.

Lana smiled and pushed the container of Parmesan across to me. I didn't look at Vaughn, but I could feel his presence at the end of the table. The sickeningly sweet scent of the roses was mixing with the scent of the spaghetti sauce and I wondered what would happen if I threw up all over the table. Would I be excused then? Somehow, I managed to sprinkle cheese across my sauce, blow on my spoon to cool a mouthful, and nod in approval.

I glanced at Lana. "Okay if I read to Cash tonight? I was thinking that I could sleep on his floor—my mattress should fit." I turned to Cash. "Wouldn't that be fun?"

"He'll never fall asleep." Vaughn's voice was firm. Was this what Lana thought made Vaughn such a good dad? Laying down rules? He was just a sick control freak. He'd probably become a cop so that he could make sure he never got caught while doing his dirty deeds.

"I will. I will!"

I kept my gaze on Lana. "The nights have been really hard, you know?" I hesitated, moved pasta around on my plate. "I start thinking about my dad, and I feel so alone . . ."

Her eyes softened. "Of course. We'll set up your bed after dinner."

"Thanks." I took a slice of garlic bread. "Just until I get more settled." Cash chattered about how we could build a fort, while I chewed slowly, nodding and smiling. I still didn't look at Vaughn. Not once. But I heard every scrape of his fork against his plate.

The window wouldn't open. I used the flashlight app on my phone to shine around the frame. Behind me, Cash was sprawled across his bed, softly snoring. Lana had drunk a lot of wine at dinner. Vaughn too. I hoped that meant they were sleeping soundly. Amber texted when she got off work at eleven, but I hadn't answered. I couldn't fake a normal conversation. Not when I was thinking about those photos. Once I had evidence and could have Vaughn arrested, I'd tell her.

There was some sort of childproof lock on the window—high up. The only way I was getting to it was if I moved a shelf of toys. Legos, musical instruments. Might as well have lined it with rat traps. The back door was too close to the master suite. I had to go out the front.

I turned the bedroom doorknob slowly, holding my breath as I stared at Cash's shape in the dark. He was still. I crept down the hallway and shoved my feet in my sandals at the entranceway. The door opened smoothly, but I used another shoe to wedge it slightly open so it wouldn't lock behind me. Before

I left the safety of the porch, I stopped and listened, let my eyes adjust. Vaughn's police truck glowed white in the driveway, moonlight reflecting on the stripes.

No movement in the house. No lights flicking on.

I moved swiftly across the grass.

It was harder to pick the lock on the shed in the dark and my fingers fumbled with the tools. Each time I broke into the shed, I risked leaving a scratch. This had to be the last time. I pleaded under my breath. Then finally a click, and the handle turned.

Hands out, I felt my way through the room, using the glow from my phone to guide me. My knee bumped Vaughn's chair. It was turned around. Had I left it that way earlier? I didn't have time to think about it. I reached for his laptop—and touched a smooth wood surface. I shone my phone at the desk. His laptop was gone. I stared at the empty space.

He must have come out here after dinner—or when I was giving Cash his bath. Did that mean that he knew I'd found out his secret? Was there a camera? I looked around the office. No lights, no small shapes. It could be hidden inside anything. I had to get out of here.

It was easier getting back inside the house. The door closed softly. I slipped off my shoes, padded through the living room, using my cell phone screen as a light. The laptop wasn't in his briefcase, or on the coffee table, or in the kitchen. I weighed the risk of sneaking into their room while they slept. I couldn't do it. He'd wake in an instant, and then how would I explain myself? Maybe I could do it when he showered in the morning. I'd make it seem as though I wanted to ask Lana something.

I was leaving the kitchen when I heard the unmistakable sound of steps. Someone was moving—slowly, carefully— down the hall. I shut off my phone and pressed against the fridge.

Vaughn's large shape came around the corner. The light flicked on, and our eyes met. He was holding a gun. I stared at the end of it, then up at him. He slowly lowered it to his side.

"What the fuck are you doing?" His voice was quiet, but hoarse with anger.

"I was hungry." I gestured to the fridge.

"I could have shot you, you idiot."

"I'm sorry." But it could have been Cash. Vaughn wouldn't shoot without checking, would he? I felt sweaty and panicked. Was this his way of warning me to keep my mouth shut?

"Well, are you eating or not?"

I pulled open the fridge, grabbed a couple slices of cheese, then some bread, and smeared butter across the pieces. I took a bite of this hastily made cheese sandwich and mumbled through my full mouth, "Lana makes the best fresh bread. I swear I was dreaming about it."

He was silent, but he'd relaxed his hold on the gun. He stepped to the side, making room for me to pass him, and pointed toward the rooms with the gun. "You better get to bed."

He didn't follow me down the hall. Moments later I heard muffled voices, sounded like a late-night news program. I didn't understand why he hadn't returned to his room, unless he was making sure that I couldn't leave again. I slid my mattress closer to Cash. His breath was soft and even, but I couldn't sleep. Every time I closed my eyes, I'd see my naked self on Vaughn's computer and think of him out in the living room. Was he panicking? If anyone saw those photos, he'd lose his marriage, his career. Maybe he was erasing everything on his laptop.

I must have fallen asleep. Hours later I woke abruptly, heart pounding. The house was quiet. He had to walk past this room to get to his own, and I never heard him. I rolled onto my side and noticed something on the floor beside me. I used my phone screen for light.

It was a plate, with a couple slices of cheese and bread. A glass of milk. He was mocking me. Letting me know he'd seen right through my lame excuse about being hungry.

It didn't matter where I slept. He could still get close.

Lana walked Vaughn to his truck at dawn. I crept out and got myself a coffee while she said goodbye in the driveway. They were trying to be quiet, but their voices drifted in through the open kitchen window. Lana said, "Be safe!" and he answered, "Always am!" I wanted to scream. He was probably driving away with the laptop.

I stayed on the couch all morning, complaining again of cramps when Lana asked if I wanted to come to the beach with her and Cash. "I'm just going to watch movies, maybe take a walk later if I feel better." I grimaced and clutched a hot water bottle against my stomach. She worried that I wasn't eating enough. I promised that I'd have some yogurt and fruit.

Vaughn had taught me something the night before. I left the TV playing to an empty house while I met Jonny a few streets down. I figured I was covered two ways—if any of the neighbors saw me outside, I'd already told Lana I might go for a walk, and if Vaughn *was* monitoring me through audio from the bedroom camera, he wouldn't know I'd left.

Jonny's truck slowed near the mailboxes where I was hiding, and I jumped into the cab, then lay down on the floorboards. We drove to the truck stop. It was one of the last places in town that still had a phone booth. In case there were security cameras, I wore my hair tucked up into Jonny's baseball cap, pulled on his work coat, and walked with a boy's swagger.

The Cold Creek police force numbered a grand total of

eleven cops, and most of them had worked with Vaughn for years. They weren't going to believe he was a dirty cop, but Thompson was new, and younger. Maybe he'd have an open mind. Maybe he'd at least look into it.

The police station operator put me straight through to Thompson. I'd expected his voice mail, a recording where I could leave an anonymous message. When he answered, "Thompson here," I thought about hanging up. Speaking to a real human was a big risk, but Vaughn could get rid of the evidence—or me. I thought of that gun pointing straight at my head.

I slipped my hand over the receiver and dropped my voice an octave, a husky sort of whisper. "I want to report a bad cop."

A long silence. Too long. I'd made a mistake calling him. He was probably signaling for Vaughn to listen in. He could be picking up another line.

"That right?" More silence. I peeked around the side of the phone booth, checking the parking lot. "What seems to be the problem?"

Was he actually listening or buying time? The police wouldn't put a trace on a call like this, would they? I didn't know how it all worked. Maybe everything got recorded.

"He's a creep. He's been taking pictures of girls with hidden cameras."

Another long pause. "How do you know?"

"I just do, okay? He has cameras in bathrooms. Like in public places." I didn't know how much to tell him. If I said the wrong thing, I could reveal my identity.

"This is a pretty serious allegation."

"I *know*," I hissed, impatient. "What are you going to do about it?"

"Well, first I need to take a statement. I could meet you somewhere—"

"No. No way. I'm not reporting him."

"I don't understand. Why did you call?"

"So *you* can find the cameras. Then you can arrest him."

"Who is the officer?"

I glanced over my shoulder and made sure no one was waiting to use the phone. "Vaughn."

He went quiet again. The dark echo of empty air. There was no background noise, not even breathing, and I wondered if he had hung up.

"And he's placed cameras in public places to take pictures of girls." His voice was quiet.

"I know what it sounds like. But, please—I'm telling the truth. He has a laptop, and an expensive camera with a long lens. He watches girls on the beach at the lake. You could catch him."

"Let's start with your name, okay?" A rig was pulling into the truck stop, the engine loud. Thompson might recognize the sound. I hung up the phone, ducked my head, walked around the side of the truck stop, and crossed the road to Jonny. My heart was racing, my head dizzy like the first time I'd tried a cigarette. I'd done it. I'd told someone, but would it matter? I couldn't tell whether Thompson believed anything I'd said. What if he *did* check into it and didn't find any cameras? What if he filed an official report about my call? Something Vaughn could read.

I had to get out of the house, and this town.

CHAPTER 8

Jonny and I sat on the floor in my dad's workshop with our backs against the wall, our shoulders bumping, and ate Dairy Queen hamburgers. He was shaking the fries around in their package, searching for the extra-salty ones. He glanced at me.

"Has Vaughn, you know, ever tried to touch you?"

"It's just the photos." I made myself take another bite of my burger, but the bun stuck in my throat, the meat tasted greasy, and I had to swallow hard.

"You don't have to run away." Jonny shifted his body so that he was facing me. He'd picked me up after riding his dirt bike and his brown hair was winging out in different directions. His T-shirt smelled of engine oil and dust. "Come live with us."

"He won't let me."

"You could go into a foster home."

"You're not listening, Jonny."

"Okay, talk to Thompson again. Tell him that *you* were the caller."

"Then Vaughn will kill me for sure." Just saying these words, the cold fact of them, made me feel sicker. I dropped my burger onto the waxy paper and wiped my fingers on my shorts.

"He can't just get rid of you, Hailey." His voice was soft.

"You want to bet? He'd make it look like suicide or an accident. He probably knows a hundred ways to get rid of someone."

I brought my knees up, pressed my forehead against the denim. "I'm running away."

Jonny was quiet for a couple of beats, his shoulder resting against mine. I could feel his blood pulsing beneath his skin, close as a brother. Sometimes I felt like I had known him even before I was born. Like we had never not been together. And I knew what he was thinking now.

"You can't go after him, Jonny."

His face flushed with anger, his eyes burning. "I could really fuck him up."

"He could really fuck *you* up. I thought about it, okay? I have a plan. Dad's dirt bike still has lots of gas. I can drive the back roads to the bus station. I'll go to Vancouver and live on the street, or in one of the youth hostels. I'll call Amber, and she can meet me. Her sister is there."

"You *hate* cities—and what will you do for money?"

I'd thought about that, too. "I'll pawn Dad's things. His knives and guns are worth a lot, and some of my mom's jewelry. Not her wedding band—I won't pawn that." I hated the idea of giving up any of their special things, but I'd find a way to buy them back.

"Then what? What about your future?"

"I'll be eighteen in a year. The house will sell, and that money has to be put in a trust for me. Lana and Vaughn can't spend it unless I'm proven dead or whatever."

"When are you going?"

"Tonight."

"Jesus, Hailey. At least let me drive you."

"No way. You have to be home or Vaughn will arrest you for helping a minor, or something crazy. Promise me you'll stay away from him? He's going to go nuts."

He shook his head, looking frustrated. "Fine, but I'm not

leaving you on the streets alone. I'll move to Vancouver too. We'll figure it out. We're a team, right?"

I leaned my head on his shoulder, took a breath. "Right."

I rolled over, checked my cell phone. Three in the morning. I grabbed my backpack and quietly swung it over my shoulders, watching Cash's sleeping face, lips parted as he softly snored, his arm flung above his head. I was going to miss him. He'd been my armor all night. We played games, I gave him his bath, got him into his pajamas, and read to him. Lana asked if I needed help and I shooed her away. "Relax, watch TV." All the while, I felt Vaughn watching me.

I'd slept in my leggings and a tank top, only needed a hoodie, and I didn't pack much.

The plan was for me to get Jonny's mountain bike where he was going to hide it in the woods and ride to my old house, where I'd take some of Dad's things and Mom's jewelry. Jonny bought prepaid phones so we could keep in touch. When I reached Vancouver, I'd call Amber.

I crept out of the bedroom, using my hand to stop the door from swinging shut, and then I walked straight into a body— hit Vaughn's chest like a wall and bounced back. He clamped his hand over my mouth and dragged me into the bathroom. It was so dark I couldn't see to grab anything. I clawed blindly for the counter.

"We don't have any stinging nettles, you idiot. You think I don't check with Cash about what you're up to? You think I don't know about your meetings with Jonny?"

I tried to twist away, but he had a strong grip on my elbow. "Stop," he growled into my ear, his hand pressed hard against my mouth. I wanted to bite him, make him release me, but I couldn't open my jaw. I hated the feel of his body against mine.

He yanked the pack from my shoulders and dropped it at my feet. "Whatever you think you found in my office doesn't exist, get it? And if it shows up again, it won't be on my computer. It will be on Jonny's."

I saw it all too clearly. The photos leaking on the internet and being traced back to Jonny. The police breaking into his house, taking his computer. His cell phone and iPad. Vaughn would collect the evidence. He could do whatever he wanted. The girls in the photos might be underage. Jonny would go to prison. Vaughn could have him hurt on the inside.

"Do we have an understanding?" I could barely move, but I nodded slightly. "Is this going to be a problem?" He pulled upward, his arm under my chin. I made a grunting sound.

No, no problem.

"Don't yell, don't move an inch." He removed his hand from my mouth. Noises behind me. He'd picked up my backpack.

"What have you got in here?" Zipping sounds as he checked each compartment. Soft thuds and rustles as some of my belongings fell on the bath mat. While he was distracted, I slid my free hand into my hoodie pocket, pulled out the prepaid phone, and quietly pushed it up onto the countertop where he wouldn't see it. Then I held my breath, praying he didn't turn on the light or frisk me. He'd feel the knife that I'd strapped to my calf. There was a heavier thump as he dropped the pack.

"You should be thanking me. You wouldn't have gotten far with any of this."

The click of the door handle, then his quiet footsteps down the hall. He'd left the door open. I picked up my pack and hugged it to my chest.

Three days later, Jonny drove the speed limit away from my old house, then gunned it when we got around the corner. I couldn't help but glance over my shoulder, even though I knew Lana, Vaughn, and Cash were at the fair. I was supposed to be with them. This morning I'd found Lana in the kitchen putting away the breakfast dishes, while Vaughn wrestled on the floor with Cash.

"I think you're right," I'd told Lana, my voice soft, resigned. Vaughn was listening, and I had to play my part perfectly. "I have to start sorting through my dad's personal stuff—I can't keep avoiding it. Maybe that's why I'm having nightmares. Can you drop me off?"

"Today? But we're going to the fair . . ."

"You don't want to do that alone." Vaughn sat straight while Cash flung himself across his back, tried to get him into a headlock. Vaughn tickled him until he screamed with giggles.

"That's sort of the point." I kept my gaze on Lana, made my eyes water. "It feels like something I *need* to do alone, and honestly, being around all of you as a family, it's hard."

"Oh, Hailey." Lana reached out and touched my shoulder. "I understand. You've to find your own way through this. We can drop her off, right, Vaughn?" She turned to look at him.

"Of course." He smiled, but I felt him studying my face. I kept my mouth downturned, chewed on my lower lip as though struggling to hold back my tears. *You just wait, asshole.*

It had been three long nights since Vaughn had threatened me in the bathroom. Three nights when I wondered if he would decide I was too much of a risk. Then it came to me.

I would still run away, but not to Vancouver. That had been a mistake. Vaughn would have the police looking for me. There'd be flyers. People might recognize me. I had to stay off the grid. Where no one would ever find me. I would live in the miner's cabin until I was of age.

Jonny glanced across the truck at me now. "You *sure* about this?"

We'd met at my house. He'd gotten my dad's old backroad maps from the workshop, while I shoved things in boxes and took photos so I could show Lana how productive I was being. I made sure to post a few on my Instagram page. #forsalesoon #estatesale #toolsandgear #makeyouroffer

Vaughn would think I was stupid—I was practically advertising for thieves. Which was the point. If I was going to rob my own house, the more Vaughn underestimated me, the better.

"Nothing else will work."

"The cabin is like fifty years old. There are bears and cougars, Hailey."

"I'll have *guns*, and I'd rather face whatever is in those woods than Vaughn."

"What about Lana and Cash?"

That was the hardest part—thinking about how they would react. Lana might freak out, and Cash was so sweet. What would this do to his six-year-old head? But I didn't have a choice.

"It's only until I turn eighteen." I'd planned every moment. Hour by hour. Still, so much could go wrong. "You should move too. Vaughn is going to be all over you."

"No way. I'm not leaving you out there alone."

"Then get security cameras—and something for your computer. Like a major firewall."

"Jesus, this is intense."

I stared at him until he looked at me. "You don't have to help me. I'll understand."

"Shut up." He reached across the bench seat, bumped his fist into my upper bicep. His way of saying he loved me, but I couldn't say it back. The words felt like a curse. Everyone I loved died. I turned to stare out the window. We just had to find the cabin and it would be okay.

The mountain would protect me. Dad had been preparing me since I was little. We were always camping. Rain, shine, or snow. Holiday or middle of the week. Dad didn't care. He rarely checked my report card, said he trusted me to see it through, and that he could teach me more than I'd ever learn within four walls. We took Jonny with us a lot of those weekends. Dad showed us how to find shelter, water, forage for berries and mushrooms. We navigated with a compass and the stars. We howled with wolves in the distance. Dad called us his pack. His wild cubs.

Sometimes Dad and I were only home for a few days before he was out in the backyard, staring at the mountain and motioning for me to come stand with him. He'd throw his arm around my shoulder, pull me close so I was tucked under the warm weight.

You feel it? The mountain's calling us, baby girl. She wants us to come home.

CHAPTER 9

Shards of glass covered the wood floors in Dad's workshop and crunched under the soles of my shoes. The gun safe lay on its side, the metal lock blackened from a blowtorch. Dad's quad was gone, same with my dirt bike. The workshop looked so empty without them. I spun in a slow circle. The fishing rods and the crossbow were removed from their holders. All the camping gear, Dad's outdoor clothing, his winter sleeping bag, knives, and toolboxes were also missing.

It was just as bad inside the house. The moving boxes were ripped open, clothing pulled out, dishes broken, pots and pans tossed, as though someone had been searching for jewelry or money, electronics. Any items they could sell. Other things were missing too, but they weren't of value to a normal thief, and the police wouldn't notice. Candles, batteries, flashlights, glue, string, water bottles, a few photo albums. The large framed photos I'd have to leave behind.

After Jonny and I had checked the miner's cabin to make sure it was still standing, we'd rushed to get everything ready. Vaughn had begun to make noise about me sleeping in my own room, and eventually Lana was going to relent. Now that I'd packed Dad's things, they were planning on holding an estate sale soon and storing my personal stuff in their garage. I was out of time.

During the week, Jonny went without me and stocked the cabin with supplies. It took him a few trips with his dad's quad and a trailer. He used his own money until he could sell my items.

Jonny and I planned the fake robbery for a day when Lana was taking Cash to a birthday party and Vaughn was giving a safety talk. Lana dropped me off with a few boxes to collect the last of the apples in the orchard. I'd told her that they made the best applesauce.

They'd think that the house was robbed the night before, and that I didn't notice right away that the front door was ajar because I was in the yard collecting apples. Meanwhile, Jonny had been moving things out, starting at dawn, when he rolled my dirt bike, Dad's quad, and his dirt bike into the gulley at the back of the property. After dark, he'd pick them up with his truck. Then he'd take Dad's bikes to a guy he knew who'd break them into parts and sell them. Same with Dad's power tools, watches, and Mom's jewelry. Jonny was going to file the serial number off my bike, paint it camouflage, and hide it partway up the mountain.

No way was I selling Dad's guns. Three rifles, two shotguns, and Dad's favorite, his .45 Smith & Wesson handgun. He loved them, and I needed them. Selling guns was too dangerous anyway. Jonny figured we'd get a few thousand for the bikes and tools. The money would be used for supplies and whatever I needed to start a new life in a year.

Jonny had left a few minutes ago after helping me fill the crates with apples. I'd wanted some time alone before making the call to Lana. I opened Amber's text from this morning. She'd sent me a photo of the sunrise. *Do you think the sun ever wishes it could sleep in?*

LOL. Maybe? I wish I could see a sunrise with you.

Me too. I miss you.

I let myself read over the conversation one more time, then I closed my messages and sat on the floor in the corner where Mom's easel used to stand—Dad said she liked the light from the window. The floor was dotted with bits of paint. I brushed my fingertips over the smooth bumps. When I walked out the door today, it would be the last time I'd be here, in our house, the last time I'd be close to my parents. My throat thickened, and I wanted to stop everything. I wanted to force Lana to let me keep my home. But it was no use. I couldn't make the mortgage payments.

I took a few quick breaths, so I would sound rushed, then made the call.

"Lana, my house has been robbed! They took everything—my dirt bike, all Dad's tools! Someone smashed through the window." I broke into sobs, drowning out her gasp of shock, her explaining that she would call Vaughn. I ended the call and moved to sit on the couch.

It was a shame that I'd shared all those photos on Instagram. That we didn't have an alarm. Too bad the lock on the workshop was old and so many people knew the house was vacant.

It could have been anyone. Anyone at all.

Lana was in the backyard playing with Cash, but she'd check on me soon. I'd spent the night and most of the morning fake-crying about the fake robbery. At the moment I was supposed to be trying to relax and watch TV. Instead, I'd turned it up loud enough to cover the sound of my voice, and I was watching them from the window while I called Amber.

"I have to tell you something."

"Okay?"

"I'm running away on the weekend, but I can't tell you where—not yet."

Silence for a painful heartbeat. She might hate the idea of having to keep a secret, tired of dealing with my drama. There were other girls with less complicated lives.

"You serious?"

"I have to get away from Vaughn."

"Stay with me." She sounded upset, her voice husky. I wished I could pack my bags and go to her. I'd seen her basement suite when we FaceTimed, the fresh flowers on the table, a bed strewn with colorful pillows. They would smell like her coconut lotion.

"I have to get out of Cold Creek. I found photos on Vaughn's computer. Of me, and other girls, naked, but I couldn't see faces. He has hidden cameras—one might be at the diner."

"No *way*." She hissed the words. "That's disgusting."

"I made an anonymous call, but I don't have any proof. Vaughn threatened me, so you can't tell *anyone*. Promise?" Cash was getting off the swing. They were coming inside.

"I promise, but Hailey—"

"I have to go. We can't text about this. Jonny will get messages to you. You can trust him. I love you." I ended the call before I realized what I'd said, and heat bloomed in my cheeks.

My cell buzzed in my hand. I looked down.

I love you too.

Five days later, I left Cash's favorite red truck on his night table, gave him a soft kiss on his forehead as he slept, and moved surefooted down the hall. This time Vaughn was on patrol—he worked one night shift a week. As a sergeant he didn't have to do nights, but he said he wanted the other officers to get a break once in a while. I had a feeling it was for different, more personal reasons. He could check his hidden cameras without being seen, watch women through lit windows.

I was careful to avoid creaky spots on the floor, but I wasn't too worried about Lana waking up. Tonight I was the one who had made her special cocktails, with a heavy hand. While she enjoyed her drink, I scooped out a bowl of ice cream for Cash, added some Benadryl, then poured chocolate sauce over the top. They would both sleep well.

The robbery had angered Vaughn. He'd questioned me so much that even Lana stepped in when I broke into tears. I wore drab clothes, rarely showered, and spoke as though in a daze. I spent all my time in my room sleeping, watching YouTube, or texting with Amber. We never talked again about my escape plan, but I felt the fear in her messages, asking if I was okay.

I confided in Lana that I was depressed about losing the last connection to my parents. I raged that someone would rob us. I bemoaned the fact that I'd asked them to wait before clearing out the house. Vaughn stopped questioning me and instead asked for an itemized list of stolen items for the insurance company. I delayed—said it made me too upset, I couldn't remember everything, I was working on it, promise. They called a real estate agent and put the house up for sale. That night I skipped dinner and went to sleep at the same time as Cash. There was no more talk of me moving back into my room, but I heard loud whispers. They were fighting. Maybe Lana would be relieved that I was gone. She and Vaughn could get back to dancing in the kitchen.

It was time. I slipped my bag over my shoulders, walked straight out the front door, and texted Jonny like we'd planned.

I'm going to run away.

Don't be crazy.

I hate Vaughn. He doesn't let me do anything.

Come to the lake. We'll talk, ok?

Text you later. Battery dying.

I shut off my phone. After I was reported missing, the cops would pull my records and see that my cell had stopped pinging when I was still in town. Jonny was camping at the lake with friends. He'd take selfies with them and post them on Facebook, so they were time-stamped, and he'd make sure he was never alone. Later tonight, he'd message me asking if I was okay, and in the morning, when he hadn't heard from me, he would call Lana. Then it would begin.

Everyone would think I'd left town because I wasn't happy. Jonny, hopefully, wouldn't get in trouble, but Vaughn would watch him closely. He'd expect me to get in touch with Jonny.

Amber was working at the diner, then she was also going out to the lake. People would see her there. If the police read our text exchanges, there was nothing that would make Vaughn suspicious that I'd told her about the photos. Just more proof that I was miserable.

I biked to the corner store, bought some chocolate bars, a can of Coke, and a bag of jerky so that I was on their surveillance camera. Then I pedaled down the side streets as though I were going to the bus station—in case any of the houses had CCTV—but then I turned onto the dark forest trails. I followed those until I reached Cooper's farm, the last big piece of private property on the way to the highway. After that it was all owned by logging companies or the province.

I left the bike at the edge of the lower field and walked the rest of the way to the barn, climbing or crawling under fences, and trying not to startle the animals. One of the dogs began barking, and I whistled high and clear. Soon a wiggling body came out to bump against my leg, then two more. Relieved that they remembered me from my past visits, I dropped my sack and pulled out the smoked salmon I'd pilfered from Lana's freezer. It was store-bought and probably farmed salmon, dyed red, but the dogs didn't seem to care. They greedily inhaled their strips and begged for more. I stroked the soft fur around the neck of the mama dog and let her lick my fingers clean. Her teats were full and swayed below her belly. She was still nursing.

Two of the dogs drifted away from me and around the

corner, back to their beds on the farmhouse porch. I followed the mama dog through the side door into the barn, dimming the flashlight I was carrying to a soft glow so I could see where she was going. Her puppies were in one of the stalls. She flopped down as I fussed and cooed over the warm bodies. Six of them altogether.

I couldn't take a nursing puppy from its mom. I sat on my heels, disappointed. The puppies bumbled over each other. In the corner, another dog was watching me. One blue eye, one brown, mouth parted in a smile. He looked young, with bright white teeth, and skinny. Maybe around forty pounds, the size of a border collie. He was shaggy, with unkempt black fur and tufted ears. His chest had a blaze of white and one of his back paws was dipped in white.

I didn't recognize him. He must be new. Lots of Cooper's dogs were dumped on the farm by people who didn't want them anymore, or were strays who made their own way over from the First Nations reservation, drawn by the animals and the other dogs. Cooper was a mean old man in a lot of ways, but every animal on his farm was always well fed.

"Hi," I whispered. "Want a treat?"

He padded over, ignoring the younger puppies, who wanted to play. He lifted his head away from one cheeky boy who was trying to grab his ear, and stepped over another.

When I reached out, he cautiously sniffed the palm of my hand, then sat and looked up at me with his head cocked like he was waiting for me to explain myself.

I offered him a piece of salmon. He delicately tugged it away from my fingers, his eyes watching me carefully while his soft lips grazed my skin. When he took it to the corner to eat, I walked to the barn door. The young dog raised his head and watched me.

"You want to come?" I patted my leg and made a kissing sound.

He didn't move. His tail didn't wag, and he didn't wiggle his body. He just stared, the one blue eye shining. I made more kissing sounds. He lay down with his head on his paws.

"Okay, boy. I can take a hint."

I watched for trucks and cars on the highway, hid in the ditch as they passed. Another hairpin corner, and I'd reached the long straight stretch before the billboard. I paused on the shoulder of the bridge, where Vaughn had picked me up the night of the lake party. I looked over the edge. The ravine plummeted almost straight down, and a creek ran through the culvert below. The woods were snarled and rocky. There were no trails. One more glance over my shoulder, and I lifted my bike, flung it over the cement barrier, and listened as it bounced down the side of the ravine.

I climbed over the edge, slid down part of the bank on my butt, holding on to roots and outcropping rocks to slow my descent. Rocks sliced my palms, gouged at the soft skin of my arms. At the bottom I found my bike. It was scraped and dented, but still worked. I hid it in the bushes, covered it with branches and debris. I'd come back for it after everything settled.

I pushed my way through the bushes and scrambled over logs and boulders until I reached a small clearing on the edge of the creek. Balanced on a wet rock, I took off my shoes, and tied them by their laces to my backpack. The water numbed my ankles as I began to hike west. My bare foot slipped on a rock, and I lurched to the side, throwing out my arms. Something fell with a splash. I checked my shoes on my backpack. Still attached. I felt my hoodie pocket. My phone! The one Dad bought me for my sixteenth birthday. He'd picked out the case, silver, with stars and moons. My photos were on my iCloud, but that phone *meant* something.

I shone my flashlight into the creek. I couldn't see through the current. I ran my hand over the dark rocks, the stones. The water turned my arms to ice up to my elbows.

A vehicle went by on the highway above. I switched off the flashlight, panicked that Vaughn had figured it out, but the truck kept driving, and soon I couldn't hear it anymore.

I had to keep walking. I moved slowly, while scanning the creek with my flashlight for deep areas and logs that could trip me. The only sound was the soft trickle of the current. I would wade up the creek for a few miles until it joined the river. Then I'd follow the rocky shoreline, and when I reached the logging roads, I'd walk east until I found my dirt bike.

The staged robbery was the last time I'd seen Jonny. We'd stood in the woods, his truck loaded, and we could barely look at one another. We'd never said goodbye before. Not like this. He punched me on the shoulder. I called him a loser. For a moment he looked scared.

"You won't be at my next race."

"You're going to do great."

"No one else knows when I'm freaking out."

"You haven't puked before a race in two years."

"Who am I going to talk to?" He didn't mean for the daily stuff—he had a lot of friends. This was about the two sides of Jonny. The one who could take jumps without thinking, and the other one, who was terrified of snakes and bats. Who felt embarrassed when people were kind to him and kept a change of clothes in his truck because he didn't want anyone to think he was a dirty farmer. The Jonny who'd had his heart broken twice. I'd hated both girls fiercely.

"Whatever. The motocross bunnies are all going to fight for the job."

"Yeah. Whatever, lame-ass." He gave me his sideways grin. Back to being cool Jonny.

"Don't forget. Two weeks."

We would meet on the mountain at a spot where we had camped with my dad last summer. By then the initial searches should have ended. There might be posters up at the bus station and places like that, but I'd be just another runaway. A statistic. Gone without a trace.

CHAPTER 10

I broke out of the woods onto the gravel and paused to catch my breath. I'd followed animal paths along the river and stuck to areas where the foliage wasn't as dense, so there was less risk of breaking plants and branches. I'd climbed rocky slopes and crossed clear-cuts thick with dried slash—tree limbs, tops, bark, and brambles tangled among the debris—and I was exhausted, my legs weak from the earlier rush of adrenaline that had come and gone. I took off my hoodie, tied it around my waist. I already felt cooler in just my camo T-shirt and black leggings.

Moonlight lit up the logging road, turning it a ghostly silver. I followed it to the right, walking along the shoulder where the gravel was packed down. The forest was quiet, with only the usual nighttime sounds, the scurrying of mice, the soft *who* of an owl, but then: A different sound behind me. Rustling. Cracking branches. Something was traveling through the bushes.

I froze.

I turned slowly, shining my flashlight around the underbrush. It picked up a glint of eyes. A shadow. The shape moved, darted behind a tree. Flash of a tail. A cougar? My heart hammered against my rib cage. No. They stalked their prey. You didn't hear a cougar until it was too late. A wolf. It could be young and hungry. Desperate. The hair at the back of my neck prickled.

With one hand I removed the knife from my belt, while with my other I shone the flashlight into the woods, moving it back and forth. A noise on the other side of me. I twisted, aimed the light. Nothing. I held my breath. Minutes passed. Maybe

I'd scared it off. I began walking again, then stopped when the glowing eyes appeared in the middle of the road directly ahead of me.

I gripped the knife and moved into a fighting stance. "Get out of here!" I wanted to sound big and ferocious, but my voice quavered. What *was* it? Was it going to attack?

The shape rushed toward me. I screamed. Then I saw the white strip of fur, the floppy ears. I lowered the knife, letting my breath out in a long exhalation.

"Jesus, dog. I thought you were a wolf!" The dog trotted to my front and sat down, stared at my pocket, and then back at my face.

"You have got to be kidding me. You tracked me for salmon?"

The dog looked at my pocket again, made a soft grumbling whine.

"I don't have any more." I looked down the road. If he'd followed my route on the highway and then through the woods, he might have left paw prints arrowing straight to me.

"Go home." I made a sweeping motion with my hand. He didn't budge. I clapped loudly. He lifted a furry ear and studied my face. I stomped my feet, raised my arms. "Get out of here!"

The dog startled, danced back, and then shot into the woods. I stayed for a moment, listening. I couldn't hear him. Hopefully he was running back to the farm.

I kept walking and soon reached the road sign warning drivers about winter runoffs and falling rocks. Just past the sign was the old wooden bridge. It had collapsed last year but the logging company hadn't fixed it yet and the only way over was by bike, horse, or foot.

My dirt bike was hidden a few feet into the woods behind the sign. I found it and mentally said thanks to Jonny, and to my parents for watching over me. I was almost free.

The headlight made strange shapes on the road as I drove

slowly, looking out for any fallen trees that might have blocked the way. I was so focused on the road that I didn't see the dog running along beside me until I caught the flash of a small dark shape. I slowed nearly to a stop, and he zipped in front of me. I hit the brakes and fell over in a slow-motion topple, with the bike landing on my leg. I looked up. The dog was standing over me, panting into my face.

I did a quick body scan. I was okay. I had been going slow enough, and the bike had pushed me against a soft bank of dirt. I lifted the bike up, checked it over. It was fine. I let out my breath and turned back to the dog, who was watching the entire process with interest. Like he hadn't just caused the crash. I put my hands on my hips. "We need to work on your timing."

We sat on the bank and shared some water—he drank from my cupped hands—and strips of my beef jerky. He licked my fingers clean, watching my face, like maybe he expected me to betray him, to snatch my hand back at the last minute. He'd learned not to trust. I got it.

I gave him another piece of jerky, then stood to get on my bike. "You can't follow me. It's too dangerous." I eyed him. He eyed me. "This isn't going to work, dog."

He stood on his back legs and rested his front paws on my thighs.

I reached down and tried to pick him up. He wriggled free with a sharp bark and a dance backward. "Then go home!" I started the bike, legs braced on each side, and revved the throttle a few times—two hard twists of my wrist—hoping the noise would freak him out. He looked at the smoking exhaust pipe, and then back at me, his eyes narrowed. Like he was *insulted*.

"I'm out of food." I held up my hands. He didn't move. "Listen, wolf-dog, the only way you are coming with me is if you learn to ride a dirt bike." I tapped the seat in front of me.

The dog leapt up, his front feet landing on the gas tank and his hind end on my lap. Startled, I reached out to hold him in place, but he was balanced perfectly. He leaned against me, his gaze on the road ahead. I didn't move. What just happened? I thought about the farm. The tractors. Maybe this dog had ridden with the workers. He glanced over his shoulder at me.

"Okay. We'll give it a try."

The headlight lit up the orange reflective tape Jonny had tied to a branch to mark the head of the trail. I tugged the tape free, then turned off the logging road, bumped down the bank, and rode carefully through the old-growth trees. I couldn't see it yet, or hear it, but I knew that the narrow animal trail was following the line of the river. I reached the next marker, removed that tape, and turned again, climbing higher until I found the ridge of rocks rising out of the ground.

When I stopped the dirt bike, the dog jumped down and began sniffing around. I could hardly make him out in the dark. I hid the bike behind a tree, hooked my helmet onto the handlebar, and got my flashlight out of my backpack. I walked softly, shining the light through the trees. The dog kept close to my heels. I wondered if he was worried about being left behind.

I pushed through shrubs and climbed over fallen logs and stones. We were at the base of the bluffs—a long slab of stone that had been formed years ago by a glacier. The flashlight beamed ahead of me, landing on the barely visible outline of a building. The cabin.

The dog moved past me and trotted toward the door confidently, like this was our home and we were just coming back from the grocery store. I followed him, but more slowly, taking in every detail. Anyone else would think the cabin neglected, dark, and cold, with the back wall, and half of each side, built into the bluff. They'd see the gray moss-covered rotten logs slotted together and think them beyond repair. The cedar shingle roof was buried under a layer of fir and pine needles. Overgrown trees blocked out the sky and any hint of sunlight.

I thought it was beautiful.

A few hard pushes, and the door creaked open. The dog squeezed through. I took careful steps, trying to avoid the gaping holes in the wood floor. Those would be my first repairs. The woodstove was rusted to a light brown. Someone had cemented around the pipe where it went through the roof, but it was crumbling in places, and water had been leaking in. I'd have to clean it and check for holes before I ever tried a fire, or I'd be smoked out of the cabin.

Nothing had been left behind by other people except a few metal containers and dusty jars that Jonny and I found last time. All my supplies were stacked in the middle—bottles of purified water, food in bear-proof containers, including fruits and vegetables. It was cool in here, but they wouldn't last long. After that, I'd be living on canned food and cured meat.

I found my lantern on top of the supplies and hung it on a rusted nail sticking out of the wall. Hands on my hips, I surveyed the rest of my equipment, and took a deep breath.

I'd done it. I was finally free from Vaughn.

For the first few days, I stayed hidden in the cabin and only ventured out briefly for bathroom breaks with the dog, who was now named Wolf. I dyed my hair dark brown with a box of color Jonny had bought for me, rinsed it out with a jug of water. When I was finished, I used my dad's old camping mirror and his clippers to cut it short on the sides and in the back. I left the bangs long so that they swooped over the side of my face and covered my eyes.

I'd acted tough in front of Jonny, but I was terrified of

grizzlies, scared of how they could tear apart buildings to get at food. I was careful when I went outside, and checked for signs that there might be one in the area—overturned rocks, ripped-off bark on the trees, scat, claw marks. I kept a rifle by the door, and another under the makeshift bed frame I'd hammered together with logs and covered with an air mattress. I slept with my dad's Smith & Wesson under my pillow.

I set about making the cabin livable. I had some of my dad's tools—not the power tools, those were going to be sold, but the basics. Hammer, nails, screwdrivers. I patched holes with duct tape or pieces of wood, replaced rotten logs, evicted spiders and bugs. My table was a crate turned upside down, and I made a shelving unit with peeled logs. I didn't feel safe unpacking much and hid anything personal under the floorboards, wrapped in plastic bags. Pictures of my parents, photo albums, some of my mom's smaller paintings that we'd stolen from my house.

My backpack was ready to go at all times with a first-aid kit and enough survival gear to get me to safety if I ever had to make a run for it. I built a latrine behind a low rock slab—so I could keep an eye out for animals. I set up a perimeter alarm with a trip wire, cans, and bells.

Jonny and I had planned for me to take one of Cooper's puppies, so the cabin was stocked with dog food, bones, and a few things that belonged to Jonny's family's dog. The first time I tossed a ball to Wolf, he watched it bounce past, then looked at me.

Fetching balls? What kind of dog do you think I am?

Treats were a different story. No matter how wild my aim, he could catch them straight out of the air. He'd leap, twist his body, and land perfectly like a cat. I got the feeling he hadn't had much affection. Neck massages and belly rubs were acceptable, but he didn't like to be held, and if I tried to kiss him, he would turn his head, or put a paw in the middle of my chest.

At night he slept on the floor of the cabin, while I lay on the bed with the lantern and read Dad's survival books. He'd taught me everything in those pages himself, but it was different now that I was on my own. I studied the pictures of track marks, the difference between a black bear's paws and a grizzly's, what to do in an attack. Every once in a while Wolf would raise his head, stare at the door, and let out a warning growl. Then he'd look at me to make sure I was paying attention. I'd reach for the handgun and wait, heart thudding. Was it a grizzly? When Wolf felt the danger had passed, he'd drop his head back onto his front legs. He never got to his feet or barked. Not once. After a few days, I began to wonder if he was just testing me.

Even in summer, the nights were cool in the mountains, and I invited Wolf to sleep with me on the cot. He ignored me and stayed on the floor, but in the early morning hours I'd feel the air mattress shift as he settled at the bottom near my feet. When we woke, we'd sneak outside for our morning business. After our first night at the cabin, I put a collar on him and attached a leash, but he wouldn't move. He planted his butt and when I tried to tug him, he rolled onto his side.

Finally, grudgingly, he let me coax him outside with treats and peed on a tree—refusing to make eye contact. Then, in a fit of stubbornness, he tossed his head while pulling backward, and the collar slipped off. He didn't bolt. He didn't walk two steps. He sat and looked at me. Point made. He never wore a leash again, but I tied one of my bandannas around his neck and he seemed okay with that. Or at least he didn't groan at me, which I'd learned was his unhappy noise.

He talked. A lot. He had different sounds for when he wanted out, when he heard something, when he wanted food, when he disagreed with me, and when he was annoyed at me for trying to cuddle. They ranged from a whine to a yip to grunts and groans and huffs.

In the mornings, he'd mark all the trees around the cabin, while I watched the woods nervously, the Smith & Wesson in my hand, rifle slung over my shoulder. When Wolf was satisfied that he'd completed his task, we'd head back inside and we'd have breakfast together. Kibble for him, cereal and powdered milk for me. Even though Wolf was skinny and hungry, he'd take a mouthful of kibble, drop it onto the floor, sniff each piece, then gently eat them.

I waited until dark to cook anything on the propane stove so that smoke didn't reveal my location, but I had to leave the door gapped for ventilation, and I was freaked that the smell would invite a few animals over for dinner too. More often than not, I just ate cold meals.

Wolf and I had hours each day, so I tested him with simple commands—sit, stay, come, wait. It only took him a couple of tries and I wondered if someone had already trained him. I worried that somewhere he had a real owner. As soon as he mastered one thing, he would stop doing it, and look at me. *What else?* I began teaching him hand signals, then tricks like touching a spot on the wall with his paw, or jumping from the chair to the bed, and picking up different items and bringing them back. He'd bark at me when I stopped playing.

After the first week, Wolf and I began to explore the area once the sun had gone down, but I still didn't venture far. I didn't want to use the dirt bike yet. I had no idea what was happening back in town and if there was a chance that they could be searching the woods.

At dawn, when the birds were beginning to sing, Wolf and I crept down to the river. Our feet and paws soft on the ground. He seemed to sense my fear, because he never bounded through the woods or sprinted ahead. If I stopped, he stopped. And if *he* stopped, I stopped.

We stayed on the rocky shore, where we wouldn't leave prints, and fished the deep, quiet pools. I cleaned my catch at the river like Dad taught me, left the head and guts behind so that animals wouldn't follow us back to the cabin. When Dad hunted, he always thanked the land, using a First Nations prayer. Some of the guides didn't like how the First Nations could hunt in different seasons and fish the river with nets, but Dad was never like that. I couldn't remember the words he'd used, so I made up my own, clutching my elk necklace, face lifted to the sky.

Thank you for the river. Thank you for this great mountain. Thank you for this bounty.

Wolf would wait until I was finished, then he liked to sit close beside me and stare at the ripples where my line disappeared into the flat surface. One morning he shoved his head under the water in the shallows and came out with a crayfish clamped in his teeth. After that, he'd nudge the back of my knees with his nose all the way down to the river, soft little bumps.

We saw deer a few times, their graceful necks lowering for sips of water. My rifle was always by my side, but I couldn't shoot one. I'd have to live on fish. Wolf tensed beside me and lifted his paw as though he were going to break into a sprint. I held his bandanna and told him no, deer were strictly off-limits. He pouted, but he never tried again. He did hunt rabbits and grouse, sometimes coming back while still licking blood from his muzzle. We didn't talk about it.

For the first time since my dad had died, I felt the darkness begin to recede. I woke up faster, my feet hitting the ground with desire for the day, to do *something*. To be out *there*. The scents of the forest, the feel of a fishing rod, the swoosh of the line whipping through the air as I cast, the slice of the lure entering the water. The trails called to me. The meadows and secret creeks lined with dark ferns and hollowed-out trees. Every breath of fresh air started to make the sharp pieces inside me soften. I hadn't realized how trapped I'd felt in town, the noises, the people, everyone's obsession with social media. I didn't care about clothes or hair or makeup. I hated politics and grown-up things. None of that mattered. I belonged *here*. I wasn't lonely, not yet, but I missed Jonny and Amber. I missed Cash waking me up in the morning, his giggle.

In case something happened to me, I kept a notebook in my backpack at all times. In it, I wrote down everything Vaughn had done. When I was finished with that, I filled pages with sketches of summer flowers—buttercups, fireweed, fairy bell. And birds I saw. Whiskey jacks, chickadees, bald eagles, ravens with their gurgling croaks. I tried to identify each call, practicing them while Wolf watched, his head cocking from side to side. I created some whistles for him and combined them with the hand signals he'd already learned.

I drew maps in my journal, of low trails that might belong to bears, meadows where I found bushes thick with gooseberries, blackberries, saskatoon berries, and vines dotted with tiny plump wild strawberries. Huckleberry bushes growing out of moss-covered tree stumps. Wolf liked to pull berries off the lower branches with his teeth, so delicately that he never burst a single one.

A couple of times I found bear scat with fresh berries in it, or Wolf would start to pace and circle around me, making a huff, huff, whine sound, and I would hurry back to the cabin.

Sometimes I pretended I was writing to Amber. I daydreamed that one day I'd show her the cabin. We'd picnic in the meadows, swim in the river together. She would love it. I thought about taking the dirt bike closer to the lake, where I could text her from the burner phone, but it was too soon. Vaughn would still be looking for me. Sometimes I even imagined I heard the drone of a helicopter in the distance. I thought of him with binoculars, scanning the forest, and me ducking and weaving through the trees. An animal running for its life.

Wolf watched the trail intently as the noise of Jonny's bike got closer. His ears flicked back and forth. He turned and stared up into my eyes.

"Good boy. Wait."

Jonny's dirt bike pulled into the clearing. The red-and-white paint was sharp against the green woods, and a welcome sight. I stayed among the trees, crouched low until he took off his helmet and whistled our call, a soft trilling tune. I whistled back. A relieved smile spread across his face—tanned, but he looked thinner, his cheekbones cut sharper.

"No one followed me," he called, running his hands through his hair and shaking it free from where it had stuck to his forehead. I stepped out from the bushes, Wolf at my heels, his nose bumping against my calf. Jonny turned in my direction, and his eyes widened. "Whoa."

"What's wrong?"

"You look so different with your hair. It's totally badass. No one would recognize you." He gave me a thumbs-up, then looked at Wolf sitting at my feet. "I thought you were getting a puppy." He got off the bike and crouched, patting his leg. Wolf didn't move.

"This one picked me. I named him Wolf." I looked down. Wolf studied my eyes. When he was satisfied that I was relaxed, he trotted over, sniffed Jonny's hand, and let him pat him before exploring the woods nearby.

Jonny got to his feet and grabbed me for a hug. We stood

like that for a while. He felt warm, solid, familiar. When he let go, he said, "You all right?"

"I'm fine. Are you okay? What is everyone saying?"

He took a deep breath. "They found your bike."

"But I hid it!" My stomach muscles clenched. What else had they found?

"A road crew was fixing the bridge and one of the surveyors was walking the river to take photos of it from a distance or something."

I could imagine it, every terrible, unlucky moment of it. The worker probably stopped to eat his sandwich, or to take a leak. He saw the glimmer of metal and kicked off the branches.

"Are they searching the woods?"

"Yeah. They found your cell in the creek too. Everyone thinks you were abducted."

"They think someone *took* me?"

"That's the rumor. Because of the highway killer."

I pressed my hands to my head, as if that could stop the tornado of panic that was hurling my thoughts around. "If they find my tracks . . ." It had been a couple weeks. Too long, I hoped.

"There was a sniffer dog, but he didn't find anything. Some people are going out by themselves on the weekends. Me and the guys have done a few searches. It feels shitty to lie to them."

"I didn't want people to think I was murdered!" I thought of Lana and Cash, how upset they must be. Cash was just a *kid*. "Did you talk to Amber?"

"I told her that you were okay. She thinks you went north. Vaughn questioned her but she told him that she'd rather eat grease straight from the deep fryer than talk to him."

"Holy shit. Why is she antagonizing him?"

"She's angry you had to leave. She told him that if anything bad happened to you, it was his fault for being so controlling and that he should take meditation classes."

I stared at him openmouthed. "He is going to *freak*."

"He's got a lot going on. There have been vigils, your poster is all over town, and you're on the news. The highway is all anyone talks about now. Girls are scared to be alone."

"Did he question you?"

"Thompson interviewed everyone at the party, so I'm in the clear, but Vaughn's been following me around. I don't even go one mile over the speed limit." He watched Wolf as he dug at a section of log. "Cooper was talking about a dog at the search. I thought he meant the puppy, but he was telling one of the cattle ranchers that he'd had a stray turn up and then disappear."

"What does Cooper care?"

"He said he was really smart, and if he showed up at any of the other farms, he wanted him back." Jonny must have seen the jolt of fear cross my face, because he added, "That's good news. He's a stray, so when this is all over you can say the dog followed you."

"How is this all going to be over? I can't just walk out of the bushes now."

"I've been thinking about it. You can say you got away from the killer. You never saw his face—or you can make up a description. It's not too late."

"It's *way* too late, Jonny. They'd never believe that."

"Then what are you going to do?"

"Stick with the plan. Maybe it's better that Vaughn thinks I'm dead."

"How will you get your money?"

"I'll figure it out when I'm eighteen. It's not my fault if they think I was abducted. I ran away, hitchhiked north or something. I didn't read the news."

Jonny gave me a skeptical look.

"I'm *not* coming back now. Even if it means I get in trouble.

You don't know what it's like to sit at the table with a man who has taken photos of you *naked*."

Jonny rubbed his hair and made a frustrated sound. "I hate him so much. I hope he gets busted one day. He'll get his ass kicked in jail."

"Yeah, me too." It was a nice idea. Vaughn being held accountable. Then he'd feel that sick shame that I'd carried around with me since I'd seen those photos. But I didn't think it would really happen, and I couldn't tell Jonny that. I needed him to believe justice was possible.

We talked for a while, about dirt bikes, the cabin, Wolf, and Amber. We made a plan for the next time Jonny and I would meet. I wanted to know about his last race, but he said it had been postponed because of my going missing. He was evasive, though, and I worried that he'd really just skipped it. After he left, dust hung in the air, the faint smell of gasoline. Wolf and I jogged after him, following his trail through the woods. I stopped partway and listened to his bike fade.

CHAPTER 11

The summer stretched into late August. My skin was golden brown, my freckles like nutmeg. Wolf filled out—and spread out. Each night he moved farther up the bed, gradually taking over my pillow and pushing me with his paws until I woke crammed against the log wall. I'd have to roll over and nudge him to the other side, while he grumbled and huffed, and we eventually settled with my body curved around his back. So tight I felt like his heartbeat was my own.

Jonny and I met one more time near the river. He snuck away from the guys at the campground, telling them he was fly-fishing the upper pools. He didn't like us not being able to text in case of emergencies—it was impossible to get a signal on most of the mountain—so he bought handheld VHF radios. I'd be able to pick up a weather station, music, and listen in on the logging companies. It had a decent range, but if there was a thick cloud cover or bad weather, he might only hear static from me. We found a private frequency and came up with the code names H150 and H250—the numbers on our bikes.

The searches were over, and most people had decided I was another victim of the highway killer, even though the police hadn't confirmed it one way or the other. I felt a strange mix of relief and guilt. Jonny said missing posters were spread around town, on telephone poles, gas stations, mailboxes. He hated walking past them. Mason had two in the diner's window.

Amber and Jonny talked, and he assured her I was okay—I wasn't a murder victim. I figured by the middle of September it might be safe for me to reach out. I could write her a letter. We might even be able to meet. The idea filled my dreams. I'd be able to touch her, hold her.

Jonny heard rumors that Vaughn had officers patrolling the highway twice a day, in case the killer struck again or my body showed up. Volunteers had searched the ditches on both sides of the highway. Jonny went to Thompson for updates. We figured that was what he would have done if this was real. Not that Thompson had much to say other than, "It's still an active case."

Those weren't the only rumors. Emily, the girl I'd seen in the diner the day Vaughn walked me out, showed up at the lake one night.

"A few people were sitting around Andy's camper drinking beer," Jonny said, "and she kept asking me if I wanted to buy anything stronger than weed. Pushing, you know?"

"So she's a dealer?"

"I think she's in deep. I checked around about her later and someone said she was a narc. She's working for Vaughn. Ratting people out for money."

"Serious?" Maybe it wasn't fear I'd seen in her face. Maybe it was something darker, an anger of sorts. Like a person might get if someone was controlling them.

"Yeah, and she asked me whether I thought you were still alive, which pissed me off. I don't care how drunk she was. Don't worry. I'm keeping her away from my new place."

In a stroke of good luck, Jonny's grandparents found an available spot at a retirement home and moved out of their old house. They offered it to Jonny to rent. It used to be a sheep farm, with a workshop, gardens, fruit trees, and chickens. He could keep his dirt bikes in the shop; the neighbors were miles away. Behind his house, trails connected with the maze of logging roads. In the future we'd be able to meet with less risk, but he still got security cameras.

"Maybe you should make friends with Emily."

"No way."

"She might know something."

He groaned. "I'll think about it."

I sped down the logging road with Wolf behind me in his seat—a milk crate that I'd fixed to the back. He was a good rider, shifting his weight when I took corners. When he was really excited, he'd stand in the crate and rest his front legs on my shoulders, huffing the wind in long snorts that he would then sneeze all over the back of my neck. Sometimes he preferred to run in the woods parallel to me, weaving in and out of the trees. Once, he was running on a high bank, and he launched himself into the crate, which nearly sent me into a crash. After that, I drove slower and learned how to brace for the impact, and he learned how to time his landing better.

First week of September, and my classmates had gone back to school. I thought about how I had once been like them, getting textbooks, finding my locker. I was glad to be free but worried about the mountain. It was hot, no sign of autumn coming. Fires were still burning up north and the air smelled of charcoal. Each morning I checked the VHF radio for the latest reports. The sky was shaded gray, while ash fell like snow through hazy sunbeams. Twigs and leaves crunched under my feet as I traveled toward the lake area. The river was running low and the timber was so dry it would only take one spark to set the forest alight.

It was early in the day, but the air was already stagnant with heat as I hid my dirt bike a mile up the mountain. I walked the rest of the way, crossed the highway through a culvert, then climbed the ridge on the other side. I wanted to check the wind and see from which direction the smoke was blowing.

By the time I reached the top—where I could look down on the highway, the entrance to the lake, and the mountain range—I was out of breath, sweaty, and gasping with thirst. Wolf and I shared some water. As he slurped from his bowl, I stroked the hot fur on his side. He'd filled out with better food. I couldn't feel his ribs anymore, and his haunches were hard muscle. When he'd drunk enough, he flopped down in the shade of a fir tree, his tongue out as he panted.

"We won't be long, buddy." He sighed, stretched his head across his legs, too lazy to even sniff around for squirrels. I studied the sky, used my binoculars to narrow in on the haze in the distance. The clouds were low and dark, drifting to the west. At the moment the wind was in my favor, but I'd keep checking the weather channel on my radio. The biggest risk was stupid people, smokers on the highway, and campers who thought they were immune to the danger.

I crawled closer to the edge of the cliff and aimed my binoculars at the lake campground. I wouldn't be able to see much through the dense canopy of trees, but I wanted to make sure no one had left a fire smoldering overnight or decided that they just *had* to have one for their morning bacon and sausages. So far it looked clear. I swooped the binoculars to the left, scanned the long-yellowed grass alongside the highway, the dust-covered bushes. I studied bits and pieces of garbage, take-out containers. Glass bottles in ditches could also start fires.

Through a thin crop of trees, where an old logging road ran parallel to the highway, I caught a glimpse of something shiny. Metal? I pulled the binoculars away from my face, wiped at the sweat dripping into my eyes, and refocused. The circle view bounced up and down. I steadied my hand, thinking it had been a trick of the light, but then a shape came into sight. The straight lines of a silver car. I scanned the binoculars down the side of it, trying to see in between tree trunks. The car was sitting at an angle. The back end low. Something wrong with a tire?

The owner was bound to come back, but they might have left something inside. Clothes, spare change, food. I grabbed my backpack and made my way down the ridge with Wolf slinking beside me. When I reached the highway, I listened for oncoming traffic, then bolted across.

It took me a few minutes to weave through the brush and follow along the logging road until I came around the corner and could see the front of the car, the silver grille shining. Tucked behind a tree, I lifted my binoculars and zoomed in on the windshield. Something dangled from the rearview mirror. I focused again. White plush, silver horn. A unicorn.

Amber's car?

I gripped the binoculars, swung them around, searching for her. Just trees and brush and the distant gray of the road. I turned back to her car, sharpened the focus. No sign of her inside the car either. Had she had a flat tire on her way back from the lake and gotten out to walk? The thought of seeing her, even for a brief instant, thrilled me.

Staying within the trees, I moved closer until I could see the full side of the car—carefully placing my feet in between fallen branches and twigs, avoiding anything that would snap. Wolf followed close with his breath hot on my legs.

The back tire was flat, a spare lying on the ground beside it, and the trunk was gapped slightly. A tire iron lay in the dirt. It was like she had just up and walked away. I crouched low, wondering if I should take a closer look inside the car—she could have passed out—but all the windows were up, and it was unlikely anyone could sleep in that heat. If I stepped out from the woods, my boots would make tracks on the dusty logging road. I gnawed on a fingernail.

A guttural birdcall, loud and familiar, ripped through the air. Ravens—fighting over something. I wheeled around, trying to gauge where the sound was coming from, but it was distorted and echoing. I found an old fir tree nearby, shimmied up the trunk, swung myself onto the first branch, and climbed until I could see over the canopy of trees.

Three ravens spiraled in large circles near the highway to the north, past the campground and on the other side of the road. They had company. Vultures. A deer carcass, maybe. I swallowed hard, clinging to the branch, bark biting into my fingers. I began climbing down.

Wolf met me at the bottom, circling around my legs and pacing, a low whine coming from his throat. I headed toward the birds, but he stayed back. His ears were down, his tail tucked between his legs. As I got farther away, he barked at me, then trotted to catch up. He followed behind my knees, brushing my skin with his nose. He was panting hard.

I had to cross the highway again and travel through the woods until I passed the campground. Within minutes, I smelled it. It hit me hard, came in on a breeze, and I bent over, clutching my stomach. Wolf whined louder, long, plaintive moans. I ignored him, pushed through the branches. They slapped at me, tore my arms, caught in my hair. My eyes watered. I breathed heavily through my mouth, tugged the bandanna from around my forehead and knotted it tight around my nose and mouth. It still wasn't enough. Tears ran down my cheeks.

Sunlight knifed through the gap between two tall fir trees, revealing an open area ahead. The ditch alongside the highway, a low bank rising on the other side. I froze. I wanted to run back into the forest, pretend I had never spotted the car. The birds screeched back and forth, driving me forward.

I stepped into the long grass. Two more halting steps, and I looked down into the space between a cluster of shrubs, to the bottom of the ditch. Cherry-red glistening strands of hair fanned across the dirt. A white hand stretched out, frozen into a claw, a raw mark around a bruised wrist, where there used to be a bracelet.

CHAPTER 12

The ravens perched on a branch above me, the vultures in another tree. Quiet and watchful. Wolf barked. The ravens screamed and rose into the air. The vultures stayed.

I looked at Amber, my hand over my mouth. Broken fingernails. Dark red streaks down her arm. Flies filled the air with an incessant buzz. My face stung with tears and I was making a strange garbled sound. Wolf took a few cautious steps toward her, sniffing the air.

"No." I held his bandanna. "Stay."

He dropped to the ground beside me, his low whine blending with the hum of flies.

Birds had been pecking at her face. She didn't look real. Like a mannequin in a horror movie, a prop in someone else's nightmare. Her skin was too white, the puncture holes and claw marks too gruesome. Her mouth was stretched in a wide grimace. She was wearing a lacy white bra, blood turning the edges brown, and her black tank top was tied around her throat. Her beaded necklaces were wound in the fabric. One hung between her breasts.

She'd been wearing jeans shorts. They were nearby, lying in a small patch of dirt as though they'd been set out that way. The top button was ripped off. I didn't want to see everything, didn't want to know the agony that she'd endured, but my eyes couldn't stop taking it in. The way her legs were spread wide, bruises on her hips. Bite marks down her side and across her chest—the slope of her breasts. One sandal dangled from her foot. The other was buried partway in the dirt. She'd dug her heels into the ground, fighting for her life, trying to push him off her dying body.

The heat and the smell were too much, my sight gone hazy and gray at the corners. I'd never felt so much evil in one place. It paralyzed me. My head and eyes pulsed from it. My blood hammered through my heart and veins all at once, a panicked stampede. Her pain and fear were imprinted in the molecules of the air. Her screams lingered.

A fly walked across her hip bone, the discolored skin. Her flat stomach was bloating with gas from her decomposing body. I wanted to brush the fly off, but I couldn't get closer to her. There would be hair fibers, boot tracks. She had to have been out here for a couple of days for the smell to be so strong. Maybe Friday night. I bit the fleshy part of my palm to hold in my cries, the hiccupping sobs. The fly settled above her groin, on what looked like a tattoo.

A small running unicorn, mane and tail blowing in some imagined wind. I'd never seen it before. But it would have been hidden by her bikini. I thought about the unicorn dangling from Amber's rearview mirror. Then I remembered the photos on Vaughn's computer. The edge of a tattoo showing on a woman's stomach. The bright colors. It had been *Amber's* stomach.

My heart was beating too fast, stabbing pains across my chest. Spasms. I sucked at the air, but nothing came into my lungs. I pressed my palm to my chest, hit my ribs. Black dots danced in front of my eyes. I sank to my knees, head bowed. *Don't pass out. Don't pass out.*

Wolf jammed his wet snout into my neck, dropped onto his stomach, and tried to squirm under my arms, licking my face. I took small breaths. I had to get it together. I had to think.

People were probably looking for her. She had a landlord, a job, friends. Her family. I didn't want search and rescue going through the woods or flying over with helicopters. And I didn't want her lying out here alone until someone found her. With the heat and the animals.

Wolf and I hiked back up the ridge. The sun beat on my shoulders, the rocks hot to the touch. I guzzled my water, poured some for Wolf. I moved to the right side of the cliff so I could see past the lake easier, checked the spot with my binoculars. The highway was quiet. The vultures and ravens had swooped back down but I couldn't shoot them from the ridge.

"Nine-one-one, what's your emergency?"

I put my hand over the speaker to muffle my voice. "I was driving on the highway and I noticed vultures circling a ditch. It smells really bad. I think it's something big."

"Would you be able to describe the location?"

"Just after the campground, heading away from town."

"And your name?"

I ended the call. Wolf and I waited at the top of the ridge—he under a tree nearby, me sprawled across the hot rock. With my binoculars I watched each truck and car that came past.

Wolf was getting impatient, whining and huffing. I tossed him part of a protein bar. He snatched it out of the air, then his body stiffened, his head cocking toward the south.

I aimed the binoculars at the bend of the road. Chevy Tahoe. White. Lights on top. The truck slowed as it drove past the campsite, then pulled onto the side. He was near Amber. Either the driver had seen the birds—or it was Vaughn, and he knew exactly where to stop.

Wolf moved close to me, and I tugged him down. His huffing changed to a grumble as he stared at the truck, his ears shifting up and down as he listened. I tried to peer inside the cab but only got reflection off the windshield. I shimmied closer to the edge. Wolf crawled beside me.

The truck door swung open. One leg stepped out, then a man. Vaughn.

He looked behind him, studying the highway. I flattened myself on the rock—hoping he hadn't seen the glint of sun on the lenses—and tugged Wolf's head lower. Vaughn turned and walked along the edge of the ditch, then stopped, arm over his mouth. He pulled a handkerchief out of his pocket and pressed it over his nose before walking down into the ditch, where he dropped to a crouch. The long grass hid him. I stared at the spot. What was he doing?

He stayed low for a few moments, then stood and walked to the truck, where he pulled out his camera—and a pair of gloves. Back at the ditch, he disappeared again. I imagined the snap, snap. His camera filling with shots. He'd be zooming in, taking photos of every part of her.

When he was finished, he climbed into the truck and closed the door but didn't drive away. He must be waiting for the other cops, the coroner maybe. I waited with him.

The police were there for hours—three other cop cars and a coroner's van. They slid white plastic suits over their clothes, but I recognized Thompson's tall shape, his black hair. He was the only one not wearing sunglasses. I liked that I could see his eyes. He seemed more real. Not like the other uniforms. And he was staying back from the ditch, from Amber. Maybe he was thinking about all the times she'd served him. The smiles and laughs they'd exchanged.

They put a tent up to block the scene from the highway and closed one of the lanes. People drove slowly as they passed by. I was sure they were taking photos and videos to share on social media. I was glad for the tent. I didn't want anyone else seeing her. The sun was going down when a black minivan pulled up. The men went into the ditch with a stretcher and carried Amber out in a body bag. I stared at the shape, watched to make sure that they were gentle with her when they slid her into the hearse. How could Amber be inside that? How could such a beautiful, alive, laughing girl end up in black plastic? She'd be taken to the morgue. They would cut her open and collect evidence. She'd be returned to her family. I thought of her sister getting the news, and tears ran down my face. The cops stayed for a while longer. Her car was towed.

The coroner left; Vaughn followed. Only one car remained. Thompson. He stood beside the driver's door. Making notes on some sort of clipboard. Paperwork.

I pressed in the memorized number on my phone, watched as Thompson pulled out his cell and looked down at the screen. His frown was clear through my binoculars.

"Thompson here."

I lowered my voice and cupped my hand over the speaker. "I told you he was dangerous, but you didn't listen to me."

A pause, silence. He looked up from his paperwork, staring down the highway. He turned around a couple of times, wondering if he was being watched. "Who is this?"

"Did you even search for cameras?"

"I couldn't find any. Without more information, I can't—"

"I'm telling you—he *has* them. Maybe he circulates the cameras around." I wanted to yell and scream, but he'd hear my voice on the ridge. Why hadn't he checked more places? Why hadn't he watched Vaughn to see if he took photos from across the lake? He could have stopped him.

"Can we meet and talk about this?"

"He *knew* Amber."

More silence. Thompson turned back toward the spot where

I'd found Amber, his shadow long behind him. "What do you know about Amber?" His voice was low and cautious.

"Everyone in town is talking about it."

"We haven't released a statement yet."

"Amber's *car* was towed. It was her. People aren't stupid."

"Did you see her with someone?"

"No, but Vaughn is always on that highway. He knew Shannon from the area, and Hailey was his niece. She's missing, right? Now Amber. He eats in the diner all the time." I thought about everything Vaughn had told me about the killer. He'd been talking about himself.

"That's it? That's all you have?" For a moment I thought he didn't believe me, but then I realized that his anger was frustration. There was something in him that *did* believe. Maybe he sensed something was off with Vaughn. Maybe he was investigating him.

"I can't say anything else."

"If you're scared, we can get you protection." How would that work? A foster home? Some sort of legal document? Vaughn could still find me.

"If you don't figure out a way to catch him, another girl will die."

I slid the phone into my pocket. Hours later, Thompson was still in his car, guarding the crime scene. The cops would be back. Maybe someone from the city. Forensics experts. But they wouldn't find anything. Vaughn had been the first to arrive on the scene. He'd spent time alone with her body. Just like he had with Shannon. Anything left in the dark was gone by now.

Wolf and I slipped down the side of the ridge and into the woods.

CHAPTER 13

I hid the bike under a tree, protected by draping branches, then checked the sky, listened for helicopters, the hum of drones. It had only been a week. The media could still be around. I brought my head back down. Too fast. The trees spun. I crouched, took sips of my water.

Wolf sat in front of me. Staring.

"Sorry," I said. "I'll do better. It's the heat." He'd woken me the last few nights with an anxious whine, pressed his body overtop mine, and licked my face while I sobbed. Each morning, he forced me out of bed, forced me to the river, forced me to keep fishing. I brought all the letters I'd written to Amber down to the shore, read them out loud, pausing over and over when I lost my breath, until I'd made it to the end. Then I ripped them into tiny pieces and let them fall like confetti on top of the water, watched the current take them away from me too.

I stood up, slowly, and walked the trail. Wolf trotted ahead. When we reached the wire fence around Jonny's farm, I found the hidden spot where I could lift the bottom section. Wolf slid under first and waited for me on the other side, his ears flicking. I crawled after him.

Jonny was working on his dirt bike in front of his shop. T-shirt, board shorts, and a backward baseball cap. He was wearing his earbuds and singing along to the chorus, humming parts. I recognized the tune. "Counting Stars" by OneRepublic. Our favorite group. For a moment I could almost pretend it was last summer and we were working on our bikes together. We'd argue over what wrench to use, the lyrics to the song. I'd make up my own and belt them out.

Lately Jonny been, Jonny been winning races
Dreaming about all the bikes he'll get for free

I found a pebble, warm and smooth in my palm, and lifted my arm to toss it at Jonny, but then his front door opened, and a girl stepped out with two mugs in her hand. Long, black, sleep-tousled hair and one of Jonny's T-shirts stopping at her thighs. Naked legs. Naked everything else probably too. Kristin Hampstead. She graduated this year with Jonny. Since when had they been together? He never said anything about her. Maybe she was a friend and crashed for the night.

She stopped in front of Jonny, and he got to his feet with a smile as he took the earbuds out. She passed him a mug, turned her face up to his. He kissed her. It went on for a while, his hand drifting down her lower back, then even lower. Definitely not just friends.

Wolf looked at me.

"Good question," I muttered under my breath. I didn't want to watch them making out, but I couldn't leave. I pursed my lips and gave a shrill whistle. Three in a row. Jonny broke the kiss and turned his head, glanced into the woods. I drifted into the shadow of a tree. He said something to Kristin, with another short kiss, and she walked inside—hips swaying as she took the steps. Jonny watched until the door closed, then went behind his workshop.

Wolf and I crept out of the woods, moving from tree to tree. We met Jonny near the woodpile, around the corner of the shop, where any view of us was blocked from the road and the house. Jonny was standing in the shade. Wolf bounced over to greet him first, then I caught up. We hugged. He smelled like gasoline from his bike, fresh-cut firewood.

"Hailey." He pulled away, face tense and eyes worried. "I have to tell you something." He was still holding the coffee mug, down by his leg, his fingertips around the rim like he'd forgotten he was carrying it. I reached out, took it from his hand, and swallowed a big gulp.

"I know about Amber. I'm the one who found her."

"Ah, shit." He was frozen for a few beats, emotions flashing across his face. Shock, horror, confusion, then sympathy. He grabbed me for another hug, tighter this time, jostling the coffee mug in my hand and splashing my leg. I let him hold me for a moment, my body stiff, but I was too close to tears. I pulled away.

"It was Vaughn. I know it was."

"What are you talking about?"

"He was the first at the scene."

"That doesn't mean—"

"He had photos of her on his computer. I *saw* her tattoo." Jonny was silent now, his face pale.

"He knew where to find her body in the ditch, and he took more photos of her—he didn't even call it in right way. She was just lying there in the heat—" I broke off, remembering how he'd crouched beside her lifeless body. Tears filled my eyes, rolled down my cheeks, dropped from my chin. "The birds had been *pecking* at her, Jonny. He strangled her with her own shirt."

"Oh, man." Jonny reached for my hand. "I'm so sorry, Hailey."

I lifted my other arm, wiped my face in the crook of my elbow, and took a few shuddering breaths. "I called Thompson. I think he believed me. I don't know."

"Jesus. What if Vaughn finds you?"

"I didn't give my name. I saw what he did to her body, Jonny. I can't sleep. I can't eat. I feel so fucked up." Jonny squeezed my hand, trying to comfort me, but nothing could. Nothing could ever fix this feeling. Vaughn had seen me with Amber. I'd put her on his radar. He couldn't take his anger out on me, and then he found her. "I want to kill him."

"Whoa." He gripped both my shoulders, looked into my eyes. "Don't do anything crazy. Let Thompson handle it, okay? They're still investigating."

"Did you hear something?"

"I got pulled in for questioning after they found Amber."

"I *knew* he was going to try to pin this on you."

"People saw me at the party. They saw me in my tent in the morning. It's fine."

I scanned the yard, took a few breaths. It was hot behind the workshop, the morning sun bouncing off the metal. I wanted to be back in my peaceful woods, at the cool river.

"Why's Kristin here?"

"She was scared last night. A lot of the girls are freaking out. It's just a hookup."

I'd never had a hookup. I'd never had sex. Amber and I had only spent five perfect hours together alone. The sum total of our relationship, but it had felt like so much more. My chest tightened, ribs pulling together as though my spine were a seam that someone had sewn closed.

A noise, the front door opening. Jonny froze. I reached for Wolf's bandanna.

"Jonny?" Kristin. She'd come looking for him.

"Yeah, one sec!" He wrapped his arms around me—a quick, painful, bone-crushing hug. "Are you going to be okay?" he whispered into my ear. "You could stay in the shop?"

I shook my head. "I'll come back next week."

"You better, or I'll go looking." He released me, scratched Wolf's neck, then disappeared around the corner, calling out to Kristin, "Want breakfast?"

I watched from the shadows as he walked back to his house. Maybe Kristin would be good for him. They'd eat, then spend the day together. They could start dating and get married one day. Jonny could have kids. A regular life. I wanted that for him. He deserved to be happy.

None of those things were for me.

I insulated the cabin walls and under the floor, shoving in handfuls of grass, pieces of bark, branches, leaves, and pine needles to fill the gaps. I found a cave nearby for a root cellar, rolled a rock in front, rigged with a pole and a rope so I could drag it away when needed. Jonny canned dill pickles, tomatoes, peaches, and fish. He watched grocery sales and stocked up on dried goods. I told him he'd make a good wife someday. He told me I would make a bad husband.

One of Dad's books suggested building a second base camp, a pit in the ground, to store survival items—water, dry food, things for starting a fire, and weapons. I chose one of the rifles and a Buck knife. That way, if someone found the cabin, I could run away.

I planned escape routes—over the rocks to the north, down to the river, or through the valley in the east. If there was a logging road where I could be trapped, I found another. I added bear bangers to the trip lines—when the line was tugged, it would pull the slide on the trigger, and release the banger. The gunshot sound would echo for miles. I looked for areas where I could make booby traps to catch anyone sneaking too close to the cabin, but I kept hitting rocks and roots and had to start over.

I didn't go near the deep pools in the lower section of the river—where I knew the local men liked to fish—but I tracked back to where they parked their trucks and carefully raided their gear, taking things they might not notice missing right away. I found rope, lures, and fishing net. Sometimes food, like bags of chips, chocolate bars, or a sandwich from a cooler. Each free meal meant my supplies would last longer.

With October came the rains, and they never seemed to stop. Gray Shawl Mountain was living up to its name. The woods were dark from the low-lying clouds, the fog that floated through the trees. My clothes were always soaked and hanging by the stove. The cabin smelled like wet fur and smoke. Damp surrounded me. I carried armfuls of wood inside to dry by the fire, and every day I scavenged for more. I ran out of propane and had to cook on top of the woodstove.

I blocked my cabin from view with branches and fallen trees, forming a perimeter wall, but the wind swept it all away. Then I ran out of rope to tie the branches together. A cedar tree blew down near my dirt bike and crashed so hard the earth shook. Wolf ran off in a panic and I chased after him. Branches cracked over my head, trees swayed, and lightning flashed across the sky. When a bolt hit a tree near the river, Wolf came back—running straight at me. We hid in the cabin, under the blankets, as the world howled around us. In the morning I inspected the damage. Parts of my roof had blown away and rain had flooded the latrine.

I buried my cans and garbage in a deep pit so that no animal could dig them up. The roof sprang a leak and ruined my baking flour. My hands were always blistered. I dyed my hair twice, hacked at it with scissors. I couldn't swim in the river, so I warmed water on the stove and took sponge baths, then wiped the mud off Wolf, combing out his snarled fur while he grumbled.

Each time I saw Jonny, he said, "I hate you being up there alone."

"I have Wolf." I told him everything was fine. He couldn't

know that I wanted to struggle. I wanted it to be *hard*. I had to exhaust myself chopping wood, hiking miles along the river, and foraging for food. I had to stay focused on keeping me and Wolf alive. Otherwise, I'd think about what Vaughn had done to Amber. Then I'd want to do something about it.

CHAPTER 14

November. Trees turned red and yellow and dropped their leaves. Frost pushed up through the dirt. The days were shorter, our long walks hindered by time and weather. I wore Dad's bulky goose-down coat and my wool-lined boots. Even inside the cabin I had to wear layers of flannel and thermal underwear. We slept with two sleeping bags and kept the stove burning.

The woods were thick with hunters. Shots rang out in the distance. I kept Wolf close to me, calling him back the moment he wandered off. Dad used to go on long hunting trips, solo or with friends, and come back smelling like woodsmoke and beer. I was thinking of him now as Wolf and I made our way back from the river with trout hanging from my pack. I'd gutted them on shore. Two were mine, the third was Wolf's. He'd grown bored with crayfish and had learned that if he stood near the currents, he could catch a leaping fish straight out of the white water.

Dad would've been impressed. I could see him giving Wolf a hearty pat on his side, roughhousing with him, and calling him a good boy. It hurt, imagining what could've been.

Wolf stopped, his body rigid and his ears swiveling back and forth, his nose lifted, huffing the air. He was trying to pick up the scent of something. We took a few more steps and he paused again, looking over his shoulder. I followed his gaze, saw nothing.

"What is it?" I whispered.

He stayed focused on the trail. The hackles around his neck

and down his spine lifted, while a low growl rumbled deep in his throat.

I slid the safety off on my rifle, kept it by my side with my finger resting on the trigger, and stared into the woods. The birds had gone quiet and the very air seemed to have changed. Was it a deer hunter? An animal? We had gone farther down the river today. It wouldn't be easy to run back to the cabin. The small hairs on the back of my neck prickled.

After a few beats, Wolf turned his head around and we kept walking, but he was tense, and stopped to listen a few times. I held my rifle tighter. Wolf stopped again, sniffing the ground at the side of the trail. I crouched. Paw prints. Big pads, with no claws showing. A cougar. Full-grown. It had followed our trail down to the river, but where was it now?

I stood, put the rifle to my shoulder, and looked around, scanning the trees, the shadows. Cougars aren't like black bears, who usually run off at the sight of humans. Or grizzlies, who rush thundering through the bush with a roar. Cougars stalk their prey or even lie in wait. You didn't get much notice before they attacked. I might be able to fend it off with my knife, if the gun was knocked clear of my hand, but one swipe from a two-hundred-pound cougar could kill Wolf.

I held on to the bandanna around his neck and stepped up our pace, while still searching the woods for movement and noise. Wolf was tight against my legs, a whine leaking from his throat. We were rounding the last bend when I saw it.

A cougar. Thirty feet in front of us, tawny brown and huge, perched on the moss-covered rocks to the side of the trail. Its yellow eyes focused on me. It lowered its head.

"Get out of here!" I couldn't shoot without letting go of Wolf, who was barking and lunging forward. I yelled again, raised the rifle with my free hand, waving it like a stick, and stomped my feet. The cougar didn't even flinch. I took a few slow steps backward, tugging on Wolf.

The cougar pushed itself to all fours and eased off the rocks, shoulders bunching and head still low. It was on the trail now and moving closer. I had to shoot.

"Wolf, stay!"

But as I let go of him to lift the rifle to my shoulder, he rushed past me, sprinted at the cougar, barking as he stopped in front of it. The cougar swatted the air and snarled, revealing its fangs.

My mind stalled. I screamed, "Wolf! No. Come!"

Wolf danced back. The cougar swatted at him again. Hissing. My finger fumbled on the trigger. I focused. Wolf was in my shot. I raised the rifle to the sky and let off a round.

The cougar backed off a few feet—Wolf was still barking and baiting it. I let off another shot. The cougar took a hard left and leapt through the woods toward the river. Wolf followed.

"Wolf, stop!"

They were gone, crashing through the thick ferns and bushes, the tangle of underbrush. Branches closed after them. I raced toward where I'd last seen Wolf, scrambling over rocks and through shrubs that tore at my hair, my clothes, my skin. Panting, I broke out of the woods and found myself standing high above the river. I scanned the trees, trying to hear Wolf over the rushing falls. Where was he? Then I saw a flash of black and spotted him in the distance.

He was chasing the cougar across an old fir tree hanging over the water. The cougar abruptly stopped and pivoted, swatted at Wolf. He yipped—a high-pitched cry that yanked my insides. I raised the gun, sighted down the long barrel, and pressed the trigger. The bullet struck the wood and sent splinters flying into the air, but it spooked the cougar. It leapt into the pool below. It popped up and swam downstream. Wolf bolted into the woods.

I hurried along the bank of the river, slipping on moss and struggling over the rocks until I reached the log. I dropped to my knees and crawled across. When I'd made it to the other side, I whistled and called for Wolf. I searched the dirt, grass, and plants. Blood drops, red and glistening. I *had* to find him. I tracked him through a meadow.

"Wolf! Come on, boy! Where are you?"

I stopped and held my breath, straining to hear over the birds and the breeze. A soft whimper. He was close. I followed the sound and found him cowering under a bush. He was panting hard, his eyes wild and panicked. I dropped to my knees and gently stroked his face.

"You dumbass. Why did you have to be so brave?" I tried to sound calm and soothing, but my throat was tight with tears. The cougar had left two gouges on his front shoulder. They weren't to the bone, but I needed to clean them. I took my first-aid kit out of my backpack and opened the sterilized pads, then held them against the wounds while I wrapped a Tensor bandage around his quivering body. It was hard not to jostle him and he yelped, his head snapping back to nip at the air, then he licked at my hand, begging for forgiveness. I rubbed his neck.

"It's okay. You can bite me if it helps."

I pulled him out, slowly, then hefted him over my shoulder. He yelped again, and I couldn't hold back the tears. What was I going to do? I couldn't make it back over the log—not with the extra weight. I'd have to circle around and hope the cougar wasn't hunting us.

By the time we'd made it downriver, I was out of breath, my shirt and hair soaked with sweat. I crossed over the river where the water was shallow and the rocks close together. I kept watch for the cougar. It could still be near. We were easy prey now.

I carried Wolf up the trail on the other side, stopping to take breaks. I thought about making a stretcher, but I didn't have my hacksaw and had no way to strap the wood together. I staggered the rest of the way to the cabin. Wolf had stopped bleeding, but he was in pain, his body trembling. I made him comfortable on the bed and cleaned the cuts and bandaged him. My first-aid kit had a bottle of CBD oil. I wasn't sure of the dose, but I dropped some into his mouth.

Wolf didn't want to eat, so I crawled in beside him, my chest and stomach against his curved back, and his haunches cradled in my lap. I stroked his head, his soft ears, his snout.

"You're going to be okay. Everything's going to be okay."

He twisted his neck and licked at my tears, then dropped his head onto the pillow. I held him in my arms and buried my face in his soft fur.

I stood outside the cabin bundled in my parka, the hood over my head and a scarf wound around my neck. The snow was a few inches deep already and coming down fast. Flurries blinded me. I tugged the scarf away from my mouth, fumbled for the mic button on the VHF radio.

"Come in, 250H. We need help. Wolf's injured. We need medicine—antibiotics." I released the mic button, waited for an answer from Jonny. *Please, please, please.* But there was only crackling static. I looked at the sky, heavy with snow. Maybe the signal wasn't getting through.

Wind whipped the snow into my face, pushed me back into the cabin. I slammed the door. Wolf didn't look up from his bed in front of the stove. I opened a packet of smoked salmon, clunked over to him in my boots. For two days I'd only managed to dribble broth into his mouth with a syringe so I could keep him hydrated. I waved the salmon under his nose.

"Try it, just a little, please?" He opened his eyes, blinked at me, and turned his face away. I lifted the bandages for another look, but I already knew what I would see. The wounds were red and puffy. I cleaned them again, applied fresh bandages, and left him by the fire.

I packed my bag, grabbing at things—food, water, emergency supplies, the radio—and shrugged it onto my back. The Smith & Wesson went into my holster, the rifle strapped to my back. Then I gently wrapped Wolf up in a wool blanket and lifted him into my arms.

We took the dirt bike until the snow got too deep, the tires spinning, then I had to abandon it on the trail. I took Wolf out of his crate and set him on top of the snow. He was more alert now, confused, and pulled himself to standing. He tried to limp toward me.

"No. Stay."

I slid the dirt bike into the sheltered area under the base of a tree, covered it with garbage bags, then with branches—however many I could hack off the nearby trees. I didn't know when I would be able to come back. I marked one of the tree limbs with Wolf's bandanna.

I trudged through snowdrifts that felt like quicksand, sucking at my boots, holding me in place until I wrenched myself free. I carried Wolf on my shoulders with the blanket over him. His head was tucked into the fur of my hood. Blinding snow blew into my eyes. My fingers grew numb inside my gloves. I breathed hard as I climbed up a hill, sliding down onto my knees, then stumbling back to my feet. Wind pummeled the center of my back, swept through breaks in the forest, and came at me from the side. I wanted to make it to the lower camp, where I could try the radio again, but the trail had disappeared. I stopped and spun around. There had to be *something* that would help me navigate. I couldn't see more than a few feet in front of me. The world had turned white.

I tripped over a buried log, and Wolf slipped from my shoulders, landing in a drift and nearly sinking out of my reach. His fur was clumped with snow. I lifted him into my arms and staggered a few more feet. I couldn't do it. The snow was coming too fast. We had to hide in a tree well. Once the storm ended, I'd recognize the lay of the land again.

My eyelashes were clumped with ice. My face stung. I found a pocket of space below a big fir tree, cut down branches, and placed them around us, weaving them together to form walls and a roof. For a marker, I ripped the bottom off my shirt and tied it to the tree. There were two outdoor emergency blankets in my backpack. I unfolded the thin silver material and used one to line the roof. More branches went underneath to keep our bodies off the cold ground. Near the entrance to our snow cave, I built a fire with tinder and broken branches that I found along the trunk of the tree. I wrapped my second emergency blanket around us.

We huddled together through the night. I tried the VHF radio over and over, but only got static in return. The fire died and I ran out of dry wood. The wind had not let up. The world grew silent as the snow built up around the shelter and cocooned us. I couldn't stop shivering.

I took my journal out of my backpack and tucked it into my inside pocket. If someone found my body, they would know who I was. They would know about Vaughn. It was getting harder to stay awake. My eyelids kept drifting closed. The VHF radio was clutched in my hand.

Wolf pawed at me and licked my face.

"I'm sorry," I whispered. "I'm sorry." I prayed Wolf would survive. My body could keep him warm for a while. He had thick fur, but he was fighting that infection, and he hadn't eaten in days. He pressed against my chest, his cheek alongside mine, breathing puffs of warmth into my neck. I wasn't cold anymore. I had no sensation in my feet or hands. Tired. So tired.

I dreamed of being at the lake with Amber. The scent of her skin. Coconut. Her hair, cherry-red fire, floating across her beautiful lips. We'd had one perfect kiss. I'd had it all in that moment. Long summer days. Swimming with Jonny. My body felt warm now. I was basking in the sun, my face lifting, soaking up the rays. I could hear our dirt bikes whizzing around the track. Louder and louder. Drowning out everything. The hum through my body like electricity.

We used to go so fast. No one could beat us.

PART TWO

CHAPTER 15

Beth

SEPTEMBER 2018

Beth pushed open the door, carefully balancing the cardboard tray of coffees, and cursed as someone bumped into her. The last thing she needed was a stain on her white blouse. She only had two good suits, rotated them religiously, and sponged them clean in her tiny bathroom.

More office workers jostled her on their way in for their Skinny Vanilla Lattes or Matcha Green Tea Frappuccinos. You couldn't turn a block in Vancouver without tripping over a coffee shop.

She let go of the door and smiled apologetically as it swung into a hipster, then she wove in and out of the crowded sidewalk, passing businesspeople, yogis, tourists with cameras. She glanced at her watch. Five minutes to get to the office. She picked up her pace, enjoying the click of her heels on concrete. Some days she still felt like she was playacting at being a grown-up.

Her cell chirped in her purse. She frowned. She would have to pause to answer it, which would delay her, but what if it was one of the lawyers? Someone with a last-minute craving for a gluten-free muffin. No. They would be too busy prepping for the meeting. She kept walking.

The phone chirped again. Stopped. Then chirped again. Only one person was that persistent. Beth tucked herself against a building, set the tray of coffees on a ledge, and pulled out her phone. Amber's photo flashed across the screen. Beth swiped to answer.

"Hey, what's going on? I'm working."

"I thought you were interning."

"Same thing." She was mostly fetching coffees and sitting in on meetings, but that didn't sound nearly as impressive. Every morning Beth walked past the lawyers in their big offices and told herself she'd belong there too one day. Okay, a lot more days. Three years and she'd have her undergraduate degree. Then she could apply to law school. She just had to stay the course.

"Are you going to church Sunday?"

"Unfortunately."

"How do you stand it?" Beth knew Amber was talking about the obligatory parental lunch after the service. Neither Amber nor Beth were particularly God-fearing, but even church wasn't as boring as passing food back and forth over a table while their mom and dad made small talk about the sermon, weather, and how the tomatoes were doing this year. Beth and Amber used to flip coins over who got to have the fake illness or last-minute shift at work.

"Since you abandoned me, I don't have a choice." Beth said the words lightly, but she meant it. She missed her little sister, even if she understood why she left.

"Sorry." Amber sighed. "I know I stuck you with it."

Beth glanced at her watch. She would have to walk and talk. She picked up the tray, tensing her fingers underneath to hold it level, and moved down the street.

"Is everything okay?"

"Can you say a prayer for Hailey?"

"Still no word?"

"Not yet." Amber's voice was vague, the tone she adopted whenever she talked about Hailey now. Beth wanted to say something reassuring, but she also didn't want to mislead her. She'd texted Amber as soon as she saw on the news that they'd found Hailey's bicycle and her cell phone. *Are you okay?* Amber had answered, *I think she did it on purpose, to throw people off track. Her uncle is scary.* Maybe, but Beth feared the rumors were probably true.

"Why don't you come for a visit? You can say a prayer yourself."

"My tires are bald. I'm waiting for my next paycheck."

"I hate that you are in Cold Creek." Only Amber would drive to the Yukon to meet friends at a music festival, then stop for gas in the creepiest town and wind up instead getting a waitressing job. For the first couple of months Amber's Instagram had been full of pictures of her doing yoga poses beside rivers and on rocky cliffs. She hadn't posted anything since Hailey disappeared.

"I don't hitchhike, but yeah, I hate it too."

That was new. Maybe Amber wasn't feeling as hopeful as Beth had thought.

"Are you moving back to Vancouver?"

"Not sure. I might still go up to the Yukon."

"And do what? Teach yoga to grizzly bears?"

Amber laughed. She never seemed to get offended by Beth's sarcasm. Or anyone's. Kids could never bully her in school because Amber just didn't care.

"I might keep waitressing. It's fun. We can't all be brilliant lawyers."

Beth heard the teasing tone, but she frowned as she walked through the revolving glass doors and headed to the elevators. "You *could* be a lawyer. You're too smart to quit school."

"You're too smart to be a lawyer. You just think it will make you happy."

"That doesn't even make sense." Beth mentally rolled her eyes. Sometimes Amber's free-spirit hippie thinking irritated the hell out of her. "I have to go. I'm at the elevators."

"I'll be at the lake this weekend—if you can't reach me. Love you."

"Love you too."

After saying goodbye, Beth slid the phone into her purse and hit the up button with her elbow. Amber didn't know what she was talking about. Being a lawyer was *everything*.

Beth watched her mom carefully lay the cutlery. She'd played her part in the charade and offered to help, but her mom would never let anyone else set the table, and they both knew it. Same thing if she tried to clean up the dishes or put away the food. It would all be declined.

Behind closed doors, Amber and Beth would giggle and call their mother "Mad Madeline"—though they never saw her react with more than a huff. They spun tales for each other. Imagined scenarios where their finely tuned mother might explode and flip the table over, sending tomato soup and cheese sandwiches crashing to the polished tile, while their father watched with his mystified expression. The one he used whenever any of them seemed upset.

Beth's mom dished out the bowls—tomato again—and sat at the table. She spread the serviette neatly over her lap and nodded. Beth's dad picked up his spoon. Beth followed.

"It was a good service today." Beth's dad—whom the sisters nicknamed "Even Steven" because he'd divided everything exactly in half for them their entire lives—said the same thing every Sunday. Beth made a soft hum of agreement, but truth be told, she'd spent most of the service thinking about Amber. Should she have lent her money for new tires? How bad were they? Beth owed a small fortune in student loans and credit cards—looking the part of a successful woman in the city was not cheap. Neither was her apartment, even with three room-mates. But she was worried. Beth peeked at her iPhone in her lap. Amber hadn't answered her morning texts.

Her mom looked over the table. "Please put away your phone."

"Sorry." Beth slid it to the side of the table, still visible enough to irk her mother. Beth might toe the line, but she wasn't above giving it a small tug. "I'm waiting to hear from Amber."

"You've talked to her?" Her dad spoke cautiously, as though feeling out the words, and he flicked a glance at her mom, mea-suring her reaction.

"She called Thursday." Beth considered whether to tell them that her sister needed tires. Amber was proud, though. She'd want her parents to think she could handle herself, and Beth didn't want to betray that. "She seems okay. She's talking about going to the Yukon."

Her mom's spoon tinged against her bowl as she slid it through the soup. "I think we're heading into another heat wave. I can't imagine what our air-conditioning bill is going be like."

Beth stared at her mother. Did she really just change the subject to *air-conditioning*?

"If you call Amber, you can ask her to come home."

"She doesn't listen to us."

"Scripture isn't conversation, Mom. Can't you just tell her that you miss her? She needs to hear it from all of us—and she needs to finish school." Beth looked from one of her parents to the other. "What if you drove up there and took her out to lunch or something?"

Her mom fluttered her hand through the air, let it settle at her throat. "It's a long way."

"We could go together."

"She doesn't want us in her life. She made that clear."

"She just wants you to accept that she's—"

"Beth." Her father's voice struck her silent. He'd only said her name, but it was enough. She'd gone too far. She could see it in the flush on her mother's face, the tremble of her lip.

"Sorry," Beth mumbled.

Her mom cleaned off the table while Beth and her dad talked—*So you're enjoying your job? They're treating you right?* She'd had more exciting conversations with her dentist. Now her mom was washing the dishes while her dad watched a documentary on ancient beekeeping. Her parents refused to buy a dishwasher. They were both teachers and made a decent living, but they donated whatever they could to the church. Their charity did not include helping their daughter with anything more than part of her tuition. They believed hard work was good for the soul.

Beth sat on the side patio, where she could see into the front and backyard, taking a moment before she had to fight through traffic. Her mother's flower gardens were exploding with color. The North Shore Mountains hovered blue in the distance. In another couple of months it would rain almost daily, and the city would turn gray, the mountaintops frosted white.

She glanced at her phone again. Three unanswered texts. Amber had said she would be at the lake during the weekend, but Beth assumed that had meant she was camping and would be back by Sunday morning. She must have decided to stay longer. Then her phone probably died, or there was bad reception. Beth checked Amber's Facebook. She hadn't posted in days.

Beth looked up when she heard a car coming down her parents' maple-tree-lined street. A police car. Black-and-white. City cops. She scanned the other houses. Her parents lived in a quiet neighborhood. She couldn't imagine what any of them might have done to warrant a personal visit.

The police stopped in front of the house across the road. Beth waited for an officer to step out, but now the car was pulling forward and turning around. They must have had the wrong address. She watched curiously. It was like Russian roulette. Whose house would it be?

The car parked in front of her parents' home, and she got to her feet, watched as two somber-faced officers stepped out. Full uniforms. One of them met her eyes, and then Beth knew.

Amber wouldn't be texting back.

CHAPTER 16

Beth settled on the patio chair, rested the plate on the side table, leaning back so the hanging baskets of flowers hid her from the media vans. Those first few days had been terrible, reporters clustered along the sidewalk, lunging forward with their microphones outstretched and shouting questions every time Beth or her parents appeared. Beth's father finally stood on the front steps and politely asked them to let them grieve in privacy. Of course, the reporters ignored him.

Since the news broke, all sorts of people had been messaging her—lawyers she worked with, students in her classes at the university, and guys she'd briefly dated. Sympathies and subtle, or not-so-subtle, questions. She gave short statements, memorized her lines.

We are trying to be strong, it's a difficult time, we appreciate the support.

Reporters took screenshots of Amber's Facebook page, all her photos, comments, memes, anything she had liked, and broadcast the selfie of Amber and Hailey together before Beth made her sister's page private. Her parents didn't understand about the relentless nature of social media. Beth hadn't even understood how bad it would get.

She found a photograph of herself taken the day before, when she'd been hauling out the kitchen trash, and had been shocked to see how much older she looked now. They all did. Except Amber. She'd never be any older than eighteen years, three months, and ten days.

Beth chewed a mouthful of tuna noodle salad, wishing she had a glass of wine to wash down the bread-crumb topping. The kitchen door opened behind her, sending out a whoosh of cool air, the soft hum of voices. It closed again. Beth stared into the backyard and listened to the scrape of shoes. She'd hoped they would keep going around to the other side of the patio, but someone came to stand beside her. Beth looked up. A dark-haired man, tall, with a navy-blue suit. Constable Thompson. One of the cops working her sister's case up in Cold Creek.

She straightened. "Did something happen? Should I get my dad?"

"No, no. I had meetings in the city. Your parents asked if I could stop by. Sorry to bother you. I wanted to take a moment to express my sympathies." His gaze slid past her to the news vans. "I can ask them to clear out."

She hadn't noticed him at the service, but it seemed the entire city had emptied itself into the church. Church members, neighbors, family. Amber's artsy school friends with their colored hair, tattoos, and body piercings. Beth had gone down Amber's Facebook friends list, messaging them individually.

She rested her fork on the side of her plate. "Did you get some food?" How many times had she said that today? *Thank you for coming. Did you eat?* "People brought so much."

He nodded. "Your mom's sending me home with a bag."

Beth thought of him driving while eating tarts, cookies, flakes of spanakopita pastry falling onto his nice tie as he mused over evidence or statements. Maybe it wasn't the first time. Maybe his fridge was stuffed with casseroles and baking from the mothers of murder victims.

The local police had been the first to interview their family. *Was your daughter having problems with anyone? Did your sister have a boyfriend? Any known drug issues?* Her parents had stuttered and stammered and looked to each other for support. Beth had sat silent, scrolling through her texts from her sister as though the answer were buried somewhere among them and she'd somehow skipped right over it.

Then Thompson traveled down to ask more questions but barely answered theirs because it was an ongoing investigation. He'd called a couple of times since. There were no suspects—at least none they'd been told about. Beth thought they should drive to Cold Creek and meet with the police. But her dad's face closed down and he said, "Let them do their jobs."

Thompson leaned on the porch railing. Beth looked away. She had a hard time meeting his eyes. She couldn't stop thinking about what he knew. He had probably seen her sister's body. There would be photos. The very thought of them had Beth waking from nightmares, sweaty and tangled in sheets, her heartbeat frantic. She'd started sleeping at her parents' house.

"When does it stop?" She jerked her chin toward the press.

"Hard to say. There's a lot of interest."

"I've read about the other cases. There's a website." Amber was one of the Cold Creek Highway victims now. Famous. Beth never understood grief before. It was a concept, something she read about. Like motherhood. Now it hollowed her, stole the breath from her chest. Her sister had *suffered*. She could imagine how hard Amber must have fought, how she would've screamed and begged. Beth's mind was a haunted house that she could never leave.

"Those sites are full of conspiracy theorists and armchair detectives. They take advantage of vulnerable people. I'd suggest you avoid reading them if you can."

"I just want answers." She *needed* them.

"We're working hard to get them. I promise. We have new

technology, more CCTV cameras. Don't give up hope. Some of the other families have found solace in support groups."

"My parents have the church."

"What about you?"

"It still doesn't feel real." She hadn't meant to tell him that. What had she been thinking? That he might turn to her and say, *Well, actually, it's not real. It's a terrible mistake. So sorry.* He shifted his weight, adjusted the line of his blazer. The movement pulled her gaze up to his face. Brown eyes. Filled with sympathy. Too much. It hurt to see that reflected back at her.

"I should help my mom." She stood and brushed bread crumbs off her skirt. "Thank you for coming. I'm sure it meant a lot to my parents." She smiled stiffly and hurried back inside.

The kitchen was spotless. The women from the church had cleaned and put everything away, stocked their fridge with leftovers. Beth sat with her parents in the living room while they drank tea. The TV was off. Her father hadn't watched the news since it had happened, but Beth would sneak peeks after they'd gone to bed, scared of what she might see, but desperate to find out if anyone had come forward. Any tidbit. She'd deleted Twitter and Facebook from her phone.

Her mom was staring into space. Her hair looked damp around her forehead, the soft bob messy, and her cheeks were flushed from heat or emotion. She kept glancing into the kitchen as though searching for more tasks. Her mom now existed between the bedroom and the kitchen.

"Why did you invite that police officer?"

Her mother slowly turned, blinked, licked her dry lips. Beth wondered at first if it was all in her imagination, the feeling that her mother was moving through thick water, and put it down to shock and grief, but then she'd found the pills in her mother's bathroom.

"We . . ." Her mother searched for words. "We wanted him to feel a connection with Amber."

Would that matter? Beth wasn't sure, but she liked the idea. Thompson working a little harder, following down every last lead, while he thought about her family waiting for closure.

Her father glanced out the window. "Are the reporters still out there?"

"Yes."

"I'll walk you to your car in the morning. If they get too aggressive, we can call the police. Just remember not to say anything. Don't react." Her dad's brows were pulled together. This was who they were now. People who tried to find ways to hide from the world.

"I don't know if I'm ready to go back to work."

Both her parents were looking at her. Who would speak first?

"You can't miss any more days." Her mother. Beth wasn't surprised. Her mom loved telling neighbors and church members about her daughter the future lawyer. Beth didn't want to think about the small hidden part of her that felt relieved about putting it all to the side.

"Maybe another week."

"You don't want to take advantage."

"It's not like I'm pocketing extra sugar packets. There's only a couple of weeks left before school starts anyway. But I might defer this semester."

"Oh, that's not a good idea, tiger. Don't do that." Her father, a lurch in his voice, as though suddenly panicked that she was about to jump out of a window.

"I'll go back in January." Beth couldn't believe they were finding this so shocking. How could they expect her to just carry on? Anything more than being in this room felt impossible. Getting groceries, mail, answering messages. Those tasks belonged in her past life.

"You can't let evil win." Her mother this time, the words a whisper, but loud enough just the same. If Beth didn't follow through, she was letting everyone down. Including God.

"You have to stay busy," her father added. "In times of tragedy, we must focus on the good. Find meaning in volunteer work. The church could always use you."

"Is that what you're going to do?"

"Teaching is important work, and the church is our family."

Right, but they weren't Beth's. Despite all their differences, she and Amber were the same in that fact. It was like they'd been playing doubles tennis and now Beth didn't have her partner. If either of them needed help deciding on anything, they consulted each other. Even minor things like a shade of lipstick, clothing, shoes. Before her first interview, Beth had held up her two suits on FaceTime with Amber and wore the one she'd picked. Nothing was done without discussion.

"I'll take your car and fill it up with gas before you drive into the city tomorrow." And with that pronouncement from her father, it was done. They were sending her home.

"If there is anything you want from your sister's room, let me know. The ladies are coming this week to pack her clothes."

Beth's hand jerked on her teacup, clinking it against the china plate. Her mother winced.

"You're cleaning out her room already?"

"The church supports many families in need."

What about Beth's need to grieve for her sister? Wasn't that important too? She wanted to fight for Amber—and herself—but all she felt was a thick blanket of fatigue.

"I think I'm going to go lie down."

"That's a good idea." Her mother stared at Amber's baby

photo on the wall, absently settling her hand on her stomach as though remembering when she had carried her safe.

"I'll make biscuits. They'll go well with that leftover stew."

Beth searched the bathroom cabinets for Tylenol, took two, then glanced over her shoulder. No footsteps. She opened her mom's makeup drawer, felt through the few products—skin cream, powder, pink lipstick. The pills weren't there. She crept across the hall and into her parents' room. On the night table she found the prescription bottle labeled *Madeline Chevalier*.

Xanax. Beth took one of the pills out and slid it under her tongue, then went down the hall to Amber's room. Most of her sister's belongings were already gone—she'd taken them with her when she moved—but Beth still had flashes of Amber sitting on the floor listening to music, meditating, or twisted into a complicated yoga pose. Beth ran her finger over the stack of spiritual books touting self-awareness, mindfulness, transcendence.

Beth plucked a photo of Amber and her from the corner of the dresser mirror. Other than the one crooked incisor they both had, they didn't look alike, and not just because Amber's features were bolder—with her big eyes, full lips, and wild hair. *She* was bigger than life, grand in her gestures, her smile. Singing at the top of her lungs whenever she heard a tune she liked.

In the photo Amber was wearing a halter top and jeans shorts. Beth was stiff and looked overheated in her graduation robe, her blond hair stuck to her forehead. Amber's hair, naturally caramel brown, was turquoise at the time, triggering a series of parental lectures about how no one would take her seriously, which Amber had said was the entire point.

During high school, they passed each other in the hallway—Amber in a cloud of lavender scent on her way to drama club or dance class, Beth with a tension headache on her way to study group. They stayed in their own lanes. Beth was proud of being the responsible, quiet one. She was proud too that Amber didn't feel the same obligation, that she felt free to find her own path. But now Amber was dead, and Beth felt the walls of responsibility close around her. She stared at the photograph in her hand. Her parents had been so pleased, took them out for a special dinner, and told everyone how their daughter would be going to university in the fall.

Beth had begun to wonder if Amber was right, that working hard to become a lawyer wouldn't make her happy. None of that mattered anymore. She was all her parents had now.

In the morning she'd let the law office know she was coming back.

CHAPTER 17

Beth moved through the crowd toward the white tent and table at the other end of the parking lot, then veered away when she noticed the network news crew. She found a spot in the shade where she could watch the First Nations drum circle. Some people were singing along, dancing. She didn't know how they could stand the heat. Her sundress was already sticking to her legs.

There were a few groups carrying banners: JUSTICE FOR THE VICTIMS! KEEP THE HIGHWAY SAFE! BRING OUR GIRLS HOME! Others were holding colorful signs with photos of victims, dates when they were last seen written in Sharpie, messages to their loved one. WE MISS YOU!

People wore yellow reflective vests. A car was parked nearby with speakers on the roof, more photos of the missing and murdered stuck all over it. She spotted Amber's photo among the others and felt a sickening rush of panic. How was she going to do this? She held her cold plastic water bottle to the back of her neck, her forehead.

Everyone near her in the shade was speaking softly. Like it would be inappropriate to laugh or raise their voice. Some of the women looked angry. Those she understood more. She locked eyes with an older First Nations woman standing with a child. They were holding a banner with WE NEED ANSWERS! painted in careful red letters over a photo of one of the victims— a beautiful girl with long black hair. Beth knew of her case. She'd died decades ago. Her family still came out for her.

Would Beth be coming to memorials with her grandchildren one day?

It had been almost a year and Amber's case was still unsolved. When Beth read online that the town had an annual memorial walk to raise awareness of the victims, she'd mentioned it to her therapist, who said, "Many people find peace in ritual. It's worth a try, don't you think?"

Beth didn't think.

She'd avoided the idea completely until she lost her apartment (an unfortunate side effect of losing her job) and found herself homeless. Maybe her therapist was right. She needed to go to the memorial for closure. Then she could get her feet under her again. She'd had a moment of doubt when she'd arrived in town an hour ago and saw the welcoming sign, but then she'd heard Amber's voice so clearly it was like she was sitting beside her. *OMG. It's pretty as a postcard, Beth. The mountains, the creek, and there's this huge elk sculpture. I call him Elvis.*

Before the memorial, Beth had driven past the house where Amber had rented a basement suite, peered into the garden that she'd loved. *I can pick whatever I want.* Her parents had arranged last summer for the landlord to ship all her belongings back. Amber's turtle bracelet that matched Beth's was missing. Thompson said it was possible the killer had kept it.

Beth glanced at her wrist now, turned the bracelet so the turtle slid to the front, the small green stones picking up the light. She'd read that killers liked to show up at the scene of the crime. Maybe the memorial walk was similar. If he was here, would he recognize the bracelet?

She lifted her purse higher on her shoulder, the weight comforting as it settled against her side. The handgun had been expensive—same with the instructor at the gun range—and it was highly illegal for her to carry it concealed. She considered both facts inconsequential.

She studied the men around her. They looked normal, but that didn't mean anything. Killers passed underneath the radar all the time. Take Ted Bundy, for example. Still, she made note of their faces.

A woman in a red dress gathered the crowd. She explained that they were to walk through town toward the highway and stop at the billboard, where they would place flowers and candles. Beth was relieved that the walk didn't go farther. She didn't want to see the ditch where her sister's body had been found. She'd seen the cross online. Someone had taken a photo, and that image, the shock of pure white against the dark woods, had sent her spiraling for days.

The woman was now reciting a poem, or maybe it was a prayer. Beth couldn't focus on the words. She bowed her head. She felt someone watching and turned to look. Police uniform. Older man, big, with pale hair and eyes. The pretty black-haired woman next to him kept pressing a handkerchief to her eyes.

Amber's voice whispered to her. *His name's Vaughn and he's such a jerk. Everyone is scared of him. He looks like the villain in a spy movie. Swear to God!*

Beth let her gaze skip past him, then bowed her head again. She was sure he recognized her. Their family photos had been everywhere online.

The woman at the front was talking about community spirit, how they had to watch out for each other, then she said, "Sergeant Vaughn has a few things to add."

The big cop moved up to the front and began to speak in an authoritative voice. "I know you're scared, and you're frustrated. We're going to increase our patrols on the highway and around the lake, but we need your help. We need you to stay vigilant. Don't travel alone if you can avoid it. Make sure your vehicles are roadworthy. Do not hitchhike. Do not pick up hitchhikers." He paused and looked around. "If you see anything strange, report it. You all know Hailey, my niece, is still missing, and I don't want any other family to go through this pain."

Beth startled. The anger that she'd been choking back for nearly a year surged forward. If he didn't want anyone else to feel that pain, then he should have found the killer *before* Amber became the next victim. He should have been patrolling *then*. He should have stopped it *then*.

She spun around and moved back through the gathering, not caring as she banged into people, who shifted away with murmurs of complaint. Her car was blocked by the crowd. She cursed, then looked around. She'd get a cup of coffee and wait. The closest thing she could see was a diner. MASON'S DINER, the sign said. It had to be where Amber had worked. She hesitated.

Behind her the crowd began to sing "Amazing Grace."

Fine. The diner couldn't be more painful than that, could it? The door gave a friendly jingle as she pushed it open. The diner was cleaner than she had expected and smelled like fresh-baked biscuits. Comfort food. Her stomach growled. She couldn't remember when she'd last eaten.

There were a few tables available, but she decided to sit on one of the red-vinyl-covered stools at the counter. The waitress, a middle-aged woman with graying brown hair and a no-nonsense voice, said, "You need a menu, hon?" and placed a glass of water in front of her.

"Yes, please."

Beth drank down the cold water, then struggled to focus on the menu. Amber had worked in this diner. She'd stood behind this counter and pressed keys on that cash register. The day she died, she'd walked out, had driven to the lake, and never came back.

When the waitress arrived to take her order, Beth impulsively ordered a burger, fries, and a milkshake. Amber's favorite meal—she was a hippie, but definitely not vegan. It arrived fast, looked good, and tasted even better. Beth shoved fries into her mouth, in between gulps of her milkshake and bites of her burger, trying to remember the last time she'd enjoyed food.

"You look like you're on a mission." She lifted her head. A bearded man was behind the counter, a cloth slung over his shoulder, his arms crossed. He was burly but not in an intimidating way. Solid. He had to be Mason.

Beth stared at him silently. His eyebrows lifted.

"Are you okay?"

"My sister." She swallowed. "Amber worked here."

"Ah." He leaned against the counter, gave her a level look. "You came for the memorial."

"Yeah." She liked that he hadn't said he was sorry, or any of the normal expressions of sympathy. She hadn't realized how much she'd come to hate them.

"So why aren't you out there?"

She shrugged. "Didn't feel like I belonged." It was probably an odd thing to say. Who would belong more than a sister of one of the victims? But he nodded as though it made sense.

"How long you in town?"

"Just the day, I guess."

"Playing things by ear?"

"I'm in transition at the moment. I'm broke, homeless." She tried for a wry smile, but she was surprised that she had told him so much without feeling embarrassed. Then again, he didn't seem like the kind of guy who would have been impressed by a future lawyer anyway.

"You looking for a job?"

"How do you mean?"

"I could use another waitress for the summer. Job's yours if you want it."

"Serious?"

"Your sister was a good kid."

Beth had planned on driving to her parents' and breaking the news that she'd failed out of school (which had led to the previously mentioned job failure). They didn't even know she was in Cold Creek. When she told them about the memorial walk, they said it was too far. Beth had noticed her mother's increasing reluctance to go anywhere. Even groceries were ordered online.

It wasn't discussed. Nothing was discussed.

She thought about the sergeant, talking about safety. What were a few extra patrols going to do? They'd given up on finding her sister's killer. They probably weren't even trying anymore. They were just waiting for the next victim. Was she going to go home and do the same? Wait for the next victim? She'd bought that gun for a reason. One that she hadn't been ready to face, but now she was here. In the town where her sister had died, being given a chance to step into the last days of her life. Beth had found no peace at the memorial. No answers. How could she go back to Vancouver without those? She stared at the bracelet on her wrist.

"Do you want me to fill out an application?"

One week later, Beth crossed the street to the motel, bone-weary after a long shift at the diner. The evening air was so thick and humid her tank top clung to her flat stomach, the long dip of her spine. She wiped at the loose hairs from her bun that curled damply against her neck and walked faster, trying to escape the hot pavement that radiated through the thin soles of her sandals all the way up to her thighs where her shorts ended. The take-out bag bounced against her bare legs with a soft rustle. She needed a cold shower and an even colder drink.

She neared the motel office window, where the manager watched from behind the desk, but Beth didn't make eye contact, something she'd avoided since the first morning when the tall, heavyset woman dressed in jeans and a man's white button-down had shown up at her door.

"Name's Rhonda. Sorry I wasn't here to check you in yesterday, Beth. I was helping at the memorial." She'd handed her two packets of coffee. "Just in case you like your caffeine."

"Thanks."

Beth had thought she'd made it clear she was ready for the conversation to end, but Rhonda had seemed in no hurry to leave. She'd leaned against the doorframe, her silver hair in a long braid that hung over her shoulder. Her skin was smooth, eyebrows dark, and Beth guessed that she'd gone gray young.

"I'm the administrator for the local crime watchers Facebook group. I also run one for the victims. I moderate the forum, stuff like that. You'd be surprised how much activity we get. From all over." Her eyes roved the room behind Beth. It was her motel—what did she think she'd see? Her gaze returned to Beth. "So, if you want anything posted, let me know."

Beth got it. Rhonda was one of those armchair detectives Thompson had warned her about. She'd probably watched every murder documentary on Netflix and downloaded *Dateline* and *Cold Case* podcasts the moment a new one was released.

She forced a smile. "I appreciate that. I have to make some calls, so if you'll excuse me . . ." She'd stepped back and closed the door, but not before catching the flash of irritation on Rhonda's face.

Beth passed the office without seeing Rhonda and having to endure any more odd interactions and continued through the outdoor hallway and around to the back. The slap of her shoes was loud. She didn't look at any of the dark windows. The motel was nearly empty. Most travelers cleared out on Sundays.

Her metal key stuck in the lock on her door and it took a few hard turns and a shove with her shoulder to get it open. The

Crows Pass was meant to look like some sort of woods lodge, with bright red doors and spindly pines planted outside each suite, but it mostly resembled a run-down summer camp for derelict loggers. Still, it had the best rates. The best location.

Amber had stayed at the same motel when she was looking for places to rent and had told Beth about the nosy manager who was always flagging her down to chat, but Beth hadn't expected the woman to be so obvious about her morbid curiosity.

As she entered her room, she glanced out the dirty window at the truck stop across the road. Semis and tractor trailers pulled out in wide swoops, their steel exhaust pipes like devil's horns. The tall neon MASON'S DINER sign blinked against the hazy evening sky. The mountains were a dark silhouette. Stars would come out soon. They were brighter outside of the city, the roads quieter. Everything shut down at ten except the pub and the one pizza joint.

It was even hotter inside the room and she dragged open the window, removing the piece of wood that had been braced inside the frame for security. Across the road, a few men were leaving the diner and walking toward the parking lot. Their laughing voices carried. When two women passed, the men turned and stared at their backsides. One of the men whistled.

They'd been watching Beth all night, asking for extra ketchup and drinks, spurring each other on while they leered. She'd wanted to dump a plate of hot food on their laps, but if she started responding like that, she would be dropping food every shift. She'd come to learn that Cold Creek had more than its share of pigs, and she wasn't talking about the kind that lived on farms. Just yesterday she'd caught an old man peeking down her shirt. How had Amber handled it? Had she laughed and brushed them off? Did she talk to her killer, serve him food?

Beth mimed pulling her gun out of her purse and aimed it at their heads. "Bang, bang."

* * *

One Xanax. It was all she'd allow herself for now. Later she'd take another to sleep. Sitting on the bed, she closed her eyes and let the little blue pill melt under her tongue. *Come on, baby. Work your magic.*

While she waited for the drug to kick in, she chewed the ham-and-cheese sandwich she'd gotten from the diner. The bread stuck in her throat. She took the sandwich apart and pulled out the meat, the lettuce. Her Coca-Cola was already room temperature and watery with melted ice, but she didn't want to walk outside to get more. The vending machine was near the office.

Her hair, wet from the shower, trickled beads of water down her back underneath the threadbare towel—so small she'd barely been able to wrap it around her body. Her legs were stretched out in front of her, the log rails pressing into her shoulder blades. Her pale face shimmered in the mirror above the desk. When she squinted, she saw Amber.

She slipped off the side of the bed to get her cell phone and scrolled through all the missed calls until she got to her parents'. Her thumb hovered over their number.

Her mom had left a voice mail an hour ago, but Beth couldn't call from the diner—couldn't risk the background noises. She took a deep breath, reminded herself to speak clearly so that her mom wouldn't hear the slipperiness in her voice, the softening.

Her mom answered her cell on the first ring. "Did you just get home?"

"They needed me to draft some documents." The lies came so easily now. Sometimes she felt like maybe it was true. Maybe in another universe she was really doing those things.

"Well, that's good." Her mom paused. Beth could feel her thinking about what to ask next, like she had to remind herself what a normal conversation was like. Last time, Beth made up stories about the lawyers at the firm, the fascinating cases, told her that the offices were floor-to-ceiling glass overlooking the city. A far cry from her current reality. She fingered the floral bedspread, looked around at the chipped desk, the worn carpet. The streaked windows.

"Tomorrow I'm sitting in on some client meetings."

"That's a big step. You deserve it." Her mom sounded so pleased Beth had to grit her teeth at the twist of shame in her belly. She just needed more time. Then she'd come up with a good explanation. They never had to know about this trip.

Beth reached over to the night table for the prescription bottle resting conveniently next to her graduation photo with Amber. She'd tucked the photo into her visor when she drove from Vancouver. Sisters on a road trip. She covered the speaker of the phone and shook out a pill.

"I should go. I have to order takeout."

Whispers in the background, something about her working late. Her mother was relaying their conversation. "Your father wants to talk to you." Silence as the phone was passed over.

"Is there anything you need? The car running okay?"

"It's fine." She tucked the pill under her tongue. The car. The stupid fucking car. *Well, Dad, it's actually stuffed with everything I own, but I'm guessing you don't want to hear that.*

"Good. Good." More whispering in the background.

"Get some rest, honey." Her mom this time, her voice distant and echoing. They'd put her on speakerphone. "Will we see you in church Sunday?"

"I have to work."

"We'll pray for you."

"Thanks." Beth hoped she sounded sincere. Or at the very least, sober. "I'll call you in a few days, okay?" She made a kissing sound and ended the call without saying goodbye.

CHAPTER 18

Beth's phone alarm pierced her skull, joined in on the party with her thudding headache, the dancing pulse behind her eyes. She rolled into a sitting position on the side of the bed. The coffee maker in the room made coffee that tasted like burned plastic, but she added double packs of sugar and creamers, and downed three cups in a row.

She stumbled to the bathroom, brushed her teeth, and scraped her hair into a high ponytail. Makeup—but not too much. Lip gloss, a bit of bronzer, and a sweep of mascara. She wiggled into jeans shorts and a white T-shirt. Breakfast was a protein bar, two Advils, and a final mouthful of cold coffee. Then she grabbed her purse and hurried across the road to the diner.

The cook was prepping for the morning rush and the air smelled of bacon, maple syrup, and sausage. Her stomach growled and she remembered her dismal dinner the night before. On her break she'd order something cheap. She tied her apron around her waist, tucked the order pad into the pocket. Mason came out of the storage room with a package of napkins.

"Morning, Beth."

She returned the greeting and set up her station. Her hands shook as she reached for the coffeepot. She hoped Mason didn't notice. He'd given her a chance. She didn't want to blow it.

They'd been open for about a half hour when two cops walked in, bulky with their bulletproof vests and uniforms. Beth recognized them instantly. Thompson, the clean-cut one who'd come to the funeral, and the *other*. Hailey's uncle. His head swiveled to scan the room, one hand on the radio at the top of his vest. Their gazes met and he gave her a nod.

Thompson stopped to talk to a First Nations family sitting at one of the tables, smiled at the baby, tickled his foot. Vaughn kept walking and slid into a booth. Thompson joined him a moment later. The diner was getting busy, loud male voices filling the air, the clomp of heavy work boots. She grabbed menus and made her way over to the cops.

"Morning, Officers."

"Beth. Nice to see you again." Thompson. He didn't seem surprised that she was at the diner. Word had spread fast. She'd been getting curious stares all week.

He gestured across the table. "This is Sergeant Vaughn."

The older man gave her an assessing look. "You're Amber Chevalier's sister?"

"Yes, sir."

"Most people around here call me Vaughn." He held out his hand, she gave it a quick shake, feeling awkward about the formality. "I was sorry to see you left the memorial early."

All those people, but he'd still noticed her. Why? "It was overwhelming."

"I'm sure it was. If you have questions, come into the station anytime."

"Thanks." But she didn't see the point. The sympathy in his face didn't matter. He didn't have any more answers than they had a year before.

"Is your family here?"

She hesitated. "No."

He glanced at Thompson, who was watching the conversation with a neutral half smile. She wondered if cops practiced them in the mirror. Or maybe he was just waiting for his coffee.

"You're not returning to Vancouver?"

How was he making these simple questions sound like an interrogation? She was beginning to feel guilty for just *being* here. No wonder Amber had called him controlling.

"My sister always talked about how beautiful this area was." She forced her face into a cheerful smile. "I'll get you some coffees."

For the rest of the time they were in the diner, she stayed on the move, which wasn't hard with the morning rush. When she took their orders, she jotted everything down, grabbed their menus, and kept their coffees full, but she never lingered, never gave Vaughn a chance to ask anything else.

Toward the end of the cops' meal, a group of guys came in and sat at the counter. They had the local look, T-shirts, jeans, baseball caps with hair winging out, or a tightly shaved head. Judging by their slow steps and haggard faces, she guessed they'd probably woken up hungover. Welcome to the club. She'd bring them a carafe of coffee and glasses of water as soon as she could.

She was walking past them, carrying a tray for another table, when one of them turned and glanced at her. Brown hair under a red ball cap, blue eyes, good-looking in a farm-boy kind of way. White shirt, tanned, muscled arms. She could almost smell the hay and fresh air on him.

Her foot caught on the edge of a stool and she lurched to the side. The tray dipped, plates sliding to the edge. She tried helplessly to right it, but he was quicker. He reached up and balanced it for her, his fingers beside hers beneath the flat of the tray. Their eyes met, and they paused, both still holding the tray. A thud, the sharp ting of cutlery, like someone behind them had set a cup down too hard. He looked across the diner and his mouth twisted in a grimace.

She followed his gaze. Vaughn was staring at him—his face

flat and cold. Farm boy let go of the tray and got to his feet. He was tall, their bodies so close she had to tilt her head to look up at him. He met her gaze, his eyes hooded and his jaw shadowed. She stepped back. He grabbed his keys off the counter, said something to one of his friends, gave Beth another look with those baby blues, and pushed open the door. She continued on to the table waiting for their food.

Seconds later there was the noise of tires squealing, and an older-style silver truck tore out of the parking lot, exhaust billowing from behind. She turned to see if Vaughn would go after him, but he was drinking his coffee and talking to Thompson like nothing had happened.

The rush cleared out, and Thompson and Vaughn had left an hour earlier, leaving a healthy tip on the table. Mason was putting away glasses while Beth refilled ketchup bottles beside him.

"There was a guy who came in with some friends this morning. When he saw the cops, he split. He wasn't even here for two minutes."

"Jonny," he said.

The same Jonny whom Amber had mentioned? Hailey's best friend. *I've been talking to Jonny a lot since she ran away. We're helping each other through it.*

"Is he in some kind of trouble?"

"Hailey was sneaking out to party with him at the lake when she disappeared." He let out a sigh, gave a shake of his head. "That girl burned bright, a real free spirit, you know? Like your sister. This morning, when I saw you over there, I remembered Hailey and Amber standing in the same place last summer." He pointed to the end of the counter. "I could see them clear as day, then I blinked and they were both gone." He looked back at Beth. "Sorry, kid. You have your own memories to deal with. You don't need to hear more from this old man."

Mason moved off to help a woman standing by the cash register. Beth stared at the end of the counter, the empty stools. For a moment she could see the girls too, their shimmering shapes frozen in the molecules of the air, but then, just like Mason said, they were gone.

By the end of the week, Beth was being driven mad by the stagnant heat in her motel room, the constant murmur of other guests' voices through the thin walls, toilets flushing, and the loud click of the ancient TV remote as she searched for a movie to watch. There had to be something happening on a Friday night. She put on a short sundress, lipstick, and walked across the street.

The pub was around the corner from the diner, a narrow building with dirty windows. Cigarette butts littered the sidewalk outside, and when she pushed open the door, her nose was assaulted with the smell of sour beer. Dark and seedy. Perfect.

She sat at the bar, ignored a group of men playing pool. One of them eyed her until it was his turn to take a shot. When the bartender came over—a gray-haired man who looked like he should be in a rocking chair somewhere, not slinging drinks— she ordered a glass of red wine and slid her ID across the bar. He barely looked at it before he slid it back.

The wine was dry and tasted like it might have been made in a bucket, but one glass turned into two as she scrolled her phone and watched a baseball game on the TV. She'd missed dinner and the drinks hit hard. She staggered down the hall to the women's washroom, kicked the door closed behind her, almost losing her balance in the process. She tried to read all the quotes and names carved into the back of the metal door, wondered about their lives.

Before going back to the bar, she ran water over her wrists, held her cool hands against her cheeks, and fluffed her hair. Another coating of lipstick. For whom? No one, but she liked the routine. The normalcy of these small moments, even if it did take her two times to get it right.

The man who'd stared at her while he was playing pool slid onto the seat next to her. *Where you from, sweetie? Need some company?* She ignored him until he muttered, *Bitch*, under his breath and left with the other guys. The bar was empty. So was her glass. She peered into the bottom.

"Now, where did *you* go?"

She slumped over the bar, rested her forehead against the warm bare skin of her arm.

"Hey, are you falling asleep?"

She looked up. Vaughn, dressed in a blue shirt, dark jeans. She squinted at him.

"I'm of age."

"I know." He sat on the stool beside her, motioned for the bartender, and ordered a beer. When he turned, his knee bumped hers. She shifted away. "You all right? This is a rough place."

"The motel was hot. I needed to get out." The bartender brought Vaughn a beer from the tap, and after Beth held up her empty glass, he poured her another wine.

"You're staying at the motel?" Vaughn gave her another assessing look. She focused on bringing the drink to her mouth without spilling it.

"For now." The words came out as *Forshnow*, and she fought back a giggle. It wasn't funny. Nothing had been funny in her life for a very long time.

"You got some troubles back home? I seem to remember your parents saying you were going to school to be a lawyer."

"I don't want to talk about it." She frowned at her glass, wiped her thumb over the condensation, realized she was spelling Amber's name, and wiped it clean again.

"Okay. We can just sit."

"You don't have to babysit me."

"This town isn't a good place for a young woman to be alone. I'm not just talking about the highway."

Beth frowned. "I'm fine."

"I know these local boys can seem harmless, but some of them . . . Take Jonny, for instance. I saw you two at the diner this morning. You don't know what you're getting into."

"I'm not getting *into* anything." Beth hadn't even spoken to Jonny, and Vaughn was making it seem as though she'd thrown herself in his lap.

"I suggest you keep it that way."

She didn't like how he made it sound like an order. Joke was on him. Hadn't he heard that if you tell a girl to stay away from a boy, it just made her want him more?

"How long do you intend to stay in Cold Creek?" There was something in his voice, some sort of tone that slipped away from her.

"Until I'm ready to move on. Is that breaking a law? Was I supposed to fill out a form?" She drained half of her wine in one gulp.

His eyebrows lowered, shadowing his eyes. "I'm sure you city girls are used to a different sort of life, but in the North, we look after each other. And I like to know what's what."

"You small-town cops don't have a lot else going on, I guess."

"You've got a smart mouth." Vaughn was looking at her like he was waiting for her to apologize, but she figured she didn't owe him anything. She hadn't invited him to sit down. His expression shifted, turned calculating almost, and she felt a jolt. What had he read in her?

"Do your parents know you're in Cold Creek?"

"What does that have to do with anything?" Dodge, deflect. She was getting good at that, and felt proud for a moment, until his gazed pinned her back down.

"I can tell when someone needs help."

"I'm fine, but I should get back to the motel." She looked away from him and cleared her throat. What was it with cops? Instead of worrying about her mental health, he should be finding the killer. Seemed to her that would be a pretty good antidepressant.

He skimmed his hand across the back of her neck, rested it on her upper shoulder, as though holding her in place. She shivered, and he murmured, "Let me buy you another drink."

CHAPTER 19

Beth had been sitting on the bed for an hour, cell in one hand, gun in the other, staring at the locked door. Her face was hot from crying, her eyes bloodshot. Water had made her stomach heave. Coffee hadn't helped either. She'd gotten so dizzy in the shower she had to sit with her head bowed while she prayed that she wouldn't pass out across the stained tiles.

Her father picked up after two rings. "Beth? What's wrong?" He was whispering, but her mother would never hear him. She slept until noon these days.

"Sorry to wake you."

"No, no," he said. "Call whenever you need."

"I'm having a tough morning."

Silence. Then, "Have you eaten? If you skip meals, your blood sugar will drop."

"That's not the problem."

"You have to take care of yourself, Beth."

She hugged her bent legs to her chest, squeezed her eyes shut, and focused on the sound of her dad's breathing until the pains eased in her stomach, but the sour taste of wine lingered. She ran her tongue around the inside of her mouth. Bitter regret with an undertone of dismal failure. She almost smiled.

"Are you and Mom okay?"

"God is taking care of us."

She didn't know how to reply. How could she explain that she envied them for being able to turn everything over, but she also hated them for it? It shouldn't be that easy.

"If you came to church—"

"I'm fine, Dad. It was just a bad moment." She brightened her voice. "The internship is great, though. I'm making a lot of new friends." She thought of Vaughn. The pub. He'd walked her home. He'd unlocked her door. What happened after? Had they talked? Had she cried? Worse? The first time she'd ever gotten blackout drunk and she'd done so in front of a cop.

She'd woken up fully clothed, but her suitcase was a mess. Her purse dumped out on the small table. She had vague memories of hearing a car alarm at some point. Had she tried to leave the room? She imagined herself stumbling around, trying to get changed, and then giving up.

"That's good, tiger—one foot in front of the other." A hitch in his voice, a clearing of his throat. "Don't forget to get the oil changed in your car soon."

"I will. Thanks, Dad. I have to go now." She rested her forehead on her knees. After a few moments she lurched to her feet. She had to get to work.

Vaughn came in for breakfast with Thompson and they sat in her section. She looked around for Mason, hoping to claim a sudden stomach flu, which wouldn't be hard to fake. He was coming out from the kitchen. She stepped toward him, but at the same moment he saw Vaughn, made an annoyed expression, and abruptly turned back around. Resigned, she grabbed the coffeepot and menus.

"Good morning, Officers."

Vaughn looked up with a pleasant smile. Would he say something? Would he admit that they'd seen each other the night before?

"Morning, Beth. Coffee would be great."

"Sure thing." She flipped over their mugs and poured them

each one, flexing the muscles in her arm so that her hand didn't shake. When she set down their menus, she glanced at Thompson. He was definitely staring at her. Jesus. What had Vaughn told him?

Vaughn talked as they drank their coffees, and Thompson listened with a serious face. They lapsed into silence when she brought over their food, thanking her with brief smiles. It was clear they wanted privacy. She was relieved—and also wondering why Vaughn was blowing the entire night off. Maybe it wasn't that big a deal. Maybe he escorted a lot of drunk girls home.

She waited to clear away the plates until Thompson went to the washroom. Vaughn was texting on his phone. She thought he was going to keep ignoring her, but then he looked up.

"How are you feeling?"

"Bit rough. Thanks for getting me back to my room."

"Don't think anything of it. Just part of my job."

"I hope I wasn't too much of a mess."

"Not at all. It's an emotional time." He got up from the table. Thompson came out of the washroom. Vaughn glanced at him. "Can you get this? I don't have any cash on me." He didn't wait for Thompson's answer before he said, "See you back at the station," and walked out.

Thompson passed her a twenty. "That should cover it." He held her gaze for a moment, but she couldn't read his expression. "Heard you met some of the locals last night."

So she was right. Vaughn had told him, and the way Thompson was bringing it up felt loaded. He was getting at something. "Not really. I only talked to the sergeant."

"You got back to the motel okay?"

Beth frowned. It was obvious she was fine—she was standing in front of him. "Sergeant Vaughn walked me." No way was she going to admit that she barely remembered it.

"That's good. If you ever need anyone else to talk to . . ." He held out his business card. "It's got all my info. Cell number is on the back." He slid his wallet into his pocket.

She took the card. "Thanks." When Amber died, Beth was furious that no cops had been patrolling that night. She'd told herself that the area was too big, they couldn't cover every mile, every minute. Now she had two cops who didn't seem to think she could cross a road by herself.

Rhonda frowned at her, looking disappointed. She stood on the other side of the registration desk. Today she was wearing a blue button-down printed with small palm trees.

"Checking out already? Was there a problem with the room?"

This was when Beth was supposed to explain why she was leaving and where she was going, but Beth felt the gaze of each victim on the posters lining the wall behind her in the break-fast room. She'd gone in yesterday for juice and a muffin, when Rhonda wasn't working, and she'd been so shocked by the display she'd walked out empty-handed. Every woman who had ever gone missing or been killed in that area had her photograph neatly pinned on the bulletin board, with little cut-out hearts, poems, snippets of quotes, and angel wings.

"No, no. The room was fine." She slid her card over to Rhonda, pretended to be focused on her cell phone while Rhonda ran it through the machine.

"Huh," Rhonda said, and Beth looked up. Rhonda pressed some more buttons, then glanced at Beth. "Seems to be a problem. Insufficient funds."

"Can you try half?"

Rhonda ran it through again. "Looks like that's okay."

"I've got cash." Beth pulled her tips from the week out of her purse, dumped them onto the counter. "That's another one hundred. I'll get the rest from the bank right now."

"Listen." Rhonda's voice turned confiding. "I get it. If money's tight, we can work something out."

"Oh, no. It's not like that. My last credit card payment just hasn't gone through yet." She waved her hand through the air. Like, you know, she'd been so busy. The thought of owing Rhonda anything made her uncomfortable. "I'll be right back." Beth pushed out the door, walked briskly to the ATM at the truck stop. She winced when she saw her bank balance. She was barely making her student loan payment.

She paid her motel bill, forcing herself to tell Rhonda that she appreciated her sensitivity and discretion during this difficult time, then she drove straight to the nearest secondhand shop. There she found a tent, a camping chair, pots and pans, a propane stove, water bottles, a cooler, and some storage containers. She bought the rest of her supplies at the general goods store, picking out whatever was cheapest. A thin sleeping bag, backpack, hiking boots, a compass that she didn't know how to use, and bear spray that she hoped she would never have to use.

She'd wanted to set up before dark, but by the time she picked up a few groceries and a six-pack of cheap beer the sun had already disappeared behind the trees. When she passed the billboard at the end of the highway, she couldn't look at it, couldn't stop wondering how many times Amber must have driven past the same warning. Did she think she was safe because she was in a car?

Beth's shoulders were tight, and her jaw clenched when she reached the campground. Here Amber had spent her last night. Here she had laughed, swum, and drunk with friends. Here she had kissed Hailey for the first time. Beth had been in her Vancouver apartment, unpacking her take-out sushi with the cell pressed to her ear, smiling as she listened to her sister describe the outdoorsy, quiet girl she'd fallen for. *She picked me a bouquet of wildflowers.*

Beth hadn't realized how dark it would be at the campsite, how the old-growth trees and foliage blocked out the starry sky, any hint of a moon. She bumped down the narrow gravel road.

Campers sitting around propane fires turned to watch her, men with baseball hats and beers in their hands, families. She found an empty spot at the end of the campground and parked.

With the engine still running and the doors locked, she reached into her purse and found her prescription bottle, twisted open the lid, and slipped a pill under her tongue. She waited, took long, slow breaths, thought of Amber. *The lake is so clear and fresh. When I swim there, it's like everything gets stripped away.*

When Beth's heart stopped racing, she grabbed her flashlight and got out. The site was small, probably only twelve-by-twelve feet, with a rustic brown picnic table. Was this the one her sister had sat on with Hailey? She would look at the photo again and try to match the view.

No one was camped on either side of the site. The flashlight picked up a thin trail leading to the lake. She pushed through the thorny shrubs a few feet until it broke out onto the lakeshore, water coming up over her flip-flops. There was no beach, no sand. The trees ended directly at the water. Across the lake, cabin lights stood out like glittering stars. Someone was softly playing a guitar. Warm water lapped against her shins. Crickets. Voices carried from the other campsites, laughter, children. She closed her eyes and listened, reminding herself of what it felt like to be a family. To be whole. She swayed her body, drifting with the waves, letting the night breeze move her hair. Her thoughts had made her melancholy, but she didn't mind. She preferred it to the hard edge of grief. She was tired, though, she now realized.

Mosquitoes attacked her arms and legs as she made her way back to her car. She didn't want to walk around searching for the bathrooms, so she went behind a bush, then brushed her teeth with water from her bottle and spit into the dirt. She rolled out the sleeping bag, spread it over the backseat, and fluffed a pillow that she'd "borrowed" from the motel. She stayed in her shorts and tank top and kept the windows down a few inches, enough to let in some air and a few wayward mosquitoes that she squished between her palms, then removed with wet wipes.

The gun was hidden under the back of the driver's seat, loaded, with the safety on. She whispered good night to Amber's photo and tucked it under the visor, then stared out the side window into the dark and munched on a protein bar, washed down with a lukewarm beer, until she stopped listening to every noise and her eyes felt heavy. Until her mind couldn't hold on to any more worries and there was no danger of nightmares. Only velvety, soothing blackness.

CHAPTER 20

Beth climbed out of the car and slid her feet into a pair of flip-flops she'd left by the door. She rubbed at her arms, surprised by the morning chill, and glanced at the lake. Mist floated across the surface in a sheer curtain, draping over the dock and the shore, making it seem as though the trees were rising from the air. As if the campsite wasn't already creepy enough.

After digging a hoodie out of her bag and wiggling into a pair of sweatpants, Beth walked to the washrooms—gun tucked into the hoodie's front pouch, making it sag. She took note of the other campers. She was the only one moving around so far. Closest to her, three trucks were parked in the same site. One with a camper, then two tents. She heard snoring. Judging by all the beer cans on the table and the dirt bikes in the back of the trucks, it was a group of guys.

She nudged open the bathroom door with her foot, then stood back in case an animal came rushing out. Silence. She crept in, hand on the butt of the gun, and checked under each stall. She didn't like the washroom, the plastic skylight, the dingy light bulb that blinked off and on. When she pulled back the thin shower curtain, a spider scurried across the black rubber mat.

She would use the toilets, but she'd shower later when everyone in the campground was awake to hear her scream for help. For a moment she thought she heard something rustling outside of the building. She stopped, her head cocked, but she didn't hear the noise again.

Beth walked back to her site, staring at shadows in the

bushes. A stump looked like a bear and a fallen tree had her panicking that it was the outstretched body of a cougar. She stiffened, every muscle in her body contracting to a hard rope. Then a small bird landed on the fallen tree.

She hurried the rest of the way. Coffee. Food. Sanity. She lifted the lid on her stove and studied the contraption. For the next fifteen frustrating minutes she attached and reattached the valve to the propane bottle, but the burner kept making a clicking sound and wouldn't light. She'd filled the air with so much propane she was praying she didn't blow the campsite up. She slammed the lid back down, then sat on top of the picnic table and ate handfuls of dry cereal.

She'd never put up a tent before. The poles kept sliding apart when she tried to thread them through the small loops, and she had to start over three times. She didn't have a hammer, so she used a rock to slam the pins into the ground. She loaded her duffel bag into the tent.

When she lifted her cooler out of her trunk, it sloshed with melted ice. She pulled out a soggy egg carton, and it tore in her hands, sending a few eggs to smash on the ground. She used the hard edge of a cup to scrape up the mess and dump it into her firepit. Now she had gross eggs oozing over top of half-burnt logs. She kicked dirt over everything.

She stared out at the lake, watching the mist drift away, and scratched at the welts on her arms. Of course sleeping next to a lake and near a slow-moving, algae-covered creek would bring mosquitoes. Swarms and clouds of them, apparently. She bent over and slapped at one that was happily sucking blood from the top of her foot. She would have to buy repellant in town.

Still leaning down, she frowned at some marks in the dirt. Paw prints? She studied them closer. Definitely paw prints. She stood up. They led to the bushes by the creek.

She spun around—and screamed. A black, furry shape was

moving around the firepit. It lifted its head and stared at her. One blue eye. One brown.

She exhaled. A dog. She'd almost had a heart attack. Where was his owner? She looked down the center road. The campground was quiet. Maybe someone had let him out so he could pee. He looked like one of those dogs who herd sheep. He could be from a nearby farm.

The dog was just standing there and watching her. Beth didn't know anything about dogs—her mom had never wanted one—and she wasn't sure if he was waiting for food or getting ready to attack. His tail wasn't wagging, but he wasn't growling either.

She whistled and held out her hand. Dogs were supposed to sniff you, right? His nostrils twitched but he didn't come closer. She frowned. He sat on his haunches. Great. Did he think she was going to make him breakfast? How was she going to get rid of him?

"Shoo!" She clapped a couple of times.

He rose and stalked deliberately toward her.

"Stay!" She held out her palm, but he'd already stopped and was nosing around in the firepit, getting ash all over his face. He licked at the eggs. "You're hungry?" She moved around the side of the site, still holding her hand out as if that would actually keep him in place.

She was at her picnic table. She glanced around. Where was the bear spray? Something to make noise. The gun seemed excessive. Unless he lunged at her. Then all bets were off.

The dog moved away from the firepit and was now sniffing around in her cooler, which she had left open. Crunching sounds. He swallowed something. Licked his lips. Her eggs.

"Hey! Scram."

He glanced at her and put his head back down. She took a step toward him and clapped louder. He didn't flinch. Instead, he lifted his paw and pushed down on the side of the cooler until it toppled forward. The water ran out. He pawed at her remaining food, sliced open a package of bacon with his toenails, and delicately tugged a few pieces out.

She watched him with her mouth half open. The *nerve* of this dog. He wasn't gulping at the food and he wasn't skinny, at least not that she could tell under all that fur, but he didn't look well brushed. He was shedding in clumps and his white parts were dirty, his underbelly muddy.

She took a few steps toward the dog with her hand outstretched. This time she would try a different approach. "Hi, baby. Can I pet you?" Her voice was sweet and crooning.

The dog eyed her warily and glanced toward the edge of the forest, his ears pricked in one direction, then the other. He had so much fur around his neck she couldn't see if he was wearing a collar. He circled around the back of the cooler, staying a few feet away from her.

She relaxed. He was leaving.

Nope. He paused in front of the picnic table with his nose up in the air, sniffing in a back-and-forth pattern. Her bag of cereal. It was still out in the open.

"No!" She made a shooing gesture with her hand. "Go away!"

The dog glanced at her, slowly lifted a paw, then placed it on the bench seat.

"Don't even think about it!" She took a few steps toward him.

He leapt onto the table, snatched the bag in his mouth, and jumped off the side. He landed so quietly he barely made a noise, then bolted for the woods.

She stared at the spot where he had disappeared. It was as if the trees had swallowed him. She couldn't even hear a branch snapping. Maybe she'd ask around the campground and make sure no one was missing a dog. Then she'd firmly suggest they keep better control of him.

The guys at the other site had emerged from their camper and were drinking coffee out of stainless-steel flasks, laughing in low voices. They looked young. One was cooking bacon and eggs on a grill. The smell made her mouth water. Why wasn't the dog bothering *them*?

They gave her curious smiles when she walked over. She spoke to the black-haired one who looked the friendliest. He also seemed familiar. She must have seen him around town.

"Don't suppose you have an extra coffee? My stove's broken."

"Sure," he said, filling a mug and handing it to her.

"Thanks." She smiled. "Do you have a black dog?"

"Nope." He shrugged and gave her a curious look. "Don't you work at the diner?" Now she realized how she recognized him. She'd seen him with Jonny. "I thought you were living at the motel." News really did get around fast. She wondered what else he knew about her.

"Yeah, it was getting expensive."

"I'm Andy." He held out his hand and she gave it a shake, then glanced at her watch.

"I better get going. Okay if I return the mug later?"

He nodded, and she felt him watching as she walked away. Would he tell Jonny she was at the campground? She tossed her head. Now, why would that matter? Stupid thought.

Beth walked around to the few other campsites—a young couple, a family—but none of them owned the dog.

When she got to the diner, Mason was in the storage room, unpacking the morning delivery. He was always the first to arrive and the last to leave. She'd seen him a few times visiting the truck drivers over at the parking lot before the diner had even opened.

"Hey, Mason, could I take some scraps after work? I moved

out to the lake campground and I saw a dog roaming around. He might be a stray."

He stood up straight. "What the hell are you doing out there?" She held up her hand to stop the rest of the lecture that she knew was coming.

"I'm sleeping in my car. Don't worry."

He gave her a look that made it clear he didn't think the car was safe either. "Keep it locked, and you can have the scraps, but don't leave them out or you'll get scavengers."

"Okay, thanks."

When she was done with her shift, she eased into her car, which was so hot she had to use napkins to touch the steering wheel and scooch forward on the seat so that her bare legs weren't resting against the vinyl. She found the local grocery store a few streets down and savored the air-conditioning while hovering near the cooler, debating her ice choices. Chipped? Blocked?

"You going to climb in there?"

She spun, startled when she saw Jonny. His arms were crossed, one hand on each bicep, legs braced, but it wasn't a defensive position. He looked relaxed, maybe even curious.

"Good idea. It's too hot." She gestured at the ice. "I don't know what's best."

"A block will last you longer."

"Thanks." She hefted one out of the fridge and set it in the cart.

"You're Amber's sister."

"You're Hailey's best friend."

He gave her an assessing look. She wondered if he'd already known that she was Amber's sister when he'd come into the diner. Did he feel the strange connection too? Did grief and pain look the same from his side?

"My friends saw you at the campground. You need some help?"

"I can't figure out my stove." She smiled. "Cooking never was my thing, but it might be nice to have a coffee without setting myself on fire."

"Don't want that. I'll come by later." He smiled back. She was struck by his perfect white teeth. Farm boy must have drunk a lot of milk growing up. He looked over her shoulder, his smile slowly melting away, the corners first, then the rest, until his mouth was a flat line. She followed the path of his gaze. Two women standing in the meat section were watching them. They turned away. Jonny was looking at her again. "Why would you camp out there alone?"

She started to get angry—why did everyone think they had a right to lecture her? Then she realized that there'd been no sarcasm in his voice, only interest. The question was genuine.

"Amber liked the lake."

"You aren't scared?"

"I guess I feel like the worst thing has already happened to me."

He rocked onto his heels, and she waited for another warning, or an uncomfortable look to show up in his eyes. Guys didn't like dealing with female emotions at the best of times.

"You like camping?"

"Last night was my first time. Backseat was kind of uncomfortable."

Now he would scoff or make some sort of decisive sound. What did a city girl like her know about the woods? Maybe he'd smirk about the backseat comment. His expression didn't change. Who was this guy? She was almost hand-feeding him opportunities to be a jerk.

"First time for everything."

"Guess so."

The moment was shifting, making room for too much

thought. The silence wide. He would walk away soon. He'd run out of things to ask her in the middle of the aisle.

She didn't like endings. Not when it was by someone else.

"I better go before this ice melts. Fix my stove, and I'll make you a drink, okay?"

He nodded again, and she pushed her cart away, focused on her shopping, picking up a couple of items. She didn't look back. If she did, he might see in her face that she was a little too pleased about the turn of events.

Her last stop was the liquor store, where she bought a bottle of cheap vodka, Coke, and some lemons. They'd have a drink or two. She'd get a better sense of him, and maybe he'd tell her more about Hailey. Maybe she'd find out why Vaughn hated him so much.

CHAPTER 21

The sun was disappearing. She'd gone for a swim, and let her hair dry in waves while she sat on the dock. Each time she heard a vehicle she glanced toward the campground road, looking for a cloud of dust, a flash of silver paint, but still no sign of Jonny. She pulled on her shorts and T-shirt and headed back to her site, then stopped. A white police truck was parked behind her car.

When she came around the side, she recognized Vaughn tapping out something on his phone. He noticed her at his window and got out with his hand resting on his gun belt.

"I see you're all set up."

She followed his gaze around her camp, irritated by his attention. Had he checked on the other sites, or just hers? The boys were working on their bikes, voices quiet. One snuck a peek at them but lowered his head right away. There wasn't a beer in sight. The music was soft.

"Something wrong?"

"Just heard you were out here. Wanted to make sure you were okay."

She had been "out here" for a grand total of twenty-four hours, half of them spent at the diner. No one in that campsite knew her and she doubted any of the boys would have spoken to Vaughn.

"I'm fine."

"Each summer we get people camping out of the park boundary." He pointed into the dense woods behind the lake. "It's private land, owned by a logging company, but some people think they're above the law. You see anything that doesn't look right, let me know."

"Okay."

He walked over to the stove, opened it up. "Make sure you have a bucket of water handy. No campfires. Not even a spark, and keep anything plastic away from the stove." Did he seriously give this same speech to everyone? He was acting like she'd never seen fire before.

"Is that everything? I was going to have an early night."

His eyebrows slowly rose up his forehead, the serious expression turning more annoyed, almost surprised. He wasn't used to being dismissed, and she regretted it for a moment. If she pissed him off, he might hold back any new information about the case.

"I really appreciate you checking on me." She forced a smile.

His brow smoothed and he gave her a nod. "You need anything, you call the—" He abruptly turned and looked toward the road as an engine rumbled into the campground.

A silver truck came around the bend. Jonny. She let her breath out, then sucked it back in when she remembered how he'd reacted the last time he saw Vaughn. Would he think she had set him up? He stopped near his friends, said something through the window. They laughed. Then he put the truck in gear and drove over to her site, where he pulled in tight beside Vaughn.

The brim of Jonny's baseball cap shadowed his face as he got out. He lifted his head and met her eyes. She couldn't tell if he was angry. He stayed silent as he leaned against the front of the truck, legs crossed at the ankles, arms flexed as he braced against the grille.

"What are you doing out here?" Vaughn didn't even try to sound polite.

"Living my best life." He smirked.

Vaughn walked toward him, then past him, looking in the back of the truck first, then into the cab. He wrenched open the driver's-side door before Jonny could say anything and felt under the seat. Nothing legal about that search.

"You been drinking?"

"Nope."

Vaughn shut the door and stood close to Jonny, nose to nose. "One fuckup. That's all I need." Vaughn said the words low, but Beth heard them and cleared her throat. Vaughn waited a second, still staring into Jonny's eyes, then turned away and walked to his truck.

He looked over his shoulder at Beth. "Keep your valuables locked up. All sorts of thieves around here. They'll rob you blind."

Vaughn backed up and came within inches of hitting Jonny with the bumper. Jonny didn't even flinch or look in his direction. His gaze was focused on Beth.

She dropped her shoulders when she heard Vaughn's truck hit the highway, the engine changing pitch. The guys at the other campsite began talking. Music filled the air. Jonny glanced at them. She wondered if he was upset about Vaughn's insinuation. Did he think she believed it?

"Wow. Vaughn's a barrel of laughs, huh?"

"More like a barrel of bullshit."

Jonny walked over to the picnic table, lifted the lid up on the stove, fiddled with a wire on the ignition, and screwed the propane tank on tight. He took a lighter from his pocket and silently showed her how to light the stove. Soft blue and gold flames flickered.

"You want me to put something on the grill?"

"Sure. You hungry? I have some hamburgers." She flipped open the cooler lid. He glanced inside, noticed the clear bag of scraps on top, and gave her a curious look. She laughed.

"Those are for a dog I saw roaming around this morning."

"Dog?"

"Yeah, a shaggy black thing who stole my breakfast."

He lifted his head and looked at her, surprised. "One blue eye?"

"That's him."

"Sure. I know the dog. He's a stray. He hangs around the campground sometimes."

"Why hasn't anyone caught him?"

He smiled. "He's fast and tricky. Trust me, he's not suffering, though. People leave food out for him and he knows how to survive on his own." He pointed to the cabins, then met her eyes. "He's not a pet. He likes to be free—and he'll bite if you try to catch him."

"How do you know?"

"Because I tried and almost lost my hand." He rubbed at his palm, then turned back to the stove. "You have any cheese to go with the hamburgers?"

They sat opposite one another at the picnic table. The lantern casting a glow. She liked that she could see his eyes—blue with dark lashes. They'd be too pretty if the rest of him weren't so masculine. The strong planes of his face, the square jaw. He hadn't shaved, his hair messy when he took off his cap and ran his hands through it. She poured him a vodka and Coke—and thought he might say no, considering Vaughn's warning, but he drank it easily. She matched him drink for drink. They didn't talk about much at first. Just safe topics. Where his family lived, what he did on the farm, how he raced dirt bikes. If Jonny noticed she wasn't saying much about herself, he didn't comment. Only thing he said was, "You have a university sticker on your bumper."

"Yeah. I was going to be a lawyer." Stupid vodka. That came

out too easily. Did he hear her say it in past tense? She steered the conversation back toward him. "Vaughn hates you."

"The Iceman."

"Is that what you call him?"

"Everyone does. Because of the way he looks." He made a circle around his face. "And his attitude. He's hassled me ever since Hailey disappeared. Before that too."

"You were a suspect."

He stared at her curiously. Not insulted. "You seem to know a lot."

"Mason told me." She didn't want to tell him that Amber had also spoken about him. He might feel self-conscious. The vodka was making her voice thick, huskier, her arms and legs warm, the muscles loose. They'd started leaning across the table toward each other. His knee brushed against her, and he didn't move it away. Male voices, laughing at the other site.

Someone yelled, "Where's Jonny?"

He looked over his shoulder. "I have to load up one of their bikes. I'll be back in a minute." He untangled his long legs, walked around his truck, and disappeared into blackness.

She fiddled with her cup, stared around. Everything looked different in the dark, but she wasn't scared with Jonny nearby. It was obvious Vaughn was wrong about him. He wasn't a killer. He couldn't be. She knew it the moment she saw the pain that came over his face when he said Hailey's name.

The roar of a dirt bike startled her. She stood, watching the other site, which was now lit with headlights. Jonny was astride a white bike, his legs on the ground. He revved it a few times, shouting back and forth with Andy, the dark-haired guy who'd given her coffee this morning. Jonny looked relaxed and easy. Like he spent a lot of time on a bike. He backed it up, walking it out with his legs, then rode it toward his truck. He stopped the bike, dropped a ramp from the back, and drove it up.

Beth stared at his hands as he anchored the bike with straps in quick, assured movements. The men she knew could text and negotiate while hailing cabs under an umbrella in the Vancouver rain. She used to think that was confidence, but Jonny had it in spades.

"Did you just steal that?"

His white teeth flashed in the dark. "I'm the bike mechanic around here. Hailey and I used to—" He broke off, the smile fading, and turned around to slam the tailgate shut. "I'm going to crash with my buddies tonight."

Beth looked at the other site. The guys were standing around their propane fire ring. She felt Jonny watching her as he brushed his hands on his jeans.

"Thirsty?" she asked him, holding up the bottle.

They sat closer this time. Beth didn't know who moved first, but somehow they ended up side by side. Jonny's arm felt warm pressed against hers, their legs touching. They'd been playing cards. He was fast, with a good poker face. She hadn't won yet. She laughed and set her last cards down. Rested her head on her arms.

"Ugh. I have to go to bed."

"I'll wait until you're locked in safe." He'd already walked her to the outhouse. Stood outside and whistled a song, then balanced her when she came out and tripped over a root. Steadied her drink. Spun the cap back on the Coke bottle so it didn't go flat. She noticed all those things. Noticed that he had a little dent at the top of his lips, that he smelled like wood and earth, but somehow in his own unique combination that wasn't like anything else. He had a lazy way of looking at her, his eyelids half-mast, but the blue would light up when he was telling a joke. When he laughed, he'd clutch at his chest, his head back, showing his tanned throat. He had a good voice. She closed her eyes a couple of times, just to hear the purr of it coming up his throat. Liquid-smooth. Her own personal bedtime story.

"You can stay in my tent." She lifted her head. "Wait. You don't have any blankets."

He gestured over his shoulder. "I've got a sleeping bag."

She laughed and gently poked him in the arm. "You came prepared." He met her eyes with a questioning look, like he was trying to figure out if she was flirting. Was she? Maybe. "Please. I'd feel safer—knowing you were close by."

"You sure? The Iceman says I'm a suspect, remember?"

"I can tell you're a good person." He looked startled and got to his feet so fast she wondered if he was leaving, but he just walked toward his truck. He grabbed a sleeping bag and tossed it into the tent. Still crouched with his hand on the zipper, he looked over at her.

"I'm not that good."

Beth curled into the darkness of her car. She'd left the windows down a few inches for fresh air and could hear him tossing and turning in the tent, the soft whisper of nylon. She imagined he was uncomfortable on the ground. Maybe he'd give up and sleep at his friends' site, but after a while the rustling stopped. He'd fallen asleep. She stared at the car ceiling, thinking.

She opened her door. It creaked loudly in the dark. The moon was full, and she didn't need her flashlight. The other site was quiet. The music had died hours ago. She soft-stepped her way over to the tent, felt for the zipper, and then realized Jonny had left it open. Was it in case she needed him? Or maybe he'd hoped for this too.

The moon was shining through the mesh roof, turning his shape to shadowy blue, highlighting the planes of his face. He was bare-chested, only his bottom half in the sleeping bag. Jeans tossed to the side. One of his arms was up over his head. He was breathing deeply but not snoring. She crept up beside his body. If he woke suddenly, would he lash out? For a strange moment she wanted to see what he looked like angry. She wanted to see all his expressions.

She hovered her finger over the indent above his top lip, then slowly, slowly brought it down, let it settle in the warm groove.

His eyes flared open. His hand gripped her wrist, and she gasped. He loosened it as soon as he recognized her, but he didn't speak a word.

She unzipped the side of the sleeping bag, slid in beside him, feeling the heat of his legs against hers. Her hair fell over his chest. She breathed in the masculine scent of his shoulders, his neck, jawline, scraped her cheek against the stubble. He shivered. She pressed her lips to his. He didn't move. Not for one count, two, three. Then his hand slid up her arm and into her hair.

The tent was already warm when she woke, birds loud in the trees nearby. She was hungover, with gritty eyes, a dry mouth, and a headache that made her squeeze her eyes shut and pray that the birds would shut up. Jonny's arm was under her cheek, his chest against her back.

"Man, I need water." His voice startled her, and she flinched. He reached over her for his boxers and pulled them on, then his jeans. She sat up, holding the sleeping bag around her chest, and noticed a cigarette pack had fallen out of his pocket. She picked it up, looking at him.

"You smoke?"

He paused from where he was unzipping the tent, and glanced

over his shoulder at her, the good humor now gone from his face. "No. I quit. It was a thing between me and Hailey. She never wanted me to smoke, but I always carried a pack, and she'd always wreck it."

The way he was looking at her, she suddenly felt like she was holding something deeply personal, a relic, and, judging by the hint of a flush on his face, he regretted telling her.

She handed him the cigarettes and reached for her duffel bag. "I'll meet you outside."

After she was dressed, she crawled through the tent opening. He was leaning against the picnic table, watching the lake, and turned with a smile. She wanted to smile back, but she was a different Beth from last night. Now, in the bright morning sun, and sober, it was all too hard.

"You're not working today, right?" He squinted at her. "We could hang out."

She looked at him, startled. She must have told him last night that it was her day off. Sure, they could hang out. Go for a swim. He'd show her around. They could get to know each other sober. What music they liked, what made them laugh. Maybe he'd tell her about some of the people in town. He'd trust her and share memories. But then what? It couldn't go anywhere.

"I'm not staying in Cold Creek for long."

He gave her a questioning look. "Okay . . . ?"

He didn't understand, and she wasn't sure if it was because he wasn't used to a girl giving him the brush-off, or if he just didn't get it. All she knew was that she felt panicked to get him away from her. If he stayed a minute longer, she would invite him back into the tent.

"Last night. It was just a thing . . . but I didn't mean . . ."

"Right." He nodded, his eyes shifting to somewhere over her shoulder.

"I like you." She hesitated, trying to find the words. "I'm not good at people."

"That's a new one." He shifted his face into a smile, farm-boy white teeth flashing, and she still couldn't tell if he was genuinely unfazed or faking. "No worries. I have to fix the dirt bike today anyway." He spun around and strode toward his truck. She took a step. She wanted to call out, *Stop. Let's do something*, but he was opening the door and then drove off with a small wave.

She busied herself around the campsite, sweeping away the fir needles that had fallen on everything, organizing supplies, tidying her clothes in the tent. The air still smelled like Jonny, some indescribable scent. Skin warmed in the sun, cedar trees, a hint of fresh-cut grass. She caught herself staring at where they'd slept, and abruptly crawled out of the tent.

The dock looked inviting, the wood glowing nearly white in the morning sun. She made a coffee, grabbed a magazine she'd bought at the store, and walked to the dock, but she only skimmed a few pages. Mostly she stared at the cabins on the other side and sipped her coffee, thinking about Vaughn showing up at the campground. The visit from the dog. Anything other than Jonny. Once, she thought she heard something in the bushes and wondered if the dog had come back. When she spun around, she caught a glimpse of something small scampering up a tree trunk. Chipmunk.

The woods were so dark and dense. It was hard to see anything farther than a few feet. The dog could be watching her right now and she wouldn't know. It was a creeper's paradise. Beth looked around, thinking. Amber and Hailey were together at the lake a couple of weeks before Hailey disappeared. Shannon Emerson had probably been at the lake all the time. What if the common denominator wasn't the highway, but the *campground*? All the local teenage girls hung out here. Someone could be watching them swimming, un-dressing in their tents.

Her sister's car had been found down a logging road. How did the killer know she was parked *there*, unless he had followed her from the campground? He even could have been at the memorial. Shannon had disappeared from a field that was only a few miles from the campground.

Everyone was so sure the killer was a trucker, but there could be someone new. Someone who lived off the grid. Vaughn said lots of people camped out of bounds, and the murders always happened in the summer. It could be a drifter, a mountain man who hated people and society. She envisioned an unkempt, bearded survivalist type with wild hair and evil eyes.

How did Jonny know for sure that the dog was a stray? He might belong to this man, who would have to drive into town for supplies. He probably had a truck or camper that could travel the logging roads. Her breath locked in her throat at the sudden image of a slow-moving vehicle, her sister standing alone by her car. Beth made herself think of something else, anything else. The sandy beach in Hawaii. The aqua-blue water.

Water. *River* water.

The night before, Jonny had told her that the lake was fed by a river that ran through the mountain. Then he pointed up behind the campsite and said something about good fishing.

If someone was hiding in the woods, parking near a river would make sense. It would provide water for drinking and bathing, fish for food. There would be signs of human activity. An old campfire, footsteps in sand, beer cans, paper, or a piece of aluminum wrapping.

Maybe her empty cereal bag.

She didn't have to hike far. She'd look around and see if she could find any paw prints to follow. Back at her campsite she scrawled a note and left it on her windshield. *Gone to hike the river.* She stared at the note. What if Vaughn came back? The idea of running into him in the middle of the woods was as disturbing as discovering any mountain man. She crumpled up the note.

She didn't want him looking for her.

CHAPTER 22

Beth shoved things into her backpack—binoculars, a bottle of water, granola bars, an apple, the compass, and the bear spray. Then she slathered sunscreen on her bare legs and arms. Her boots were new, the leather smooth and stiff, so she pressed a Band-Aid around each heel and did a few lunges, rising on her heels, then down on her toes, trying to make them more flexible.

She entered the woods where she'd seen the dog disappear, and followed a narrow trail, ponytail swinging, shoulders back. It wasn't long before her face and neck were sticky with sweat. She'd taken off her shirt, tied it around her waist, and was now hiking in a black sports bra—she kept the gun in her backpack and the bear spray hooked to her front belt loop.

She stopped to whistle a few times, called out, "Come here, boy!" and clapped her hands—she'd read that loud noises scare off bears, but it hadn't seemed to worry the dog back at the campsite. She was hoping he'd recognize her voice and come looking for more food.

She drained the last of her water within the first hour and had to keep stopping to adjust the straps of her backpack, which were rubbing her shoulders raw. Her legs and calves were beginning to turn pink—even in the woods the sun streamed through the branches like iron swords and she'd sweated off all the suntan lotion. Her shorts kept her cool, but she hadn't thought about how her skin would get scratched and that the forest was thick with blackflies. Soon her arms and legs were streaked with blood.

The underbrush got even more dense as the trail narrowed, brambles and thorns on either side, fir trees crowding together. She was dying of thirst. She knew the river ran through the forest somewhere off to the west. She held her compass, turning one way and then the next. The arrow wavered at *W.* She glanced up, saw the path she'd have to follow. Was it even a path? She readjusted her backpack and hiked on. The air grew cooler the deeper she got in the forest.

She heard something in the distance. Wind? No, it was the rush of the river. Now she was walking faster. When she reached the top of a hill, she could see through the trees and down into a gulley. She stopped when she caught a glimpse of dark green water. *That* was the river?

She'd imagined the river to be wide and flat, with a sandy shore. Not a wild undulating beast that cut its way through the land. The banks on either side were sheer rock and steep gravel inclines. Snarled logs crisscrossed over deep pools and underbrush lined the river, forming an impenetrable wall. No one could camp there. Maybe the river flattened higher up.

She kept climbing. When she reached a ridge that had been logged at one time, she staggered over to a rotten tree trunk, gray from the sun. The clearing was wide and covered in slash like bony toothpicks. Stumps were blackened. Fireweed and berries fought for survival.

She tried to massage her aching calves, but that set the sunburn aflame. She settled for stretching her legs out in front of her and resting her feet. When she took off her pack, her shoulders were red, with white stripes where the straps had protected her skin from the sun.

She turned her face to the cloudless blue sky. An eagle let out a screech that startled her through her spine. She pulled out her binoculars and watched the eagle swoop, then lowered her view to the valley below. She didn't see any obvious places where someone might camp.

She put the binoculars away, then used her shirt to pat sweat off her face. Checked her watch. Eleven. She'd been in the woods for two hours. It felt like a lifetime. She tied her shirt over her head like a bandanna, then started back down the trail. Enough was enough.

She thought that going downhill would be easier, but as she continued, the sun moved higher and now hung directly above her head. How much longer until she made it to the campsite? She glanced at her watch. Noon. If she kept walking at the same pace, she'd be out of the woods before the hottest part of the day. As soon as she got back to her site she was going to leap into the lake. She stopped to pick berries for moisture in her mouth, and realized she was staring at a small, overgrown animal trail that ran alongside the blackberry bushes. Maybe deer used it to get to the river for water. She gave the backpack a little lift, adjusting it on her shoulders, and winced at the bite of canvas against her throbbing sunburn. She pushed through the greenery.

She emerged onto an outcropping, stood with her hands on her hips. She admired the view of the river below for a few moments and felt glad for the fresh air, the greenery. It had been good for her to get out of her rut, even if she hadn't found anything. She let out her breath in a long sigh.

Behind her, a sharp sound. A stick breaking. She spun around. A deer, soft-eyed and gentle, strolled through the timber, lifting its hooves delicately. Beth gasped at how close it was—it saw her, then sprinted away, bounding over trees, crashing through the bushes.

Beth stood still, her heart racing, and laughed to herself. Maybe the deer was a sign from her sister. *You don't belong in this forest. Go back to the city, Beth!*

She had dropped the compass in her surprise. She bent over now to get it, and the pack shifted on her shoulders, throwing her off balance. One of her heels came down on the mossy rocks and skidded off to the side. She fell onto her knee. She pushed her hands into the moss, trying to grab on to something, but it all came apart. Her boots slipped. Now she was on her stomach.

She slid over the cliff edge, grabbing at twigs and branches and roots, the hard rock. She almost caught herself, then the root broke away from the dirt, and she was plummeting down.

She was freezing. She reached for the blanket to tug it over her shoulders, felt only air. Something was pulling on her from behind, jerking her back. She opened her eyes, moaned, and sucked in a mouthful of water. She gasped and spluttered, shifted onto her side. She tried to sit up. Everything tilted and she lowered herself toward the rock—most of her body was in the water.

Barking. The rasp of a wet tongue across her cheeks, her forehead. Rough, insistent. She turned over, then startled when she saw the black dog. Was it *him*? She held out her hand, but he danced backward. He grabbed the side of her backpack in his mouth and yanked hard.

"Hey! Stop it!"

She slowly sat up, clutching her head, and squinted at the sun. Her hand felt sticky. She pulled it away and sucked in her breath when she saw the blood, and instantly regretted it because of the shock wave of pain stabbing her ribs. The dog had bounced out of her reach and was sitting nearby. One ear twitched at her.

"I've been looking for you." Speaking hurt. Her mouth tasted like blood. She stared at him for a long, wavering moment, leaned over, and puked. She bent over the river and scooped water into her mouth. When she tried to stand up, she wobbled, and stumbled backward. She thought for sure she was going to fall again, but she threw out her arms for balance.

She shrugged her wet backpack off her shoulders, groaning with every move. She took out another shirt, which was also wet, and pressed it to her head. She looked at the dog.

"Thanks for waking me up." His tail thumped. That was new. Last time he had ignored her. "Are you with someone?" He thumped again. The mountain man? He could be watching her. She turned and looked into the forest, scanned the shadows, stumps that looked like hunched people. "Is anyone out there?" She was greeted with silence.

"I've lost my mind." She started to shake her head, then grimaced at the wave of nausea. It took her a couple of tries before she was able to bend and fill her water bottle. She hesitated, thinking about bacteria. The river was running fast though. That was good, right? It had to be okay. She drank in big gulps, then attached the bottle to her backpack. The dog watched.

She began to pick her way over the rocks. She thought about how far she was going to have to walk to the campground. Did she even know the way? She stopped at the shore.

"I'm so fucked."

She bent over to puke up the water she had just drunk. The dog bolted into the woods, but he stayed at the top of the bank. As if he were waiting. When she walked toward him, he yipped, spun around, and started down the trail.

She stopped, thinking. Was he leading her back to the campground? Maybe she was crazy. Her head throbbed. The trees around her kept merging. She closed her eyes, waited for her balance to come back, then she took a tentative step toward him. He wagged his tail. Okay. She'd let him play leader. He seemed more certain about where he was going than she did.

It took all afternoon. She stopped a few times to sip her water, pausing between each mouthful to make sure she could hold it down. Every time she glanced over her shoulder, eyes scanning the forest, the dog would yip impatiently, and she'd continue on, but she found herself moving slower and slower.

She sank to her knees and leaned forward on her hands, bracing herself, but her arms sagged, and she collapsed onto her stomach in the middle of the trail. The ground was cool under her body. Her breaths felt ragged. The dog barked in her face.

"I need to rest," she said weakly. "Few minutes."

The dog wouldn't shut up. He barked incessantly, coming within inches of her, nipping at her boots, then leaping backward.

"Go away!" She scrabbled up a handful of dirt and tossed it at him, but he didn't run off. He grabbed on to her backpack strap, dug his feet into the ground, and began yanking and growling, twisting his neck. She moaned and cursed at him but pulled herself to her knees.

The dog pounced forward, still aggressively barking.

She got to her feet, weaving, and stumbled after him. When the trail started to look familiar, she realized she was close, and she quickened her pace. She was panting hard, almost gasping. Then she remembered the gun—at the top of her pack. She stopped, and with shaking fingers she removed the bullets, and shoved the gun to the bottom of her damp backpack.

She broke out of the trail, staggered onto the campground road. She looked behind and the dog was standing at the edge of the forest. He spun around and disappeared.

"Hey, you okay?" A shout. She looked up. The black-haired

guy from the other site. They'd cooked bacon yesterday. It had smelled so good. She had really wanted a slice of that bacon.

She slumped to the ground.

Beth woke to noise. Pale green walls, a TV hanging in the corner, a white board with red writing—the day nurse's name, the date, Beth's last vital check, the attending physician's name, and a cheerful smiley face.

The noise again. She turned her head to the right. Jonny sat sprawled in a chair, watching her with his chin in his hand, a paper cup in his other.

"Brought you a coffee. It's on your stand."

"Thanks." Her voice felt dry, husky. She slowly sat up and reached for the coffee, wincing as her body stretched. She couldn't stop thinking about what it had felt like to fall from that cliff, the sensation of nothing under her feet, hands grasping at air. The strangest thing was the feeling of disappointment when she woke at the bottom. She'd thought that if she ever came close to death, she would feel her sister nearby, maybe hear her voice, but it was only the dog.

Jonny got to his feet and passed her the cup, made a few adjustments to her bed so that she could sit up. She took a swallow, rested her head back. Was it only this morning that Jonny had left her campsite? She imagined how she looked to him now. The nurses had helped her into the bathroom to wash the blood out of her hair. She'd studied herself in the mirror, shocked at her pale face, the dark shadows under her eyes, the ugly bruise along her temple. Turned out head wounds bleed a lot, but the cut wasn't as deep as she had feared. She only needed a few stitches. The area around it was swollen and hurt to touch. The mother of all goose eggs.

She blinked at him. "How long have you been here?"

"Just a few minutes."

"Your friend tell you?"

"Andy? Yeah."

She remembered the ambulance ride, the jerkiness of the stretcher as the paramedics bumped it over the curb and pushed it into the hospital. "I owe him."

"Don't tell him that. He'll have you buying him dinner."

She looked over and met his eyes. Was that jealousy? She couldn't tell. His voice was teasing, but they'd left things so awkward. "I could offer him a burnt hot dog."

He laughed. "That's still better than hospital food. I broke my ankle a few years ago and needed surgery. Hailey snuck in DQ milkshakes and hid under my bed every time a nurse came to check on me."

"Nice. You had your own delivery service."

"She was just trying to get out of school," he said with another easy laugh. "She always wanted to be outside, and skipped classes constantly, but she got good grades."

"How did you become friends?"

"We were kids, she taught me to ride. We liked doing all the same things." He rubbed at a worn spot on his jeans. Beth imagined them riding dirt bikes, going out to the lake, jumping off the dock. She could hear the echo of her laughter. She was a ghost, always around him.

"Amber and I didn't have much in common, but I think that's why we got along. I didn't have to worry about her stealing my clothes." A comforting warmth spread across her chest, a memory of Amber flipping through her closet. *Why is everything gray? You need more color!*

"Family is different."

"Mine is a mess." She sighed. "I've been lying to my parents for months. They don't know that I dropped out of school. They don't even know that I'm in Cold Creek."

"No kidding." His eyebrows lifted.

"I can't seem to make myself care anymore." She drifted into silence. She liked that he didn't ask for more details. He took a sip of his coffee, his long legs crossed at the ankles. He'd been like that in bed, she remembered. Never pushing her past her limit or rushing ahead. It was this easy sort of dance. She wished they were in a darkened tent again. Using their bodies to talk.

"I stopped racing for a while," Jonny said. "It seemed stupid, shallow. Who cared about winning a trophy when my best friend was gone? It took a while to get over that."

"How did you?" She watched his face, the play of emotions.

"It bothered me, that I was letting Hailey down. She used to come out to every race, no matter what, and I started thinking that maybe I should have as much faith in myself as she did."

Beth thought over what he'd just said. "Amber was such a hippie. She'd probably tell me that I'm on a spiritual journey now and I need to go with the flow." Beth waved her hands in the air, then brought them to the prayer position at her heart center. "Namaste."

He smiled. "Maybe you could open a yoga studio."

"Ha. Don't make me laugh. It hurts." She let out her breath, releasing some of the emotion that had tightened her throat. "Amber really liked Hailey."

"Hailey liked her a lot too. She was upset they couldn't see each other."

"Why was Vaughn so hard on her?"

"That's the bullshit part of it all. We pulled some crazy stunts, but Hailey was *good*. She kept me away from drugs, and she was always busting up my fights. She was my voice in the dark, you know? That person who gets you through when you can't see the way."

Beth thought over his words with a pang of longing. Amber

had been her voice. Maybe that was why she had felt so weight-less since she'd died. Unanchored. Lost.

"We got stuck in a silver mine when we were kids," he said. "I freaked about bats and Hailey told me to stop being such a baby." He laughed. "She dragged me out of there, talking the entire time about how she was never going to let me forget that she was the brave one."

"She sounds great."

"She wasn't afraid of anything." He said it with so much ad-miration that Beth felt even sadder for him. In the end, being brave hadn't been enough, had it? He realized that hard truth at the same moment she did, his smile fading. "Anyway, she re-ally liked Amber. Vaughn saw them together. He flipped out."

"Is he homophobic?"

He shrugged. "I think he just didn't like Hailey having fun."

Beth turned over all this new information in her mind like stones at the beach, searching for something to scuttle out. Who else might have seen them together?

"I was thinking about how most of the girls had been at the lake at some point. Like that's where *everyone* goes. I wondered if the killer has been watching them there."

"How do you mean?"

"What if he's in the woods? Vaughn said there's lots of illegal camping. That's what I was looking for. Signs of someone living out there. Maybe by the river."

"Whoa. Your brain is moving too fast for me." Jonny shook his head. "If someone was living out there, then a hunter or dirt biker would have seen him by now."

"I don't know. When I woke up at the bottom of the cliff, that dog was licking my face and barking. He led me back to the campsite. If he was really a stray, would he do that?"

"Okay, what kind of drugs are they giving you?"

"I'm serious. He has to belong to someone."

"No one could live in those mountains. Not even an experienced guide." Beth was surprised to see a shimmer in Jonny's eyes. He blinked a few times and cleared his throat. Then tossed his coffee in the garbage with a thump.

"Hey—I didn't mean to upset you."

"It's okay, but I should let you rest." He got to his feet.

"You don't have to go." She blinked, her eyelids drifting closed. She was so tired. The weight of all this. The ghosts of Amber and Hailey crowding the room.

She felt him squeeze her hand. "Hang in there."

When she opened her eyes to say goodbye, he was already gone.

CHAPTER 23

They kept her in for another night and her duffel bag was in the
room when she woke. The nurse told her that a young man had
dropped it off, along with her keys. Her car was in the parking
lot. She didn't ask for a description. She knew it was Jonny. She
looked at the items he'd packed: shorts, tops, toiletries, underwear, and bras. Strangely, she wasn't embarrassed. She felt comforted. Maybe that was how people with boyfriends felt. Like
they had someone looking out for them.

She'd gone through her backpack the day before, pulling out
the damp items to dry on the hospital room heater, and was
relieved that the gun was still wrapped in a shirt at the bottom.

Now she put everything back inside and thought about how
none of it had helped her in the end. She smiled when she saw a
few teeth marks in the nylon fabric. Her dog angel.

A noise at the door, someone clearing their throat. She closed
the flap on her pack and looked over her shoulder. Vaughn. Her
body stiffened.

He came farther into the room. "Glad to see you are up and
about. I checked on you last night, but you were asleep."

A spider of fear skittered across her shoulders. He had been
in her room while she'd been *sleeping*. The nurses had given her
drugs. She remembered nightmares, dark shapes, falling.

She moved around to the side of the bed. "I didn't know."

He sprawled, uninvited, in the chair beside the window, and
set down a couple of magazines. Fashion magazines. "Wasn't
sure what you like to read." His legs were stretched wide, black

boots with a thick tread, his arms crossed over his chest so that his biceps bulged. It would look casual to most people, but somehow it felt aggressive. Like he wanted her to see how large he was, how unhurried. He had all the time in the world—and it was focused on her.

"I'm leaving today, but thanks."

"You need a ride?"

"I have my car."

He studied her. "You could have died in that river."

"I could die anywhere."

"Hiking in those woods alone, without experience, wasn't smart." His scolding tone was beyond patronizing. How did his wife stand him?

"I'll be more careful." Maybe if she humored him he'd feel like he'd done his job.

"I heard you had a visitor yesterday."

"Isn't a hospital supposed to be private?"

"Not much stays private in this town. If you two are dating, that's your choice." He held up his hands, then said casually, "He used to date Shannon Emerson." He watched her lower herself slowly to the bed. He smirked. "You didn't know that, huh?"

"It's a small town."

"She was at the field that night with him. Somehow she ended up alone."

She frowned. "That doesn't mean—"

"You think all these girls are just *unlucky*? He came into the diner every few days, and, sorry, sweetheart, but the burgers aren't that good. He had his eye on your sister."

Jonny had sat in that chair. They'd talked easily about Amber and Hailey. He had made her feel comforted, reassured. She'd have sensed something was wrong with him when they got drunk together. She would have *known*. She couldn't have slept with her sister's killer.

"Everyone probably knows everyone in this town. Doesn't mean anything."

He got to his feet. "Sure. Bet Amber thought the same thing. Unless you want to join her, stay away from him. I don't want to have to pick through your bones." It was macabre, the way he said it, shockingly brutal, and judging by the glint in his eye when she sucked in her breath, it hit exactly as intended. There was nothing she could say against such ugly words.

"You take care, now." His shoes squeaked on the floor as he spun around, his strides long.

After he was gone, Beth sat on the edge of the bed for a few more minutes, then grabbed her bag and slung it over her shoulder. On her way out, she took the magazines and left them on the nurses' desk.

Her car was full of gas. She'd only had a quarter of a tank the night she drove home from the diner. Jonny had filled it up. She stared at the gauge. Why hadn't he told her about Shannon? It had to be a lie. Vaughn was manipulating her, for some reason. Maybe to get at Jonny.

She eased out of the hospital parking lot, sucking in her breath when her tires rolled over a speed bump. Her ribs were bruised, not broken, but they would still take a while to heal, and she'd have to come back to get the stitches on her head removed. The doctor told her that she needed to be careful not to get another concussion. She promised to avoid more cliff-diving.

Midweek, the campground was nearly empty. One family was in a site close to the entrance, and a truck with Alberta license plates and a camper was in a middle site. Three large men stood around their barbecue, drinking beer and admiring their dirt bikes.

She was disappointed to see that Jonny's friends had left the campground. She'd come to think of them as protectors. Or at least they weren't strangers. Jonny might not believe there was a mountain man, but she wasn't convinced. Either way, that dog was still out there.

She walked slowly around her site and the shore but didn't see any paw prints. She'd bring more scraps in case he showed up. He deserved a burger—a *steak*—after saving her life.

She crawled into the tent to change, pausing to stare down at her things, all rumpled and out of order. What had Jonny been thinking when he went through her clothes? Did he feel as though he were violating her privacy? If she'd been going through his things, she would have stopped to smell his shirts, maybe pulled one over her head to keep. She decided to leave her clothes the way he'd left them, unfolded, tossed loose from their straight little lives.

The vodka bottle was on its side in the cooler, the remaining liquid leaked out. She'd picked up another on the way back. Drink in one hand, and the bottle of vodka under her arm, she walked down to the dock and sat in the middle on the warm wood planks. She hugged her knees to her chest and wondered if Amber and Hailey had sat in the same spot.

Three women. Two dead, and one missing. Jonny had an alibi for when Hailey went missing, and if there had been any *real* evidence he was involved with Amber's or Shannon's deaths, the cops would have arrested him. It was just Vaughn's obsession. Jonny hadn't even tried to get Beth alone. She was the one who invited him out to the campsite, and into her tent.

Still. Why hadn't Jonny told her about Shannon? She thought for a moment and picked up her cell phone, hovered her finger over the keyboard. It's a bad idea to text a guy when you're feeling emotional. Especially if you're high on pills and maybe a little bit lonely.

She quickly tapped out, *Thanks for dropping off my car*, and hit send before she could overthink it. She was being polite. If he answered, great. If he didn't, oh, well.

She picked up the vodka bottle and swirled the liquid around. The Coke was at her campsite in her cooler. Seemed a long way to go for something she didn't need. She pressed the rim to her lips and drank it straight, then dropped onto her back, legs dangling into the cold water, and waited for the alcohol to hit her blood and mix with her painkillers.

Goodbye problems, hello oblivion.

Her face was wedged against her backseat. She tried to sit up and sucked in a sharp cry at the pain in her ribs. Right. Forgot about those. She pressed her hands to the side of her head and winced when she made contact with her stitches and the lump that was still very lumpy.

She closed her eyes until the pain receded, then she sat up *slowly*, taking stock of her body, her car, the heat pressing in around her. Her hair felt sweaty. She was still dressed in yesterday's clothes. Her feet were filthy. Sand and dirt were in her bedding, on the seats, the floorboards. Somehow she'd gotten dirty footprints on the dash. Like she'd kicked her feet up. Having herself a nice day at the beach. She stared at the marks, willing herself to remember. When was she in the front seat? What else had she done? Her gaze landed on her cell phone.

Oh, no. Had she texted anyone? She couldn't remember if Jonny had messaged her back. She had a vague memory of checking her phone and being angry, or maybe sad. If luck was on her side, she would have been smart enough not to act on those feelings. She tapped the home button. The screen was black. She glanced at her watch—not on her wrist. She must have left it on the picnic table. The sun was up, but the air was cool. She guessed it was early.

When she reached for the car door, she realized it wasn't locked—it wasn't even closed properly. She ran her hand under the front seat. The gun was still there. She pushed the door open the rest of the way and stumbled toward the bathroom. She stopped to retch a few times into the bushes, crying out every time her ribs expanded, then kicked dirt over the remains.

Toiletries finished, she unearthed half a bottle of lukewarm water from her cooler, and drank it down in two hard swallows. She found her watch. She had to leave soon for her shift.

She brushed her teeth, rolled her hair into a messy topknot, with sections loose to hide the stitches, patted some makeup gingerly across the bruise, and dug through her clothes until she found a pair of clean shorts and an oversized white T-shirt. Hopefully the shirt wouldn't irritate her throbbing sunburned shoulders. She swallowed a painkiller—and, after a moment's consideration, a nibble of Xanax—then slid behind the wheel of her car.

The engine wouldn't turn over. She tried the key again. Nothing.

"Shit, shit, shit." She pounded her fists on the hot steering wheel. Was there any limit to how stupid she had been last night? When she hadn't closed the driver's door properly, it must have kept the interior light on, which drained her already-weak battery. Now she had no water, no food, no phone, and a dead car. If she didn't get to town, she was going to lose her job too.

She got out of her car and had a look around the campsite. The family at the entrance had left their tent. Their car was gone. The truck with Alberta plates was also gone, but they still had chairs around their barbecue. They were probably riding their dirt bikes.

Beth tossed a few things into her backpack, tucked the gun into the side pouch, pulled the flap down, and headed to the highway. Trucks passed, a couple of cars. If anyone wondered why a girl was walking along the highway—*that* highway—no one stopped to ask.

It had only been ten minutes, but her ribs were so uncomfortable she could only take shallow breaths, and her lips were already dry and cracked. She licked them again.

When she heard a vehicle slow behind her, she rested her hand on the backpack strap near the gun, then peeked over her shoulder. A cop car. She dropped her hand. Vaughn? This was getting creepy as hell. Could a cop be charged for harassment?

The car slowed beside her. "You need a ride?"

She looked through the open window. Thompson.

She sighed with relief, nodded. "That would be great." The doors unlocked with a click and she slid inside the air-conditioned interior, wincing as she pulled the seat belt across her chest.

Thompson reached behind the seat, then handed her a bottle of water—cold, *perfect* water. She drank it so fast she got brain freeze. She rubbed at her forehead.

"Thanks for picking me up. My car battery died, and I couldn't charge my phone."

"I'll give it a jump-start." He did a fast U-turn in the middle of the highway and drove back toward the campsite. "You shouldn't be walking alone."

"I wasn't hitchhiking. I was going to ask someone in the cabins for help."

"Still not a good idea." He frowned, the sun shining on his inky hair, slicked back like he'd showered not long ago. The sleeves on his uniform shirt had crisp lines.

"I didn't think hanging around the campsite was any safer."

"Yeah, well, you shouldn't be there either."

"Please." She held out a hand. "Save your breath. I've already heard it all from Vaughn. God, it's like he's appointed himself my personal savior. Does he visit everyone in the hospital?"

"He cares about the people who live here."

Beth snorted. "Not everyone."

"Why do you say that?" He shot a sideways glance at her and it was obvious he was trying to seem casual, but she saw how his eyes narrowed.

"He hates Jonny, *really* hates him. He thinks he killed Amber." She was too high to be talking, but she couldn't hold back. "Is that why no one has found her killer? Is he even considering other suspects? I thought cops weren't supposed to get tunnel vision." They were bumping down the road into the campground.

"Vaughn's not the only investigator on this case."

She glanced at him. "I trust Jonny."

They were at her car. Thompson pulled in and got jumper cables out of the trunk. Beth sat behind the wheel and followed his instructions. When her car started, Thompson gave her a thumbs-up. She left the car running and got out. He was putting away the cables.

"Thanks. Hopefully I won't be too late for work."

He nodded and gave her a thoughtful look. "What you said about Sergeant Vaughn turning up wherever you go? I'm sure he's just watching out for you, but if you're uncomfortable being alone with him, or if something ever doesn't feel right, call me."

"*Nothing* about this town feels right, Thompson." She pulled open her door, wincing as her rib cage complained, and lowered herself into her seat. "Who do I call about that?"

She closed the door before he could answer.

Mason eyed her. He had a hand towel thrown over one shoulder and an order pad tucked into his apron. "You sure you're up for working today?"

"I've got this."

"Maybe start with wiping down the booths." He looked uneasy, like she might drop a tray or mess up everyone's orders. He might not be wrong. She'd gone to the bathroom, splashed cold water on her face and neck, touched up her makeup, but she still felt shaky.

She moved over to a booth, cleaned the table, rubbed at some ketchup that had spattered up the wall and onto one of the picture frames. "Where did you get all these old photos?"

"Came with the diner. Hailey's father gave me the history of them all. He knew everything about the area. Every mountain, river. Hailey was just like him."

Beth studied the row of photos, stopped at one black-and-white shot of a small log cabin with smoke drifting up from a metal pipe. It looked as though it were built straight into rock.

She moved closer and tapped the glass. "What's this?"

"The cabin? Miners used it, but that silver mine stopped operating years ago. Probably collapsed or grown in by now." The door jingled and he moved off to help the customers.

Later, when Mason was working in the stock room and Beth's phone was charged up, she checked her messages—and cringed as a series of texts loaded. One after another. All to Jonny.

I said THANK YOU. The polite thing is to answer back.

Where are you? Are you ignoring me?

I need to ask you something.

Did you lose your fucking phone?

Okay, now you're just being a dickhead.

He'd never responded. Her words sat naked on the screen. Little green bubbles of disaster. She squeezed her eyes tight and shook her head. Stupid, stupid, stupid.

CHAPTER 24

Beth needed something a little more sustaining than vodka. Walking into the store, she heard the rumble of loud engines and turned around. A few trucks, dirt bikes in the back, blew past with their music blaring. She waited until they had all gone. None of them were Jonny's.

"Going to the pit," the cashier said when she asked.

"Pit?"

"Yeah, the old gravel pit. It's a motocross track. They race every weekend."

Beth paid for her groceries with her crumpled tips and got the cashier to draw a map on the back of her receipt. She wouldn't talk to Jonny. She just wanted to see him race.

The road wound through stretches of dark forest with no houses in sight. She was beginning to think that she'd gotten lost when she came around a sharp corner and found trucks lined up and down the gravel road. Some were new, others old, with dented sides and huge meaty tires covered with dust. Several of them had trailers attached, currently empty. Guys milled about, but there were girls too. Bikini tops and jeans shorts.

When she got out of the car, she heard the dirt bikes. They sounded like a thousand angry wasps, a powerful droning hum that filled her body with a strange anticipation. She walked to where a bunch of people were standing. A radio was playing country music. Some of the crowd had brought chairs and coolers, umbrellas for shade. She spotted a guy standing near a keg selling beer and used the last of her tips to buy one. She gulped the frothy, cold liquid as she pushed through the group of people and looked down into the pit. Ten motorbikes were going around in a circle, up and down hills, plumes of dirt chasing them like dragon's breath.

One rider was well in the lead, and when he soared over a big mound of dirt, he was so far in the air he was only holding on to the handlebar with one hand, his entire body out behind him, then somehow he got into position, the bike hit the ground, and he went right up the next bank.

She gasped out loud. The girl next to her glanced over with a friendly smile. "Right?"

"Who is that?"

"Jonny Miller." The girl sounded surprised, as though everyone knew his name, and turned to give Beth a longer look. Her eyes focused on the faint bruise on Beth's temple and her eyebrows lifted. "Oh! You're the new waitress. You're staying at the lake campground, right? My older brother, Andy, he helped you . . ." She pointed at Beth's head, then looked awkward.

"Yep. That's me."

"Cool." The girl took a sip of her beer. "First time at the pit?"

Beth nodded. "I didn't know people rode like that."

"They're not all that good. Jonny's the best." She pointed to the bikes trailing after him. "No one can catch him." She looked excited, her cheeks flushed. "He knows tricks that only riders in the professional circuit can do. He could go pro, but he keeps turning them down."

"Why?"

Her proud expression turned sad. "Because of Hailey McBride. Jonny won't leave until her body's found." Her eyes widened. "I'm sorry. I forgot your sister . . ."

"It's okay. I know you weren't being insensitive." She watched Jonny for a moment. "It's sad that he's put his life on hold like that."

"Jonny feels like it was his fault because she'd snuck out to meet him at the lake, but she was always kind of wild and did her own thing. Living with the Iceman must have been a nightmare for her." She glanced at her. "Guess you've met Vaughn."

"Unfortunately. Did you go to school with Hailey?"

"Yeah, but I didn't know her that well." She shrugged. "She only hung out with Jonny."

"That must have been hard when he had girlfriends."

"He's not the girlfriend type."

What did that mean? Did he sleep around with different girls all the time? He hadn't seemed like a player to her, but maybe her radar was off. She was blinded by their connection.

"I heard he was dating Shannon when she died."

The girl's friendly smile disappeared, and her eyes narrowed. She stepped back. "I don't know anything about that." She pushed her way through the crowd.

Beth's eyes followed the girl's pink tank top as she made her way down to the end of the track, where a cluster of guys stood around Jonny. She recognized Andy. Jonny had taken off his helmet and was wearing sunglasses, a black motorbike jacket, racing pants, and black boots. He was still astride his dirt bike, legs long on either side, one hand resting on the handlebar. She didn't know anything about bikes, but his looked big and powerful.

The girl was talking. They all turned to look up at Beth. She lifted her beer in a greeting. Jonny started his bike and rode off, dust following in a cloud. Was he really going to ignore her like *that*? Right to her *face*? He seemed to be heading behind the pit. Another road?

She got in her car and drove around, spotted Jonny loading his bike into his truck. He'd taken his coat off and was just wearing a T-shirt and his racing pants. As she got out of her car, he lifted a beer out of a cooler behind him, pulled the tab, and took a long swallow.

He sat on the tailgate. "Shouldn't you be taking it easy?"

"I'm okay. I wanted to thank you for bringing my car."

"You came all the way out here to say that?"

"No . . ." She looked around at the deserted road, the constant whine of dirt bikes still in the background. How was she going to phrase this? There wasn't any easy way to ask someone if they were a liar. She met his eyes. Indigo blue in the sun, the rest of his face in shadow.

"I'm sorry about the texts last night."

He met her eyes. "I didn't answer the first one because I was working. When I got to my phone later, you'd fired off those others. It didn't seem like a good time to talk."

She looked down at her dusty toes in the flip-flops. "I was upset. Turns out painkillers and booze don't mix. Who knew?" She cracked a smile, but he didn't smile back.

"Why were you upset?"

"Vaughn showed up at the hospital. He said you dated Shannon Emerson." She searched his face for his reaction.

He sighed, shook his head with disappointment. "We went out a couple of times, but she liked one of my friends better. They were together at the party."

"You must have been angry."

"Not at her, but I was pissed at my friend. We argued, I got drunk and passed out in the front seat of my truck." He put a hand on his heart. "I've got witnesses."

"Why didn't you tell me?"

"I don't usually hand out a list of girls I've slept with. But now that I know you're investigating me, I'll make sure to keep you in the loop, okay?" His tone was sarcastic, but there was hurt in his eyes, and in the way his chin lifted. Then anger flared in the blue depths. Her relief had shown on her face and made her initial doubt that much worse.

"I don't think you're the killer."

"Am I supposed to feel good about that?"

"I'm sorry, okay? Vaughn just has this way of messing with my head."

"You're kind of good at that yourself."

She flinched. He had a point, which stung. "That morning at the campsite, I didn't mean for it to sound like I was just using you for a fun distraction. I *like* you, but I panicked."

"No big deal. You're leaving at the end of the summer anyway, right? I don't want to get involved with someone else I'm going to lose."

Someone he was going to lose. She heard the truth in the steeled edge of his voice. He liked her, and it scared him. She wished she were braver, wished she could tell him that he was the first guy she'd ever stayed the entire night with—she always left after, had treated sex like a trip to the doctor. A necessary requirement for occasional physical relief of tension and stress.

"I just . . . I don't know what I want."

He raised an eyebrow. "Yeah, I got that." He sighed and swung himself back up into the truck, lifted a tool out of a metal box, and began wrenching something on the bike wheel.

"Is it true that sponsors want you to race for them?" He flicked a glance at her but kept working. She had probably earned that, should leave well enough alone. Still, she had to ask.

"Are you staying in Cold Creek because of Hailey?"

He stood up, spinning the wrench in his hand as he watched her for a moment.

"You want to go for a ride?"

They rode up the mountain together in his truck, traveling logging roads that looked as though they'd been washed out by decades of winter rivers, with long gouges cutting across them, potholes so deep Beth heard the bumper scrape. Jonny's expression was calm, his hands relaxed on the steering wheel, tapping out a beat along with the radio.

She took sips of the beer he'd given her and wondered why she was so attracted to him. Was it the mystery? Or the thrill of doing something out of her comfort zone? No, it was more than that. There was a goodness about him that she wanted to drink in. The kind of guy who would run into a burning building for you, or dive underwater. Who stayed loyal to his friend, even though she was never coming back. Beth rubbed her hands down her legs, smoothing out goose bumps.

"You scared?"

"Maybe a little."

"Nothing to worry about. You're with me." He gave her one of his sideways smiles that plucked at her stomach muscles. The truck slowed and he pulled into a clearing.

He handed her an extra helmet—a smaller one. She didn't ask who it belonged to, not even when his hands grazed the skin on her neck as he checked that she had it on tight.

When he rolled the dirt bike down the ramp from his truck and motioned for her to climb on behind him, she hesitated. Jonny's eyes met hers through the visor on his helmet with a teasing glint. No way was she going to be the girl who chickened out. She slid her leg over the seat, rested her thighs on either side of his hips, and wrapped her arms around his hard stomach.

He put the bike in gear and rode down the center of the road. He was fast, so fast she felt the wind steal the breath out of her throat and her heart press back against her ribs, but she wasn't scared anymore. His body was warm, his shoulder blades flexing. He tapped her leg, showing her how to shift her weight when he turned. She squeezed her thighs tight when the bike skidded around a curve in the road. He gave it more gas and they surged forward. The bike straightened.

Over his shoulder he yelled, "When in doubt, throttle it out."

"What does that mean?" she yelled back.

"Sometimes when you're losing it, you just have to power up and go with it."

She pressed her cheek to his back and closed her eyes, let the roar of the engine and the speed wipe everything away. It was a rush, the spike of fear, the thrum through her body.

They rode for an hour, until she stopped gripping him so hard and started admiring the view. The woods were cooler than in town, and the sides of the logging roads were covered in dusty ferns, bushes, and wild huckleberries. The sun was dappled through the trees on the road in front of them, opening to the occasional logged area with fallen timber, stumps bleached white.

They circled back to his truck. He parked the bike and she climbed off, wobbling on her legs with a laugh. She pulled off the helmet, ran her hands through her messy hair, feeling shy as he watched her. She didn't want the day to end but didn't know how to keep it going.

"We should have brought something to eat. I'm starving . . ."

"We can get your car, then I'll make you dinner at my place," he said. "What do you think?"

She smiled. "Perfect."

His house was a surprise, with white clapboard, a front porch with a set of sky-blue Adirondack chairs. The lawn was mowed, the garden beds in front of the house weeded and tidy. The vegetable garden was organized in neat lines, some plants tied to stakes. She imagined him kneeling with his hands in the soil, pulling out fresh carrots or potatoes. She'd thought him a boy, but he was more settled and grown up than most men she knew back in the city.

Each corner of the house had a security camera, and one above the door. She turned her head, spotted another one on the workshop. Dirt bikes were expensive, and he probably had tools too, but she wondered if the security had more to do with Vaughn than with possible thefts.

She followed him inside, padded across oak floors sanded down to a soft finish. His furniture was simple, a cedar-slab coffee table, a worn leather couch, and a 1950s-style kitchen table with aluminum legs and a sparkled orange Formica top. He saw her smile and shrugged.

"It was my grandma's."

So were his avocado-green cups and plates, she learned as they ate outside on the porch. The evening light bathed their bare feet with gold where they were kicked up together on the railing. Once in a while the side of his foot drifted against hers. She never moved away.

After they cleaned up, working together in a comfortable silence, he took her to his garage and pulled out a kid's dirt bike that he'd fixed for a neighbor. She laughed when he said he was going to teach her how to ride, but she stopped when he held out the helmet.

"What? You don't think you can do it?"

She snatched the helmet from his hands. "How do you start this thing?"

She lay on her side, head in the crook of his arm, her back against his chest. The steady thump of his heart reverberated through her. The night before it had been dark when they stumbled to his room, her hand in his, neither of them talking, and then only murmurs under the blankets, the whisper of his husky voice.

He shifted behind her and yawned. They would have to speak

soon, acknowledge what had happened, and what it meant, but she didn't know. Was she really going to stick around in this town? Was she going back to school? Could she be the kind of girl who changed her life for a guy? She was here to find closure, not a boyfriend, but judging by the way Jonny's hand was drifting down her arm, settling softly on her hip, the night meant something to him.

His bedroom had been another surprise. No posters of dirt bikes or naked girls. No empty beer bottles on the nightstand. Instead there was a map of the world with colored pins—places she assumed he wanted to visit—and travel posters. He also had a few tastefully framed photos. One was of him fishing in the river, his head thrown back in a laugh. She was almost sure Hailey had taken the photo but didn't want to ask. There was a photo of the two of them, their faces tight together and turned upward. A selfie. They looked tanned and happy, with the hint of bare shoulders and water in the background. The lake.

"I'll get us some coffees." He rolled off his side of the bed. She heard him moving around behind her, opening drawers, closing them softly.

He walked across the room in long strides. She peeked at him over her arm, which was tucked partway under the pillow. The sheets were lemon-scented and crisp-white. She wondered if he washed them in preparation for having a girl over for the weekend. Maybe one had already stayed the night this week. She pushed away the thought.

Now he was pulling on his jeans, tugging them up his long, muscled legs. She glanced away. The drawer on his side table was half open. She moved closer to the side of the bed to close it—and paused when she noticed a black cell phone. His iPhone, with the blue case, was sitting on top of the table. She looked up at him.

"You have two phones?"

He followed her gaze. "It's dead. Me and Hailey had prepaid phones so she could call when things were bad with Vaughn." He stepped closer to the drawer and picked up the phone, staring at it. "I forgot it was in there. I'll charge it up and give it to one of my brothers."

"Hailey had to sneak around that much?"

"Vaughn is an asshole. That's why I told you to stay away from him."

"Did he hurt her?"

"He got rough a few times."

She held his gaze. Maybe he was lying. Maybe he was a drug dealer and needed a burner phone, but he was obviously upset. His mouth was tense and his eyes glassy.

"I'm sorry."

He nodded and blinked a few times. "You take sugar and cream, right?"

"Yeah." After Jonny left the room, Beth rolled into a sitting position with the sheet around her body, running her hands through her hair to untangle it. She glanced at the door, then looked up at the selfie on the wall, focusing in on Hailey's bright green eyes, her pretty smile. She couldn't imagine what it must be like for Jonny to know that Hailey's body was still out there somewhere. Alone. If Beth didn't know where Amber was, she'd lose her mind.

"I wish I could find you for him," she whispered into the empty room.

CHAPTER 25

Jonny seemed fine for the rest of the morning, while they drank their coffees in bed, while they showered together, while he made bacon and eggs, but that was the crux of it all. He *seemed* fine. Beth had done enough pretending in her own life to know when someone was faking.

Their footsteps crunched on the gravel as he walked her out to her car. She thought they would kiss, but he pulled her in for a quick hug that ended with a vague, "Text you later?"

For a moment she wondered if he was being distant because he still thought she didn't know what she wanted, but when she looked in his eyes all she saw was sadness.

"Are you okay?"

"Seeing the phone . . ." He hooked his thumbs into his belt loops, showing a strip of golden brown skin. Just last night she'd run her fingers along that line. So intimate. So close.

"Brought back memories," she said.

"It just hits me hard sometimes," he said. "And I need a couple of days to get my head together, you know? But I don't want you to think I'm trying to get rid of you."

"I don't think that. We'll just play it by ear, okay?"

"Cool." He stepped back, giving her room to open her door.

She smiled and gave a wave as she drove off. When she was out of sight, she dropped the smile and frowned at the road. What did he mean, *cool*? It was what Beth had wanted. Non-committal. But now that Jonny had denied trying to get rid of her, she was starting to wonder if that was exactly what he was trying to do. She couldn't follow her own thoughts anymore.

She turned the radio up. Fine. If he wanted space, she'd give him space.

Beth stacked dirty dishes into the plastic tub, wishing the day was over already so she could get some sleep at the campsite. She was thinking about her conversation with Jonny. What would it be like to be a suspect in the disappearance of your best friend? He'd called Hailey his voice in the dark. Beth smiled, remembering the memory he had shared—Hailey dragging him out of the silver mine.

Beth hoisted the tub onto one hip and glanced up at the photo of the miner's cabin. She still couldn't shake the feeling that the dog belonged to someone living on the mountain. They could be using that cabin. Hailey and Jonny had found the mine a few years ago. It couldn't be *that* hard to locate the cabin. Tomorrow was her day off. She could look for it then. Beth thought about texting Jonny for more details, but he'd made it clear he needed space.

After work, she drove to the small local history museum and pretended to look around. The clerk didn't know anything about abandoned mines. Unfortunately, he knew a lot about logging, and the declining forestry industry. When Beth finally escaped, she found a coffee shop with Wi-Fi and Googled on her phone until her eyes burned. There was one reference to a silver mine in an ancient newspaper article, the wording stiff and overly formal, and the description of the topography was confusing—*Black Bear Bluffs, the Deep River Pools, Burnt Fir Tree, Horseshoe Trail*, and comments like, "along a pine-edged meadow of wildflowers."

She used the library's printer to make copies of some satellite maps and a few rough drawings of decommissioned logging roads.

That night she sat by a lantern and pieced the maps together. The Black Bear Bluffs were a rock formation that ran perpendicular to the river, starting from its widest point. She guessed those were the "deep pools" the newspaper had mentioned. Maybe the Horseshoe Trail led from the river to the cabin, which had to be built into those rocks. It didn't look far away, but she'd learned during her last hike that the forest could be deceiving. She needed to be prepared.

Jonny texted at ten. The chirp surprised her as she dozed in the backseat of her car.

Long day, heading to sleep, hope you're okay.

She read over his message a few times, but she wasn't sure if he wanted an answer. He hadn't phrased it like a *real* question. Was he checking in out of politeness? Before she could overthink it, she tapped out, *I'm fine ☺ Someone kept me up late last night so I'm going to bed too!*

She waited for a few minutes, but he didn't text back.

In the morning she made herself choke down some mushy oatmeal. Then she coated herself with bug spray and slid her feet into cotton socks. Loose-fitting hiking pants would protect her legs, and a long-sleeved shirt would cover her arms. She pulled her ponytail through a baseball cap. Two bottles of water went into her backpack. Sunscreen. Plus an emergency blanket. She attached bear bells to the straps and hung a whistle around her neck. The handgun she tucked into the side pouch and practiced pulling it out, but felt silly, like she was playing at being a cop.

She drove her car up the logging roads until they got too narrow and rough, then she parked and started walking—following the map she'd made. The bush was thicker than she expected, and the terrain steep. Her quads and hamstrings burned from the strain. After an hour of hard hiking, she was down to her sports bra—the shirt tied around her waist—and she'd unzipped the bottom half of the pants, so they made shorts. The air smelled sooty from forest fires, black smoke blowing west. It gave the sky a heavy feeling and muffled the woods.

The sun rose higher. She'd been following the river for what seemed like miles on an overgrown logging road that ran above it when she noticed a natural dam. The fallen trees were old, the wood long grayed, forest debris crammed against them. Ferns and huckleberry bushes grew out of the mossy, rotten parts. She pulled out her binoculars. The curve of the river matched the area she had marked on her map, but there were probably a thousand bends to this river. Still, it was worth a second look.

Nearby she found a narrow deer trail that cut through the brush. She crawled under logs, and picked her way through the forest, grasping at roots and branches on the steep bank. When she reached the bottom, she quickened her pace alongside the shore, leaping from rock to rock, until she found a shallow area. She waded to the other side, and narrowed her eyes at some rock cliffs that jutted out over the river upstream. They could be the start of the Black Bear Bluffs, but how was she going to get to them? The shore ended, and the dirt bank rose straight from the water. She wasn't risking another fall. She'd look for another away around.

She turned and headed into the woods. She kept straight until she saw a way through the trees to the north. It should curve toward the bluffs. The trees were sparser now and there wasn't as much underbrush to force herself through, but she stumbled when her foot caught on a root. She glanced down. Something pale and long. Bones, and there were more scattered around. She froze. Human? She forced herself to look closer. She saw a rib cage, not big, but she couldn't tell with the other pieces. Moss had grown over some, and dirt obscured the rest. There was no skull.

Then she spotted the jawbone. Long, with a row of teeth. Too many to be human. The panic settled to a hum. Something had died in that spot, maybe a deer, but it wasn't Hailey. Still, she had an uneasy feeling. It was the way the trees shrouded her. The quiet of the forest.

She moved on quickly, her steps fast as she weaved around the timber. So fast that she couldn't pull back when she stepped onto something that gave way with a loud crack. She crashed through dirt and branches and landed hard on her back, staring up at the sky.

She stayed sprawled out, sucking at the air until she caught her breath. She rubbed dirt from her eyes, spat some out of her mouth. She must have fallen into some sort of hole, a natural erosion.

She sat up straight and saw the branches that had fallen with her. They'd been cut. This was man-made. A trap—maybe dug by a hunter. She got to her feet, clawed at the sides of the pit. Chunks of dirt crumbled in her hands. She jammed the toes of her boots into the walls and tried to pull herself up, but she kept falling backward. She stopped. There had to be a better way. She could use the gun to dig steps into the soil, or create an angle with extra dirt, like a ramp.

Noise above. Something walking? Animal or person? She held herself still to listen. Twigs snapping, the rustle of leaves. She tugged the handgun free from her backpack and pointed it toward the sky. Sniffing sounds, moving around the pit. She followed with the gun. What the hell was it? Bear? A black nose appeared over the edge, pink tongue lolling. The rest of his furry head came into view. One blue eye, one brown—her granola thief, the black dog.

He let out an excited yip that ended in a long warble, then turned to look over his shoulder. A slim figure stood in the shadows, just out of sight. The mountain man.

"I have a gun," Beth shouted.

The shape stepped forward. The sun slanted across his shoulders, blocking his face. He raised something in his hands. Beth's finger trembled on the trigger. The shape took another step closer, and the sun shifted away, flashing for a moment on cheekbones, a mouth. It was a girl. Black hair cut into a ragged pixie, windblown. Green eyes stared down the barrel of a rifle.

Beth knew those eyes, but it couldn't be. She stared back, took in every inch of the girl's face. The arched eyebrows, proud chin, and flared nostrils. Copper-colored eyelashes. Her skin was dirty and tanned walnut-brown, but it didn't hide her freckles. Hailey McBride.

PART THREE

CHAPTER 26

"You alone?" Hailey flicked her eyes to Beth, then around the forest, her finger still on the trigger. Another rifle was slung across her back, and a knife was in a sheath on her hip.

"Yes." Had Hailey been living in the wild for a *year*? It didn't seem possible. She looked too healthy. Her faded shirt showed muscled arms, sinewy, and her legs were lean in her shorts.

"Give me your gun."

"I'm not going to hurt you."

"The gun—or find your own way out of the pit."

Beth thought it over, but she didn't have much choice. She needed Hailey's help. She'd have to hope that Hailey wasn't a complete psycho. Beth made sure the safety was on and threw her gun up over the edge.

Hailey bent to retrieve it, then shoved it into the waistband of her jeans shorts. She stared down at Beth. "Hold on." She turned and disappeared.

Beth heard the snapping of branches, a soft grunt, then the knobby end of a large log appeared over the edge of the pit. Beth ducked back as the log slid down and lodged itself vertically just a few feet from where Beth stood, pressed against the side of the pit. She climbed it like a ladder, bracing her feet on broken branches and gripping the rough bark that fell off in chunks. Hailey stood above, the rifle pointed at the ground. When Beth reached the top, she rolled onto her back, catching her breath. The dog nudged her neck with a damp snout.

"Hey, boy." She reached up to pet him.

"Wolf, get back here." Hailey whistled sharply and he came to her side.

So the sheepherding dog was called Wolf. Well, that made about as much sense as the rest of this situation. Beth moved into a sitting position, rubbed at her bruised shoulder.

"How did you find me?" Hailey demanded.

"I wasn't looking for you. I had no idea you were even alive. I'm Beth—Amber was my sister." Hailey didn't seem surprised. In fact, her expression was blank. Beth thought about how she had felt followed in the woods before, how the dog had found her. The footsteps around her campsite.

"You've been watching me." She must've gone through her car, her purse, read her ID.

Hailey's silence was answer enough.

"Everyone's been looking for you. Jonny thinks you're dead!"

Hailey still didn't answer, but there was a flicker of something in her eyes. Guilt? No, she was watching Beth like she was waiting for her to put the pieces together.

"Oh, my God. He knows you're here." His grief had seemed *so real*. More real than this moment, standing in the forest, looking at a girl who was supposed to be dead.

"You haven't answered my question."

"I was looking for the miner's cabin. Jonny mentioned it once, and I saw the photo at the diner." Beth looked at Wolf. "He said the dog was a stray. Guess that was a lie too."

"Jonny's been keeping you safe. You don't know what you're getting into."

"Then *tell* me."

Hailey lifted her chin, defiant. "Vaughn had pictures on his computer, other girls too. Amber. He has hidden cameras everywhere."

Beth felt sick. She knew exactly what Hailey was getting

at—she could see the fear all over her face. She believed Vaughn was the killer. Could it be true? There was shame there too. That was why she ran away. She might have been abused. Amber had hinted at problems. Then another realization—Amber had *known* that Hailey ran away. That was why she'd been so evasive.

"Why didn't you tell someone?"

"I tried, but he threatened me. And there were no faces in the photos. I didn't know Amber was one of the girls he photographed until I found her body . . ." Hailey stared at Beth's wrist where her bracelet had slipped from under her sleeve. "Her bracelet was gone."

Hailey had been the one to find Amber. Her face showed the horror of what she'd seen. Beth wanted to scream and rant and cry. Her trusting, sweet sister, who wanted to see the world, who was funny and charming. Who never wanted to hurt anyone.

"You have to tell the police."

"He *is* the police. Why are you not getting that? I told Thompson that Vaughn was in your room that night. I've made anonymous calls. It doesn't *matter*. They'll never catch him."

"My room?"

"When he walked you home from the bar, I was in the parking lot. I had to set off a car alarm to get him out."

Beth tried to take in all the information that was being shot at her. She remembered the distant sound of a car alarm, how her clothes had been all messed up in the morning. Did Vaughn take photos of her too?

"You said Vaughn has hidden cameras? I'll find them."

"Do whatever you want, but leave me out of it." Hailey dragged branches over the pit, kicked dirt and leaves on top of them, then stood on the edge and brushed her hands off. Beth watched, confused. Should she help? Were they done talking?

Hailey adjusted the straps of her backpack and looked at Beth. "If you tell anyone where I am, Vaughn will kill me."

"I won't, of course I won't, but you have to give me *something*. I need more information."

Hailey reached into her front pouch and pulled out Beth's gun, gestured for her to take it. Beth stepped forward and tugged it out of her hand. She wanted to grab on. Wanted to make Hailey stay. Wolf watched, as though he sensed her internal struggle—and he didn't like it. She backed away.

"There's a girl," Hailey said, chewing on her lower lip. "Emily. She's a dealer. People say she's a narc for Vaughn, but I think she hates him. If you talk to her and she's wearing a perfume that smells like spicy oranges, then she's definitely been inside his truck."

"How do I find you again?"

"You don't." Hailey walked through a narrow gap in the trees, Wolf at her heels, and she was gone. Beth waited a few moments, then took a few steps through the trees after them. Was the cabin nearby? Maybe she could see it. She stopped. There were no trails; there was nothing to follow.

The sudden noise of a dirt bike cut through the forest, sent birds flying up from trees. Beth lunged at a nearby bush and hid behind it. She felt ridiculous a moment later when she realized the sound was heading away from her. Hailey was on the move.

Beth sat on her picnic table and watched the glowing sun sink in the sky, toasted its descent with vodka. It was a miracle she'd made it out of the forest before dark. The trees had closed in on her, blocking out the sky, the sun. She'd gotten off track and lost the trail for over an hour. Finally, she found a ridge where she could stand on a stump and scan the mountainside below that stretched out in variant shades of green. When she realized she'd come up the east side, she picked her way through the slash, weathered logs, and branches spread like brittle bones all down the hillside, until she found her boot tread in the soft dirt. From there she worked backward.

She'd shredded her pants. Left locks of her hair on branches. Scratched her face. Lost her sunglasses on the trail. But none of that mattered. That wasn't what made her feel unable to move, her arms and legs heavy. She was at the bottom of another mountain, but this one was steeper, and more dangerous. She had a suspect in her sister's death, and no way to prove it.

She checked her phone, her finger hovering over her last text message with Jonny. She hadn't heard from him all day. She thought he had wanted space because he was upset, but he was probably scared because she'd seen his other cell phone. He'd lied to her. She wanted to give him a piece of her mind, but she wasn't ready yet. Tonight she was getting drunk. Otherwise she'd have to think about how he kissed her and how she told him things she'd never told anybody. How she'd felt like he was the only person who understood how much pain she was in. Then she'd think about how for a brief, sparkling, hopeful moment, when she saw Hailey's face, she'd imagined that maybe Amber was alive too. Maybe she was hiding with Hailey, and the police had made a mistake. But Beth had come down the mountain alone.

She took another swig of vodka and stared at her blank cell screen.

CHAPTER 27

Hailey

I hit the trail hard, taking chances. Beth was already on her way back through the forest to her car. Worse, what if she was looking for the miner's cabin? I didn't think she would find it, but just in case, I'd grabbed my escape bag before I left. Would she go into town or straight to Jonny's house? The handheld radio had stopped working last week—the batteries run dry. I had to get farther down the mountain where I had cell service to call him. Then I'd ride back to my lower camp and hide overnight. I clenched my jaw. How could Jonny be so careless?

I'd *spoken* to her. Beth. Amber's sister. They had that same crooked tooth. That same fluid tone of voice, the soft cadence. Their words each flowed into the next like connecting lakes. Their musical laughs. I'd heard Beth's when she was with Jonny. That night of drinking.

Wolf shifted in his crate, trying to balance. We were going fast. We rounded corners, jolted over bumps. Sunlight sliced through trees, casting shadows that distorted the ground and hid roots. I'd been riding for ten minutes when something grabbed the tire from underneath and flung the bike sideways. I was airborne, then crashed hard into a rock. I lay still, gasping. The wind was knocked out of me, but nothing seemed broken. I rolled over. Wolf was gone.

"Wolf?" Silence. I pushed up onto my knees, shouted, "Wolf!"

He slunk out from between a few shrubs, gave his head a shake that made his ears flap.

"I'm sorry, boy." I felt his body for blood or broken bones, then buried my face in his neck. He grumbled into my ear. When we parted, he looked down the trail, then at me.

"Okay, okay." I crawled over to the bike, lifted it up. "Dammit." The clutch lever was broken and hanging from the now-bent handlebar. I checked it over. Wolf watched me with his head tilted. I wouldn't be able to start the bike unless I had a steep hill and a lot of luck.

I rolled my bike behind a tree and covered it with branches. My shoulder hurt, and I'd scraped the side of my face. I gingerly felt along the raw spot, wincing when I touched a bruised area. How was I going to get a lever for my bike? Then I remembered the truck with Alberta plates and dirt bikes in the back that I'd seen at the campsite last time I was spying on Beth.

It took an hour to walk to my lower camp, where I'd hidden the old mountain bike Jonny had given me. It was late afternoon, the heat still thick in the woods. I paused for a rest, shared some food and water with Wolf. He ran behind my bike as I pedaled the rest of the way. When I finally reached the outer edges of the campsite, warm evening light was slanting through the trees. I patted my pocket and made sure the pepper spray was in place. Some campers let their dogs run free. I'd been more careful since Wolf had gotten into a fight with a German shepherd.

I crouched near the entrance where I was able to get a couple of bars of cell service and called Jonny's burner phone. No answer. He was either working at his parents' or Beth had already called him. I shot a text to him—using the code we'd agreed on if I was ever discovered.

Got the part you wanted. Will be in touch with price.

He would be freaking out, wondering what was going on, but now he'd know I was safe and hiding out at my lower camp. Or at least I would be after I stole the clutch lever.

The forest sloped down toward the lake, so I could walk

along the edge above the campground, staying hidden in the trees, and check out all the sites below. Andy's truck was gone. He and the guys often camped out during the summer. I never stole from them.

I found the site where the men from Alberta were camping. Three of them, sitting in lawn chairs and drinking beer around a propane fire ring. It would be a while before they went to sleep. I continued along the deer trail until I was closer to Beth's site. Her car wasn't there yet.

The first morning she had camped at the lake, I recognized the university sticker in her back window. I'd seen it the night I was waiting outside the motel to catch a glimpse of Amber's sister, who Jonny had told me was working at the diner. When I'd heard Vaughn's voice, I hit the ground hard, and then watched as he helped Beth to her room, his arm around her waist as she stumbled. After he hadn't come out for a while, I'd found an expensive car, pulled on the handle and slapped my hands on the hood until I'd set off the alarm. Vaughn had rushed off, and when I sneaked in her window, I found her sprawled on the bed, with her dress pulled up around her waist. Vaughn had been taking photos. The gun in her purse had been a surprise.

With my backpack for a pillow, I rested against the trunk of an old fir tree. Wolf sat beside me, his nose testing the air and his ears flicking. I chewed my nails and worried about Jonny. After I got my dirt bike fixed, I'd ride the trails to his house and find out if he was okay.

Beth's car drove through the campground and slowed to a stop near her tent. I crept alongside the creek with Wolf. We watched through a wall of ferns while she ate a sandwich, then poured vodka into a red plastic cup. She was sitting on her picnic table, staring out at the lake and holding her cell. She glanced at it a few times, but she didn't text or make any calls.

She poured another drink. Then a couple more after that.

No mix. I remembered how shocked and upset she'd looked when she realized that Jonny had lied to her.

It was getting dark, and her head was drifting lower, her body weaving. She set her phone down on the table. She got up, crouched behind a tree, and then stumbled to her car.

I waited fifteen minutes, then crept along the shore of the lake, around the back side of her car. I brought my head up slowly and peeked through the side window. She was on the backseat, curled into a ball, with her eyes closed and her arm hanging limp.

Wolf and I shared some of her fruit and a slice of cheese and a bun. She didn't have many clothes, nothing suitable for living on the mountain. Her bottle of pills was still hidden in the side of the tent. She was running low. Outside the tent, I froze when I heard a vibrating sound, a soft hum. Something was glowing on the picnic table. Her phone. I scrolled through her history. She hadn't called the cops or Jonny. No text messages to him—not recently. There were others. I skimmed them. If she woke up in the morning angry, she might call the police about Vaughn.

I tucked her phone into my pocket.

The rednecks were still drinking, but most of the other campers had turned in. Wolf padding at my heels, I kept to the shadows and drifted through a site with a blue tent. They had a posh-looking SUV, and their gear was new. I found a few bags of chips, a flashlight, a knife, some toilet paper, and a cooler full of hot dogs and steaks. My hands skimmed over the items without making a rustle, my feet whispered across the ground, my breath was soft. I tossed Wolf a weiner, and he snatched it out of the air fast and silent, his teeth barely clicking together.

At another site, I picked up a lighter, boxes of Kraft dinner, a long-sleeved shirt, and a package of marshmallows. I tucked what I could into an extra bag I had in my backpack and slung it over my shoulders. When I was finished, I moved back to the hill above the campsite and watched the rednecks drink for the next hour.

I liked being near the lake this time of night. The quiet campground. In a couple of months the weather would turn, and Jonny would begin to urge me down from the mountain. He wanted me to go to the Yukon. I rolled on my back, looked up at the starry sky. I'd thought I was hallucinating last winter when I'd opened my eyes in the middle of the snowstorm and saw Jonny's blue ones staring down into mine. *Hailey? Wake up.*

It had been a snowmobile that I'd heard. Not our imagined dirt bikes. My radio calls had gone through, crackling, disjointed, but enough, and he borrowed his dad's snowmobile, rushing out to save us. When he got close, he'd heard Wolf howling. He'd taken us back to the cabin, wrapped me in blankets by the fire, then warmed me with compresses and broth. Wolf got the same treatment, including antibiotics. Jonny's dad had a bottle for their farm animals.

When Wolf and I were stronger, Jonny took us to his place. We built a bunker in his workshop, but we mostly stayed inside Jonny's house, and hid if anyone showed up. Over the winter I helped Jonny fix bikes and we painted his helmet. Blue flames. We watched movies, played cards, and I checked on Cash through Lana's Facebook page—she'd never set it to private. We were safe and warm, but I'd missed my mountain. My cabin. How could I leave?

I rolled back onto my stomach and watched the campers from Alberta. When the last two stumbled to bed, I slid on a pair of leather gloves, took my wrench out of my backpack, and double-checked the knife in my calf holster. I left Wolf at the head of the trail guarding my mountain bike. He gave me a few complaining growls, but I didn't want him to get hurt.

I waited another ten minutes in the shadow behind their camper. The lights were off, blinds closed. No movement.

Loud snoring. I slipped around to where they'd parked the dirt bikes. I had the bolt off and was beginning to remove the clutch lever when the camper door flung open and slammed against the side. I tugged the lever free and dropped to my stomach.

A hulking shape was shining a flashlight around the site. His body was clear in the cast-off beam. Tall, with a shaved head, and a series of tattoos down both biceps. He would be violent if he caught me. He was searching for something on the picnic table—knocking over empty beer cans, letting out long burps. He picked up a cell phone. The bright screen lit up his face as he swiped at it roughly, muttering to himself.

The glow disappeared. He'd put the phone away. The flashlight shone at a tree near him. His steps were heavy as he stumbled over to the edge of the site, unzipped his pants, and began to let out a loud stream of urine, while burping again. When he finished and was trying to zip his pants up, he dropped the flashlight. It shone in my direction like a compass arrow. I held my breath.

He bent to pick up the flashlight, and for a moment it seemed as though he were turning back toward the camper, but he must have sensed me, or wanted to do a final check on his bike, because he spun around—and shone the light straight at me.

I ducked, and, gripping the clutch lever, sprinted through the woods. The dense bush grabbed at me, blocked my way, sent me into dead ends. I had to zigzag. For a big drunk guy he was moving fast, boots thudding behind me, his breath huffing out in grunts like a bear.

I glanced over my shoulder—and stepped into the stream, dried out except for the thick, tar-like sludge at the bottom. My foot sank. I lurched sideways and hit the ground, dropping the wrench and the lever. Before I could take a breath, the guy was on me. A hard punch to my guts, my lower back. Flipped over. A fist to the face—shock of pain, a rattle of teeth.

Barking noises. He turned to look. Knee to his groin.

The man grabbed a handful of mud and smashed it into my face, filling my mouth. I choked on the grime, trying to spit it out before it slid down my throat. Wolf was growling and attacking the man. He screamed and kicked out. Wolf yelped. The man stood to kick him again.

I felt around in the mud, grabbed the wrench, and in one motion I leapt to my feet and clubbed him across the head. He grunted but didn't go down. He knocked the wrench free of my hand. He was pulling his shoulder back, ready to punch. Wolf soared through the air and latched onto his arm. The man screamed, trying to shake him off as he spun around. I lifted a rock out of the mud and slammed it against the back of the man's head. He fell to the ground. Wolf landed, still growling, twisting the man's arm in his teeth. I pulled him away.

I looked down at the man, faceup, the flashlight beside his open hand. I nudged his big body with my foot, bent over and listened. Breathing—and no blood on his skull. His shirt was ripped on his arm and Wolf had punctured the skin, but none of the wounds were gushing. I used the guy's flashlight to find the wrench and lever. "Wolf, let's go."

We ran back up along the creek. Each step jarred the breath out of my chest, my bruised ribs. My face felt swollen, my lip puffy. I tasted blood. He would guess that I was male, maybe young, but it was still a problem. He'd report the theft. He'd have dog bites.

Beth's phone vibrated in my pocket as I ran. Someone was calling her.

CHAPTER 28

Beth

Beth startled awake at the sharp rap on her back window. She sat up, clutching the blanket to her chest, which was only covered by a thin tank top. She recognized the face peering at her. Thompson. Once he'd met her eyes, he averted his gaze like he was giving her privacy.

"Can I talk to you?" he said through the window.

She nodded and pulled her hoodie on before clambering out. She felt exposed in her yoga shorts, no makeup, messy hair. She self-consciously brushed strands away from her face.

"Sorry to wake you," Thompson said. "There was an incident at the campsite last night."

Beth froze. Had another girl been hurt? "What happened?"

"A camper interrupted someone trying to steal their dirt bike." He pointed toward the campers from Alberta. "A man was assaulted. Did you hear or see anything?"

"No. I went to bed early."

"Okay." He looked over her shoulder at the empty bottle of vodka, and the solitary cup. Party for one. "If you remember anything, drop by the station or call and ask for me."

"Sure." She gave him a tight-lipped smile. Was this the moment she should just blurt out that she had found Hailey? She couldn't do it.

Thompson walked away with a small wave. She watched as he talked to the other campers, then she turned back to her site. She wanted to check her texts, and maybe set up a meeting with

Jonny. But there was a problem. The phone wasn't on her back-seat. It wasn't in the front either. She checked the floorboards, under the car, the picnic table, the tent, the dock, and the bathrooms. She'd had it before she went to bed, but she couldn't remember after that.

She pressed her hands against the side of her head, squeezing at the headache and trying to think. There had been a thief at the campground, and now her phone was gone. She dropped her hands and scanned the ground, all the way to the shoreline, and around the trees at the perimeter. Dog paw prints, and beside them, boot treads. Hailey.

When Beth walked into the diner thirty minutes later—showered and sober—Mason was putting cash into the register. He glanced over with a smile. His brown eyes were twinkling, radiating warmth that she didn't feel she deserved. Hailey's secret weighed heavy in her.

"You ready for the rush?"

"You bet. I just have to slip into the bathroom first." She washed her hands, fussed with her hair, and applied lipstick, while glancing around for a hidden camera. She fixed her shoe strap and looked under the toilet. She refilled the toilet paper, grabbed a paper towel, and wiped around the mirror, the window. No strange bumps or drilled holes. No objects out of place.

How was Vaughn getting away with this?

One hour into her shift, and her edginess hadn't eased. She was watching for Jonny or any of his friends, watching for Thompson and Vaughn. Each time the door opened, her head snapped around and her heart kicked into high gear. She was forgetting orders, spilling water.

Mason stopped her behind the counter, his large hand on her arm. Warm and solid. She wanted to lean into him. "You okay?"

"I'm sorry. There was a robbery at the campground. It was close to my site."

"Damn, kid. I didn't know. Why don't you take a quick break."

"You sure? It's busy."

"I have to protect my customers." He smiled. "Go on. Step out into the alley and get some fresh air. That's an order."

She gave an apologetic laugh and saluted him on her way outside. She propped herself against the brick wall and studied the dumpster. Did Hailey scrounge for scraps? She'd survived for a *year*. Beth thought about all the jars of vegetables and fruit she'd seen at Jonny's house. She'd teased him about his homemaking skills. Now she realized he'd been doing it out of necessity.

Male voices were coming down the sidewalk. Beth watched the entrance to the alley and startled when Jonny, with his friends, crossed in front.

"Hey!" she shouted, and he spun around. He made a motion to the other guys, then walked down the alley toward her, his hands in the front pockets of his jeans. He moved casually, his legs loose, a soft breeze blowing his long, surfer bangs off his forehead, showing his eyes. He had a great face. A wonderfully, perfect, *lying* face. She wanted to punch him.

"What are you doing back here?" He leaned against the wall beside her.

"I'm on a break." She noticed the damp hairs around his neck and remembered when they'd showered together at his house. He'd washed her hair, running his fingers through each strand, kissing her under the rush of water. It couldn't have all been a lie.

"I called you last night," he said. "Texted you this morning too."

"I didn't get it. I can't find my phone."

"You need a cell out there. It's not safe."

"I think it was stolen." His concern made her angry again. He knew Vaughn might be a killer and he never told her. She wanted to shout at him, but she wasn't sure how to tell him that she knew his secret. She wanted to delay. "Did you hear about the robbery at the campsite?"

"Yeah." He snorted. "Can't wait for Vaughn to blame me."

"Where were you?"

He frowned, shot her an annoyed glance. "At home. I told you I needed some time."

Yeah. Time to grieve over Hailey's supposed death.

"Well, while you were *thinking*, I hiked up the mountain. I was looking for the old miner's cabin, but I found a bigger surprise."

"What are you talking about?" He pushed himself away from the wall.

"Hailey."

"That's impossible." He was staring at her like she'd lost her mind. Of course he was going to deny it. He didn't trust her, didn't really know her, but her anger was turning to rage.

"She told me about Vaughn. I know you've been helping her."

The fear went out of his eyes and now he looked pissed off. "Hailey disappeared."

"Stop it. I *know*, okay? I won't tell anyone."

"You don't know what you're getting into."

"It was my sister who was murdered, remember?"

"Go back to Vancouver before you get hurt. Face up to your parents."

Rage, thick and bitter, coated her throat. He was using what she'd said in the hospital. Twisting the knife. "It's not me you're worried about—it's *her*."

He held her eyes, and for a moment she thought he was going

to keep pretending that Hailey was dead, then he looked away from her.

"Don't make me choose."

"I'm not making you do anything." But it stung, mostly because she already knew who he would pick, and why wouldn't he? Hailey was his best friend. He'd proven that he would do anything for her. "Did you help me because you wanted to make sure I couldn't find her? Is that what it was all about? You kept throwing me off track."

He met her eyes. Would he admit it now? Would he say Hailey's name?

"That's not what happened. I saw you, walking into the motel. I thought . . . you're so beautiful. I wanted to stop and talk to you, but I didn't want you to think I was a creep. I didn't know you were the new waitress that all the guys were talking about until I saw you in the diner."

She remembered that flare of recognition she'd seen in his eyes when she'd almost dropped her tray on him. That connection. She wasn't wrong. There was something between them.

"Can you come to the lake tonight? It's safer to talk there."

"I'm working late. My dad's building a new barn."

"Whenever. Just come to the campsite. You owe me an explanation."

He took off his cap and ran his hands over his hair, agitated. "Fine." He spun around and left the alley, turning away from the diner. Was he going to find Hailey? What other secrets did they share? She listened until Jonny's loud truck drove away, then hurried into the diner.

Jonny's friends had ordered when she was outside, and now she had to bring them their food. She wondered what he had told them about his sudden departure. She recognized Andy, who'd helped her twice at the campsite now. She set the plates of eggs and bacon in front of him and his friends.

"Thanks for rescuing me the other day."

"Can't ignore a damsel in distress." Andy smiled. The other two guys dug into their meals, but she could feel them watching. "Come by our site next weekend. Have a beer."

The door opened behind her and a rush of warm air hit her legs. Heavy footsteps, then, before she could turn around, Vaughn's hand clamped down on Andy's shoulder.

"Are you giving this young lady a hard time?"

The smile disappeared off Andy's face. "No, sir." He stared at his plate and mouthed, *Fuck you*. It was barely on his lips, but Vaughn must have caught something, because his fingers curled into Andy's shoulder hard enough to make him flinch.

After a beat, Vaughn removed his hand and turned to Beth.

"Coffee when you get a chance, please."

Vaughn was staring at her with those cold eyes, but she couldn't make her mouth work. She wondered if she might faint. Hailey was *alive*. He had photos of girls. Amber. He had spied on her, stalked her. Hailey thought he was the killer. Vaughn frowned, suspicious of her silence.

"Of course." She led him over to a table, swallowing hard and trying to get her breath under control. She had to get herself together or he was going to realize that she was terrified of him. She grabbed the carafe and held her arm stiff to stop the shaking while she poured.

"Thompson said you didn't hear the robbery." He tore open a sugar packet, dumped it into his cup. "Must have been a lot of shouting. The victim got hit pretty hard."

"Didn't hear a thing. Want the usual eggs?"

"Sounds good." He glanced back at the guys. None of them looked in his direction, but their voices were lowered, and she knew they could sense his attention. Andy scowled under his cap.

"You still hanging out with Jonny?" Vaughn looked back up at her.

"No," she blurted, then she felt another jolt of fear. Had he been watching the diner? He might have seen Jonny go into the alley. "We had a falling-out."

"Everything okay?"

"You're right. He's not the kind of guy I want to be involved with. We're just really different. Anyway, you didn't come in here to listen to my problems."

"Hey, the police are here to serve, and you're one of us now. I dropped by the campsite yesterday to check on you . . ." Another shiver went up her spine. He had been looking for her.

"I went into town for groceries. Probably just missed you."

"Hm."

She glanced over her shoulder. "Kitchen's getting busy. I'd better get that order in." She moved away before he could ask anything else.

While she served him and the other customers, she made sure to be in a rush each time she stopped at his table. After he was done eating, he asked for another coffee, but he must have gotten a radio call, because he tossed down some money and left before she could bring it.

She watched his white truck pull out of the parking lot, then made sure all her tables were taken care of and walked over to Andy. If Jonny wouldn't tell her what she needed to know, then she was going to have to get creative. She dropped into the empty seat near Andy and slid their bill to him.

"I need to ask you something."

He handed her a twenty, eyeing her from the side. "What's up?"

"I want to buy some weed."

"Just like that, huh? Vaughn's got his eye on you."

"I know." She made a disgusted face. "He's an asshole."

Andy took the last gulp of his coffee. "Like I said. Not a good idea."

"I'm going through a shitty time, okay? I need something to help me sleep, and I heard there's a girl who sells. Emily. How can I find her?"

"You seem to know a lot." He narrowed his eyes. "Why are you asking me?"

"I don't know where she lives."

He glanced at the other two guys. One gave him a shrug, and the other was texting.

"She works at the blueberry farm. She's there every day—her grandparents own it." Andy stood and grabbed his jacket from the back of his chair. She caught the scent of woodsmoke and thought about Jonny. She hoped Vaughn wasn't out looking for him. Andy stayed behind while his friends pushed out the door. When she met his eyes, he looked worried.

"Don't get Jonny in shit. He's had enough trouble."

"I won't."

"Good." He picked up his keys and joined the others in the parking lot. Their big trucks roared away. Andy had his phone to his ear. She wondered who he was calling.

The air had cooled with the sun drifting behind a cloud, but the pavement was still hot as she made her way to her car, first checking the parking lot for Vaughn. A quick Google search, and she had the address of the only blueberry farm in Cold Creek. They were closing soon.

Beth turned off a dusty country road at a white sign with a cluster of blueberries painted on it and a cheerful YOU PICK!

The shop was pale blue with white shuttered windows, and

the door gave a little tinkle as she pushed it open. Behind the counter, a girl was tying ribbons on baskets of blueberries. Products were displayed on wood shelves around the shop—jams, syrups, blueberry-patterned teacups. Emily was wearing a purple tank top with the same logo that had been on the sign. Beth had expected her to look harder. Maybe bleached blond, arm tattoos, and a lot of makeup, but if this was Emily, she was petite and dark-haired, with a posture like a ballerina's. Graceful arms.

"Let me know if you need anything?" Emily glanced up as she fiddled with the basket in her hands. She seemed tired, or bored. Beth's face felt hot and she was beginning to second-guess her entire mission. How could she ask a stranger something so personal?

Then Emily took another look at her. "Are you new in town?"

"I'm Beth." She came closer to the counter. "Amber Chevalier was my sister."

"Oh." Emily's eyes widened. "I'm sorry." Her expression was changing from surprise to confusion. Next would be suspicion. Beth needed a smoother opening.

"She always talked so nicely about this town. I wanted to see it myself." Beth looked around the shop, admiring. "She mentioned a blueberry farm she loved."

"Really? I don't remember her coming here."

"Did you know her?"

"I saw her around." She pushed a basket of blueberries across the counter. "Here—on the house." She reached for a small bottle of sanitizer by the cash register, squeezed a few drops into her palm. Beth caught a glimpse of the label. Blood Orange. The spicy orange scent Hailey had mentioned. So, it must have been Emily in Vaughn's truck.

"Thanks." Beth rested her hand on top of the basket but didn't move toward the door. She couldn't leave until she found out what Emily knew about Vaughn, but she wasn't sure how to open up the conversation. The anger that had driven her here didn't come with instructions.

"I also wanted to talk to you. . . ." She looked into Emily's eyes, trying to use hers to somehow express urgency and also understanding. "Vaughn is creeping on me."

"Yeah?" Emily crossed her arms across her chest, instantly wary. "What's that got to do with me?"

"I heard he did the same to you."

"Who told you that?"

"Friend of a friend."

"They were lying." She looked at Beth's purse on the counter. "Are you recording this?"

"No. I don't have my phone." She opened her purse. "Check for yourself. I'm not here to cause you trouble. I just want to stop Vaughn before he picks up another girl on the highway."

"You think he picked up *Amber*?"

"She would have trusted him." Emily looked so shocked that Beth wondered if it had been a mistake to share that part. She didn't want her warning Vaughn.

"You shouldn't go around saying stuff like that."

"Are you scared of him?"

"*Everyone* is scared of Vaughn."

"Yeah, but you have better reason. He took photos of you." It was a chance for Emily to deny it again, but her expression shifted. The wariness turned to anger.

"I don't know what you're talking about."

"I won't tell anyone—I swear. But I need to figure out if he's the killer, and if you don't help me, then another girl is going to die." It was a guilt trip, but desperate times called for dirty tricks, and she'd dig into an entire bag of them to catch Vaughn.

Emily held her gaze for a few beats. Now Beth saw the tough

side of her. There wasn't fear in her face, or any sort of embarrassment. She was weighing her decision.

"My grandparents need me. I'm the only one who can help on the farm."

"Okay. . . ." Beth waited. This was going somewhere.

"I don't make much money. I get it other ways." Emily paused, one eyebrow raised, but Beth still wasn't fitting the pieces together.

"You mean selling marijuana? I know about that."

"I sell a lot of things." Emily held her hand out. "Pay up."

"You're blackmailing me?"

Emily rolled her eyes. "If you want to know about Vaughn, it will cost you."

"I don't have a lot. . . ." Beth pulled out all her tips, dropped them on the counter. Emily counted the bills and tucked them into her pocket. Then she looked at Beth's bracelet.

"What about that?"

"No. That's special." Beth hesitated, then tugged off her ring, an emerald surrounded by diamonds. "The diamonds are small, but real." Her parents would be upset. The ring was a graduation gift. But if Beth could use it to solve her sister's murder? They'd *have* to understand.

Emily took the ring and slid it on her finger, held her hand up to the sun coming through the window, then turned back to Beth. "If you tell anyone we spoke, I'll deny everything and say that you're lying. I won't make any official reports against Vaughn. Understand?"

That wasn't good news. Beth wouldn't be able to back up her evidence if she went to the police, but maybe they would have other ways to get Emily to share what she knew.

"A couple of years ago, he caught me being friendly with one of the truck drivers in his rig. . . ." She gave Beth a look. Right. Emily hadn't been playing Scrabble. "I figured it was Mason who told him I was working the area. He'd seen me around when he was delivering takeout."

Beth nodded, thinking about all the times she'd seen Mason leave with a brown paper bag full of food for a hungry driver who had to hit the road again. Mason never sent any of the girls to the truck stop because of the highway killer. "Did Vaughn arrest you?"

"No. It was weird. He let me go with a warning. Then he picked me up walking one day and said he wanted to talk to me. He drove me out to a place across from the lake and told me that he had a better way for me to make money—if I stopped hanging out at the truck stop."

"Photos?"

"Yeah, but it wasn't a big deal. The photos never showed my face. I just had to lie on the ground and pose like I was sleeping." Beth felt a sick wave of fear. Didn't Emily understand? Vaughn had wanted her to lie still. Like a body.

"Did he ever do anything . . . ?"

"He never touched me. Honestly, I didn't get why he wanted the photos, because he didn't seem turned on. Maybe he used them later." She shrugged. "Then I guess he got bored of that, so he started paying me for other stuff. Like information on who was partying where and with who."

"Are you still doing that?"

Emily shrugged again and reached for the sanitizer and rubbed it over her hands and in between her fingers. It was like she was literally trying to cleanse herself of guilt.

"Sometimes. Once he wanted me to put a hidden camera in the women's change room at the pool." Beth had been working really hard not to pass judgment, but she couldn't keep her mouth shut about that one.

"You *helped* him?"

"None of my business what he did with that camera." She

returned Beth's look with a hostile one of her own. "He gave me a lot of money—it helped pay for a new well on the farm."

"Does he know that you sell drugs?"

"He likes that I can tell him who's buying. But he doesn't want me at the truck stop. He caught me once last fall and he told me he'd arrest me if he saw me there again."

Beth felt anger coating her throat like she'd eaten something vile, but she couldn't spit it out. If everything Emily had said was true, then Vaughn was more than capable of being a killer.

Beth wondered when he'd set his sights on Amber. Had he offered her money in exchange for photos too? Would Amber have done it? Beth didn't know what was worse—the idea of Amber posing for him, or that she thought it was a possibility.

"You really won't make a report? Thompson seems like a good cop."

"Are you kidding me?" Emily dropped her arms, her pixie face twisting with anger. "Did you listen to *anything* I said? I'll never testify against Vaughn. He didn't make me do anything I didn't want to do, and that money *helped* me. I'm not staying in this town forever."

"Okay, okay. Sorry."

Emily came around the counter, brushed past her, leaving behind the faint scent of orange musk, and walked to the door. She flipped the OPEN sign.

"We're closed."

Beth stopped on the other side of the door. "If you change your mind . . ."

Fear had returned, pinching Emily's mouth until there was a white line etched around her lips. "Don't come back. I'll call him next time." She closed the door.

Beth heard the quiet snick of a lock. Somehow, she'd become the dangerous one.

CHAPTER 29

Hailey

Wolf leapt down from the back of my bike and loped ahead, taking shortcuts, then appearing suddenly, his tongue lolling. I pumped my legs. Sweat soaked through my shirt, the band of my baseball cap. I rubbed at my face with my arm, and tasted blood. I'd reopened the cut on my lip.

Jonny would be leaving for work soon. I rounded a corner, sailed over a jump, and landed on the lower part of the trail with a thud that pushed my breath out in a painful whoosh. My ribs still hurt. So did my pride. When I made it back to my dirt bike last night, I couldn't loosen the clutch cable. On top of that, air had leaked out of my front tire. I'd missed the puncture when I checked it over the first time.

I slowed my pace, coasting down the bank behind Jonny's property and weaving through the edge of the forest. The slam of metal. His truck door. Now his engine roared to life. I stopped by the fence and watched through the trees as his truck disappeared down his driveway. I tossed my bike to the ground and grimaced as my ribs compressed. I rubbed at the bindings. I'd have to wait. I was too sore to go anywhere else, and I needed him to buy a patch kit for me.

Wolf and I settled into the shade of a tree and tore into one of the bags of chips I found last night, shared a cold hot dog. Wolf rested his head across my legs. I dozed but jolted awake when Wolf lifted his head, ears flicking as he stared at the road.

A vehicle. Jonny hadn't been gone long, maybe thirty minutes at the most. I got to my knees, ready to run if it was Vaughn.

The noise was louder. Jonny's truck flashed silver along the road. He was speeding. The pitch of his engine slowed to make the turn into his driveway, but he was still going fast. I glanced up the road. No one was following. Why was he driving so crazy? Jonny hit the brakes in front of his house, and the tires slid. Dust blew up in a soft cloud. He leapt out and disappeared into his shop. Wolf looked at me. I shook my head and gave him a signal to stay. Jonny was acting strange, and I wasn't moving until I knew it was safe.

The workshop's big doors opened. Jonny rolled his dirt bike out and started it up, heading straight for the trail at the back of his property, the small locked gate. He never looked up at the road. He wasn't trying to outrun someone. He was going to search for me.

The dirt bike stopped. The metal clink of the gate lock. Then a minute later Jonny's blue helmet came into view. He was standing on the bike pedals, arms flexing as he navigated the bike up the narrow trail. I motioned to Wolf and he trotted out of the shadows and sat in the middle of the trail where Jonny would see him. Jonny stopped the bike, got off, and removed his helmet.

"Wolf? What are you doing, buddy? Where is she?" He gave our whistle and looked around the woods. I stepped into the sunlight. His eyes widened. "What happened to your face?"

"I wiped out on my bike, then I stole a clutch lever and got caught."

"That was *you*? That was really stupid, Hailey."

"Telling Beth about the silver mine was stupid."

"I told her a story about how you *helped* me. I had no idea that she'd try to find you. I'm upset too, okay? I'm supposed to go by the campground tonight so we can talk." He did look worried, but I wasn't sure if it was because she'd gone looking for me without telling him, or because he liked her.

"You shouldn't have gotten involved with her."

"That's between me and her." He crossed his arms over his chest.

"Dude, she's not your type. She didn't even know how to light a barbecue."

"So what?" He narrowed his eyes. "Did you take her cell?"

"I didn't want her to call the cops."

"Give it back. She would have called the cops already if she was going to do that. It's time you got off the mountain anyway. You promised."

"I said after the summer."

"You could have been seriously injured wiping out on your bike, and then this?" He pointed to my face. "Vaughn is going to figure it out—*someone* is going to figure it out."

"Not if your girlfriend backs off."

"She's trying to find out what happened to her sister."

"And I'm trying to make sure the same thing doesn't happen to her."

"You should talk to Thompson again."

"Why? He didn't do anything after I told him about Vaughn going into Beth's motel room. Cops stick together."

He fumbled with his helmet, let out a long sigh. "What parts do you need?"

"A patch kit for my tire, and I can't fix the clutch alone."

"You could stay in the workshop."

I shook my head. "Too risky. I'm not leaving the woods."

"Fine, but I have to work late at the farm. I'll try to get back before dark. Stay close. We'll ride up and fix your bike. Then I'll go see Beth. Give me her phone back."

"It's with my bike and my gear."

"She's not safe without it."

"She's got a gun."

"Right." He thought it over. "We'll get it tonight." He stepped forward, grabbed me for a rough hug that pulled me off my feet, and scraped my face against the stubble on his chin.

He pulled away. "Keep out of the campsite. Meet me back here later."

I found a gulley near Jonny's house and spent most of the day catching up on sleep. A few times I opened my eyes and spotted Wolf sitting on the bank, looking over the forest, guarding me. Some crows fighting in a nearby tree woke me up. Wolf padded over and nudged me, letting me know he was glad I was finally awake. I rubbed his head, then pulled Beth's phone out of my pack and slowly scrolled through the photos of Amber that I hadn't seen before on Facebook or Instagram. I looked up at the sky. Now I could give Beth back her phone.

When the sun set, I made my way closer to Jonny's house. He should be done with work by now, but there were no lights on in his house and his truck wasn't in his driveway.

The battery on my burner phone had died. I checked Beth's phone. Dead too. I calculated the risk. I hadn't seen any movement on the road or in the surrounding woods. Wolf would know if Vaughn was sneaking around. I'd go into Jonny's house and use his landline.

I punched in his security codes and kept the house lights off. I'd made it into the kitchen when headlights flashed up on the road. I turned, ready to meet Jonny at the door, and glanced one more time out the window, expecting him to be heading up the driveway. The headlights had stopped moving—red and blue flashing ones were now behind him. He'd been pulled over.

Wolf grumbled when he realized I was leaving him in the house and tried to push past my legs. I stopped him with a quick hand motion, then snuck out the back door, and dashed across the gravel and into the woods that blocked the view of the house from the road.

A few yards in front of me, Jonny's shape was outlined in Vaughn's headlights as he stood against the driver's-side front panel of his truck. His back was to me, so I couldn't see his face, but I felt his fear. His hands and legs were spread while Vaughn patted him down.

"Don't fucking move." Vaughn pushed Jonny's head down so that his cheek was pressed against the hood—even though Jonny hadn't spoken and wasn't resisting. "Stand there."

Vaughn circled the truck and lifted the cover on the back. He shone his flashlight around. There were sounds of metal scraping against metal as he dragged something closer.

He whistled. "Nice tools. Expensive. Did you pay for all these?"

"Yeah."

"I bet you don't have receipts."

Jonny remained silent. I crept closer, climbing the bank. I stepped on a stick and froze. Vaughn came around the front and pointed his flashlight at Jonny.

"You think you can make a run for it?"

"I didn't move."

Vaughn walked toward him with his hand on his sidearm and I tensed, ready to rush out, but he had stopped at the driver's door, which he opened to continue his inspection. He found Jonny's helmet and took it out, let it roll off his hand and hit the gravel while he stared at Jonny.

Jonny's face looked flushed even in the dark, his mouth twisted in anger, but he didn't say anything. Vaughn set his boot down on top of the helmet and ground it into the gravel with a smirk. I could hear the crunch of the sharp gravel against the paint—the blue flames we'd spent hours designing.

Vaughn left the helmet on the ground and turned back to the truck. He searched through the glove box, yanked out papers, checked the console and under the front seat.

"Well, look what I found." He stepped away from the door, holding up a small bag of white powder—his flashlight shining on it. "You've upgraded yourself to drug dealer."

"That's not mine!" Jonny's head lifted off the hood. "You put that in my truck."

Vaughn strode back to him and smashed his head down on the hood. Jonny's legs sagged but he stayed upright.

"I told you not to move. You're a little pissant. Nothing but white trash. You even smell like shit." He leaned over and sniffed Jonny's hair. "Just like I thought."

I pulled my knife free, held it in my hand, but I didn't know what to do. If I threw it and missed, Vaughn would come after me. If I succeeded, then I'd killed a cop—major bad news.

A rock. I'd try that first. I found one by my feet and heaved it into the woods. Vaughn drew his gun and spun in that direction. He waited, tense and quiet. The only sound was Jonny's ragged breath. Vaughn took a couple of steps toward where the rock had landed.

I crouched low in the bush and crept closer. I was only a few feet behind Vaughn now. Did I dare run for the truck? A branch snagged on my shirt, snapped. Jonny's eyes widened when he saw me. He coughed to cover the noise. Vaughn turned back around.

"Didn't I tell you to keep your mouth shut?"

"I know you took photos of Hailey." Jonny was looking into my eyes as he spoke. "She told me everything. Pervert." Vaughn kicked him between the legs and Jonny dropped to his knees, gagging and coughing. Vaughn used his boot to push him down, then he sat on his back, wrapped his hand in his hair, and ground his face into the dirt.

"You trying to resist me, you little punk? You trying to go for my gun?" He jabbed his fist into Jonny's ribs—two times, hard. Jonny grunted, gasped for air.

I shimmied under the truck. Screw it. I didn't care. I was going to kill Vaughn.

Jonny was spitting out dirt, laughing in a crazy way. "Fucking pedophile." Why wouldn't Jonny shut up? He was making things worse.

Vaughn was kneeling on his back now. The click of handcuffs. "You're under arrest."

"What for?"

"Possession of a controlled substance. That's just for starters. I'm going to make sure you stay in prison." Jonny laughed again, but his eyes were angry when he met mine under the truck.

He mouthed, *Get out of here.*

"Where's Hailey? What did you do to her?" Vaughn's knee pressed into Jonny's kidney.

"Don't know . . . where she is." He groaned out the words, gasping.

"You were with her that night. I know you were."

"She never showed."

Vaughn smashed Jonny's face into the ground again. Rock hit bone and a wound opened above Jonny's eyes. His nose was already bloody, same with his mouth. The color dark in the dim light. I wiggled forward on my belly. One inch at a time.

"Stop!" Jonny was talking to me, not Vaughn, but I had no intention of leaving him here to goad Vaughn into killing him. It was like he wanted to be punished.

"You're going to get caught." Jonny was still staring at me, blood dripping into his eye. *I don't care*, I mouthed back, and I made a throat-slitting motion.

Vaughn laughed. "For doing my job?"

"Take me in," he said to Vaughn. "Take me to jail." He was trying to get Vaughn to haul him out of here. Away from me.

Static crackled from Vaughn's radio. Vaughn hesitated, then pushed himself up, leaving Jonny flat on the ground. I crawled under the axle, using the tire to hide me—my face inches from Jonny's. Vaughn was sitting inside his car, talking into his radio. Had he reported Jonny? Maybe I was the only person who knew he'd pulled him over. He could do anything he wanted with no witnesses.

"I'm going to cut him," I hissed.

"Get the fuck out of here," Jonny slurred through his broken lips. "If he catches you, then this last year was for *nothing*." He turned his head to look at Vaughn's car. "You have to clear out my place. Get rid of the burner phone. And find Beth. Tell her what happened."

"I can't leave you."

"He won't kill me. He wants me blamed for everything."

Tires on pavement, an engine. Another car was coming down the road—and the lights would reveal me. I rolled into a ball and tucked myself close to the big tire. The car slowed and stopped.

The engine idled. A door opened, slammed shut. Vaughn got out of his car next, also slamming the door. "What are you doing here?" He sounded pissed off.

"You weren't answering the radio." Thompson's voice. Good, unless it turned out that he was also a dirty cop. I peeked around the side of the tire.

"Mr. Miller here was speeding."

"What happened to his face?"

"He was resisting arrest."

"He's lying!" Jonny yelled from the ground. "He just wanted to beat me up."

"Found drugs in his glove box. Looks like a few ounces of cocaine. I'm bringing him in."

"He planted it!" Jonny shouted. "I don't deal—ask anyone."

"That's enough out of you." Vaughn stalked over to Jonny, dragged him up by his cuffed arms, and led him toward his car. Jonny stumbled, his balance off. They moved out of my sight.

The sound of a door opening. Noises, like bodies grappling, a grunt of pain, then the door slammed shut. Vaughn and Thompson walked a few steps away—but closer to me.

"He looks bad," Thompson said. "You should have a doctor look at him."

Vaughn grunted. "He's a drug-dealing dirtbag. He tried to run. He had it coming, believe me. Get this truck towed. I want it in the impound."

Vaughn drove off. I waited for Thompson to walk back to his car, but his steps were going in the opposite direction. He opened the driver's door of Jonny's truck. It sounded like he was searching, but he was being more methodical than Vaughn. What was he looking for?

I tensed, my fingers digging into the earth. Finally, Thompson's boots crunched over to his car and the door closed. I didn't have much time.

I shimmied to the back of Jonny's truck, rolled out, and crawled into the woods until I was hidden by the trees. Then I got to my feet and sprinted toward Jonny's house.

CHAPTER 30

Beth

Beth waited for hours. She stared out at the lake, annoyed with herself for being disappointed. Jonny didn't trust her—and maybe he was right. Why was she keeping the truth to herself? She should tell Thompson. He needed to investigate Vaughn. But she kept circling back to the other reality. If she *did* tell Thompson, then she was putting Hailey in danger.

She felt lost without her phone. She was sure Hailey had stolen it, the bike parts too. Those fresh paw prints she'd seen by the lake were a dead giveaway. Plus she'd heard someone at the diner say that the Alberta man had been bitten. By midnight, she gave up on Jonny and huddled in the backseat of her car. She took a Xanax, and when that didn't work, took another.

The next morning, dry-mouthed and groggy, she got ready for work. When she opened the driver's door of her car, she paused, trying to understand what she was seeing. Her cell phone was on the front seat. Black screen. Dead. Hailey had returned her phone.

Beth looked around but the campground was silent. She would charge the phone at the diner and see if Jonny had texted her.

By the time she got into town, the morning rush was well underway. She hurried inside and called, "Sorry!" at Mason as she wrapped her apron around her waist. "Car problems."

He frowned. "Again?"

"Yeah, I left the interior light on. So dumb." She fussed behind the counter, grabbed her notepad, and shoved it into her pocket. "What are the specials today?"

He pointed to the chalkboard. "Pork patty breakfast sandwich. We talked about it yesterday."

"Right, of course."

"You sure you're okay? Have you spoken to Jonny?"

She paused, menus in hand. "No. Did something happen?"

"He was arrested last night. Vaughn pulled him over, found drugs in his truck."

Drugs? She'd never seen Jonny take anything stronger than vodka. "Is he in jail?"

"His parents are bailing him out this morning."

She glanced at the clock, then back at Mason, but he read her mind.

"I need you here today. It's going to be busy—and that boy will be sleeping most the day. Seems he resisted and paid the price. Go after work. You can take him some food."

The day was endless. She watched the door, hoping some of Jonny's friends would come in so she could get information, but there was no sign of them, and she didn't know the other townspeople well enough to ask. The diner seemed subdued. They all felt trouble in the air.

When she was finished, Mason put together a care package for Jonny—soup, muffins, a slice of pie, burger, and fries—and told her it was on the house. "Tell him to come back in soon."

She grabbed her purse and drove to Jonny's. His truck wasn't in the driveway, but it was possible the cops had impounded it. She knocked on the door. Silence. She knocked again, harder, then called his cell from her phone. It rang inside, then shut off abruptly. Now she was angry. She was standing on his porch with an armful of food for him and he was *ignoring* her?

Beth looked up at the security camera in the corner, stuck her tongue out, then walked down to the end of the porch where the kitchen window was open a few inches.

Stretching with one foot on his patio chair, she shoved the food inside onto the counter, then heaved herself after it. Jonny came around the corner—and stopped.

"What are you doing?"

She slid the rest of the way off the counter and held up a cardboard container. "Food."

He was wearing faded jeans, no shirt, and a lot of bruises. One of his eyes was swollen and rimmed a dark purple, almost black, and his cheek was scraped like it had been dragged along the ground. His ribs were splotched several shades of blue and he was holding an ice pack to them. How could one cop cause so much damage and get away with it?

"It's hard to chew."

She blinked back tears. "It looks awful." She came closer, grabbed his free hand, and slipped her fingers through his. She didn't think about whether she should touch him. How he had walked away from her. How he hadn't texted her. Jonny made her forget every bad thing.

"You need to report him."

"I tried." He slipped his hand out of hers and sat at the kitchen table, sucking in a breath at the pain. "Soup smells good."

She didn't know if he had pulled free because of her touch or her words. To cover her awkwardness, she got a bowl out of the cupboard and served him the chicken soup. He picked up the spoon, swished it around half-heartedly, and didn't lift it to his mouth.

"What's going to happen?"

"I was charged for drugs and theft. I have to go to court."

"Was it true? Did you have drugs?"

"Vaughn planted them."

She sat across from him, relieved that they weren't his, but worried about how he was going to get out of this mess. It would be his word against Vaughn's. Jonny studied her face, his eyes dark blue, jaw tight. Was he upset that she had asked about the drugs?

"I had a patch kit for Hailey's tire," he said. "She crashed trying to get down the mountain. Now my truck is impounded, and the kit is locked inside."

That's why he was tense. He was finally admitting Hailey was alive, admitting he'd had a part in her disappearance. That had to mean he trusted her.

"I can help."

"You can't get involved. I'll figure something out."

"I'm already involved."

"I lied to you, Beth. About a lot of stuff. You should hate me."

"Please don't tell me how I should feel. Nothing in my world has made sense for a long time. When people see me, they see Amber. They want to know how I'm coping, how my parents are coping. What they really want are all the horrible details. You didn't treat me like that—and, yeah, our situations are different. But we've both lost someone."

"I know you want to solve Amber's case, but I have to protect Hailey."

"What about you? Who's looking out for you?"

"My parents found a lawyer." He leaned back in his chair, wincing. His ice pack had melted, the blue gel turned slushy. She found a fresh one in the freezer and handed it to him.

"Hailey has your cell phone," he said. "I was going to give it back."

So it had been Hailey. Beth nodded. "I found it this morning."

"That's good." He let out his breath. "She took my bike, so

she's getting around. She'll circle back to me when she thinks it's safe. She was under the truck when I got beat up."

Beth tried to imagine how Hailey had felt watching Vaughn hurt Jonny. She must have been out of her mind with anger and fear. Beth felt that way just at the idea.

"I'm glad she didn't do something crazy."

"Yeah. I was scared she was going to kill Vaughn." He pushed himself up from the chair and hobbled over to the couch, dry-swallowed a couple pills from a bottle on the coffee table. Then he lay down, lifting his legs onto a cushion with a groan. "God-damn, that hurts."

She picked up the soup and set it on the coffee table. His eyes were drifting shut. The new ice pack was pressed to his ribs. "Sorry I'm being rude," he mumbled. "Tired."

"It's okay." She found a knit throw on the chair and draped it over him. His mouth lifted in a faint smile, his free hand reaching up to graze hers. A soft thank-you.

"Get some rest," she whispered.

She sat in the armchair, staring at the bottle of pills on the coffee table. His breathing deepened. She studied the faint patterns of mottled green and blue across his rib cage. Knuckles, the hard edge of the boot, a square tread. Vaughn had kicked and stomped a man handcuffed on the ground.

She imagined Vaughn hitting her sister. She wouldn't have stood a chance. No woman would, against that strength. The only way to fight back was to beat Vaughn through trickery.

She needed to get him alone.

Beth left Jonny's house before he woke up, and that night at the campsite she didn't text him. She'd made it clear she was on his side. The rest was up to him. In case Hailey came through the campground again, Beth left water and granola bars on the picnic table. Curled up on her backseat, she listened for footsteps, but the only creatures she could hear stirring were crickets and frogs.

In the morning, she checked her messages. Jonny still hadn't texted. Stubborn boys and their misplaced heroics. She had a quick shower and rushed to the diner. The sun was already high in the sky, and she kept her car window down, letting the air blow her hair wild.

The old-timers up at the counter griped about the record temperature and complained to Mason that he needed to turn up the air conditioner, which was already working overtime. Beth piled her hair into a bun and draped cold cloths around her neck whenever she had the chance. She hustled through the diner, refreshing waters and iced teas, blending milkshakes for whining kids, and delivering ice cream that began to melt before she could get it to the table.

She was sure Vaughn would come in and gloat over Jonny's arrest and she turned her head to check the parking lot so many times she had a crick in her neck. He missed breakfast, then lunch. She had almost given up when his truck pulled up outside near the end of her shift.

A few men gave him dirty looks as he walked in alone, his shoulders back and his hand on his gun belt. Beth wondered if they'd heard—lots of people seemed to know Jonny and his family. Vaughn either didn't notice or didn't care about that reaction. He slid into his usual booth with a pleasant smile as he glanced at Beth.

She brought him coffee and a menu. While she poured the hot liquid, she tried to work up the nerve to start a conversation, but he beat her to the punch.

"Your shift must be ending soon." Startled by the sudden rasp of his voice, she dripped coffee onto the table. While she wiped at it, she glanced at him through lowered eyelashes.

"Yeah." She thought quickly. How to get him alone? Maybe in his truck? "As soon as I get off, I have to walk to the gas station. My car is on empty, and apparently the truck stop pump is broken." Customers had been complaining about the inconvenience all afternoon. It was perfect, if he took the bait. She looked out the window. "I've been dreading it. It's so hot . . ."

"You need a lift to the gas station? I've got a jerry can."

She chewed the inside of her cheek like she was thinking it over. "I don't know . . ."

He leaned back against the booth. "You heard that Jonny Miller's been arrested." It was a statement, not a question.

The coffeepot was getting cold and there was a diner full of people waiting for their orders, but she had to see this through before she lost the moment. "Heard something about that."

"I told you that he was trouble." There was a cruel glimmer in his eyes as he watched her closely. She couldn't figure out if he wanted her upset or grateful.

"I didn't know he was into drugs. You were right." She wanted to choke on the words, but it was obviously what he wanted to hear. He nodded and took a sip of his coffee.

"I'll have a plate of Mason's meat loaf, and when you're done, we'll get you that gas."

"I don't want to be a bother."

"I don't want you walking around alone." Like he owned her. Like it was up to him what she did. *You're a psychopath and I'm going to prove it.*

"I appreciate that."

When she hung up her apron and told Mason behind the counter that Vaughn was giving her a ride to the gas station, a strange look floated across his face.

"What are you up to, kid?"

"Nothing. He offered." Then she grabbed her purse and left before Mason could say anything else, but she felt him watching all the way out the door, his arms crossed over his chest.

Vaughn opened the truck's passenger side for her. While he walked around the front, she hit the red record button on her phone and held it in her hand, hidden behind her purse.

The police truck was smothering hot. Vaughn blasted the air conditioner, aiming the vent on her bare legs. She shivered, and even though she couldn't see his eyes behind his sunglasses, she had the feeling he'd done it on purpose. As they pulled away, she adjusted her jeans shorts, let her fingers absently rub at the top of her thighs. Vaughn flicked a glance at her legs.

"How's it going at the restaurant?"

"Good. I like Mason."

"Are you going back to Vancouver at the end of summer?"

"I'll go home, but I might give up on law and do something with the arts. I like fashion."

"That would be a switch."

"I've always liked clothes. I used to have an older boyfriend—I met him in the mall. He said I could be a model, and my parents freaked out. They made me break up with him."

"Sounds like they wanted to keep you safe."

"Do you think I could model? I get lots of likes on Instagram."

"Be careful online. Predators use social media." He looked over at her. "Your sister posted a lot of photos. We don't know if someone was following her that way."

"Are you trying to scare me?"

"I'm trying to stop you from getting hurt."

"Is that why you became a cop? You like saving women?"

He looked at her. "What are you getting at?"

"I want the police to put more hours on my sister's case." She slid her leg higher on the seat, twisted toward him. "You can help me . . . and maybe there's something I can do for you?"

He pulled over so abruptly that her body jerked forward and the seat belt tightened painfully against her chest. She tried to loosen it, struggling with the release.

"I don't know what game you're playing, but you need to smarten up. There's a killer in this town, and you're just his type." He opened the side door. "Get out. You can walk back." At the last second, he latched on to her wrist hard, twisting until her cell dropped into his hand. He checked the camera, swiped his finger across, and deleted the video. He passed the phone back.

"Recording someone without their knowledge is illegal." He pointed at a garage. "They'll have a jerry can you can use."

He left her on the street rubbing her sore wrist. He'd pressed her bracelet into her skin, made a faint pattern with the links. It had to be a message. *Back off or end up like Amber.*

CHAPTER 31

Hailey

I forked up the last piece of pie and dropped the plate onto the floor for Wolf. He sniffed it, tasted the lemon, and gave me a side-eye. I shrugged. He huffed and began licking the flakes of pastry and leftover cream. He ignored the smears of lemon filling.

Jonny opened his eyes slowly. "Beth brought that pie for me."

"Losers sleepers."

"Doesn't even make sense."

"Doesn't make sense that she likes *you*. Why didn't you open the door for her? She climbed in that window like she was Romeo and you were Juliet."

"You were spying again."

"I was checking on you. You've been sleeping ever since she left."

"You been in the house since yesterday?"

"I took off for a while last night, made sure Beth was safe, then came back. Someone has to protect your sorry ass." I'd been too restless to sleep much. I read his magazines, used his Facebook profile to look at new photos of Cash and Lana.

"Ha." He inched himself into a sitting position, wincing. "God, that hurts."

"You didn't answer my question. Why were you ignoring her?"

"You were right, okay? I shouldn't have gotten involved

with her. I'm trying to spare her this mess." He pointed from him to me.

"I would be offended if I didn't agree with you."

He nodded, but it was more like he was trying to remind himself, and I knew he hadn't ignored Beth's knocking because he wanted her to go away. It was the opposite. Unfortunately.

He gave me the once-over. "You okay?"

I nodded. "I filled up the gas on the bike from the barrel. Can I use it until we fix mine?"

"Yeah. I'll get your patch kit when I get my truck out of the impound, but it'll be a couple of days until I can ride up the mountain."

"Vaughn needs a taste of his own medicine."

"Stay away from him."

"You know he's just getting warmed up. Next he's going to figure out a way to get a search warrant for this place. We need to cover the bunker in the workshop." The last thing we needed was for Vaughn to find my winter hiding spot.

"Andy wants me to fix his truck. I'll get him to park over it."

"Check the security recordings and get rid of any clips of me."

"Did it as soon as I got home from jail. I wanted to see if there were screenshots of Vaughn pulling me over, but it was too far up on the road. Can only see headlights."

"You should have Andy stay for a couple of nights. Vaughn is going to try to frame you for something worse. The more alibis, the better."

"What are you up to?"

"Nothing. I just know that Vaughn didn't expect Thompson to show up the other night. It stopped him from finishing whatever he really had in mind."

Jonny nodded, thinking over what I'd said. "I'm worried

about Beth. She wants revenge, and she has that gun, you know? Can you watch out for her?"

"Yeah. No problem. I'll make sure she doesn't go near him."

Unlike Jonny, I wasn't worried about Beth. Vaughn wasn't going to touch her, because I was going to kill him myself. I remembered Dad standing in our driveway, burning weeds with a blowtorch. He'd said, "You have to kill them at the roots, or they'll just keep coming back."

Staging a suicide would be hard. Making it look like an accident would be even harder. It had to be a robbery gone wrong. The diner at night made the most sense. There was an alley, I could cut across the woods without being seen, and I was familiar with the layout. I didn't want to mess up Mason's life, but if things went according to plan, the worst that might happen was he'd have to buy a new door.

Vaughn was on patrol every Thursday night. The timing was perfect. I left Jonny's dirt bike at the end of the highway, with Wolf guarding. He'd grumbled at me, annoyed that he was missing out, but I bought his forgiveness with a bone from Jonny's freezer.

I jogged through the forest, dressed in black, and wearing a knit hat. My face was covered with dark grease. The Smith & Wesson pressed into the skin on my hip, the holster chafing. I didn't stop to adjust it. I felt high on adrenaline, sharp and ready to fight.

Vaughn had this coming. For Amber. For Jonny. For *everyone* he'd hurt or had been going to hurt in the future. When I reached the parking lot across from the diner, I crouched behind a truck.

The diner was dark inside. The neon sign hummed and crackled. The truck stop was quiet, with a few rigs parked.

None of them were running at the moment, but they could start up at any time. Some of the drivers liked to sleep during the day and make their runs at night, when the roads were clear. Hunched low, and avoiding where the sign lit up the pavement, I moved across the street and into the alley. I slid alongside the bricks, still hot from the day's sun.

I'd have to be quick. As soon as I pried off the lock and opened the door, the alarm shrieked. Slamming the alarm with the butt of the pistol until it silenced, I slipped inside the diner. In the darkness, I made out the shape of the cash register on the counter. I yanked it free, knocking some glasses and condiments onto the floor. I dropped the register and stomped on the keys. Now to run outside and hide in the dumpster until Vaughn showed.

The wail of a siren right outside the building. Flashing lights bounced through the windows, spun across the walls. One car or two? I couldn't tell, but they'd gotten here fast. They must have been in the area. They'd catch me if I tried to slip out the door. I'd have to hide. I scrambled across the floor and slid under a booth.

"Police!" Vaughn, already at the back door. He'd come through the alley.

I wedged myself tighter under the booth, gun ready, and watched Vaughn's legs come into view. My eyes narrowed as I held up the gun and aimed. He was moving, shining a flashlight into each corner.

"Come out with your hands up!" he shouted. His legs turned one way, then the other. He was scanning the room. More lights flashed on the walls. Backup had arrived. They would come in the back door. I couldn't escape. Then I remembered the ceiling tile Amber had told me about.

Vaughn stood in front of the counter, close to the end, and checked the dining room area.

I crawled forward, gun held in front of me, and shot the row of drinking glasses behind him, the mirrored wall. He ducked behind the counter, returning fire. Then I aimed for the light fixture above his head, globe-style, heavy. The bullet struck the chain, sending the fixture to shatter on the floor. He grunted.

As I raced down the narrow hallway, I emptied the clip behind me. In the storage room, I climbed the shelving unit. It took two tries before I found the right tile. I pulled myself inside.

Boot steps below me. Heavy breathing.

"He didn't go out the back . . ." Vaughn said. "I would have seen him pass."

"He's got to be in here somewhere. Check the cooler." The other man sounded like Thompson. They were moving away. A door opened and slammed back against a wall.

"Come out with your hands up!" Now they were in the bathroom.

I wiggled sideways until I was resting on one of the cross boards. It was sweltering in the attic and sweat dripped into my eyes, blinding me. I got into a hunched position and walked forward on the boards, careful not to make any noise. I scanned every corner for a glimmer of daylight. Amber had said she was able to blow her smoke outside. I *had* to find that vent. Finally, a bright spot at the far end.

When I got closer, I lifted the screen off and shimmied out, then dropped onto the roof. The tar paper was warm and sticky on my hands. I looked over the edge. The ground below was too far away for me to jump. I leaned back and looked around.

At the end of the building, a piece of old plywood sat on top of the roof like it had been discarded after a repair. The next roof belonged to the truck stop bathrooms. Still hunched over, I made my way to the plywood, slid it across the two roofs, and slowly crawled over.

Now I was farther from the diner—and still screwed. I might be able to jump off the back, into the shadows and out of sight from the street, but there was a good chance I'd hurt myself. Then I'd still have to run through the woods to my bike without the cops catching me.

The sound of a diesel engine starting made me drop to my belly. Then it gave me an idea. I peered over the edge of the roof again. I could see through the windshield of the semi, parked on the other side of the lot. The driver was watching the diner as he put the truck in gear. He'd probably heard the gunshots and wanted to get out of here before the cops blocked him.

I waited until he swung wide and close to the truck-stop roof, then I took a running leap and landed with a jolt on top of his shipment. I clutched at the metal tie-downs, expecting him to hit the brakes or to see one of the cops running out yelling for him to stop, but the truck kept moving. Two other cop cars with lights and sirens flew past and screeched to a halt in front of the diner.

The rig passed through town, bringing me close to the beginning of the highway. When he stopped for a red light, I checked that no one was behind us, then I slipped off the back, using the cables to lower myself down. I launched myself as he pulled away.

The ground rushed up at me, dirt, rocks. I fell hard, rolling a few feet and knocking the wind out of my chest. My hands hurt, my wrist felt like I'd bent it backward, and I'd scraped my knees. I stayed still for a moment, catching my breath, surprised I'd made it, and listened to the rig disappear down the highway. The road was silent. I leapt to my feet and started running.

CHAPTER 32

Beth

Beth nursed her coffee, bitter without milk, and watched mist drift over the lake. It would be a peaceful image if she weren't so broken up inside. What was she going to do? She'd made everything worse by trying to trap Vaughn. She rubbed her wrist. She could *still* feel his grip.

Jonny didn't know about her pathetic attempt at espionage—and she wasn't going to tell him. After twenty-four hours without any messages, he'd texted last night.

Sorry for the radio silence. I've been recovering. You okay?

I'm good. Need some company?

Andy's over. We're having a few beers.

Cool. I had a long day, so I'll probably go to bed early.

Have a good night.

She tried to not obsess. Tried not to be stung. He was just keeping his distance because he thought he was protecting her. Meanwhile, she'd gone and put a target on her own back.

She hadn't been lying—she was tired—but she barely got any sleep. She'd replayed the car ride with Vaughn in her head over and over, and the only other set of campers had partied late. She hadn't minded the music that played until after midnight, though. She'd felt less alone.

Now the morning silence was suddenly broken by the crunch of tires. She looked over her shoulder. Someone was driving into the campground. The engine was loud. Jonny?

She got to her feet and listened as it drove past the other sites. It seemed to be heading toward her. The truck came into sight. Red. She couldn't see through the windshield, only the reflection of the forest, but she recognized the camper. It looked like Mason's truck. She'd seen it parked a few times in front of the diner, but he normally drove his Harley to work.

The truck parked, the driver's-side door opened, and Mason climbed out with an apologetic smile.

"You all right?" he said. "You look scared half to death."

It was strange seeing him here. Her boss. She'd never seen him anywhere other than the diner. She thought of her bathing suit pieces hanging on the line to dry, the string bikini.

"Sorry, yeah. I'm kind of jumpy." She moved to the side to block his view of her clothes. "It's creepy now that most of the other campers have cleared out. What brings you by?"

"The diner was broken into last night."

She frowned. Did this mean she was out of a job? "Oh, no! That's terrible."

"Yeah. There was a shoot-out, but no one was hurt. Vaughn thinks it was the same person who robbed those campers from Alberta."

Beth thought about Hailey. Was it her? But why? Breaking into the diner would only bring more attention, and that seemed like the last thing she needed right now.

"So the diner's closed?"

"For a few days. I could use some help on the cleanup. How's the battery?" He nodded toward her car.

"It's been shaky. I haven't tried it yet this morning."

"Let me have a look."

"Thanks. I appreciate that." She slid behind the wheel, popped the hood, and turned the key when he asked. His shadow moved underneath the crack in the hood. She thought about her dad.

He'd be upset that her car wasn't running right. She felt a rush of shame that she hadn't called her parents for days.

"When's the last time you checked your oil?"

Good question. She'd meant to do it before she left Vancouver weeks ago.

"I don't know."

Noises as Mason checked, metal scraping. He made a disapproving sound.

"You're pretty low. You can't drive or you'll kill your engine."

Mason closed the hood with a bang. She got out to talk to him as he pulled off his gloves and put them back into his tool kit. "I'll give you a lift."

"Thanks." She gave him a relieved smile.

"No problem. I'll drive you back later and we'll fill up the oil." He put his hands on his hips and shook his head. "I'm glad I checked on you."

She thought of Amber, stopped down a lonely road, waiting for someone to help her. Then she imagined herself with smoke billowing from her hood. That's all it took. Bad timing.

"Me too."

Once they were on the highway, she thumbed through her messages, wondering if Jonny knew about the break-in. It would be rude to text him in front of Mason, who had started telling her more about the damage. She'd wait until they were at the diner. She slid her cell phone back into her pocket and realized she'd left her keys in her car's ignition. She grimaced. Just her luck.

Mason glanced over. "I know some tradespeople who can fix the walls and replace the windows. We'll be up and running soon."

"Half the town will probably show up with hammers."

He laughed. "There's some good people here."

"How did you end up in Cold Creek?"

"I was in a biker club for a while. Nothing too hard-core, just a bunch of guys who liked to ride Harleys. I'd cook at the clubhouse and they always seemed to enjoy my food. Eventually I got a job cooking at a logging camp and scraped together enough money to buy the diner." He shrugged. "The rest is history." He glanced over at her. "I bet your parents are missing you."

"They don't know I'm in Cold Creek. I didn't want to scare them."

"I wouldn't blame them for being worried."

"I don't want to go home until I have answers."

"Answers?"

"I want to find Amber's killer. I think she knew him. . . ." She looked at Mason, considering whether she could share her suspicions. He might tell Vaughn, though.

"You don't think it was random?"

"Amber was smart. She wouldn't have gone anywhere with a stranger."

He was staring at the road ahead of him. "Why do you think he picked her?"

She rubbed at some scratches on the dash, upset by his question. She didn't like thinking about the killer choosing Amber, watching and waiting, like she was a toy on an assembly line that he could snatch up when he was ready. "He knew that she didn't have people in the area. Maybe he thought no one would report her missing. Freaks like him prey on vulnerable girls." She turned her attention away from the dash and looked out the window, the trees whipping past.

There would never be another summer when the heat didn't fill her with dread. Never a walk in the woods when dry riverbanks, the quiet of a gravel road, and dusty ditches with long grass didn't make her think about her sister's murder. It was all twisted and ugly, dark and evil.

"You're probably right." He reached over to adjust the radio and brushed against his coffee cup, knocking it over. Coffee poured out on the console, filling the cupholders, and splashing her too. She jerked backward, swiping at the hot spots speckling her legs.

"Damn, you okay?"

"Yeah. But it's all over the seat."

"There should be some napkins in the glove box."

"Okay." She leaned over, pushed papers around in the glove box. "I don't see any."

"Hang on." He slowed and pulled over onto the side. "Maybe in the door pocket?"

She looked down, but there were only receipts and chocolate bar wrappers. Movement, a flash of shadow coming toward her. Her head slammed the window with a sickening thud. She gasped, clutching her skull. Mason. He was attacking her. She had to get out. She scrabbled for the door, but he had a painful hold on her hair, yanking her back. She pried at his hand, his fingers.

Branches scraped the windows, the windshield. They were in motion, the truck bumping down a logging road. Her head pounded. Bright lights, sparks, exploded in her eyes. Made the world thick and greasy. She grabbed at the back of her head, her hair, trying to relieve the pressure from his grip. With her free hand, she undid her seat belt. The truck jerked to a stop.

Something warm was dripping down the side of her face. Her vision blurred. Nausea swarmed up her throat. She spun in her seat, clawed at his face. Her fingertips met something wet and soft. His eye.

He roared—and let go of her hair. She grabbed the door

handle, fell out of the truck, and hit dirt, flat on her back. The air rushed out of her lungs. Her teeth clacked together.

Arms, legs, emerging from the truck. He landed on top of her like a spider, sat astride her hips, his face full of rage and slick with sweat, his mouth open—a giant maw.

One, two, three hard punches to her face, her mouth filling with blood, dirt in her eyes, heavy hand clamping down over her lips, grinding against her teeth. Blue sky above. Then it tunneled into gray.

Her last thought was of her parents.

CHAPTER 33

Hailey

Crouched among the trees, I watched as Beth climbed into Mason's truck. He started up the engine and the two of them backed out of the campsite and drove away. Beside me, Wolf whined. He was anxious, staring up the road after Mason's truck, then back to me.

"I know." Every single guy I knew seemed to be obsessed with helping Beth. I'd been one second away from whistling to get her attention when I'd heard Mason's truck roll in. Now I'd have to find some other way to get a message to Jonny and let him know that I was okay. When I'd jumped from the semi, I'd cracked the screen on the burner phone, and it wouldn't turn on, but riding to Jonny's house was a risk as long as Andy was staying there.

Wolf slipped out from my side, skirted along the shore, nose to the ground. He stopped in front of Beth's car where Mason had been standing and sniffed along the edge of the hood. I whistled for him, but he kept pacing around her car with his hackles up, then he trotted over to where Mason's truck had been parked. He looked up the road again, his ears cocked.

I followed Wolf's path along the shore and came out in front of Beth's car. I touched a drip of engine oil on the bumper and rubbed it between my fingers. I'd seen Mason check the oil and assumed that was the problem. Her keys were still in the ignition. Had she been high again? While she slept the other night, I'd reached right into her car and put her cell on her seat.

I slid behind the wheel and popped the hood. The oil was close to the full line and looked clean. The battery connections were tight. I got back inside, left the door open in case I needed to jump out. The car started right away. She only had a quarter tank of gas, but that was enough to get to town. Why didn't she drive? I glanced around the car, found a few coins in her console, and tucked them into my pocket. I would try to call Jonny from a payphone after dark.

A photo was slipped into Beth's visor. I pulled it out. Amber and Beth. I recognized the picture from Amber's Facebook page. I traced the curve of her beautiful face with my finger.

Wolf put his front legs across my lap and whined as he stared into my eyes. I scratched his neck. He pawed at my chest. His whine grew more intense, shifting into a higher pitch.

I looked at him, then down the campground road. Beth had looked surprised when Mason drove in, so she hadn't expected him. He'd shown up early, when no one else was awake.

How did he know she would need a ride? The diner wouldn't even be open.

Amber had also worked for Mason. She also had an unreliable car—tire problems, in her case. If Mason had stopped to offer her a ride, she would have accepted. Anyone would have, me included. But Mason was one of the good guys. It couldn't be him. It just couldn't.

A year ago, I was in Vaughn's truck, hurtling down the highway to the lake. I tried to remember what he'd said about the killer. One sentence spun out of the darkness.

He's already looking for his next victim.

Going to town was risky. Vaughn would be on high alert. Or maybe it would be good timing. He wouldn't think the thief would go near the diner again so soon. I rode the trail fast, my eyes focused on every bend, each dip in the dirt. Jonny's bike was heavy. One wrong jump and I'd launch Wolf—and myself—into the air. There had to be a good reason Mason was giving Beth a ride. She was probably helping him buy cleaning supplies for the diner. Still, the thoughts kept coming. Why did he even have a camper on his truck? I'd never known him to go on trips, hunting or otherwise.

On the outskirts of town, I hid Jonny's dirt bike in a cluster of trees, then Wolf and I jogged to the forested area across the street from the diner. I pulled out my binoculars.

Mason was at the front counter. He was doing something to the cash register, probably trying to get it working again. I couldn't see Beth. Time ticked past. The sun rose higher, reaching through the trees and heating up the forest. Thirty minutes later Mason was sweeping the floor, making piles of broken glass, righting overturned chairs. Still no sign of Beth.

Another fifteen minutes passed. The anxiety in my stomach bloomed. She wouldn't be in the kitchen or the storage room. The diner was closed, and nothing was damaged in those rooms.

Mason's truck was in the alley, close to the back door. Like he wanted to keep an eye on it. I stared at the camper. The curtained windows. I wanted to look inside, but someone might see me. I watched the diner's front window for another twenty minutes.

This was wrong, every part of it. Beth was in trouble. Mason had done something to her. I waited for a few cars to pass, gave Wolf the signal to stay, then walked across the road with my shoulders hunched. I stuck to the alley wall, inched closer to the truck, and looked into the front.

Beige plaid fabric. Tidy. A tree-shaped sanitizer dangled from the rearview mirror. No purse or girl's clothing. No blood.

I climbed up onto the rear driver's-side tire, braced myself against the wall of the camper, and peered through the dirty window. The curtains blocked my view of most of the interior. I glimpsed floor and part of the bed area. I pressed my ear to the glass and softly said, "Beth?"

No response.

I climbed down, returned to the woods. If Beth wasn't in the camper, maybe she was trapped at Mason's place. He lived on a big piece of property miles past the lake, off a dirt road that led to the second peak of the mountain. It was within a half mile of where Dad had crashed his truck. Only a month before the accident, I was with Dad when he dropped off tools that Mason wanted to borrow. Mason met us at the bottom of the driveway. Now I wondered what he had been building. He'd given the tools back after the funeral.

I needed help. I swung the binoculars over to the truck stop. Three rigs parked close together. The drivers were standing around, coffees in hand.

"Stay," I told Wolf. He grumbled, then found a spot in the dirt, and dug a shallow hole. He flopped down with his head across his front legs. "I won't be long."

Following the forest around the bend, I waited until traffic had cleared before running across the road and hiding among the rigs. Making sure no one had seen me, I crept around the back of the trucks until I reached the phone booth. The men were focused on their conversation.

I dropped one of Beth's quarters into the phone. Thompson took a long time to answer. I was about to hang up when I finally heard his voice.

"Thompson."

I pressed my mouth close to the receiver, muffled it with my hand. "Beth, the new waitress at the diner, is missing. Mason did something to her car so he could give her a ride, but she didn't show up with him. He's taken her somewhere."

A pause, then, "How do you know this?"

"Doesn't matter. You have to search his camper."

"Last time you called, you said Vaughn was the killer."

"Vaughn is a pervert. I wasn't lying—but Mason's done something to Beth. Swear to God. Just check it out, please? Or I'm going to talk to him myself."

"Stay away from Mason. Let me deal with it."

"She could be *hurt*."

"Stay *away* from him, all right?" This time he hung up first.

I went back to my spot in the woods where Wolf was waiting. He got to his feet, tail wagging, and bumped his snout into my face when I crouched to ruffle the fur on his neck.

"Good boy."

Resting my back against a tree, I kept my binoculars aimed at the diner. The sun was high now and scorching hot, even in the shade. My hair was damp with sweat under my cap. I took it off, wiped at my forehead. Wolf and I drank my last bottle of water, sun-warmed.

A cop car turned onto the road and rolled to a stop in front of the diner. I held my breath, waiting to see who got out. Black hair. Tall, with narrow shoulders. He wore dark mirrored sunglasses. Thompson.

He *was* going to follow up on my report. I checked the cop car, making sure Vaughn wasn't with him, and then up the street. No sign of backup. I focused on Thompson again.

He was at the diner door now. He paused, looked right then left. I scooched lower. Did he sense I was nearby, watching?

After a moment, he slid his sunglasses up onto his head, and entered the diner.

CHAPTER 34

Beth

She woke to black. Woozy, semiconscious, delirious with pain. Her head was heavy and throbbing, a helmet of agony. Where was she? She was lying on a floor, contorted into an uncomfortable position. She tried to open her eyes, which were so swollen she could only squint.

Her tongue was thick as it pushed against the fabric balled in her mouth. She choked on saliva and blood. Her back was arched, her hands tied to her ankles behind her back.

Panting, she lay still, listened hard. Traffic sounds in the distance. Was she by a road? She felt movement, vibration around her. She was in a vehicle—the camper? She pushed forward and came up against a hard surface. She lifted her head and slammed into something. She gasped. Nausea and dizziness. Fresh air was coming from somewhere. She wiggled backward and hit another obstacle. She was in a box or a crate. Maybe a closet. She tried to scream but could only moan and grunt, then dissolved into sobs that made her gag, her body shuddering. She was alone, helpless. No one knew where she was. No one would notice she was missing.

She found the spot of air, pushed her nose against it. Coolness. Outside air? Wherever she was, he'd wanted her to breathe. He was saving her for something. Horror swelled. She thrashed, kicking and twisting until she was exhausted and panting and couldn't struggle anymore.

The movement stopped. A truck door opened. She could

hear it through the ventilation somehow. Did that mean someone could hear her scream? She waited, ready to fight in whatever way she could if he was coming to get her. She imagined him dragging her out. Imagined him cutting her with a knife, stabbing into her flesh. Her breath was too fast, she was going to hyperventilate. She tried to focus, tried to remember any self-defense lessons she'd taken.

Time passed. He hadn't come. Where had he left her? She stared into the darkness. She had to pee and finally, when she couldn't wait anymore, she had to go in her shorts. Maybe he'd hate that. Maybe he'd beat her for it. Maybe that would be a blessing. He wasn't going to let her live. She already knew that. Whatever he was planning, she wasn't going to walk away from it.

Beth thought of Amber, closed her eyes as tears leaked out, and prayed to her sister. Prayed for her to send help. She repeated it over and over, a mantra of desperation. She didn't know how long she had been trapped. She was sure she had a concussion. She drifted into a hazy sleep, then woke to the pounding in her skull. Beth had never experienced pain like this. Nothing had ever prepared her. She wanted to step outside of her broken body.

Voices. Coming closer. She lifted her head, tried to listen through the small air hole. The voices were deep-pitched. Men. She stilled. She needed a plan. If he opened up the box, she could pretend to be dead. She'd rear up and smash her head into his face.

"Vaughn looked over everything last night." Mason's voice. Distant, like he wasn't standing close to the camper.

"I just needed to confirm the point of entry." The other voice was familiar. Thompson? The point of entry. What did that mean? She couldn't think properly, the pressure in her head moved her thoughts around backward. Door. The diner door. The truck was in the alley.

"You're alone today?"

"Gave the cook the day off. I was going to let Beth work a few extra hours, but she didn't show up."

"You didn't go to the campsite?"

She rocked her body, but she couldn't stretch her legs and barely made a soft tap. She tried to moan loudly, straining her throat muscles, and bringing noises up from her chest.

"No. Came straight here. Why?"

"She's missing. Her tent, her car, everything is still there."

Wait. Someone had noticed she was gone. Someone *had* called the police.

"Did you check with Jonny? They had an argument the other day. She came back upset."

"Really?"

"Yeah." Mason was lying, sending Thompson in the wrong direction. Beth shifted her weight, pushing her body back and forth. If she could make the camper rock, Thompson would notice. Her shoulders were hitting the side, but the noise seemed muffled, like she was cocooned, her box padded. He'd made it soundproof.

"I'll give him a call. I'm sure she's fine, but we've got to follow up." Thompson seemed so calm, so unconcerned. How could he believe Mason's lies? She wanted to scream. "Noticed you parked in the alley today. You need help unloading something?"

Beth held her breath. *Please let Mason say something suspicious. Please let Thompson insist on checking the camper.*

"It was just a few tools, already got them inside. Thanks, though."

Silence for a moment, then Thompson said, "Your eye okay? It looks sore."

"Got some debris in it when I was sweeping." Mason cleared his throat. "If you don't mind, I really need to get back . . ."

"Sure. Let me know if you hear from Beth."

"Of course. I'm worried about her too."

Thompson was leaving. *No, no, no.* Beth stretched her body and strained at the ropes, her shoulder muscles tearing, the skin on her wrists burning, but she had to get Thompson's attention. She choked on her saliva, retching and gagging, her eyes streaming. For a paralyzing moment she thought that was it for her. She was going to suffocate, alone in a box, but she finally got some air through her nose and caught her breath. Just in time to hear footsteps moving away.

Beth woke with her head crammed into a corner. She'd fallen into an exhausted sleep. Her mind had shut down with shock. Now the camper was moving. She didn't know how long they'd been on the road. Hours? Seconds? Every mile brought her closer to her death.

She thought of the police showing up at her parents' door to tell them they'd lost their daughter. They'd be alone now, forever.

Mason. All this time it was Mason. She'd worked with him, talked with him. Breathed the same air. Laughed and smiled. She'd been so grateful when he gave her a job. Hailey had never guessed the real killer. No one had, and he was *there* the entire time. Front and center.

The truck stopped. The distant slam of the door. Now a closer noise, a lock clicking open. The camper door. Footsteps, scraping sounds above her. She attempted to roll onto her side so she could hit him in the face with her forehead, but the top was opening, and she was blinded by brightness. Something came into view, blocking the light. She blinked. Mason's eyes, his beard hovering right above her, then his fist coming down.

She woke on a concrete floor. Hands moved her roughly.

Her arms flopped. She was untied, but her muscles felt numb, tingly. She'd lost circulation. She was still gagged, and her skin was cold. Then the sudden realization. She was naked. She rolled onto her knees, and something hard came crashing down on her back. She fell flat, her face scraping against the concrete. Hands picked her up, flipped her over. She was looking up at Mason.

He towered over her with a metal rod in his hand. A camera hung around his neck.

"You're going to pose for me."

Beth shook her head, her palms out in a plea. She begged him with her eyes.

"You're the first one I've had time with." He sounded so pleased, sharing this news like she was supposed to be honored. "The others happened too fast. I had to take their photos after they were dead. Then I built the cooler in the camper. My lucky day when you walked into the diner." She stared at his face, his mouth moving, saying these angry, terrifying words. This couldn't be the end of her life. She was only twenty-one. She wasn't supposed to die like her sister. She was supposed to avenge her. She was supposed to fix her family.

Mason tucked the rod under his arm, raised the camera, and aimed it at her. He pressed the shutter. She blocked her face with one hand, tried to curl her body up and cover herself with the other.

"That's good," he said. "I like that."

CHAPTER 35

Hailey

Thompson chatted briefly with Mason. Then he walked away. I watched in disbelief. Should I go to Mason's place, or stay here? I paced along the edge of the woods, indecisive. Wolf watched me. Around noon, I caught motion behind the diner's windows. The CLOSED sign moved like Mason was checking it. Nothing for a few minutes, then the side door opened. He was getting into his truck. He had waited a long time and I wondered at his patience. The idea that he might dump her body turned my legs to liquid, but I couldn't follow him on the highway. My indecision melted away. I had to get to his house and hope she was still alive.

I rode the bike recklessly, Wolf balanced with me, taking turn after turn. As I neared Mason's property, I passed the spot where Dad had crashed. The bark on the trees was still scraped from when his truck had launched into the air. I'd never understood why he was going so fast. I'd never known him to speed. He didn't normally even take that route up to the mountain. Now I wondered if Dad might've stopped at Mason's to retrieve his tools and seen something. Something bad. I swallowed hard.

After the next bend, I cut across the road, jumped a ditch, and made the bike climb a hill so steep I had to use my feet to balance. The tires spun at the top, churning up dirt. Wolf leaned against my back. We coasted down the other side into a hollow and parked beside the creek.

I told Wolf to guard the dirt bike, gave him the last bone, and hiked up the hill as fast as I could in the direction of Mason's house. I was still wearing my backpack, and I had gloves on. I wasn't leaving fingerprints behind. One knife was in my ankle sheath, and the other on my hip. I didn't know what kind of weapons Mason might have. I wished more than anything that I had my gun, but I'd used all my ammo when I was trying to ambush Vaughn, and I couldn't take the time to get more.

Mason's house sat in a small clearing surrounded by trees. I surveyed it from the edge of the forest. Small, rustic, wood siding. No signs of life. Behind the house, at the end of a second driveway, there was a large metal building. A garage. Mason's truck was parked in front. He'd backed it in like he had to unload something from the camper. My stomach did an ugly flip.

I used my binoculars to check the house. One security camera by the front door. I'd have to avoid it. I moved from tree to tree until I'd reached the garage. The engine on the truck was still ticking.

The building was old, with rusted sheet metal on the sides, a half-moon-shaped roof, and a foot of concrete foundation aboveground. I pressed my ear to the metal side and heard muffled sounds. Scraping, then a clinking sound. Chains? I pressed my hands to my eyes and rocked back on my heels.

What was I going to do? I wished Jonny was here. I wished I had my dad with me.

I crept around to the front of the building. The door was cracked open a sliver. A stone had lodged under the bottom. Silence. The clinking sound had stopped. I crouched low and stayed to the left of the door so that if he pushed it open, I would be behind it.

I inched closer, peered through the opening. My knees buckled. Beth stood naked on a stool. A noose hung around her neck. Her head drooped and her blond hair was a messy veil over the side of her face. Some of the strands were streaked with blood. Her hands and feet were free, but there were red marks around her ankles. Ropes were on the floor.

She was alive. She was still alive.

The noose was tied to a chain dangling from a roof beam. He was standing to the side of her with a camera. He grabbed her under the chin with his free hand. Her eyes were wide, and she was gagged, lips pulled back. Her body twitched and jerked as she shivered.

I twisted my finger and gently pulled the door. Mason was still focused on Beth. If she saw me, she might cry out. Could I hide somewhere? There were workbenches on either side, toolboxes, crates and barrels. At the back of the garage I spotted his Harley-Davidson. I pulled the door open a little more—testing whether the hinges would squeak—and slipped through. My shirt snagged. I reached down, fiddled with the fabric. If he turned, he would see me.

Mason was pacing around Beth, shifting his stance each time he took a photo, and holding the camera in one hand like this was some sort of sick fashion shoot. Long red marks lined her ribs, arms, and legs. I'd seen those marks before. On Amber. Then I saw the metal rod on the floor by his feet. He'd beaten Beth before I got here. He was going to beat her again.

My shirt finally tore free and I crawled over the rough concrete to a darkened corner, where I fit behind a barrel. I slipped my hand down and slowly removed my knife from my belt.

Mason froze, like an animal in the forest, and twisted his body. I held my breath. He was walking toward the door now. I tucked my head, hunched my shoulders, and made myself small.

He opened the door and looked around. I prayed that Wolf hadn't followed me, prayed that I hadn't left any footprints. After a long moment, he shut the door tight.

I watched him as his gaze skimmed around the room, then he focused on Beth. She was moaning, trying to stand straight. She lost her balance and fell off the stool. Now she was choking, legs kicking out, her hands clawing at the rope around her neck. Mason grabbed her and set her feet on the stool. She swung her fist, trying to punch him, but he easily stepped back.

"Do that again and I'll let you die." Now I realized his plan. She was forced to endure the suffering or hang herself. Beth stood with her chest heaving and tears running down her face. I wanted to signal to her to stay calm, that I was going to save her, but I couldn't risk it.

Mason picked up the metal rod, and still holding the camera, he began walking around her. He slapped the rod against her butt, and she cried out, jerking to the side and nearly falling.

I instinctively reached out to help her, my hand grasping at air, then I snatched it back. I wasn't fast enough, though, and Beth noticed, her eyes staring blindly at the corner. She groaned. I held my finger to my mouth. She blinked slowly.

Mason hit her again with the rod across her butt and she leapt forward, only stopping herself with one toe before she swung forward. Mason lifted the camera and took some photos of the marks he'd left on her skin. He got closer, zooming in on the red pattern.

I couldn't just sit here and watch. He could hit her hard enough to kill her. She might get knocked off the stool and choke. But I couldn't throw the knife from a seated position. I had to stand, and I had one shot at it—if I missed, Beth and I might both be killed.

Mason hit her again. The fleshy smack echoed in the garage. Beth's eyes were squeezed tight with pain, but then she opened them. Some emotion I couldn't fathom came over her face. Dark and determined.

Beth's legs tensed, and when Mason came around the front,

she kicked out. He turned at the last moment and her foot missed, sending her body spinning off the stool. She was moving too fast to put her foot back down this time, and her neck jerked as she spun helplessly.

I didn't think. I just moved. Rising to my feet, I leaned back, and, focused on Mason's broad back, threw the knife with all my strength. At the last moment, he moved, dancing around her spinning body. The knife struck his shoulder.

He roared, dropping his camera and the metal rod.

Beth's face was turning red. Blood-red. She was choking.

Mason reached behind his head and yanked out the knife. He whirled around and saw me, his mouth gaping in the middle of his messy beard. His surprise was already turning to rage.

He lunged toward me, my knife gripped in his hand. I didn't have time to pull my other one out from my ankle sheath. I ran straight at him, dropped, and kicked his legs. He crashed onto his back. Beth was still spinning. I reached out and booted the stool to slide beneath her feet. Mason was rising. In one motion, I snatched up the metal rod from the floor, leapt into a standing position, and struck him with all my power across his head. The rod bounced back from the impact, sent vibrations up my arm.

He fell to his knees, weaving, but still conscious. "Haywire," he croaked. "Look at you, alive and kicking." He laughed, a maniacal sound that sent shivers down my spine.

I rushed at him with the rod. He swung up and the knife missed my face, but his arm hit me in the chin. The force knocked me down. The metal rod rolled from my hands and I slid into Beth's stool. She was back in the air, jerking, making a retching sound. I grappled with the stool.

Mason was reaching for me, holding my knife out like a dagger. I turned onto my back and booted him hard in the nose, felt the cartilage give under my heel, then scrambled to help Beth. Her toes landed on the stool. I couldn't beat Mason in a knife fight—his reach was longer than mine. I felt for items on the workbench. What could I use for a weapon?

"I called the cops," I panted. "They'll be here any second."

He swiped the blood from his broken nose. No laughing this time. His eyes were on me, measuring. I reached for a long section of chain he had on the bench and swung wide, wrapping it around his wrist. I yanked him toward me. My knife slipped out of his hand and skittered to the far end of the building. I bent over and pulled my other one from the ankle sheath, held it in front of me, ready to attack. But Mason wasn't coming after me, he was turning toward Beth.

He brought his foot back to kick the stool. Beth swung her body and locked her knees around his head, pushing herself up to keep pressure off her neck and squeezing him hard. He punched at her legs.

I plunged my knife into his back and wrenched it out.

Mason twisted around. I slashed across his neck, cutting his jugular in one long gash. He made a choking sound, a frothy red bubble at his lips as he clutched his throat. Blood spurted through his hands in a dark stream. He collapsed to his knees, then fell sideways, and sprawled out with his eyes wide and shocked. One last gurgle leaked from his body.

Beth's feet had landed back on the stool. She was staring at Mason and sobbing through the gag. I pushed one of the barrels closer and sawed at the noose. The fibers were thick, but finally the rope snapped. I wasn't strong enough to hold her, but I tried to use my body to slow her fall. She toppled forward and hit the cement with a heavy thump. She didn't move.

I jumped off the barrel and removed the gag, wet with her saliva and blood. I patted my fingers against her bruised cheeks. "Hey, wake up." Her eyes fluttered open and she took a heaving gasp, then another, choking and wheezing. "Easy, slow breaths."

She clutched at my wrist, panicked as she looked around. "Where is he?" Her voice was raspy and sore-sounding, but she could talk. That was good news.

"Gone. He's dead." She dropped her head back, eyes rolling. "Don't pass out again, please. Beth? Beth?" I touched her neck, felt for her pulse. She took a gulping breath. Her lungs and heart were trying to catch up. Her skin was so red and bruised. What if her throat swelled shut? I had to get help. Mason would have a phone inside. I got onto my knees. Her eyes opened.

"Don't go," she whispered.

"I'm going to call 911 from his house. I'll pretend to be you."

"It has to be my voice." She winced as her throat contracted. "They'll listen to the recording. Help me walk."

I thought for a moment. Could I carry her? She wasn't much bigger than me, but she'd been hurt. She should stay still. She reached out and pinched my calf. I gasped.

"Do it, Hailey."

"Fine. But if you pass out, it's not my fault." I slid my arm under her neck and gently lifted her to a sitting position. Her body weaved, her eyelids flickered, but she held on and nodded when she was ready for the next step. I got to my feet, dragging her up with me. She staggered, and I gripped her around the waist, then we slowly limped to the house.

We made the last few wobbly steps and I opened Mason's door, scared for a moment that he might have rigged a trap or bomb of some type, but nothing happened. The inside of the house was dark, with wood paneling and brown linoleum.

In the kitchen, I let Beth slide to the floor, pulled a bag of peas out of the freezer, wrapped them in a towel, and held the cold pack to her neck. "You kicked ass in there. That leg move? It was like watching WWE."

"Are you being nice to me? Have I died?" she whispered.

"Shut up or I'll gag you again."

She snorted, but I knew she was grateful for the dumb joke. I didn't know how else to deal with everything that had just happened. Mason's bleeding body in the garage. Beth naked in front of me. I pulled a blanket from the couch and wrapped it around her. "It's going to be okay," I said, with a serious voice this time as I looked her in the eye. "It's over."

She rested her head on her knees and started to cry. I rubbed her back. I couldn't make her feel better. She needed help beyond me.

"You have to get to the hospital. I'm going to find the phone."

She lifted her face. "You can't let Vaughn see you."

"I don't plan on it. I'm going to remove the security cameras." I would have to take Mason's computer or whatever he had been downloading the recording onto, which was stealing evidence, but Beth didn't seem to think about that part, and I didn't want to bring it up.

I found Mason's landline on the coffee table in his living room. I glanced down the hall. The bedrooms must be back there. Maybe an office.

Beth wasn't looking good, her face pale in the places that weren't bruised purple and bloody. I pressed the numbers and held the phone to her ear. She spoke in her raspy, damaged voice to the operator. "Help, I need help."

I gnawed at my fingernails and looked out the window as she finished telling them as much as she could. She nodded at me when she was done.

"He has knife wounds in his back. You'll have to explain everything." I wiped my knife with a paper towel, removing any fingerprints I'd left in the past.

I pressed her fingers around the knife. "They'll want this."

"I'll say he cut me down. We fought. I got the knife away from him."

"They're not stupid."

"They'll be distracted. I'm the victim, not a suspect."

"Vaughn will be looking for proof that I was one of Mason's victims."

"I'll say he talked about you."

"Yeah, okay, that's good." We didn't have much time. I got to my feet and ran down the hall. Three rooms. One looked like storage with cardboard boxes, one was a spare bedroom with a small bed, and the last one was an office of sorts with a filing cabinet and a desk. On top of the desk I found an iPad. I searched around but I couldn't find a computer. I'd never seen him with a laptop at the diner. I had to hope the iPad was all he used for recording security video.

Back in the living room, I opened the front door. No sirens yet. I stood on a crate on the porch and ripped the security camera off the wall. It left a few small holes, but the cops wouldn't know for sure what had been there.

Beth was slumped in that ugly blanket. I crouched in front of her.

"I need his cell phone. Did you see him with it?"

"I can't remember."

"I'll check the garage before I leave." I walked to the door and looked back at her. "You'll be okay. The ambulance will be here soon."

"I've never seen where Amber died. The ditch."

"Okay . . ." I stared at her, one hand still on the door handle. She was mumbling, and I worried that she was going into worse shock. Some sort of concussion side effect.

"I know there's a cross," she said. "But I couldn't go there. Why do people do that? She was dumped there like a piece of garbage." She was holding my gaze like she wanted me to make sense of it all, but I didn't know what to say. I wasn't good at those sorts of conversations.

"I think it helps them."

"Helps?" She choked a bitter laugh. "What could it help?"

"They want her to know she isn't forgotten."

Her eyes filled with fresh tears and she swallowed, then winced. "They didn't even know her."

I bowed my head, nodded because it didn't matter what I said. She was exhausted, in pain, and there was nothing that was going to fix those wounds. Sirens trilled in the distance.

"I have to go."

She looked at up at me. "Be careful."

"Of what? We killed the big bad wolf." I made a face at her, then dashed out the door and sprinted toward the garage. I found Mason's cell phone in his back pocket. His body was cooling, his eyes turned blindly to the side, the blood a wide black pool. I thought of Amber.

I looked down at him. "I hope you rot in hell."

The sirens grew louder as I jogged through the woods. Soon red and blue lights were flashing through the trees. Wolf jumped all over me, frantic with his kisses and warbles of relief.

"Hang on. We're going to go fast." I hopped onto the bike, and Wolf landed in his crate. We were on the logging road in under a minute. I hoped the sirens would drown out the noise of my bike. I skidded around a corner near where my dad had crashed, and caught my breath, but then an invisible hand righted my wheel. I was straight and heading out of the curve. I'd made it.

CHAPTER 36

Beth

Hailey was gone. Her hiking boots had stepped out of sight, the door closed behind her, and now Beth was alone. In Mason's house. She pulled the blanket tighter around her shoulders. She didn't want strangers to see her naked, beaten body. She retched onto the floor, crying as bitter liquid slid up her damaged throat.

She had to think, had to remember not to slip and reveal anything about Hailey. Hot tears stung the cuts on her face. Hailey had saved her. She hoped she got away.

The sirens were closer. Right outside now. They sounded like a long scream that went on and on. She pressed the palms of her hands to her ears, noticed more blood, her raw wrists.

Her body was a live wire of sensation. Her skin felt open to the air. She'd pretended to Hailey that she was okay, that she was managing the pain. Hailey wouldn't have left her alone otherwise. Then she would've been caught. Maybe it shouldn't matter, now that Mason was dead. But it felt like it mattered even more, like Hailey was the last reason to hang on to this world.

One of the sirens stopped in front of the house with a sudden *whoop*. Lights reflected on the wall. The door burst open. Vaughn appeared with his gun drawn. "Police!"

Beth shrank against the cupboard, tried to lift her sore hands. "I'm alone."

Vaughn was looking around, gun drawn, his legs braced. "Where is he?"

"Dead," she rasped. "In the garage." He moved farther into the house, speaking into his radio. She didn't understand the codes, the fast words. She thought he was going to check on her, provide first aid, but instead he was walking quickly down the hall toward the back of the house. She rested her head against the cupboard, confused and dizzy with the pain. More sirens were outside, but Vaughn was still in the other rooms. Noises at the door. Paramedics.

A man and a woman in uniform. They knelt beside her. Opened their medical kits. Speaking to her gently, they checked her pulse. She imagined it leaping in jagged lines. She watched the hall. Vaughn's big shape was coming back now. His gaze skimmed over her. He conferred with another officer who'd come through the door.

The paramedics lowered her and put a mask over her face. She tried to breathe deeply, but her throat was closing, and she clawed at the mask. The female paramedic murmured soft words, telling her everything was going to be okay. She closed her eyes. More police. More voices. Thompson was here, kneeling by her side and talking to the paramedics. He held her hand.

Thompson helped them load her into the ambulance. They gave her something in an IV and the loud pain became a hum. Equipment swayed as they took the corners fast, a paramedic speaking into the radio. Words she didn't understand. They rushed her into emergency, pushed her through swinging doors where doctors and nurses clustered around and called out instructions. She was sent for a scan, stitched up, bandaged, and soothed. She floated through it all. At some point she was wheeled into a room and she must have fallen asleep, because when she woke up, Vaughn was sitting in the chair beside her bed while a nurse checked her vitals.

The nurse looked at Vaughn. "Don't tire her out. She needs to rest her throat." She squeezed Beth's hand. "Hit the call button if you need me." Beth wanted to stop her, wanted to beg her to stay, but she was out the door with a swish of her scrubs.

"You're a brave young woman," Vaughn said. "Looks like you had a hell of a fight."

She squeezed her eyes tight. She was hanging, spinning around and around. Mason was coming at her with that metal rod. "I don't want to talk." She never wanted to think about it again. She was going to ask the nurse for more drugs. She would live the rest of her life high.

"I just have a few questions."

"Why isn't Thompson here?" Her body felt so light, like she was drifting away from herself. The nurse. She must have given her more pain medication.

"Where's Mason's cell phone?"

"Don't know. Didn't see it."

"Did he talk about any of the other victims?" Vaughn sounded distant, but he was sitting so close. How did he make his voice move around the room?

"Amber." She could barely get her name out, like every damaged tissue in her throat had swelled at once, locking her sister's name into her body, holding her close.

"Anyone else?"

She had a plan. She had to remember. "Hailey. He said he killed her."

"Did he say what he did with her body?"

She shook her head. He let his breath out in a sigh, then rested his hand on top of hers. She hated the warm weight of it. She wanted to slide her hand away, but it was pinned down.

"I hope we have more answers after we finish the search of his property. Did you look into any of the other rooms? After you made it from the garage to the house?"

She shook her head again. Her eyelids were so heavy. *Don't say anything else. He'll trick you. Tricky, tricky.* She pulled her hand away, fumbled for the call switch. "I need water."

"One more question. Why did he cut you down without securing your wrists and feet?"

"I was pretending. To be unconscious."

"You slit his throat. Sliced his jugular. He bled out in seconds. That takes a lot of strength." He was staring at her, trying to shock, looking for the lie.

She pressed at the call switch, but her strength was fading. It took two times for her to find the right spot. To make it buzz. He didn't help. "Go away. I'm tired."

"I'm going." He stood and walked toward the end of the bed. Then he rested his hand on her ankle, where Mason had tied her up, and squeezed the bandages. She gasped, and the sudden spasm of pain in her throat forced her into choking coughs. "We'll talk another time."

He walked out as the nurse came in.

Light shone through her eyelids, a soft glow, then the scent of antiseptic, plastic, and sickness. Beeping noises and movements. A warm hand skimmed across her knuckles and held her fingers. She lifted her eyelids, blinked a few times to clear away the dancing white lights. Her mom's face came into view, blond bob untidy, some strands tucked behind her ear, some falling forward onto her face. The lines around her mouth were deep, her blue eyes watery.

"Beth." She cupped her face. "Thank God."

Beth lifted her hand to the bandages at her throat, wincing as the IV tugged in her arm. Her tongue felt thick and there was a strange ringing in her ear. Hospital. She was in the hospital. Vaughn had been in her room. She remembered crying.

Doctors and nurses touching her. How many days had it been? One? Two? Night blurred into day. She'd woken up over and over again.

"Don't move." Her mom adjusted the pillow. "Are you thirsty?" Beth nodded, and her mom lifted the straw to her mouth. She held the cup with her other hand. It was shaking slightly. Beth stared, fascinated by the soft tremor. Butterfly wings. The pain-killers ran through her body and gave her a floaty feeling. Later there would be a headache and nausea. But for now it was good.

"I told them not to call you." The words tumbled out of Beth's dry mouth, hung suspended in the air. Her mom flinched and took a few steps closer to her dad at the end of the bed. So tall. Like an oak tree. Gallant and strong. Except today he just looked tired.

"Sorry." Beth grabbed at her thoughts, sandwiched them to-gether. "I didn't want to scare you. I wanted to tell you myself."

"Constable Thompson called." Her mother stared at Beth's IV as though she were worried eye contact might set her off. Or maybe it was just painful to look at her face. Beth hadn't seen the bruises yet, but her eyes and lips felt puffy, her cheek-bones ached, and it hurt to speak. Even her teeth throbbed. Beth eased up on the pillow so she could sit straight.

Her mom lifted her gaze. "We don't understand why you were here. The internship . . ."

"I lied, Mom. I dropped out of school. I was failing all my classes."

Her mom's mouth parted. Her dad blinked, then blinked again.

"You lied?" Her voice was hushed. The first stabs of guilt were stirring in Beth's stomach, but she had pharmaceutical courage running through her veins.

"We don't talk. We never talk about anything important."

"You don't *tell* us anything." Her dad still looked stunned. One hand over his heart.

"You don't *ask*."

"We were giving you space."

"Space? For what? I couldn't go to class. I couldn't do anything. I thought I was going to lose my mind."

"My God." Tears poured down her mother's face in long rivulets, the mascara now inky streaks that bowed around her mouth. Beth watched, startled.

"God has nothing to do with it. I don't understand how you can go to church after what happened to Amber. Why didn't God protect her, Mom? That's the real lie. There's no heaven. No mercy or angels. She's just a bunch of bones. She's *gone*."

Her mom's chest was rising and falling in quick gasps, but she was still holding her emotions in tight, her arms wrapped around her body. Beth wanted to shake her loose.

Her dad moved closer. "Beth, you've always been so independent, pushing us away, wanting to do things on your own. We love you, honey. We've always loved you. If you don't want to go to university anymore, we will deal with it. You can move back home."

"You're not angry?"

Her mom pulled tissues out of her pocket and blew her nose. "I am *furious* with you for coming to this awful town. I hate that you lied to us. I hate that you have been living at a campsite. You risked your life, and for what? Were you trying to punish us? You don't think we suffered enough?" Beth had never heard her mother speak with so much force. Her teeth were gritted, and her neck muscles corded. Mad Madeline was leaking through her mother's carefully constructed facade.

"I couldn't do it anymore. I couldn't pretend."

"Pretend *what*?"

"That I was perfect. You always wanted everything to look so good. Our house had to be tidy. We had to wear those little dresses to church. We had to volunteer, and handwrite thank-you notes, and sing in the choir. You took our report cards to church and showed everyone."

"I was proud of you!"

"Stop it, Beth. Stop all of this." Her dad let out a big sigh, ran his hand through his thick hair, almost fully gray now. "Maybe we should have been open about a few more things, but we go to church because it helps. Believing is a choice, Beth. You fault us for trying to find peace?"

"I just don't understand how you *can*."

"We wake up each day missing her. We go over everything we could have done differently. We count the years until our own deaths when we will see her again. We go through photo albums, and we sit in her room. We cry at night. Is that what you need to hear?"

"Yes," she whispered. "I need to hear all of that."

"We can only step through a door if you open it." Memories tangled with feelings and Beth didn't know what was true anymore. Had she shut them out? Was she the one who closed people off?

"I should've tried harder with Amber," her mom said. "But she was always skipping school and running off with her friends. I was tired of fighting."

"You should have brought her home."

"She never returned our messages. We thought that she needed a couple of months to get it out of her system and then she'd see how hard it was on her own." Her mom's voice cracked.

Amber could have missed that party. She could have left with someone else at the lake. How many moments could her death have been avoided? There were a thousand scenarios.

"I can't talk anymore." Beth couldn't stop the tears from filling her eyes, the horrible, sickening realization that Mason's death had fixed nothing. The pain was still the same.

"The doctors say you will be in the hospital for a few days," her dad said, "but after that, you still need to be watched closely. We'll bring you back to Vancouver with us."

"I'm not ready. I have a campsite, and things to deal with."

"We can pack your site."

"I said I'm not *ready*. Things aren't magically fixed now that Mason is dead. I've made a mess of my life. I don't want to be a lawyer anymore. I don't know what I want." Pressure was building in the room, coming loud and fast like a thousand voices all talking at once.

Leaving Cold Creek meant leaving Amber behind. It meant *living*. Beth wouldn't see Jonny or Hailey again. She'd have to deal with things. She'd have to get a job and a future.

"You don't have to decide today. We'll stay in town."

Beth's vision blurred with fatigue as she looked up at the ceiling. She let her eyelids drift closed. Sleepiness settled over her like a weighted blanket.

"The car broke down," she slurred to her dad, forcing her eyelids open so she could look at him. A nurse had come into the room. She was fussing with the bag, adding something to the IV. Warmth enveloped Beth's hand. Her dad's large palm closing over her fingers, a cocoon.

"I'll have someone look at it."

"Get some rest." Her mom's voice. Soft, but firm, like when she used to tuck her in at night. She'd always turn off the light, even though Beth hated the dark and would lie stiff under her blanket until Amber tiptoed into her room and turned the light back on. For a moment she could see her sister's face hovering over the bed, eyes dark and serious. She was saying something about Hailey. Beth tried to speak, to ask if she was okay, but she couldn't open her mouth. The last image that floated through her mind was Hailey running through the woods.

CHAPTER 37

Beth

Thompson arrived the next day with a quick knock on the door to alert her before he strode in, dressed in a navy suit, hair neat. "How are you feeling?" He sat in the chair near the window.

"Like a psychopath tried to kill me." Beth's throat felt better with the swelling going down, but she was still getting headaches and blurred vision. She wiggled upright.

"Well, I'm glad he didn't succeed. Are you okay? I don't just mean all this." He pointed to her bandages and the IV. "I mean in here." He tapped his head.

He was the first person to ask her that, and the sudden rush of tears to her eyes was embarrassing. Especially because his niceness was probably a trick so she would trust him.

"I haven't been able to process it all."

"There are some great counselors you can speak to through victim services."

"What about victim rights? I didn't appreciate Vaughn interrogating me."

"Sergeant Vaughn?"

"Is there some other Vaughn?" Then she realized, from his confused expression, that he hadn't known Vaughn had come to the hospital. "Guess your communication isn't so good."

"He probably hasn't had a chance to brief me yet."

"Sure." She gave him a look that made it clear what she thought of his justification.

"I'd like to ask you some questions."

"What's the point of this? Mason's dead."

"We still have unsolved cases."

"Did you find Amber's bracelet?"

"Not yet. But we haven't finished searching Mason's property."

They'd be looking for graves and bones. Personal belongings. Amber's purse had never been found. Beth wondered what he'd done with hers. In the end, her gun hadn't helped her. She tugged the blanket tighter around her body. "Did Vaughn find anything in the bedrooms?"

"What do you mean?"

"Before you got there, he searched the house." She thought about how Vaughn had gone straight down the hall. Like he knew where to go. He'd asked those strange questions too, about whether she'd gone into the other rooms. Maybe she was remembering wrong.

"How long was he there alone?"

"I don't know. It's all hazy. He burst in and didn't even stop to see if I was okay. Then he was sitting there when I woke up." She pointed at the chair. "He was saying horrible things, asking about how I killed Mason, and about my sister. I don't want to talk to him again."

"You don't have to. But I'm a good listener. Can you take me through everything?"

This time she had better answers prepared.

Beth blinked a few times, waking from a nap, and then let her eyelids drift closed again. She'd go back to sleep where no memories could chase her down. A noise, someone in the room on her right side. She jerked her eyes open, turned to look. Jonny standing by her window, his face pensive as he gazed out at the mountains. The purple bruises on his jaw had turned a soft yellow. She cleared her throat and his head snapped around. They met eyes, then his gaze drifted from the bandages around her throat to the cuts on her arms, then back up to her puffy eyes and lips. The nurses had washed the blood out of her hair, but the stitches were an ugly reminder.

"How did you get past the cops?"

"Thompson let me through. A lot of reporters are hanging around."

"Guess I'm famous. Yay, me." She pumped a fist in the air and regretted it when the IV tugged at her skin. She dropped her hand back down.

"You didn't eat breakfast."

Hadn't she? What time was it? She glanced at her breakfast tray. The oatmeal had congealed, the brown sugar a murky puddle. It looked like she had managed a few sips of coffee, but she only remembered the exhaustion, the way her body sank backward into the pillow.

"You were right about the food. A burnt hot dog would be better."

"I should've brought you something."

"I'm just happy to see you."

Their eyes held for a moment, then he moved to sit in the chair beside her bed, sliding it closer. He entwined his fingers with hers and rested his forehead against her arm. "When I heard what happened . . ." His lips grazed her skin as he spoke, a warm sensation that traveled up her body. "If you hadn't killed him, I'd have hunted him down myself."

She tensed, and he must have felt the motion, because he lifted his head and met her eyes, his blue ones almost black in the hospital lighting. "I'm sorry. We don't have to talk about it."

She glanced at the door, then whispered, "Hailey," and his mouth parted. She pressed her fingers to his soft lips so that he wouldn't ask questions. "She saved my life." She didn't know who might be in the hall. She didn't need a doctor or a gossipy nurse overhearing.

"She okay?"

"Think so. I made her leave before the cops came." Beth reached up and touched the bandage around her throat. "When I get out, I'll tell you more."

"Aren't you going back to Vancouver?"

"Do you *want* me to leave?"

"I don't want you caught up in all the lies. This vendetta that Vaughn has against me. He's pulled my brothers over, and my dad," Jonny said. "He's looking for anything."

That wasn't really an answer. She stared at him, and he flushed, dropped his gaze to their clasped hands.

"Let me get this straight," she said. "You're worried that if we started dating, he might give me a speeding ticket?"

"I don't know *what* he'll do. That's the point."

"You don't need an excuse to tell me that you aren't interested in a relationship, Jonny."

"That's bullshit—it's not about that."

"I'm not going to talk you into something you obviously don't want." She tried to tug her hand loose, but he wasn't letting go. "Don't worry. We had our fun. I get it."

"You *don't* get it. You're free. You can leave this town, but I can't."

"What if I don't want to be free?"

"You have a big life waiting for you. I don't want to be the guy you regret later."

"I think I already do." He looked stunned, his body giving a slight jolt, but then he nodded, once, twice, as though reminding himself that was what he'd wanted. Her anger.

A nurse appeared at the door. "Everything okay?"

"Yes, he's leaving." She gave her hand another tug, and Jonny finally let go. "I'm not feeling well." She turned her head into the pillow. Jonny murmured his goodbye. She listened to his steps fade out of the room.

The nurse adjusted her IV. "I didn't know you and Jonny Miller were together."

"We're not." She scratched at the bandage on her wrist. She wasn't going to cry. Not in front of this woman who would tell everyone. "Can you give me more painkillers?"

"You're on quite a bit—"

"Please. It really hurts."

"Okay." Her voice softened, and she patted Beth's hand. "I'll see if I can get you something."

It had been two weeks. The bruises had mostly healed, the stitches had been removed. The flashbacks and nightmares continued to be a problem, which had bumped her Xanax use up to an alarming amount. She'd need a refill soon.

She chewed another one as she sat in her car, parked down a narrow logging road. Her backpack was filled with supplies, water, and a map. She'd brought orange tape to mark the trail.

Her cell felt warm in her hand. She'd lied to her mom again. They'd agreed to meet back at the motel in a couple of hours. They thought she was at the doctor's, and considering her recent vow of honesty, they'd be extremely pissed that she was about to search for Hailey. It was important, though. She was going to help her get away from Vaughn once and for all.

Beth's parents had offered her money to get settled again. She'd share it with Hailey. They'd find a place in Vancouver that accepted dogs. They could both start over.

She headed down the trail. It felt good to get some fresh air and sun. She hadn't had much activity since getting out of the hospital, but she pushed herself along. Thompson had been there almost every day. She claimed shock to get her out of explaining some of the gaps.

They'd found Amber's bracelet at Mason's house. She'd asked for it, and was told someday, once they were finished their testing. The police were checking his DNA against other cold cases and still digging up his property. Thompson said it could take a while.

A trail of trees decorated with orange tape behind her, Beth followed the bank of the river until the cliffs eliminated the shoreline. She must be close to the bluffs. She had to go deeper into the forest. Her footsteps were muffled by a blanket of fir needles and moss. A bird gave a piercing cry, and she looked up, recognized a cedar tree where a branch jutted out in a horseshoe shape. She'd seen it before, lying on her back at the bottom of the pit and staring up at the sky.

She searched the ground for indentations. There, in the shadows of a large tree. It was subtle, the very slightest disturbance on the forest floor. She bent over, brushed the leaves away, and scraped at the dirt until she found the branches woven together under the surface. The pit.

Now she had to find the cabin. She'd only been walking a few minutes when she entered a small glade, the forest floor covered with ferns and salal bushes. Her boot caught on something. She froze, looked down. Was that . . . twine? She followed the length of it with her eyes. Some sort of trip wire? She eased her foot away. She wasn't going an inch farther. She didn't know what else Hailey had set up. Land mines? Anything was possible with that girl.

Beth took off her backpack and drank some water, then she whistled a few times, varying the tone and length. No answer except for birds. Time to step things up.

"Help!" she yelled. "Help! Wolf! Come here, boy!" She kept calling, turning in circles, hands around her mouth to make her voice carry. Something rushed through the bushes. She leaned over and grabbed a stick. A shaggy black body bounded out from behind two trees with excited yelps. He danced around her legs, panting in an openmouthed smile. She dropped the stick.

"Hey, there, Wolf. Want a cookie?" She offered him a Milk-Bone from her pocket, which he took gently, set on the ground, sniffing it and then crunching it loudly between his white teeth.

Hailey appeared through the trees, a rifle at her hip. She was frowning, her eyes concerned. She looked Beth up and down. "You hurt? You were calling for help."

"I didn't want to yell your name."

"Why are you here?"

"To make sure you're okay." Wolf leaned against Beth's leg. She scratched his neck.

"You hiked up the mountain injured?" Hailey was still frowning. "What if you'd fallen again? You could've asked Jonny."

"I'm better—and Jonny and I aren't talking."

Hailey lowered the gun. "What happened?" Beth wondered why he hadn't told Hailey about their conversation in the hospital. Did it mean he had regrets?

"Why don't you ask him?" When Hailey raised an eyebrow, Beth realized how childish she sounded. She relaxed her shoulders and rubbed Wolf's head until he groaned. "We just want different things. I'm going back to Vancouver soon. You should come with me."

"You're kidding, right?"

"No. I can help you."

"I'm fine. Jonny brought me another dirt bike for my lower camp."

"So now you two are stealing bikes?"

"It was his old one." Hailey frowned. "What's your deal? You came out here to lecture me on my life choices?"

"I'm offering you a way *out*. I told Vaughn that Mason admitted to killing you, but I don't know if he believes me. I heard he's been at the scene every day looking for evidence."

"They're probably searching for Mason's cell phone and iPad."

"Do you think there's anything on them? Like pictures?"

"I don't know. They're locked with passwords."

"It's weird that both he and Vaughn were into taking photos of girls." Beth and Hailey held gazes as they thought about what that meant.

Hailey opened her mouth to say something but stopped when Wolf let out a low growl. His gaze was focused on the direction Beth had arrived from, ears pointing straight, and his body stiff. His lips were twisted into a snarl, showing white fangs.

Hailey's hand tightened on the rifle. "Get behind me."

"What is it?"

"Footsteps. You were followed."

Beth didn't need to be told twice. She hurried over. "Give me a weapon." The cops had confiscated her gun during the investigation and her bear spray was still in her backpack, sitting out of reach on the ground.

Hailey reached down her leg, fumbled for something under her jeans. Beside her, Wolf was still growling, the fur around his neck and spine standing up in a long ridge. He looked as though he were about to bolt into the bushes. Hailey gave a short whistle and he froze, one ear flicking in her direction, and then front again.

Vaughn stepped into view.

CHAPTER 38

Hailey

"So you are alive." Vaughn's eyes were almost bulging in rage, his pale skin flushed and sweaty. He was wearing tactical gear and a black baseball cap. "I fucking knew it. You set this all up."

"I found your disgusting pictures." I wanted to sound tough, but I heard the quaver in my voice. The butt of the rifle was wedged into my shoulder, the sight trained on Vaughn's chest. I hadn't had time to get my ankle knife loose for Beth. Wolf's deep growl vibrated through the glade. He let out a sharp bark.

Vaughn rested his hand on the butt of his gun. "If he makes a move, I'll shoot him."

I heard the quick exhale in Beth's throat, felt my own tighten. He would do it. No doubt about that. Would he shoot me next? He couldn't. Beth was a witness. Then I realized that people already thought I was dead, and Beth probably hadn't told anyone where she was going.

Vaughn looked at Beth. "Thanks for that tape marking your trail." So that was how he found us. Beth had marked her route. If we got out of this alive, I was going to smack her.

"You can't arrest me," I said. "I haven't done anything wrong."

"I want Mason's phone and iPad."

"I don't know what you're talking about."

"Give me what I came for, and I'll walk away."

I laughed. "You won't leave me alone. You'll kill me."

"I could kill you now if I wanted."

Beth stepped out from behind me. "I told Thompson that

you've been taking photos of girls. He's talking to Emily right now, and if anything happens to me, he'll know it was you."

"Emily is a messed-up girl with a drug problem," Vaughn said, crisply. "And whatever Hailey told you is a lie. She tried to blackmail me, threatened to frame me with photos she took herself, and when I wouldn't give her money, she ran away."

"No one is going to believe that," I said.

"No one will believe *you*. You lied to the entire town for a year. You *and* Jonny, and now you're a murderer. I know you killed Mason."

"You're crazy." I kept the rifle pressed to my shoulder.

"Mason made mistakes." Beth's voice was angry, not scared. She was going to provoke him. "You've made mistakes too. People are going to know you're a dirty cop."

Vaughn flipped the snap off his holster and rested his hand on his gun, the muscles in his forearm corded. "No one is going to know anything."

"Stop!" My finger was tense on the trigger, aching to pull, but if I missed, or only injured him, he'd shoot us for sure. "She's lying. We don't have proof of anything. Just arrest me and let her go. You said it yourself. No one will believe us, right? I'm just a liar and she's a drunk."

Beth shot me a look from the side. "I'm not a *drunk*."

"I saw the empty vodka bottle." I blinked at her, hoping she realized my jab was an attempt to buy time.

"It wasn't just me!"

"Please."

"Shut up, you two," Vaughn snapped.

Wolf was barking, a sharp incessant noise. Vaughn was becoming more agitated. I could see it in his face, in his hand tightening on his gun. I couldn't hold on to Wolf's bandanna without letting go of the rifle. Then, like I feared, he bolted forward.

I dropped the rifle and threw myself on top of Wolf, but Vaughn had already let out a shot. The noise was deafening. Echoed in my head. A hot sting on my shoulder. Wolf was fighting to get away from me, snarling at Vaughn. Beth was screaming. I looked up.

Vaughn was crossing the glade toward me. I needed to make a move. Beth dropped to the ground beside me, her hand pressing on my shoulder. "You're hurt!"

I looked at where my shirt was torn, the bloody gash. A flesh wound. Nothing deep.

"Run. Take Wolf to the cabin—at the base of the bluffs."

Vaughn was closer, and Wolf was losing his mind—twisting and snarling. He broke from my hold, rushed at Vaughn, who stopped with his legs braced wide and both hands on the gun.

"No!" I picked up a rock and threw it at Vaughn, hitting his wrist. His hand jerked, throwing his shot off. Wolf yelped and spun around to look at his back end, confused.

Vaughn aimed again. No time to dig in the branches for the rifle.

"Get out of here!" I shouted at Beth as I sprinted toward Vaughn and hit him across his muscled forearm. His shot went wild. I bolted past him. Vaughn spun around and gave chase.

It sounded like a bear was crashing through the woods behind me. Heavy footsteps, branches snapping, but that was good—I could keep track of his location. It would have been easy for me to slip into the darker parts of the forest, go off-trail, take a thousand different routes that would have sent him stumbling and lost, but I wanted him to follow me. I wanted him to travel along the animal trail where I'd stashed a flare gun and set traps. I had more guns at my lower camp.

After I'd saved Beth and escaped to the mountain, I'd

worried that Vaughn would figure it out and come looking for me. I'd been prepping for that possibility for the last two weeks.

I found a rhythm, shoving bushes out of the way—breaking some, kicking up moss and dirt so that he would easily be able to see my footprints—and managing my pace so I didn't get too winded. Vaughn was strong. He'd be able to match my endurance. But I knew these woods.

Beth and Wolf. Their names kept pace with me. I hoped Beth had listened and didn't try to follow Vaughn. I didn't know how far she'd be able to carry Wolf, or how badly he was hurt. Did she know any first aid? Thinking about Wolf made me run faster, my breath chuffing.

No heavy steps behind me, no trees crackling. Had I lost Vaughn? I glanced over my shoulder and tripped over a root. In one motion, I scrambled forward and jumped back onto my feet, but I'd hurt my elbow and knees. Blood dripped down my shin.

I saw the fir where I'd hidden a few things. I grabbed the lowest branch and hauled myself up. I found the knife and flare gun that I'd stuck into the crook of two branches. I waited. The woods were quiet. I strained my ears. If he'd gone another way, I'd have to track him.

Footsteps, coming closer. He wasn't running as fast, his pace steady, but he didn't sound out of breath, more measured. Like he felt confident that he would find me no matter what, and I was so angry I almost swung down and kicked him in the face right then. I was sprawled as low as I could get on the tree, my body stretched flat along the limb, but it was as though he sensed me. He slowed to a walk, his head turning one way, then the other. He was holding his gun out, firing stance. He knew I was nearby. I waited until he was in the right position.

The flare gun was in the palm of my hand, slippery with

sweat. He was almost under. Now he was moving past—his stride was too long. He'd be out of sight soon. Aiming at his back, I pulled the trigger in one quick motion, gripping the branch with my other hand so that I didn't fall. The flare struck the ground behind him and exploded. The air shook. Smoke rushed around me. Vaughn dropped to his knees, spun around with his gun out, and fired.

Bang.

I clung to the branch.

Bang, bang.

Did he have more ammo on him? He was at the wrong angle for me to attack. The throwing knife was in my right hand, but I would probably only hit his shoulder, best-case, and then I'd have given away my position.

He rose to his feet, gun out, looking around. His body was alert, his arms locked into position. He was staring at each tree, each shadow, scanning back and forth. He'd look up soon.

No way could I get to my feet. I'd have to hope my aim wouldn't be off. I gripped the knife, narrowed my eyes, held my breath, then flung it. The blade spun and flashed—he was stepping to the right, turning around. The blade connected with a soft thud.

I'd gotten him in the fleshy part of his thigh.

He looked up, straight at me—gun rising. I leapt to the ground, hit the dirt hard, and rolled back onto my feet. I ran. I pumped my arms, knees lifting high. The jump out of the tree had jarred my bones, sent sharp pains up my legs. I didn't know how deep my knife had gone into Vaughn's thigh, but I could hear him thundering behind me. It hadn't slowed him down.

A loud crack rang out and a tree branch blew up beside me. The trail crossed over a smooth stone plateau, then narrowed on the other side, and sloped into a long hill. I was running, dirt and pebbles loose under my feet. I lost my balance partway and skidded onto my back. I looked up. He was standing on the stone plateau, aiming down. Another loud crack, and I rolled to the side, throwing myself into the dense underbrush. I got up and kept running.

A few minutes later, maybe ten, I couldn't hear him. I felt like I was bleeding from a thousand small wounds. Rocks had scraped at my arms and legs. Sticks stabbed me. Ligaments were torn, tendons vibrating with strain. My lungs begged me to stop. Sweat was dripping down my face and into my eyes.

The trees bunched close together here, the forest thickening and blocking out the sun, the mountain cupping its hand around me. I was almost there. I slowed to a trot. The small clearing where I'd set up my lower camp was empty. I found the tree that I'd marked, dug up the duffel bag, and pulled out the rifle, slid off the safety. I looked over my shoulder.

The woods were quiet. I'd wait a little longer, then I'd have to go back and try to find him. Maybe the knife had done more damage than I'd thought. I grabbed a bottle of water out of the bag, crawled on my knees behind a tree, and gulped it, dumping some on my face and hair.

Footsteps. I shrank against the rough tree bark, braced the rifle on my knee, dialed in the focus to a tight round circle. Vaughn came into view. Blood had soaked through the front of his pants leg, the material wet and glistening. He was breathing hard, looking around.

I tightened my finger on the trigger. He was turning away. I needed to make this shot count, had to get him in the heart. I thought quickly, but not quick enough. He'd found my duffel bag. His body was blocked now by a stump as he leaned over to rummage through my supplies.

If I shot now, I'd hit a tree.

He stopped and looked around him. He was still behind the

stump. His breath had lost the ragged, desperate edge, seemed more even and calm. He was regaining his strength.

"I'm wearing a bulletproof vest, so you better be sure where you hit."

I choked back a gasp, my finger slipping from the trigger. I lifted my eye away from the scope, taking in the wider image. He was staring up into the trees, then scanning the ground, peering into the shadows. "Let me guess, you have traps set. Little surprises for me? It's the only reason you'd stick around." He aimed his gun to the left, then swung far to the right, and gave a low laugh. "Which one of us will break first, you think?"

I'd have to try for his head. But he was moving, ducking behind a tree, then sliding to the next. Only the top of his black cap showed, then a flash of skin. If I took off running again, he would follow, but he might not pass directly over the dirt pit. My second surprise.

I stepped out from behind the tree, holding the rifle in one hand, and pointing it down. It was risky but I didn't think he'd shoot me—at least not right away.

"You win."

He slowly stood, his firearm raised, and glanced over my body. "You're giving up."

"I can't . . ." I pressed my hand against my chest. "I think I broke my ribs." I staggered, sinking the gun barrel into the earth like I was so weak I had to use it for support.

"Throw the gun away from you."

I lowered it the rest of the way to the ground, gave it a little kick that sent it sliding.

He eyed me. "You carrying any knives?"

Should I lie? He might search me. I lifted the tail of my shirt and tossed my knife.

"Turn out your pockets," he said. "Pull up your pant leg."

I hated giving up the knife strapped around my calf, but I had no choice. I tugged it free and threw it near the first one.

"That it?" he said, eyeing me.

"Yeah." If he didn't fall into the pit now, I was as good as dead. I took another struggling breath, rubbed my wounded arm over my mouth so it would look like I was bleeding.

"My lung," I wheezed. "I think I punctured my lung."

"Stand here." He motioned with the gun to a spot in front of him. The pit was between us. I'd have to walk closer, then stop so that he'd come the rest of the distance. I stumbled forward. It wasn't fake—my legs were weak and cramping from the run. I stepped onto the dirt, and when I thought I was near the edge of the pit, I rolled my eyes back into my head and dropped.

"Goddamn it." Footsteps running toward me. I'd landed on my side, couldn't see him. I kept my breathing shallow, waited for the sound of the branches snapping. He was only a couple of feet from me. Why hadn't he fallen yet? Was I in the wrong spot? Then, finally, everything shifted and slid—but the ground was breaking around me. I was too close to the edge. I clutched at roots, felt his large body hit the back of my legs, and then he was grabbing at my ankles as he went in. My hands slipped from the roots and I fell with him, clods of dirt raining down upon us.

He landed beside me, then rolled so he was sitting on top of me, with his arm across my throat—just enough pressure to hold me still. If I moved, I'd choke. His head blocked the sky.

I clawed at his face. He swung his gun across my forehead, bolts of pain and white lightning behind my eyes. I sagged.

"Freeze!" The voice came from above. Male. Another cop. Maybe Thompson. The arm lifted from my throat. I gulped air. My head was pulsating, the ache stretching around and squeezing like it was filling with blood.

"You're under arrest for assaulting an officer." Vaughn was

still astride me and breathing hard. He looked over his shoulder. "I found Hailey. She just tried to kill me."

"No!" My voice came out husky, winded. "He's lying."

Metal noises. Vaughn was undoing his handcuffs. He turned me over, rough and fast, so fast that my face slammed into the dirt. He snapped the cuffs on one wrist, then the other.

I wanted to argue, wanted to explain to Thompson, but Vaughn yanked on my arms, his knee digging into my hamstrings. I cried out, and my mouth filled with dirt. He gripped me under my shoulders. Thompson leaned over and lifted me out—Vaughn pushing from behind. Thompson laid me on my stomach. Noises behind me. He was helping Vaughn out of the pit.

I turned my head. They were standing a couple of feet away. "Don't leave me alone with him. He shot my dog—Beth ran away. They need help!"

Vaughn shook his head. "Hailey faked her disappearance. Jonny was probably in on it. Beth found out somehow. I had a hunch she was lying about what happened with Mason, so I followed her up the mountain. When I confronted Hailey, she stabbed me." Vaughn pointed to his thigh where the blood was seeping through his pants.

"It was self-defense!"

Vaughn looked at Thompson. "I'll take her in."

"I'll do it," Thompson said. "You're hurt." Thompson reached down and pulled me up by my waist, helping me to my feet. I staggered from the sudden rush of blood to my head.

"You have to believe me. He beat me up."

Vaughn snorted. "Convincing, isn't she? That's how she got me into her trap."

"You should've called for backup."

"You telling me procedure, Thompson?" Vaughn's voice deepened. The two looked at each other for a long moment, then Vaughn nodded. "We'll talk about this later."

"It was me. I phoned you." I twisted to face Thompson. The words rushed out. "He was taking photos of me—not just me. Other girls too."

"Shut the fuck up." Vaughn stepped forward, but Thompson moved in front of me. Vaughn got right up close to him. "What do you think you're doing, Officer?"

"Protecting the witness, *sir*. You're out of control."

"I'm out of control? What do you call defying a senior officer? Go ahead and report me, destroy your career. I'll have you working a desk if you're lucky." Vaughn moved around to grab me, but Thompson quickly rotated us so that I was still behind him.

"She's not going anywhere with you."

"Tell me you aren't believing this shit! She's delusional." He gestured around the woods. "She's been living like an animal. She needs a psych evaluation."

"I don't know. Her story makes sense. I've been watching you, Vaughn."

"Is that so?" He was so close he was almost nose-to-nose with Thompson. The muscles in his neck were tight. He smelled of sweat and blood.

"You're threatening me?"

"I don't make threats." He shoved Thompson in the chest, sending him stumbling backward. Thompson let me go, and I fell to my knees, off balance. Thompson launched himself on Vaughn, grabbing him in a bear hug, tackling him. They rolled around, grappling for Thompson's gun.

I got to my feet and ran awkwardly over to my gear, my hands cuffed behind my back. There, one of my knives. A shot rang out. They were still struggling. I couldn't tell if one of them was hurt. I dragged my foot over the knife sheath, trying to get the knife out.

"Get your hands up."

I froze, but Vaughn wasn't looking at me. Panting, nose bleeding, he was standing over Thompson and pointing a gun at his head. Thompson's lips were slick with blood, a cut open on his cheek and one above his eye. He slowly put up his hands.

"Vaughn. Don't do this. You'll go to prison for years."

"They'd have to prove it was me first, Thompson. I've got a crazy girl." He gestured at me with his head. "And while she was resisting arrest, she got my gun from me."

"I already started a report on you—I knew you were dirty. There'll be questions."

"Doesn't matter. I can make them go away. You think you're the first person to try to bring me down?" He cocked the hammer. "Sorry it had to work out like this, Thompson."

CHAPTER 39

Beth

Beth slid one arm under Wolf's stomach, the other around his back end, then hoisted him up into her arms and half staggered, half ran into the woods. She wove through the trees, hoping they blocked her from view. She searched the shadows ahead for the bluffs. Was she close? She'd gotten disorientated. Everything looked the same. Wolf whimpered, then turned silent, his body quivering. Scared he was bleeding out, Beth stopped behind a cedar, and eased him to the ground. When she reached for his side, he snapped at her, his teeth clicking together. She yanked her hand back and tugged her shirt over her head, wrapped it around his snout.

"Stop it. I'm trying to save you." He growled and struggled but he couldn't open his mouth. She gently pressed her fingers across the fur on his side, and at his muffled yelp, she knew she'd found the source of his pain. She spread his fur with one hand, found the long, deep gash, and cringed. Blood. Torn flesh. She took a steadying breath.

"It doesn't look bad. You're going to be okay." She had no idea if he was going to be okay but figured it was a bad time to explain to him that she didn't know anything about injured dogs.

Beth unwound the bandanna from her hair, wrapped it around his midsection, and applied pressure. Over her ragged breathing, she tried to hear where Vaughn and Hailey had gone, but she couldn't make out any noise. She hoped Hailey was okay.

"Okay. We can do this." Beth hesitated, then loosened

Wolf's muzzle. When he didn't bite her, she loosened it more so he could pant, then scooped him up again.

She looked at the sky, trying to track the position of the sun, but she couldn't see it through the canopy of trees. She kept going, slowing to a walk. Wolf's body was getting heavier by the minute, and her shoulders and back ached. She adjusted Wolf's weight and he let out a whine, a sad sound that stabbed her ears. Her arm felt damp where his back leg was resting. He was still bleeding. She pushed on, stumbling through the brush. She heard rushing water.

The trees thinned and she broke out of the woods at the edge of the river. She'd gone in the wrong direction. She looked up and down the shore. No sign of Hailey or Vaughn. She crouched and set Wolf down, one reassuring hand on his back. She sucked in some breaths.

The river looked shallow in that section, rocks visible under the water, light patches of sand. Where were the bluffs? They should be upstream. She remembered the wide pool, the cliff, the steep bank. Maybe if she was out farther into the river, she could see around the bend.

"Hang on, boy. I'll look and come back for you." Wolf whined, struggled to his feet, and took a few hobbling steps. "Stay." She held her palm out like she'd seen Hailey do.

Wolf halted, but his eyebrows were furrowed, his ears flat. She took a few cautious steps into the water, gasping at the cold. She glanced over her shoulder. Now Wolf was standing on a rock, his back leg lifted with only the toes touching, that whine still leaking out.

The stones were slippery. She waded slowly into the icy water, placing each foot carefully, arms spread for balance. When she got closer to the middle, the undercurrent began to push against her knees. She shielded her eyes from the sun, scanned the bank upstream, then down where it ran deeper—

and, judging by the white froth, a lot faster. In fact, it looked like it went through a gorge. She turned to check on Wolf and realized he'd followed her into the water.

"No. Stop!" She held out a hand. "Stay. Good boy." But he was still trying to get to her, awkwardly hobbling on three legs as he scrambled over a rock. She made her way toward him, lurching through the water. "Stay!" He barked, four frustrated yelps.

She was close enough now to reach and touch his snout, while trying to make some sort of sound that would soothe a dog, but she'd extended herself too far. Her left foot slipped from its boot, lodged between two rocks, and her ankle twisted. She landed on her side in the water, going under. She lifted her head, coughing and gasping. She grabbed at rocks, struggling to get to her feet, but the current was too strong. It pushed her downriver like she was on a slide.

Wolf hopped toward her, barking wildly. The water picked him up and now he was swimming, his paws scooping at the water. He was being rushed past her.

She lunged and hooked her arm around his neck. He turned his body. Then she realized he was pulling toward shore—and he was a strong swimmer. Maybe they had a chance.

She kicked with Wolf, using her free arm to plunge into the water and propel them forward. The water was running too fast and so cold her legs were numb. The shore became trees, then rock as they floated past. They'd reached the high rock bluffs of the gorge.

They were going to go through the chute.

The rapids bounced them up and down and she held on to Wolf, both of them trying to keep their heads above water. They went under a couple of times, but she clung to his neck, and they surfaced again. Once, when they were caught in a whirlpool, he was wrenched from her arms, but when they circled around, she got hold of him.

They spun through the gorge, cliffs forming jagged walls, until it opened into a wide pool. Logs hung over one side, and she reached for the branches as they were carried underneath, but the wood was brittle and broke off in her hands.

Her kicks grew weaker and her teeth chattered. She thought of hypothermia. How long did it take? Maybe it was already happening. Wolf was barely paddling. They were floating, spinning helplessly, bobbing. She stopped fighting, wound her hands under Wolf's bandanna, and hoped that if she passed out she wouldn't drag him to his death.

When she heard gunshots, she jerked and floundered in the water, twisting her head around so she could see the shore. Wolf also began to thrash, his paws slapping the surface.

She spotted a tree hanging over where the river narrowed. The branches drooped into the water like a net. If they kept at the same speed, she might be able to arc toward it and latch on. From there it was only a few feet to the shore.

Too fast or too slow, and they'd miss what might be their last chance.

"Come on, boy!" she shivered out of her cold lips. "Go!" She sliced at the water with her free arm, touched a rock with her foot, and used it to push them forward—powering all her muscles and energy into that singular moment. Wolf must have heard the desperation in her voice because he was leaping forward like a horse in the final moments of a race. The tree was within reach.

Beth's body was aimed in the right direction, fighting the undercurrent that still wanted to yank them farther into the depths. She could make out each branch, and now she noticed a large rock under the tree. She reached up—her hand touched the branch. She held on tight, got her feet onto the rock, then pulled the rest of her body up with one arm. Her other was still grasping Wolf's bandanna. He was in the water, clawing at the rock, eyes frantic.

"Stop!" Either he lost strength or he understood, because his body relaxed, and he was now floating. She locked her arm around the branch and used the other to haul him up beside her onto the rock. Without any sort of thank-you, he clambered over her, jumped from the rock into the shallow water at the shore, and limped onto the sand. Then his adrenaline must have given out, because he collapsed onto his side, tongue lolling and ribs heaving.

Beth followed, sliding off the rock and wading over to him—then sank onto her knees. He whimpered and snapped his head around when she bumped against his hind leg. The cold had stopped his bleeding, but the gash was big. His leg quivered when she ran her hand down it, and he licked her arm. She looked up into the woods as she rubbed her own leg with her other hand, trying to get her circulation going. No more gunshots. What did that mean?

Wolf watched her face as she got to her feet, stumbling as the blood rushed back to them. Her clothes were stuck to her body, hair roping across her face.

She held up her hand. "Stay."

Wolf rested his head on his front paws, his eyes still watching her intently, but it was clear he was exhausted, and his sides heaved. Beth staggered in the direction of the gunshots, her eyes scanning the forest. She took a trail that ended in a wall of trees. When she turned, a breeze drifted under her nose. A faint scent. Something familiar. Gasoline?

She pushed through the bushes and found a red gas can and a dirt bike.

The second escape route. She had to be near Hailey's lower camp. Beth crept forward and peered down into a gulley through a gap in the trees. She caught sight of Hailey below in a small clearing—her hands cuffed behind her back. Some sort of standoff. Vaughn was looming over Thompson with a gun.

Beth's only weapon was the dirt bike. She thought fast. If she pushed the bike through the trees, she could start it when she was coasting down. It would distract Vaughn.

It sounded simple, but the bike was heavy, and her muscles were weak. By the time she reached the gap in the trees, Thompson was on the ground, his face bloody and his hands above his head.

Vaughn stood over him.

A deep breath, and she pushed off. The bike was huge, and she almost crashed when it rolled over a root, the tire jumping. She dropped one foot onto the ground, careened dangerously to the other side, and corrected it at the last moment.

Thompson, Hailey, and Vaughn looked up as she hurtled through the brush. Vaughn's arm swung in an arc and he aimed the gun at Beth. She hit the ignition switch. The bike roared. The front wheel lifted, and she shifted her weight forward. She shot down the hill.

Thompson kicked Vaughn in the crotch. Vaughn bent over with one hand between his legs. He lowered the gun, but it was pointed at Thompson again, who was trying to roll away.

Beth was almost at the bottom. Only a few feet away. The front tire of the bike hit a dip, launching her off the seat. But she kept her grip on the handlebars and aimed the bike at Vaughn, and felt the thud of his body being crushed underneath. The bike flipped. She was flying. Flashes of trees, sky, then she hit the ground, sliding forward on her stomach. Breath rushed out of her lungs, dirt filled her mouth, and her teeth snapped together. She had a final second to remember the doctor's warning about another concussion before she swung her arm up to protect her head and slammed into a rock.

Search-and-rescue arrived on all-terrain vehicles. A red helicopter hovered overhead. Thompson shouted orders into his radio. Beth had gone into shock and was lying on her back with her arm, scraped and bleeding, across her chest. Her teeth chattered as one of the rescuers put a blanket over her. Somewhere behind them, Hailey was complaining on her stretcher.

"I can walk. I have to get my dog." Chopper blades whooshed through the air as they flew Vaughn out of the woods. If he was being airlifted, he must be in rough shape. Beth was worried that he might die. They'd never get answers. Never see him punished.

"The searchers have already found your dog." Thompson's voice was thick and nasally through his swollen nose. "They're giving him first aid."

"He'll run away."

"He's too weak." Beth was in a neck brace and she only had a view of Hailey's legs, which were kicking as she tried to twist off the stretcher.

"He's probably bleeding to death! I told you not to leave him."

"I had to save you!"

"I didn't ask for help!" More sounds of a struggle. "Let go of me!" The rasp of ripped fabric, a man's voice, yelping in pain. Flesh hitting something. Hailey was fighting a paramedic.

"Stop!" Thompson's voice.

"Wolf *needs* me." Grappling noises, a frustrated yell from Hailey, then a confusing silence. Beth waited, thinking that Hailey was planning her next move, but her legs were still.

A female paramedic knelt beside Beth, adjusted one of the

straps, and said, "They gave her something so she can rest. She'll be okay."

Beth closed her eyes. They could both rest now.

Beth shuffled into Hailey's room, dragging the IV pole alongside her. She'd adjusted her hospital gown to cover up as much of her bruises as possible—underneath the thin fabric she looked like she'd rolled in purple and blue paint. At least she hadn't broken any bones. Not *hers* anyway. Vaughn was a different story.

Hailey sat propped up against pillows, arms crossed over her chest. She frowned as Beth came in. "I'm too tired to talk. The nurses keep waking me up." They'd been in the hospital for two days, and from what Beth had overheard, Hailey fought the nurses about everything, wouldn't take her medications, and refused to see her aunt. The latter had surprised Beth. After a year, why didn't she want to connect with her family?

"I just wanted to know if you've spoken to Thompson."

"He's been here every day. It's annoying." Hailey was looking at her with her chin up, like she was daring Beth to say different.

"They arrested Vaughn." Beth paused. "But I guess Thompson already told you."

"Yeah."

Beth didn't know what else to say. She didn't want to go back to her lonely room. She glanced around Hailey's. It was the same size, but Hailey had more flowers, bunches of bouquets. Maybe they were from Jonny.

He'd texted Beth once since she'd been in the hospital. *I can't believe you ran over Vaughn. You're my hero.* Then, moments later, in another bubble, as if he'd had to think about it first, he'd written, *If you need anything, let me know.*

Like Beth was a neighbor who wanted him to water her

plants while she was on a little vacay at the hospital. She didn't text back.

Hailey's bag was on the chair. Beth wondered where the clothes had come from and realized Jonny must have gotten them. She remembered how he had done that for her.

Wait. Was Hailey's bag half *un*packed, or half packed? Beth glanced at Hailey and caught the wary expression in her eyes. Now Beth got it. It wasn't that Hailey was unhappy to see *her*, she was unhappy about Beth being in this room.

Beth looked around again, slower. Hailey's IV dangled loosely from its pole—her hand resting over her wrist. Her dinner tray was empty. The pudding cup sat on top of her duffel bag. Beth moved over and quickly dug around—forks, knives, a juice box, a hunk of bread.

"Hey! Get out of my stuff." Hailey was off the bed now, pushing her away.

"Are you trying to leave?"

Hailey yanked the bread out of Beth's hand. "That's none of your business."

"You're running away again."

"I'm not running anywhere. I'm going home."

"The doctors haven't cleared you, have they?"

Hailey rolled her eyes. "I'll be fine. They fixed what needed to be fixed."

"What about Wolf?"

"He's recovering with Jonny."

"So now you're going to walk out on everything? What about the court case?"

"They have enough evidence. They don't need me."

"You sure about that?"

"I have to get out of here. I can't breathe with all the noise. Nurses coming in and out. Visitors."

"You mean people?"

"Yeah, fucking *people*." Hailey was sliding on her jeans, turning around to remove her hospital gown and tug a shirt over her head. "We're not the same—you and me. You have a family to go back to. You still have your parents."

Was that the problem? Hailey couldn't see a future for herself?

"You can't go back to the miner's cabin. Everyone knows that's where you were living. They won't leave you alone. They'll want to take pictures of you, with you. You'll hate it."

Hailey wasn't listening, just grabbing at things—the blanket from the bed, rolled into a ball. Now she was studying the electric cords like she was thinking about how to use them.

"The nurses will call the police."

"I'm not under arrest."

"The cops want you to stick around."

"I don't care what they want."

Beth was getting angry. How could Hailey be so blind? Didn't she see what this would mean? "What about Jonny?"

Hailey shrugged herself into a hoodie and jammed her feet into the dusty work boots she pulled out from under the chair. She swung the loaded bag onto her shoulder, pressed a baseball cap onto her head, and began to move toward the door.

"He's safe now that Vaughn's gone."

"Except that you're ruining his life."

Hailey spun around. "That's not true!"

"He's turned down racing opportunities, a chance to travel! You've seen the maps all over his bedroom walls. You think those are just because he likes looking at them?"

"He hasn't missed anything. He would've told me." But Beth could see the doubt growing in Hailey's eyes. She was wondering if Beth was right. Maybe Jonny had his own secrets.

"You *know* how loyal he is. He's the reason you can keep

living on the mountain. While you're doing what *you* want, you're stopping him from having anything *he* wants."

Hailey looked down at her boots. Beth moved closer and stood in front of her.

"He will never leave you alone out there." She softened her voice. "You need to think about that. Whatever you decide? You're deciding for the both of you."

Hailey just shook her head. Beth couldn't see her face, whether she was crying or whether she was angry. She didn't know what else to say to reach her.

"I'm going to go," she whispered. Hailey didn't glance up. She stood motionless. Beth could tell she was thinking hard. She wanted to tell her everything would be all right. But how could Beth really know? Hailey would see through her words and recognize them for the half-truths they were. Neither of them knew how this was going to work out in the end.

Beth quietly left the room. She didn't turn to see if Hailey slipped into the corridor, her bag over her shoulders. She didn't wait to hear the sound of her boots striking linoleum.

What happened next was up to Hailey.

CHAPTER 40

Hailey

I put the last of the coffee grounds into the maker, pressed brew, and listened to the steady dripping sound. Soon the kitchen smelled of fresh coffee. I found two mugs, filled them both, and left one on the counter while I doctored mine with sugar and cream—a luxury. The fridge was dismal, but I found some cookies in the cupboard. I sat at the table, quietly munching and sharing pieces with Wolf, who was partway under my chair and had his head resting on my foot. Every once in a while he'd give me a complaining huff and a nudge with his snout. His leg was shaved, the bullet wound stitched neatly in a long line. I told him he'd have a cool scar.

The toilet flushed at the end of the hall. Thompson was awake. He walked into the kitchen, rubbing his hand over the top of his hair and squinting in the dim light. Thankfully he was wearing pajama bottoms and a T-shirt, or the upcoming conversation would be awkward.

At the counter, he fumbled for his glasses and shoved them onto his face. Another yawn, and he reached his arms up in an overhead stretch. His back cracked. I sipped silently at my coffee. Wolf was wagging his tail, a soft whisper on the floor, as he tracked Thompson.

Thompson noticed the coffee mug on the counter. He lifted it to his mouth and took a long drink, then turned around. "I like my coffee stronger."

"I'm not a barista."

"Clear on that." He sat across from me.

I pushed a couple of cookies over to him. "You only have one piece of bread left. The cheese stuff."

"You know I have a front door."

"Climbing the tree was more fun. I get bored."

"Get some better hobbies."

"Should I take up knitting? Needles could be interesting." I made a stabbing motion in the air. "Or maybe crocheting. Don't they have hooks?"

"Enough. What's going on?"

"Is Jonny in trouble?" When Thompson interviewed me in the hospital, I only filled him in on the basics: Vaughn threatened me when I discovered he was taking nude photos. I was scared, so I ran away, and hid my bike at the bottom of the ravine. My cell fell into the creek. I didn't realize that it would look like I had been abducted. I was very, very sorry.

I told him that Jonny didn't know where I was hiding, but then I couldn't explain that I'd witnessed Vaughn planting the drugs without admitting Jonny and I *did* have contact.

"You swear he didn't help you, and so far we haven't found any stolen goods at your cabin, so we have no reason to believe that you are responsible for any of the local thefts." Jonny had already gone up and cleared out everything. No one but me would ever know which items were stolen from my old house. The personal items were hidden, and Jonny recovered them all.

"What about the drugs Vaughn said he found?" I asked.

"The charges are being dropped."

"Did you hack into Mason's iPad and phone yet? What's on them?"

"That's part of the investigation. I can't discuss it."

"You wouldn't even have them if I hadn't given them to you."

"We would have had them *weeks* ago if you hadn't stolen them."

"I had *reasons*." Unfortunately, I hadn't been able to hand them over without admitting that I had helped Beth, but I told him that when I arrived at the garage, she had already killed Mason. A plan we'd agreed on, whispering together in the emergency room after I woke.

Thompson let out his breath, looked up at the ceiling like he was trying to decide if he should trust me, or was asking God to get me out of his house. He met my eyes again.

"Vaughn was letting shipments of drugs go through the truck stop—for a price. Mason found out somehow, either witnessed it or heard about it. In exchange for his silence, Mason wanted Vaughn to take photos of girls for him. Likely it was a way for him to have power over Vaughn and minimize his own risk of being caught. It doesn't seem like Vaughn was interested in the photos himself. He just wanted to keep his job, his family, and his cushy life."

Money. That was what it all came down to? He sold our bodies for money. He'd walked around his big house and gone on expensive vacations that he'd paid for with things that didn't belong to him. Our privacy, ourselves.

"Did he know Mason was the killer?"

"He says he didn't, but we're still going over each case. I think Vaughn had his suspicions, especially after Amber was murdered."

I thought about all the cautions Vaughn had given me about riding my bike out to the lake. He knew I was on the killer's radar because he had been feeding him photos of me.

Thompson took a sip of his coffee, set the mug down. "There's something else you should know. Mason kept all his security video on a cloud. Looks like your dad caught him building that compartment in his camper, and there was an altercation. Your dad got away, but Mason followed. We found a damaged truck grille and front bumper in Mason's garage. There were traces of blue paint. We think it matches your dad's truck. We're waiting on forensics."

"Mason ran him off the road." I said this slowly, absorbing the truth of it. I'd suspected that Dad had been trying to get away, but I hadn't imagined that Mason could have actually *caused* the accident. He'd killed my father. Any lingering guilt that I had over taking another person's life ended instantly. I had let Mason off easy. I should have made him suffer.

"Vaughn wrote up the accident report, so we'll open that investigation again and check that it wasn't part of the cover-up."

Vaughn was the one who told me about the crash. Over and over he implied that it was my dad's fault that I was alone. He'd wanted to break our bond. Vaughn had destroyed so much, but my dad was something he could never steal from me. Dad was with me all the time. I saw him as I watched Wolf catch fish. I thought of him as I built a fire on a cool morning. Every move I made had in some way been shaped by my father. I imagined him standing on a cliff overlooking the river, his arms raised to the sky, cheering that Vaughn had been caught.

"Beth says that you need my statement. That I have to testify."

"We need everything we can to build a solid case against Vaughn."

"What about Emily?"

"So far she is denying everything. Your aunt wants to help but she doesn't know much. She was horrified when we found the hidden camera in your bedroom. She wants to talk to you."

"Yeah, so she can tell me that she hates me for ruining her

life." How was I going to face my little cousin Cash? Would he cry or ignore me? Vaughn had been the only father figure in his life. Lana had been so happy. She'd lose everything now. She'd have to start over too.

"I don't think you're giving her enough credit. She's just glad you're alive."

"It's not that simple." Lana would have questions. She'd want to understand things I didn't even understand. I fed Wolf more crumbs, stroked his muzzle. The velvet of his ears.

"You want to run away again." Thompson gave me a steady look. "That's what this is about. You're trying to tell yourself that no one cares about you, so then it's okay."

"So, what, you're a shrink now?"

He leaned forward. "We need to make sure these charges stick, or his lawyers are going to find ways to get him off. You called me when I was still at the scene of Amber's murder. You saw him go into Beth's motel room. I need to know *everything*, Hailey. Dates, times, places."

"It's hard." I rubbed at my hair, the short strands. Talking meant feelings.

"Yeah, it is. You went through a lot. But Vaughn can't hurt you anymore."

I gazed down at Wolf. He set his chin on my knee, leaned his weight into my leg, and met my eyes with a little huff. He always knew exactly what to say. I turned back to Thompson.

"I'll do it."

"Great. We can go down to the station. I just need a shower."

"I want to tell you now. When you aren't in uniform."

He stared at me across the table. I stared back. He got up, refilled his coffee and mine. While I added sugar and cream, he pulled out his phone and set it on the table.

He swiped his finger across the screen, opened the recording app. "This is a victim statement with Hailey McBride. August fifteenth, 2019." He nodded at me. "Whenever you're ready."

One breath. Two breaths. I wasn't in that kitchen. I was stalking across an open field. I had a rifle on my shoulder. I lowered my eye against the sight, focused in on my prey.

"I was coming home from the lake. It was dark. I heard a truck behind me. . . ."

CHAPTER 41

Beth

Beth came to a stop, a dust cloud behind her tires. She'd parked beside Jonny's truck. His front door clapped. Hailey appeared on his porch, Wolf beside her. She limped down the few steps with Wolf at her heels. Jonny was over by the barn, working on a dirt bike—another one beside it. He paused to watch Beth get out of the car, wrench in his hand.

"Thought you left town." Hailey crossed her arms over her chest. Wolf trotted to Beth, tail wagging. He sniffed her hands. She ruffled his ears, rubbed his head. Hailey was silent, observing. Beth took another moment to scratch Wolf.

"Thompson told me you were here. I wanted to say goodbye."

Hailey looked past Beth to her car, where the trunk was partway open and tied down over her camping gear. "You pack about as good as you set up camp."

"I see you haven't lost your sunny personality. How's the return to civilization?"

Hailey shrugged. "I'm getting used to it."

"Big adjustment."

"I'm not an animal."

Beth raised an eyebrow. "You sure about that?"

Hailey laughed—the sound surprising Beth. She'd never heard her laugh before. She'd never even seen her smile. Hailey looked more like the girl on her "missing" poster now. Her hair was back to its natural color and smoothed into a boyish cut that glowed copper in the sun. Faded jeans shorts hung on her small hips, and a white tank top showed her tanned arms. The bruises had faded. Hailey took the last few steps, stopped at the bottom, and leaned against the railing.

"You staying here for good?" Beth said.

"For now. Jonny wants to travel, so I might stay with my aunt. We've been talking. She needs help with my cousin."

Beth tried not to react to the news about Jonny. It didn't matter where he was going. She had her own plans. "Before I leave, I'm going to visit Amber's cross." She rubbed at her arms. The breeze lifted strands of her hair and brought with it a hint of fall and damp leaves. Things to come.

"Cool." Hailey looked away, paused. "Those are wild roses." She pointed to a green bush at the front of the house with red berries clustered on vines. "They're finished blooming, but the rose hips will last for a couple of months and feed the birds. Wild roses are tough. You can mow them down to the roots, or set them on fire, and they'll still come back. They never stop living."

"So, basically they're weeds."

Hailey frowned, still staring at the bushes. "Something like that."

Beth had the feeling that she had messed up. Hailey had been trying to tell her something, and she'd let her down. She hadn't understood. She'd wanted this goodbye to go well. Hailey had saved Beth's life, and she was her last connection to Amber. She didn't want to break it.

Beth took a couple of steps closer to Hailey, reached for her hand, and lifted it toward her. She dropped Amber's bracelet into her palm. Hailey stared at the gold chain.

"What's this?"

"She would want you to have it. You found her. You took care of her." Hailey looked up at her suspiciously. Beth laughed. "Jesus, I'm not proposing."

"Good, because you're not my type."

"I'm *everyone's* type." Beth earned a smirk that time and thought Hailey might keep sparring, but she folded her hand around the bracelet.

"Does this make us sisters?"

"Something like that."

Hailey smiled. "I'll get Jonny for you." She turned around and walked over to the bikes, where Jonny handed her a helmet. He glanced at Beth and said something to Hailey. Beth shoved her hands into her pockets.

Jonny strode toward her, his motorbike boots giving him that familiar swagger. He stopped in front of her, his eyes locked with hers.

"Guess you don't have time to go for a ride."

She couldn't tell if he was serious or if it was some sort of icebreaker. "My parents are waiting at the motel. My mom is probably on her tenth cup of coffee."

"Gotcha." He was quiet for a moment, his gaze aimed over her shoulder toward her car, and she didn't know if she should say goodbye, but then he let out his breath and looked at her. "I'm sorry for being an asshole. A lot of stuff was coming at me. I didn't deal with it well."

"Me neither." She studied her hands, like she was holding the key to making the next words easier. All she saw were chipped fingernails. "I have to see a doctor. I'm hooked on pills. Maybe I need rehab. I don't know. Something."

He didn't seem surprised, and she realized he already knew about the pills and the drinking, but she didn't feel ashamed. She wasn't perfect. She didn't want to be perfect anymore.

"After that?"

"I don't know." She glanced over at Hailey, who was astride her bike, one leg braced on the ground, the other on the foot pedal. "Everything's still screwed up, but I'm trying."

"Trying is good. Can I call you sometime?"

She jerked her head back toward him. He wanted to talk? Did she want that? She'd gotten used to thinking they were a one-way street that had ended in a wall. Now he was looking at her with a guarded expression like he knew she might shoot him down, but he was ready for it.

"What if I ask you to visit me?"

"I've got a truck." He stepped closer and leaned in until his cheek was next to hers—a smooth slide of skin—then brushed his lips against her ear. "When in doubt, throttle it out."

She was hit with the memory of when he took her riding on his dirt bike, her arms tight around him, how wild and free she'd felt when he took those sharp corners. Faster and faster.

"You bet, farm boy."

Jonny smiled as he backed away, the whisper of his breath still traveling from her ear to her neck. He slipped his helmet over his head, only his eyes visible, and walked to the bikes.

Beth got back into her car, sank into the seat, and rolled down her window to let the hot air out, but she didn't want to leave just yet. They had started their dirt bikes, the motors roaring, blue exhaust filling the air. Hailey led the way, Jonny followed, and Wolf loped behind.

They were at the edge of the forest. They would disappear out of sight soon. Beth held her breath. Hailey's bike merged into the shadows, leaving a haze of dust from the trail.

At the last second, Jonny looked back at Beth, then he rode after Hailey into the woods.

Beth's tires crunched on the soft gravel shoulder. The car vibrated as she slid the gearshift into park. She sat for a moment and stared out the windshield at the ditch, the green shrubs, tree boughs that touched the ground, long, yellowed grass. The engine ticked as it cooled down, the air conditioner hissing. She wanted a Xanax, but she had handed them all over to her mother.

She closed her eyes. Long breath. Short breath.

The door hinges squeaked loudly in the still summer air, her palm nearly burning on the metal frame. She clutched it, steadying herself, then took a few clumsy steps down the side of the road. She focused on the sound of her flip-flops and the hum of a fly near her ear. The grass was so thick and long that she didn't see the white cross on the other side until she was standing in front of it. If Hailey hadn't noticed the ravens that day, Amber might never have been found.

Pressure built in Beth's chest, a sob escaping in a strangled breath that she couldn't hold back.

Someone had placed a photo of Amber in a plastic sheet and pinned it to the top. Beth didn't recognize the picture. Amber was sitting on a tailgate with some guys, her mouth open in a big smile as she held out a beer, cigarette in her other hand. It was a bad photo. It made her look like a party girl. Like someone who would end up dead in a ditch. Beth reached to rip it off, then stopped. Amber was *happy* that night. Someone wanted to remember her that way.

Beth sank to her knees, grass soft around her, vines scratching and grabbing at her skin. The base of the cross was crowded with flowers, some in vases. Plastic ones and real ones that had dried. She picked up a fallen teddy bear, rubbed the moss and dirt away, and put him back upright. Letters and cards were left in plastic bags or pinned to Amber's cross. Beth pulled one free and read the poem inside about a life gone too soon. Her eyes burned with dripping mascara and suntan lotion. She pulled another one free. A letter from someone who knew Amber through the diner, who'd loved her cheerful smile. Beth read them all. From people who'd never met Amber and people who had. Words of regret and sorrow. Prayers, and Beth didn't feel the anger she had expected. She felt comforted that they remembered her sister. She looked back at the photo of Amber sitting on the tailgate, her smile. Their shared crooked tooth.

"I'll never forget you." She stopped and cleared her throat. It felt strange to be speaking out loud to the silent woods, the empty air, but she had to hope that, somehow, Amber would hear her. "You loved nectarines, and you ate them until they gave you stomachaches. You painted your toenails pink in the summer and red in the winter. You liked Taylor Swift and knew the words to all her songs. You wanted to write a book about traveling and the people you would meet. You thought that unicorns must have been real at one time and you were angry that they were gone. You believed in heaven and you said death was only sad for the people left behind." Beth stopped again and took a few breaths. "I'm going to choose to believe the same, okay? I'm going to believe that you're at peace and I'll see you again."

Beth's vision slowly came back into focus as she stared at one of the bushes growing in the ditch. She frowned when she noticed the thorns, the red berries. She plucked one of the berries so she could see it closer, rolled the oval shape between her fingers, breathed in the sweet scent. She looked around. The bushes were everywhere, covering where Amber's body had rested. The vines tangled in the trees, sprawled through the ditch like rolling smoke.

Wild roses.

EPILOGUE

I followed her out of the ditch to her car, my steps drifting over hers. I settled in the passenger seat beside her. I hoped she would keep the window down. It made her hair blow across her face and she would brush it away with that quick flip of her hand, the air pushing against me. The closest we could touch. Her eyes were softer now, still glassy from tears, but with that look that the lake got after a bad storm. All rippled and then nothing. Flat. Calm. I'd heard everything she'd said, of course.

We were able to do that, dip in and out. Not always by choice. I'd been with her at the diner, the motel, and when she was in his garage. I'd wanted to help, wanted to scream in his ear and claw at him, but he could never hear us—we had tried before. The most I could do was try to hold her soul's light when I saw it leaking from her body as she twisted from the rope, spinning in circles, the colors fading with her breath. I'd cupped my hand around her light, kept it warm, then she made that small gasp, and it came back to her, all soft yellow with blue tinges.

Once, Hailey almost saw me in the forest. She'd looked so pretty, her hands quietly slicing into the river and scooping up water to drink. Her soul's light was pink, but she'd be furious to know that. She'd want it to be black or red.

Usually I stayed away from Hailey. Her memories of me still had the sharp focus of first love. She had been mine too. I would cry, but I couldn't do much more than make a sound that was somewhere between a breathy gust of wind and an eagle's call, and if I got too close, she felt me like a razor running across her skin. That day at the river, I came up beside her, needing to be in that small space that existed between us and the living. Sometimes, if we were lucky, and we timed it right, we could send them a scent, the words of a song, or a little thought to bring them comfort. In this moment, though, she was bending over, and I was bending over, and then for a startling second my shadow was mirroring hers in the water. We shimmered together for a beautiful heartbeat, and then I rushed backward, and my wind blew the surface of the water clear.

She sat there for the longest time, staring into those depths. What I wouldn't give to tell her that I was with her. Wolf saw me, that much I know for sure. His head lifted, his ears turning, and he'd looked straight into my eyes. It wasn't the first time. Wolf and I had walked together in the woods before, watched over Hailey while she slept. He liked it when I made the grass move so he could pounce at imaginary rabbits.

As Beth drove on, clouds blew over the sun, and a light drizzle turned the faded pavement to charcoal. The air through the window was tinged with the scent of ozone, a summer thunderstorm. Violent and unpredictable. She would need to leave town soon to beat the weather.

The car passed through a shape standing in the middle of the road. Beth didn't see it, but she shivered and turned up the radio, a frown flickering across her face as though she were trying to figure out where the strange sensation had come from. I turned and watched the woman with the backpack on her shoulder, a hoodie over her bent head, and shorts with cowboy boots.

She stuck her thumb out. A blue truck appeared from the shadows and slowed beside her, the chrome grille like shark's teeth, headlights bleeding through Beth's rain-streaked rear window. The passenger door opened, and the girl jogged toward the truck. She was stepping in, long legs climbing up. Then the road went dark. Their journey had ended years ago.

We had reached the end of the highway. A First Nations girl was crouched on the side of the road near the billboard, her arms around *her legs, her face ravaged with tears. Black straight hair, dark eyes, and a red dress. More women came and stood behind her.*

Beth was talking on her cell. Her voice was gentler, less angry, as she spoke to our mother, but I felt the fear tingling under her skin. She was wondering if she could do it, if she could get through without me, but she would, and she had our parents now. They were waiting at the other end of town. Once they connected, she'd follow them to Vancouver.

I looked behind me at the women and watched as, one by one, they stopped whispering, stepped back into their stories, and disappeared. Those women had grieved with me, had been the ones to cradle me when I was lost, torn from my body, cast into the nothing land, but they knew I didn't need them anymore. Not like I had. That's how it goes sometimes. People move on, even those whose lives on earth had ended.

I turned back to Beth. We had only a short time left. I could feel myself wavering, changing. My hand flickered over hers. Did she feel my love? Did she know that for me there was no more pain? No more sorrow or anger? I hoped so. She'd done it. She'd set me free.

In front of me, the road turned white, expanded to a beautiful light. The most beautiful light I'd ever seen, drawing me forward. I was there, then I wasn't.

Dear Reader,

When I begin the process of creating a new novel, I typically try to avoid being influenced by real events, but sometimes there are crimes so disturbing that they linger in my mind for years. One of those for me is the Highway of Tears in Northern British Columbia, where women have been murdered or gone missing since the 1970s. To this day, most of the cases remain unsolved. When I was a teenager, the highway was a terrifying reminder to never hitchhike, of how dangerous it can be when you're traveling alone in a remote location. The image of a desolate road haunted by the lost souls of women, searching for answers to their deaths, stuck with me. I found it comforting to change history and write an ending where justice was served.

Out of respect for the victims, their families, and the RCMP, who have worked and continue to work on the Highway of Tears case, I didn't want to use that highway, or any of the towns involved. Instead, I created the fictional town of Cold Creek, the Cold Creek Highway, and the campground by the lake. The details of the crimes, the characters in my novel, and the events that take place have sprung from my imagination, but it continues to be a terrible truth that Indigenous women experience a disproportionately higher rate of violence and homicide than the average woman in Canada. There are several important groups bringing awareness to this national crisis. You can read the final report of the National Inquiry into Missing and Murdered Indigenous Women and Girls on the MMIWG website at www.mmiwg-ffada.ca.

To learn more about the Highway of Tears, and the significant work being done by Carrier Sekani Family Services (CSFS) to prevent violence against women, visit their website at www.highwayoftears.org.

The RCMP's investigation into the highway murders, Project E-PANA, began in 2005 and is still active today. If you have any information that could help, contact BC Crime Stoppers at www.bccrimestoppers.com or call the 24/7 tip line at 1-800-222-8477.

This story may trigger disturbing memories in victims of crime. If you, or anyone you know, needs support, please contact the Canadian Resource Centre for Victims of Crime at www.crcvc.ca, or your local crisis center.

All best,

Chevy Stevens

Acknowledgments

There is a reason this book is dedicated to Jennifer Enderlin, my patient, astute editor, and Mel Berger, my equally esteemed agent. I feel very lucky to have worked with both of them from the beginning of my career, now more than twelve years ago. This book was the hardest for me to write. Not so much the work itself, but the finding of the story. They never pushed. Never made me feel terrible for my fumbles and false starts. Mel would say, "The book will be done when the book is done."

Guess what, Mel? You were right! It's finally done. Yes, I promise I'm working on my next, and Jen, you are simply the best and cooler than the rest.

Carla Buckley, my dearest friend and critique partner, who has read sections of this book nearly as many times as me. Thank you for always being just a FaceTime session away and answering the thousands of emails that I send you when I am approaching the end of a book. You're the yin to my yang. The butter on my toast. The lid to my pot. The sugar in my coffee.

Beth Helms, who lent me her name, makes me take a second look at the hard stuff that I would really rather avoid, and keeps me entertained with her witty texts. I've learned so much from you. Most of which can't be repeated in here. I look forward to our next sloth-cation.

Robin Spano, thank you ten times over for being willing to read a draft while dealing with a young child at home in the midst of the COVID crisis. I know how precious each minute of your day is, and your insightful feedback and positive encouragement is always appreciated.

Ingrid Thoft, my sister-wife, we have been separated for far too long. I look forward to the day we are reunited and can drink Grasshoppers in the sun at the Hotel Valley Ho.

Roz Nay, my favorite, pretend archnemesis, you know what you've done.

At William Morris Endeavor Entertainment, I'd like to extend my gratitude to Tracy Fisher, Caitlin Mahony, Carolina Beltran, Sam Birmingham, Anna Dixon, and James Munro.

At St. Martin's Press, Brant Janeway, Katie Bassel, Lisa Senz, Kim Ludlam, Tom Thompson, and Erik Platt. Erica Martirano, one day we will hang out in matching corgi pajamas, eat chocolate, play with dogs, and gossip about celebrities. Thank you for all your help with all the things. Mike Storrings, you did an incredible job with this gorgeous cover. David Cole, you have now copyedited six of my books and I remain in awe of your keen and thoughtful eye.

Raincoast Books, my appreciation for everything you do for me in Canada. I'd also like to thank my foreign publishers and translators, who share my stories around the world.

On the research side, my thanks to Corporal R. Jo for answering all my text questions, even when they were lengthy scenarios that probably sounded very strange out of context. BJ Brown, for the helpful phone calls and emails. Steve Unischewski, for the dirt bike information. Any mistakes are most assuredly mine, or the result of my taking creative license.

Connel, as you said, you've been down this road with me a few times now, and you are a great copilot. Thanks for keeping our family intact and for all the times you bring food to my desk, answer random research questions, listen to my panic attacks, and assure me that everything is going to be fine. Yes, you can go fishing on Sunday. We both know you were going anyway.

My darling Piper, Pipster the Hipster, Pipes, Pipsqueak,

Kitten, you fill my life with joy and laughter. I'm sure it isn't always easy being the daughter of a writer who stays in her office for hours at a time, but I love our cuddle breaks, your jokes, and your performances. You are a great kid and I am proud to be your mother. Please don't write about me one day.

Ziggy and Oona, thank you for keeping me company while I write and cleaning up all my dropped crumbs, but please stop barking at the Amazon delivery drivers, the UPS driver, the squirrels, the crows, and imagined monsters. You make it hard for Mommy to think.

To my wonderful fans, your support allows me to keep doing what I love, and your emails, messages, and Facebook comments keep me going on the hard days. Finally, a big thank-you to all my friends and family, who make my life about more than words on paper.